THE LEPER KING

ALSO BY SCOTT R. REZER

LOVE ABIDETH STILL

SHADOW OF THE MOUNTAIN

THE LEPER
KING

†

SCOTT R. REZER

—for donna
who taught my heart to
express its deepest thoughts

CAST OF CHARACTERS

Kingdom of Jherusalem

Baldwin IV: *King of Jherusalem*

Sibylla: *sister; wife of Guion de Lusignan*

Isabella: *half-sister*

Agnes de Courtenay: *mother of Baldwin and Sibylla; former wife of King Amaury; wife of Reynald Grenier, Lord of Sidon*

Joscelin de Courtenay: *brother of Agnes; Seneschal of Jherusalem*

Baldwin V *(of Montferrat) (called Baudinouet): son of Sibylla and William of Montferrat*

Barons of Kingdom

Balian: *lord of Ibelin and Naples; husband of Maria Comnena, Dowager Queen*

Baldwin: *lord of Ramlah and Mirabel, brother of Balian*

Amalric de Lusignan: *knight; later Constable of Jherusalem; Master of Order of Sion*

Guion de Lusignan: *brother of Amalric; knight; later Count of Japhe and Ascalone*

Reynald de Châtillon: *former Prince of Antioch; lord of Kerak and Montreal; Regent*

Humphrey II: *lord of Toron; Constable of Jherusalem*

Humphrey IV: *grandson*

County of Tripoli

Raymond III: *Count of Tripoli; Prince of Galilee; cousin of king; Regent*

Principality of Antioch

Bohemond III: *Prince of Antioch; cousin of king*

Clergy
Alexander III: *Pope/Bishop of Rome*
William: *Archbishop of Tyre; Chancellor of Jherusalem; historian*
Heraclius: *Archbishop of Caesarea; later Patriarch; member of Order of Sion*

Military Orders
Templars
Othon de Saint-Amant: *Master of Templars; member of Order of Sion*
Arnaud de Torroge: *succeeds Saint-Amant as Master*
Gerard de Ridefort: *Seneschal; later Master; member of Order of Sion*
Hospitallers
Jobert: *Master of Hospitallers*

Muslims
Salah ad-Din: *Sultan of Egypt and Syria*
Ismat ad-Din Khaitan: *wife*
Turan-Shah: *brother of Salah ad-Din*
Taqi ad-Din: *nephew*
Farrukh-Shah: *nephew*
Imad ad-Din: *secretary to Salah ad-Din*

† PROLOGUE
1174

Thou hast prepared a table before me against them that afflict me.
Thou hast anointed my head with oil...
—*Psalms 22:5*

Incense filled the great dome of the ancient church. Sunlight and candle flame set the air of the Holy Sepulcher to a golden illusory glow. A solemn procession of monks bearing smoking censers wound its way through the crowded nave, chanting the words of a holy invocation.

The Patriarch of Jherusalem stood before the altar, surrounded by his ecclesiastical audience, reading the mass, his words echoing throughout the sanctuary. Baldwin, the fourth of the name, knelt before him, waiting for the oil and the crown to be set upon his head. Words and murmurs of prayer mingled around the boy, enveloping him in the protective shadow of God's holiness. The Patriarch dipped a finger into the oil and made the sign of the cross over the head of the young king.

...In nomine Patris, et Filii, et Spiritus Sancti. Amen.

It was an auspicious day for the crowning of a king: the fifteenth of July—the day Godfrei de Bouillon had captured the city of Jherusalem seventy-five years before during the First War of the Cross. The day the heathen hordes of Islam had fallen to the valiant armies of Christendom.

The archdeacon of Tyre shifted his weight from one foot to the other. Blood flowed back into the deprived appendage. Sharp needles of pain lanced into his toes. William winced. Even for the midst of July, the heat was unbearable. He was suffocating under the burden of the thick vestments of his office. A bead of sweat slid torturously slow down his back. Amidst the prayers of so many righteous men, he lifted a silent, selfish plea of his own to the heavens.

1

His gaze wandered over the faces of those gathered around the church. Most were members of the kingdom's High Court that had presided over the assembly only two days before to elect Baldwin as his father's successor. The Seneschal, Milon de Plancy, and the aged and venerable Constable, Humphrey of Toron, knelt at the king's left and right hand. Milon held the royal banner, Humphrey, the crown and scepter. At the officers' back, in their customary tabards of black and white, stood the masters of the Hospital and the Temple, Jobert and Othon de Saint-Amant. The rest of the crown vassals watched in attendance, including a dozen or three of the minor lords from around the kingdom. The most conspicuous by their absence were Count Raymond of Tripoli and Prince Bohemond of Antioch, the king's close cousins. It was particularly odd that they were not present, if not suspicious, even if the northern lords seldom involved themselves with the coronations of Jherusalem's kings. Some would see their absence as treason.

Not surprisingly, he found Baldwin's mother, the strikingly handsome, Agnes de Courtenay, among the attendants. She had managed, at long last, to find her way back to court on the arm of her most recent husband—the fourth—Reynald Grenier of Sidon. She stood next to the king's beautiful sister, Sibylla, another recent return to court. Although only a year older than Baldwin, she had spent most of her life secluded away at the convent of Saint-Lazare in Bethany, but word of her father's death had brought her back with her mother. Baldwin had seen neither of them much in his short life; therefore, he hardly knew them. William, on the other hand, knew them well and had little regard for either woman.

Sibylla was young and spoiled and given to bouts of selfishness; Agnes, on the other hand, was a hanger-on. Ever since the Church annulled her marriage to King Amaury, she had sought to find a way back to court. The Papal Father—as Amaury demanded—legitimized her children, but she remained reduced to her former status of Countess of Japhe and Ascalone. Other than its income, it was a meaningless title since the lands remained in the hands of the king. A pope's decree robbed her of the title of queen and separated her from her children. What Agnes desired now was a means to power a little closer to the throne. Sidon was too far from Jherusalem and her son. William feared how she might use Baldwin to gain just that, power.

Agnes caught his eye before he could look away. She smiled demurely, seductively. He glanced away, uncomfortable by that wanton stare. There always seemed to be some rumor floating around the kingdom about Agnes' many indiscretions.

2

THE LEPER KING

With so many proud and noble personages in attendance, William found it hard to determine who might prove to be a friend or foe for the young king. Friends he would need, for certes, if he were to reign effectively. Only yesterday, the High Court had argued about the rights of succession or the need of a Regent for a king still in his minority.

A week ago, it would hardly have mattered. William had been both friend and tutor for the thirteen-year old prince—before King Amaury suddenly and unexpectedly died of illness at such a young age. A week ago, no one would have thought to place the burdens of kingship upon the shoulders of a boy suffering from the early effects of leprosy.

There were few who knew of the king's incipient illness; his symptoms had not advanced beyond the numbness of his hand and arm, and the few sores on his feet that he hid beneath clothing and bandages. William was all too familiar with the tragic story of the young prince's illness—he was the unfortunate soul who had discovered it. God willing, the grace of Heaven would fall upon Baldwin and he would recover, allowing him to reign long, well, and prosperously.

Kyrie elision... William prayed, whispering. *Lord have mercy...*

If Baldwin should fail, the kingdom would decline into civil war. May God have mercy on them all if that should come to pass.

* * * * *

Moonlight silvered the olive trees in the abbey of Notre Dame du Sion outside the walls of Jherusalem. Othon de Saint-Amant, master of the Order of the Knights Templar, pulled his cloak over his head and slipped quietly through the garden to the appointed place. A breeze stirred, rustling the leaves. Shadows shifted among the trees. The abbey bell sounded, calling the monks to Compline.

He had grown used to these late night meetings in the last three years since becoming master of the Templars. In so doing, Sion entrusted him with secrets few men knew: the truth about the origin and purpose of his order, and a long held secret that had reached even to Rome to bring the Pope himself to heel. Secrets that revolved around the man he had come to meet.

"Your late," a voice whispered.

Othon turned sharply. A cloaked figure detached itself from the near shadows of the abbey wall. A hood hid nearly all of the man's face. Only a mouth was visible framed by a neatly trimmed black beard, a curious oddity given the current fashion at court. "I was detained at the palace," he said. "I couldn't leave."

"Is there a problem we should know about?"

"It was nothing," Othon answered tersely. His cloaked companion said nothing, but he could feel his calculating stare upon him. "The Constable called a meeting at the last moment. The old boar wanted to discuss a matter of the kingdom's southern defenses."

Othon looked around the garden suspiciously, wary of any one who might be watching.

The man in black suppressed a short laugh. "Don't worry, my friend. We will not be disturbed. I warded the garden against intrusion. Were you followed?"

"I know the protocol, *Messire*. No one saw me leave the city," Othon said and turned into the garden to walk beneath the trees. His companion followed.

As a servant of the crown under King Baldwin III and King Amaury I, and then, as a Templar Knight, there were few things Othon truly feared. Amalric de Lusignan was one of them. Too many privileged young lords had gained prominence in the kingdom in the last few years; ambitious men who were new to the East and thought the world lay before them, waiting for them to claim it at will. Lusignan, however, was not like the little men of his generation. He was not particularly handsome or charismatic—although he supposedly had caught the eye of the king's mother, Agnes de Courtenay, for a time—but a man of subtle power. A power made more powerful by the secret brotherhood that moved in the shadows of the government, manipulating events to their own will. Even at his age and position, Othon was still nothing more than a pawn on the table.

"Amaury's death has caused us a setback. Our plan had nearly come to fruition when he decided on that fool's errand of a campaign to regain Belinas from the Turks. His foolishness has cost us dearly." A restraining hand caught Othon by the arm. "Someone else of the sacred blood must be found to take Amaury's place; perhaps, someone with an even better claim to the throne of David."

Othon stopped and drew closer to the other man. For all the shadows, he might have been talking with a ghost. "What of Baldwin? There are few men who can keep this kingdom together under one rule."

"Baldwin is only a child," the darker man said, his voice touched with the razor edge of fine Damascus steel, "and, a leper. He will never beget children to inherit the throne. He is a liability. We need another king."

Othon's nostrils flared with sudden fury. He raised an accusatory finger. "The Templars are the sworn guardians of the *sangreal*. I will not see him so casually cast aside just for the sake of expediency."

Amalric de Lusignan drew himself up to his full height, forcing Othon back against a tree. Instantly, what seemed like an unseen hand grasped Othon by the throat. He gasped, unable to breathe. He forced himself not to panic. In the corner of his mind that he had trained to the discipline of calm, he recognized the use of magic; he was not surprised—he had seen its use before. This was different, however. It was darker, more sinister. Its practitioner had not even lifted a finger to employ it.

"Your Order, *Messire*, exists to do the will of Sion. You would do well to remember that," Lusignan whispered harshly. The hold on Othon's throat suddenly fell away. "But do not trouble yourself over much about our young king, my good Othon. We have no need to hurry."

A shaken Othon raised a hand and rubbed his throat. "What does the Order plan to do?"

"De Plancy must be dealt with first and a new Seneschal set in his place—one of us or, at the very least, someone sympathetic to our cause who can keep our young king in check. But not now—perhaps, when the campaigning season has slowed. Salehdin is prowling the desert, kicking up sand on the border. He is as twitchy as cat with a mouse. An assassination just now might cause him to act prematurely."

"What do we do until, then?"

"We watch and we wait, Othon," said the master of the Order of Sion, "as we have ever done."

* * * * *

The sun set over the western desert of Egypt in a globe of shimmering fire. The souks and shops across al-Qihara had closed; the mosques stood open, filling with waiting worshippers. The *mu'adh-dhin* wailed from atop the minaret, calling the faithful of Islam to prayer.

There is no god but Allah, and Muhammad is the Prophet of God.

Salah ad-Din Yusuf ibn Ayyub knelt in his small private room of the vast palace, deep in meditation. Two of his Mamluks stood by the doorway, garbed in yellow and gold, mute and impassive as stone. The sound of trickling water called to him from the garden. In this land of heat and dust and sun-blasted stone, it was a treasure; the one luxury he permitted himself. The room was simple enough and plainly decorated, austere by western standards considering the untold wealth of the fallen Fatimid Khalifate. As a man of humble origins—a Kurd from beyond the Great River—his needs were simple and not given to excess.

The wail of the *muezzin* called from high and above, echoing through the courtyard. He shook out his prayer rug before the *mihrab*, the niche in the eastern wall of the room facing holy Mecca, and bowed his head; he murmured the words every faithful Muslim was bound to recite five times a day. The words washed over him and through him, striking the chord of his thoughts and emotion. As a man of the Faith, he found comfort in his devotion to the teachings of the Prophet. It gave him a sense of purpose, of being, a sense of oneness with something greater than himself. It cleansed his soul as though with fire.

Allah had favored him for his devotion. His star was in its ascendance: three expeditions against Egypt under the tutelage of Shirkuh, his grizzled old uncle; commander and wazir of Egypt; now sultan or *al-malik*—king. Only three years ago, he had abolished the weak, heretical Shi'ite Khalifate in al-Qihara and restored the Egyptians to the religious obedience of Sunni Islam. The pupil had become the master. Where his uncle had been a spark of flame, ready to ignite the realms of Islam for the sake of Baghdad, he had become the fire, consuming and unquenchable. Allah willing, the call for *jihad* would sweep eastwards, uniting all the lands of Islam under the war-banner of the crescent moon, and drive the desecrating infidels of Urshalim back into the sea.

He was reading from the Qur'an by candlelight when his secretary, Imad ad-Din al-Isfahani, arrived with food and drink, and a message. Yusuf reached for the silver *káffe* service and poured himself a small cup. He took the sealed letter from Imad and looked up at him inquiringly.

"From our agent in Urshalim, Highness," said the slim dark man, bowing over the sultan's hand.

Yusuf set the unopened missive casually aside on the silver service and leaned back on a bolster. "What does it say, my friend?" Imad ad-Din looked at him uncertainly. Yusuf laughed. A rarity for him, he knew. "I pay you handsomely to know what goes on for me."

His secretary plucked a piece of fruit from the tray and took a seat on the floor. "The Ifranj have crowned the boy king."

"Have they elected him a Regent?"

"No. They are so divided and mistrusting of one another they can't even decide which of them would best lead them."

"So they choose a boy to fill the throne of men, instead," Yusuf remarked, sipping his *káffe*. "And in so doing they grant me a gift beyond worth."

Imad raised an eyebrow. "And what gift is that, Excellency?"

Yusuf sat up swiftly and gracefully as cat, and plucked a grape from the tray. "Time, Imad: Time. *Ya Allah* these Nasrani are stupid."

"Or arrogant."

The flame of his anger flared; he quenched it with a smile. "Yes—and very arrogant. Let them be. Urshalim and the Ifranj can wait," he said calmly, and reclined again. He weighed the grape in his hand. "Nur ad-Din has long kept me from Dimasq. I doubt his eleven-year old son will have the same success. Once my brother puts down the revolt in the south and I have brought Suriya to heel, I can choose when and where I will finally drive the infidels into the sea."

He popped the grape into his mouth, savoring more than just its juicy sweetness. "I want you to immediately send a letter of condolence to our brother Al-Malik Bardawil in Urshalim on the death of his father."

Recognizing a dismissal, Imad ad-Din rose and bowed. "Is there anything else you require, Excellency?"

Salah ad-Din—Salehdin to the Ifranj—returned to a kneeling position and picked up the Qur'an to resume his reading. "Once you send the letter, send word to the commanders to assemble the army in the eastern delta—in case the Ifranj prove stupid or arrogant enough to proceed with their planned invasion."

JHERUSALEM 1176

† CHAPTER ONE

For thou hast regarded my humility, thou hast saved my soul out of distress. And thou hast not shut me up in the hands of the enemy...
—Psalms 30:8-9

Deus lo volt! Deus lo volt! Deus lo volt!
For the second time in as many weeks, Baldwin listened to the assembled knights of his kingdom as they shouted the familiar paean of the Pope's Holy Wars on Islam: *God wills it.* Their voices rose again, shouting their praise for him. Soiled with the blood and gore of battle, he stood up on the small platform of shields and spears the knights held aloft on their shoulders. Pulling off his helmet and coif, he raised his sword, acknowledging the echoing shouts of their acclaim.

At midday, the combined armies of Tripoli and Jherusalem had swept down upon the garrison of Damascus and crushed the Sarrazins. Three days before, the army had set out to raid the small villages about heavily guarded Damascus, hoping to draw out the Muslims towards the Beka'a valley. Salehdin was campaigning in the north, avenging the second attempt on his life by the Assassins of Masyaf with a siege on the impregnable stronghold. His brother, Semsedolus, commanded the army garrisoned in Damascus. It seemed an opportune moment to remind the sultan of Frankish presence in the land. Semsedolus had taken the bait.

Feigning a retreat into the fertile Beka'a, the Muslims pursued the army of Tripoli under their commander, Raymond of Tripoli, towards Ba'albek, and into the trap set for them. It had been an excellent strategy. Even old Humphrey the Constable who usually commanded such things had commended its merit. Archbishop William's endless

8

lessons on such figures of history as Caesar and Hannibal, Alexander and Charlemagne, had proven useful after all.

Taking advantage of the steeply terraced slopes of the valley, Baldwin's heavily armored knights rolled down over the Sarrazins, crushing them with the sheer force of their momentum. The Franks caught the Sarrazins on their eastern flank, pinning Semsedolus' unsuspecting army between the Litani River and their only means of escape.

The pounding hoofbeats of two thousand horses combined with the deafening battle cry of the Christian knights, thrilling through his body. The thrill, though, was short-lived as the first line of the charge slammed into the Muslim lines with a terrifying noise; at a given signal, Raymond's army turned on their pursuers and drove into them.

It was a slaughter: the battlefield turned to a sickening ruin of broken bodies, horseflesh, and far too much blood. The heat made a terrible stench of the dead. Semsedolus barely escaped with his life along with a few surviving Mamluks. Warfare had turned out to be far more different than Baldwin had imagined it to be. Nor was he entirely sure if he liked it. He had received only a shallow sword-cut where a huge, swarthy Arab had somehow managed to cleave a hole in his chain mail with a vicious stroke of a sword. A moment longer and it could have been far worse—or so the Master of the Templars kept reminding him—had not Humphrey cut the warrior down with his mace.

A small victory, perhaps, but it sent a clear message to the hordes of Sarrazins massed about his kingdom. Just as he, and his uncle, Joscelin de Courtenay, the new Seneschal had intended. *This long have you come against us; but no longer. You will not drive us from this land. Arm yourself, and prepare for war.*

Despite the obvious adoration, there were some among of his knights—too many, he thought—who refused to look directly at him on account of the disease slowly beginning to deform his face and body. No one spoke of it; no one ever considered it. Neither was it ever far from the private thoughts of those closest to him. Among his warriors he was determined not to cower behind a veil; warriors often saw far worse in the bloody aftermath of war. Still, too many refused to look upon their king. No matter, as long as they vowed to remain loyal and serve him with their much needed arms.

A small thin man with bright grey eyes met him as he leapt down from the shields and took the man's forearm in his. The Syrian sun was hot and unrelenting to men weighed down in chain mail and thick padded gambesons. Baldwin wiped the back of his gloved hand across his sweat and blood-spattered brow and met Raymond's stare with a slight smile.

"You... you still think it unwise of me to break the truce with the Sarrazins, cousin," he said, trying to control the stammer that was so reminiscent of his father. He struggled with his impediment, but at least it gave him the outward semblance of a man who thought out his words carefully and purposely.

In the two years since he had come to the throne, he had quickly learned how to use his thoughtful silence to his advantage. Lesser men began to think twice before engaging him in conversation. Men like the Count of Tripoli, however, used tact. Raymond was no fool. He took his time answering, trying not to appear critical of his young king. After all, Raymond had forged the unsteady peace of the last eighteen months.

"I think my king is well able to decide what course of action he thinks is best for his kingdom."

In the days following Milon de Plancy's mysterious murder a year and a half before, the High Court chose Raymond as *bailli*, or Regent, of the throne during the king's minority. Baldwin had not taken offense at the sudden change of policy; it had given him time to study the mood of his barons towards him and to decide how he would handle the reins of government. He learned that whatever his Court thought of his disease, they respected his right as a prince of the blood to rule.

"You didn't answer my question, my lord of Tripoli."

"Does my king require me to answer?"

"No; only if you choose to."

A howl of laughter erupted among ranks of the lesser knights as they gathered up the spoils left by the defeated Sarrazins; a brief scuffle ensued over the golden bridle of Semsedolus' horse, slain by a spear thrust to its heart. Raymond ignored the argument. He pulled off his mail coif and stuffed it into his helmet under his arm.

"I am concerned that your uncle's council was given more in the hope of revenge for his long imprisonment by the Muslims, than as a carefully planned strategy of war."

It was true that Joscelin had only recently been released from a prison in Aleppo as had Baldwin's kinsman, Reynald de Châtillon. Bohemond of Antioch had demanded that the lord of Aleppo release them as a condition for his help against Salehdin's siege of Aleppo. Joscelin vowed he would have his vengeance, but it was not the reason Baldwin broke the truce between the Christians and the Sarrazins.

Baldwin's hand strayed to the hilt of his sword. It was a boyish reaction to his anger and he knew it. He forced himself to calm and let his hand fall. "You were a prisoner not so long ago. You know the torments he endured. Revenge would hardly seem an unexpected sentiment of his council, but I assure you, cousin, my actions are mine, and mine alone. And ones… and ones"—he paused briefly, schooling his halting tongue to his will—"and ones that men who are far more experienced in the craft of war and diplomacy should have employed before now. If we can draw Salehdin away from his siege on Masyaf, perhaps we may be able to gain the friendship of the Old Man of the Mountain."

At the mention of Masyaf and its reclusive master, Baldwin saw the reaction he had expected on Raymond's face. His dark brows gathered in a thunderous cloud, but the storm did not break. The servants of Masyaf slew Raymond's father when he was only a boy. It was certainly reasonable that he should despise the friendship of a man he considered a murderer; but times demanded unreasonable actions.

"I caution you, Highness," the Count of Tripoli said coolly, "not to put too much hope in a friendship with Sinan or his Assassins."

"We need whatever allies we can find."

"Not if you abandon—" Raymond started to argue, but caught himself. "Not if you abandon this new-made war and sue for a renewal of the truce with Salehdin. Send me to him and he will listen. He is a man of honor. He will keep the peace."

"For how long, Tripoli?" Joscelin de Courtenay said, coming over to them. He was a tall man, and handsomely made for a man his age: a masculine image of Baldwin's mother. "Six months—a year? Salehdin holds nearly all of Syria and Egypt in his hand. While we have sat back abiding your truce, Salehdin has strengthened his position against us. Once he surrounds us, he will strike. Even Bohemond saw the wisdom in defending Aleppo against him."

Raymond ignored Joscelin. He made his appeal to Baldwin. "Wait a little longer. The call for a new holy war is sweeping across Europe. It is only a matter of time before new knights answer the call. Let the truce stand for a season longer."

"No, my lord Raymond," Baldwin said. "I appreciate—the kingdom appreciates—your service to the crown during your Regency. I am… I am not a boy anymore. I must do as I think my father would have wanted."

"Your father would have wanted—"

"Enough, my lord. Enough," Baldwin said, holding up a gloved hand. "It has been a long day and I tire easily—a symptom of my ailment I'm afraid. Take heart, cousin. It's not likely that you'll have to contend too much longer with me as your king, but until then, I need your sword and your loyalty to defend our people."

Properly rebuffed, Raymond fell to his knees and pressed the back of Baldwin's hand to his mouth—his undiseased left hand he noticed. All around them, Templars, knights, and Hospitallers alike, stopped what they were doing and stood watching. One by one, without really knowing why, they all began dropping to their knees, ready to pay homage to their sworn king simply because one man had done so. Lastly, his uncle went to his knee and took his other hand in his. Their reverence struck Baldwin dumb.

"I have sworn to defend you and serve you with my life," said Raymond, bowing. "Forgive me, Highness, if I have betrayed your trust in me with my words. God forbid that any evil should befall you. Here and now, I pledge my life and fealty to you anew. And may God strike me down if I fail you."

At once, a thunderous cry of acknowledgment erupted across the Beka'a, echoing repeatedly like a storm breaking over the land. "*Deus lo volt! Deus lo volt! Deus lo volt!*"

* * * * *

Tyre was an ancient city, its foundations set down in the dawn of memory. It was already old when Hiram lent his aid to Solomon to build his fabulous Temple to God in Jherusalem; it was older still when it dared to defy Alexander's march of conquest. Actually, Tyre was two cities: the older city on the mainland that Alexander destroyed in his arrogance and rage, the rubble of which he used to build a causeway to capture the newer fortress that lay proud and indomitable upon its island in the midst of the sea.

The people of Tyre rebuilt their city, though; others destroyed it again; and time saw it built anew. Boasting of several large caravansaries and exceptionally clean bazaars, fountained plazas, and an aqueduct that ran from the mountains to the sea, Tyre sat like a jewel in the crown of the kingdom of Jherusalem, its magnificent cathedral the pride of the Church, rivaled only by the Holy Sepulcher.

While the army billeted in the city, Baldwin sat patiently in a room of his private house, waiting as his doctor, Abu Suleiman Dawud carefully examined his wounds and sores. They were not alone. Archbishop William stood in the slanting sunlight of a window, reading from a book. A servant moved about the room inconspicuously.

Dawud gently probed the edges of the lesions with the point of a lancet. In the past two years, the sores had grown worse, particularly on his extremities and his nose. Fortunately, for him, the pain proved minimal at this stage of his illness. Dawud breathed heavily through his nose and shook his head; he continued without word. Baldwin closed his eyes as Dawud rubbed his sores with oil mixed with quicksilver. He felt nothing, only numbness—until the doctor gently wrapped the bandages about his hands and feet. The bandages smelled faintly of attar of roses. It helped mask the odor of decaying flesh.

Dawud swatted at his hand without glancing up as he tried to scratch his nose. Baldwin chuckled softly at the mild affront to his royal person. To an Arab Christian, Frankish titles of rank—even a king's— meant little. Six years ago, his father had hired Dawud as Baldwin's personal doctor. His devotion had kept him on even after Amaury's death. His quiet presence and careful ministrations were reassuring; it gave Baldwin hope that perhaps by some miracle of God, he might survive his illness.

"How… how bad is it, Dawud?" Baldwin said, drawing on his cotte as he stood stiffly. On the other side of the room, William closed his book and leaned back against the window frame, listening.

Dawud wiped off his instruments with meticulous care and set them down on a cloth to pack them away. He glanced at Baldwin. "I would say that another hand span closer and Semsedolus' mamluk would have cleaved you asunder. It was a foolish venture if I may be so bold to answer."

"I didn't mean the sword-cut and well you know it."

Dawud inclined his head with a slight smile at his cleverness. "My humble apologies, Highness." He turned his attention once more to the last of his knives, dunking it repeatedly in water, and set it down carefully.

"Humble apologies, indeed," Baldwin muttered under his breath, smiling. "If—"

"What is the prognosis of the king's leprosy, Master Dawud?" William said from his vantage point by the window. The cleric's question clipped the wings of the rising levity in the room.

Dawud lifted his dark gaze to the Archbishop, and then turned to Baldwin. Unbidden emotion played mercilessly across the old doctor's face. He fought visibly to maintain his expression of trained detachment. His gaze broke and fell. "It is not good, my lord Bishop," he replied. A spot on the floor suddenly seemed to draw his entire attention. "There is no longer any doubt that he has leprosy. The sickness advances rapidly now. The numbness he feels in his feet will only worsen until the muscle grows too weak to support him; the ulcers will eat away at the flesh and bone until nothing remains. That we can hide, perhaps even slow, but his face will continue to deform; blindness will eventually follow—though I pray it will be several years yet."

The words struck a terrible blow to Baldwin's sense of false hope: a hope that his illness would not advance into his adulthood. Instead, his adolescence had only worsened his condition.

The world went grey, then blinding white. An arm bore him swiftly up. Had he swooned? A command focused his gaze, coming to bear on his two companions. The voice belonged to Dawud. Baldwin was speechless.

"Sit, your majesty. Sit. It is the quicksilver. The dizziness will pass in a moment."

"Can anymore be done for him?" William asked.

"Continue treatments with ointment. Keep the sores clean and bandaged. Hot springs may help, and time in a more favorable climate. The coastal cities would be best."

"And nothing more?"

Dawud paused with his usual Arab penchant for the dramatic. "Abdicate the throne and retire to private life; though I doubt any of your loyal subjects would dare suggest it aloud. At the very least, appoint a Regent to hold the reins of the kingdom."

The last remnants of the medicinal haze burned away from his mind. Baldwin glared up at the small, grey-bearded man and his taller, more robust, tonsured accomplice. Even in his fit of despair, he wanted to cry out against his doctor and Chancellor. Instead, he silently cursed both men. What he heard sounded like a carefully rehearsed speech meant to sway him to their purpose. Certainly, they were concerned for his well-being—of that he had no doubt; but this went beyond mere concern. The only two men in this kingdom of vipers he could truly trust—except, perhaps, with the addition of his uncle—and they were plotting against him.

He wanted to scream—or laugh. "Enough," he shouted. "I… I am not a child who cannot see what you are doing. If you think it best for me to renounce my throne, then find me a man among my lords who *can* hold it in my stead. Find me a man who will bind the kingdom together, rather than bring it to the brink of civil war with their petty bickering and squabbling every time we need to make a decision. Otherwise"—he paused, having to catch his breath—"otherwise, I'll thank you not to bring the matter of my abdication up again." He cast a narrow gaze at both of them as though it was a spear. He stood up nimbly, gathering all his energy about him, feigning a strength that belied his sickness. "Now, doctor, if you're done brooding over your patient like a mother hen, I'm sure you have other matters to attend to."

Dawud pulled a sour face, but made his obeisance without argument. Gathering up his instruments, he drew off his small cap, touched a hand to his brow, and left the room.

When the door closed, Baldwin turned slowly towards the Archbishop of Tyre and grinned slyly. "That was foolishly played, my lord Bishop. Will you always treat me as a child?"

William held a hand to his mouth and made a slight cough. "Is it true what I hear from the soldiers—that it was you who led the charge?"

Baldwin stood up to his full height. He had grown another hand or so; he was taller now than Father William. "I am king now."

William laughed incredulously. "What were you thinking?"

"The army needs to see that their king is not some fragile invalid without skill of leadership—at least, not yet. If I cannot... if I cannot lead them in battle, then it will be as if I do not hold the crown at all."

William shook his head. "But to lead them in a useless skirmish simply for the sake of rustling Salehdin's feathers I find reckless and foolish. What if you were unhorsed and unable to remount?"

Baldwin reached up to scratch his scabbed nose. He remembered Dawud's silent admonition. A man must have the ability to control his impulses. "If I need advise on matters of war, then I will ask of those best qualified to answer. You are my Chancellor, your Eminence, not my Constable."

"And so I would like to remain, but it will prove most difficult if you insist on leading charges yourself needlessly. You have no need to prove yourself before your people. They believe in you. You are the anointed king. For them, that is all that matters. That you are a leper is of no consequence."

William had the uncanny ability of turning the most heated of arguments with a word. Baldwin smiled wryly. A silence descended in the room; and lengthened still more. He glanced furtively at his former tutor and wandered casually towards the window. William stood mutely; he folded his hands in the sleeves of his habit.

"Is something troubling you, Baudinouet?"

Baldwin smiled at the seldom-used sobriquet. It meant 'little Baldwin' and was given to him in honor of his father's brother who was king when he was born. When asked by a subject what gift he would give to his new godson, the king jested in reply, the Kingdom of Jherusalem. No one, however, even then, had expected him to become king. It was another of those subtle gestures that William made use of to reconcile their arguments.

15

"It is nothing."

"Nothing," William chuckled softly at his back, "has a curious way of usually being something."

"I have no desire to argue with you, Father William."

"If you won't let me be Constable, then at least allow me to be Chancellor and give you advice if I can."

That won a cough of laughter from him, but no more. "*Touché*, my lord Bishop. *Touché*." Below the window, Baldwin watched a squad of mounted knights pass by on the narrow street. He picked out the insignia of Lord Reynald of Sidon among them. They were knights of his mother's husband: his knights.

"Your Highness?"

"Do you think children suffer for the sins of their parents?"

"I'm sure they have and do. But our Lord taught that the blind man was born blind that the power of God would be shown." William paused, letting the silence have its due. "Perhaps God has some purpose for your affliction that He has not yet revealed. We are all vessels created for His use."

The long line of soldiers turned the corner and rode out of view. "And what if the vessel is too weak to bear the weight of His purposes?"

William chuckled softly. "Our Lord gives us no more than what we can bear."

"Do you honestly believe that?"

"If I didn't, I would be a poor minister of God's word, indeed. And one far less humble than God expects of me."

Baldwin grasped the sill of the window and held it tightly. He stared at his bandaged right hand. "Surely God must see that the kingdom would be better served by a king with a strong sword-arm."

"Not if a sick leper would serve Him better."

Baldwin closed his eyes. "To what purpose, William? To what purpose?"

"His own—to test our faith."

"And how do I know if my faith is strong enough?"

A hand touched him, squeezed his shoulder. "Embrace your weakness and allow God's strength to sustain you. Only then can you truly begin to live."

* * * * *

Dimasq was an oasis of stone and palm set amidst the barren harshness of the desert; at its center, an emerald garden watered by a thin finger of the Barada and the palace of the sultan from which he ruled over all of Suriya. At least, that was the sultan Salah ad-Din's ambition, if he could ever bring the troublesome Suriyans to heel.

Turan-Shah stood before him, immobile, mute, and defiant. Salah ad-Din Yusuf stood abruptly. The fresh red scar running along his cheek into his beard—a reminder from the Hashshashin that his life could become forfeit at anytime if he did not end his war against Masyaf and its master— itched terribly. He fought the urge to finger the wound. Grabbing a handful of dates from a bowl, he descended the steps of the dais.

Walls of shadowed lattice and dark, brooding stone, with touches of living green softening the monotonous blank faces, circled the courtyard garden. A fountain showered diamonds in the pure golden sunlight among the citrus trees. The water set the garden to the enchantment of music. Behind the many lattices, prying eyes watched, glad for the discreet concealment they found. Intrigue was like coin to those who knew where to find it. Dimasq was a city full of intrigue.

Salah ad-Din stood before his brother. They were nearly eye-to-eye with each other. Turan-Shah was older; he was taller; he was stronger. Popping a date in his mouth, he walked slowly around Turan-Shah; his brother turned with him, ever watchful, wary of the swift and sudden punishment he knew should come to him.

Although it was a twisted turn of fate that saw Turan-Shah born the elder, it was his own keen intelligence and the favor of their father, and of Allah—may his name be praised forever—that set Yusuf above his brother as lord and master. He never let Turan-Shah forget it, just as he never forgot his brother's unequaled skill with a sword. It bound them together as one. It was a fact that made this interrogation a particularly uneasy situation.

"So, brother, you were bested by a leper who is no more than a boy—you, my most able commander. Worse, you lost the army I gave you to garrison Dimasq."

"No doubt the Ifranj will claim it was a greater victory than it was."

"Why should they not—you are already claiming it was far less a loss. Yet, the Ifranj cut your horse down beneath you and slew your Mamluks. You barely escaped with your life. I wonder, brother, what you would consider a loss?"

Turan-Shah ground his teeth. "We were lured into an ambush."

"In a place you had no reason to be." He popped another date into his mouth.

"What would you have had me do, brother? The Ifranj dogs were raiding the villages about the city, baiting us, knowing we had to defend them."

Salah ad-Din slowed and stopped, facing his most trusted emir. He folded his hands behind his back and raised himself up on his toes. "And so you obliged them with a chase into the Beka'a. I left you to defend the city, not to make war upon its enemies. Imagine my alarm at hearing that the Ifranj drew out your army and slew it nearly to a man. I can hear the rumors now that will fly: Salah ad-Din forced from a siege on Masyaf after only a week because of his fear of the *sheikh al-Jebel*. I caged Sinan like a bird in his fortress, but I had to let him go so I could return to Dimasq. I need Aleppo and Masyaf in my grasp if I am to hold Suriya."

"What was I suppose to do about the villages?"

"Leave them to their fate, brother," Salah ad-Din said. "*Ya-Allah*. You are a fool, Turan-Shah. This land has seen war for years uncounted. They are used to such destruction at the hands of invaders."

"I thought—"

"You thought that this was an opportunity to gain higher favor with me. What am I to do with you, brother?"

At a glance, the disgraced emir fell at his feet, baring his neck to the sword. "Slay me for my failure, brother. Let the dishonor of our house be removed with my blood."

Yusuf turned away from his brother in disgust, his back stiff. "Get up, you fool. You are no good to me dead, especially after the loss of so many needed soldiers. It would be better for us both if you found death and Paradise at the point of an Ifranj sword, rather than on mine. Now leave me, before I reconsider the gift I have given you and change my mind."

Once his brother had gone, Yusuf paced the small, enclosed garden, thinking. He had underestimated the leper king: for one so young, Al-Malik Bardawil ibn Morri had more genius than did all his fancy lords. He understood the game of war. Without a truce with the Ifranj, it forced him to fight a war on two fronts. A war that he was unsure he could win.

For the last two years, his plans to annex Suriya to his domain remained thwarted by a succession of Regents for Nur ad-Din's son and heir, as-Salih. The prince's current keeper, the eunuch Gumushtekin, holed up with the young boy in Aleppo, and was unwilling to surrender. Between Dimasq and Aleppo stood an even greater threat in the person of Rashid ad-Din Sinan, the infamous master of Masyaf and the Hashshashin.

The feud between them was as old as Islam—a situation not unlike the one the Nasrani were embroiled with between al-Rum and Byzantium. Certainly, neither Isa nor Mohammed had envisioned such struggles for the leadership of their faiths. While Salah ad-Din fought for the dominance of the Sunnis, Sinan defended the beliefs of a small group of Shi'ites comprised of a militant extremist brand of the Ismaili sect that favored the use of fear and terror to gain their objectives.

Gumushtekin and Aleppo could wait—they would fall as had Dimasq in time, Allah willing, but the *sheikh al-Jebel* could not. Thrice Sinan had sought to take his life; thrice he had failed, but barely. Either he had to destroy the lord of Masyaf, or he must make peace with him. He was not sure which would be the easier task. First he would deal with the Suriyans and the master of Masyaf, then he would consider how best to handle the new threat in Urshalim.

Tossing the last of the dates into the air, he reached for his sword. The blade rasped from its sheath and cut cleanly through the air with a whisper. Two halves of a date fell at his feet. He flicked the halves aside with the toe of his boot as he would his enemies. Holding the sword level, his gaze slid along the length of the blade as he controlled his anger. At the point of his sword, his gaze lifted beyond, to the walls of shadowed latticework and the secret world it hid from the world.

He turned abruptly.

A small figure—no more than a child's it seemed—stood before him, swathed all in black, a mirror of his own self. A hand reached up and drew back the veil, revealing a face that beauty had once favored highly, but had since been touched by the hand of time. She wore a slender gold fillet encrusted with jewels. It sparkled in the sunlight. It reminded him of her high position in this place.

"My lady Ismat," he said, taken back by the unexpected intrusion on his solitude.

She inclined her head in obeisance. Her dark eyes looked up at him, smiling. "My lord Salah ad-Din."

"This is an unexpected pleasure," he said. "Would you see my garden?"

"You mean see what you have made of it since taking the city," she said, appraising a small blossom. She glanced at him. "It was mine before, made for me by my husband as a gift."

He chuckled softly. "I promise I have only added to what your hand has already graced."

They walked along the narrow path, pausing every so often to share a thought about the garden. He waited her out, letting her direct the course of their conversation. She came to the point almost at once.

"I've heard you have need of allies."

He smiled, a rare accommodation, especially to a woman. "So, it's true, then, that the walls have eyes and ears."

"Always, my lord, in a city such as Dimasq." She ducked beneath a low hanging branch. "But it hardly takes a servant's eye at the lattice to see what is plainly obvious."

He had heard that the Lady Ismat ad-Din Khaitan was a woman of uncommon wisdom. She was direct as well; a quality he respected, in men, and in women. "I see the Lady Ismat is as wise as she is beautiful."

Her laugh was a delightful sound. "You have no need of empty flattery, my lord, to gain my allegiance."

"I merely give you what is your due," he said. He plucked a blood-red rose from an arbor and handed it to her. "What do you propose?" He too could be direct.

"Nur ad-Din was a good man and a faithful husband, but I did not love him. He lacked passion—you are a man of passion, are you not, my lord?"

"Given a reason to be—certainly."

"Then I see no impediment to a marriage between us."

"*Marriage?*"

"My husband is dead. I am a widow," Ismat said frankly. "According to the laws of the Prophet, I am free to marry whomever I choose. I have rank and wealth, my lord. I would make you a powerful ally. I offer you my most humble self and the alliance of the harem."

Yusuf raised an eyebrow. He stroked his small pointed beard, running the hairs through his fingers. "You make a convincing argument, my lady. But what I have need of most, is men with arms, and a lasting peace in Suriya."

They had completed their circuit of the small garden and stood at the entrance of the courtyard. Ismat reached up and recovered her face, hiding away the treasure of her handsome beauty behind the black veil of anonymity.

"Do not underestimate the alliance of the harem, nor should you take lightly its enmity. Too often men fail to realize how vulnerable they are when they lie in the arms of a lover. Do not be such a man, my lord Salah ad-Din Yusuf. We can be more deadly than any Assassin."

* * * * *

Baldwin sat in a narrow windowsill of the tower, his knees drawn up under his chin. The tower stood atop the southern wall of his house; once it had served as a minaret, a place where the priests called the Faithful of Islam to prayer before the armies of Christ had taken the city. It stood now unkempt and unused, except for the swallows that made their nests along the top of the walls. Occasionally, he left crumbs of bread for the doves. He had no crumbs today.

He had come here often when he lived with the Archbishop during his years of tutelage. Of course, as a prince it had been simple enough to slip away from the not-so-watchful eye of his tutor William. As king, guards always followed him about in case Assassins lay in wait. Slipping their protective yoke was not as easy now, but nor was it impossible as he had proven today. He needed time alone, despite the threat of Assassins. He had no doubt that even a king could not escape a scalding for his foolishness.

The sun was high in the afternoon sky, burning through layers of thick haze. From the tower he could see the dome of Saint-Mary's Cathedral, and beyond, glimpses of the green-grey sea, white with the foam of waves.

Looking out over the city, he thought of his hero, Alexander— Sikander, as his riding master, Dawud's brother, Abu 'Khair, called him in the stories he often told. Alexander had been barely twenty when he had ascended the throne of his father and began his march of conquest across the world. He did not have to contend with the curse of leprosy, though. He wondered if Alexander's generals had ever had doubts about his abilities.

Alexander's mother Olympia certainly never did. Just as Baldwin's own mother had none, despite his illness. A woman he barely knew; and yet, she was proving to be one of his staunchest allies. First, they had had to learn how to be friends, though; perhaps, later, there might come genuine affection.

The only mother he had ever known was his stepmother, Maria Comnena, his father's queen and widow. He felt a measure of comfort with her, but she had retired from Court to live out her days in Naples. He envied her that. Perhaps that was why he had been so angry with Dawud and William. Abdication was the one thing he desired most, and the one thing he could not contemplate—at least, not yet. If the kingdom ever gave him a real choice, he would like most to seek out the lepers of Saint-Lazare and live among them as their equal.

Alexander had chosen to make the world his empire and Tyre had been but one of many cities that had fallen to his ambition; all Baldwin wanted was peace and privacy, neither of which was his.

What manner of kingdom was this that God had given them that the only man worthy enough to govern it was a leper? Despite Father William's opinion to the contrary, it was more than he could bear.

A sudden voice caught his ear, a child's, drawing his gaze down and down; it echoed distantly from a courtyard beyond the turn in the road.

There, the answer to his trials seemed clear. He closed his eyes, wondering what it would be like if he leaned just a little too far out over the sill... and fell. How easy it would be, so quick, so simple. It would be but a short flight—only the space of a screamless gasp, the briefest moment of utter, surrendered pain. Then, peace and calm: Paradise. It would be a release from all his cares—freedom from the burdens of mind and body and soul. Or, would he be condemned to Hell for seeking a coward's death.

He could feel himself leaning, almost giving into his fantasies of death. Just now, Heaven and Hell seemed not to matter. Only that his present life had passed. Voices whispered to him, promising that God would be merciful. All he had to do was lean too far and he would be free.

Suddenly, he was falling—or rather, floating, gliding gently downward towards the pavement. He was wrong. There would be no sudden stop, only a release of what kept him bound to his flesh.

A hand, light, yet firm, touched his brow, drawing him up and up, back into the window. He blinked, and the images dissolved into silence and nothingness. He had not fallen after all—only dreamed. He sat gazing at the bright blue sky. The room had grown dark with shadows.

A voice whispered in his ear. *God gives us no more than what we can bear.*

"Father William..." he called, but he knew that the voice belonged to no man. It was a woman's—or an angel's. He turned expectantly, but no one was there, only the breeze off the sea, teasing his hair into elflocks. He shuddered as an icy tingle crept up his spine.

Slipping from the windowsill, he gathered up his discarded cloak, and with a last suspicious glance towards the window, climbed down from the tower to find other, more cheerful company in the hall below.

† CHAPTER TWO

What shall we do to our sister in the day when she is to be spoken to?
—Canticles 8:8

Agnes de Courtenay was not a vindictive woman—at least in her opinion—but the satisfaction she felt being back at court after so many years was, in short, nothing less than vindication. She understood the envy the petty lords and clerics of Jherusalem had for her—or was it fear? The de Courtenays were a well-connected family of high rank; and such connections usually translated into power and influence, even for a landless family from lost Edessa.

It had galled the lords of Jherusalem to know that a woman of a dispossessed family had won the hand of a king—no, not a king then, but a prince. King he had become only after they had demanded he put her aside in fear that she would become queen. They were fools—all of them. Let them wonder now how she might deal with them with her son on the throne, and she one of his closest advisors and her brother the Seneschal. She would make them rue the day they had forced her aside: For the sake of vengeance, of course.

She glanced towards the door, wondering what kept her son. It was usual for him to be late; he liked to keep his lords on edge to remind them who was king should they choose to forget. From her place of quiet vigilance beside a pillar in the Tower of David, she could survey the hall, keeping watch on those in attendance. Wisely, all the lords of the realm had chosen to come celebrate the return of the king and the victorious army of Jherusalem. The hall stood clean and decorated as if for the Easter or Christmas festival. The servants had beaten the dust from the tapestries and rugs the day before; banners hung from the roof, representing all the great families. The treasures of Jherusalem were set about the hall to add a sense of pageantry to the festivities: a reminder of the kingdom's past glory and, hopefully, its future under its young king.

Light and darkness competed for dominance in the palace: the haze of sunlight slanting from the high, narrow windows of the Tower, darkness in the form of deep shadows that crept from the walls. In its midst stood the huddled courtiers, most clustered about the pillars lost in the shadows. Her husband, Reynald Grenier of Sidon, stood by the doorway, deep in conversation with the Seneschal and Archbishop Heraclius of Caesarea. Agnes wandered purposefully towards the vacant throne. An echo of voices followed, murmuring at her back. Wearing a gown spun from the finest cloth of gold, she turned a few heads; a few more eyed her with obvious disdain. She glared back at them.

"You are the most beautiful woman here, my lady," a voice whispered in her ear. A hand guided her towards the shadows. The voice belonged to a tall, dark man who was achingly handsome. Where others had chosen to wear tunic, cotte, and hose, he wore the chain mail of a knight overlaid with the blue and white tabard of the House of Ibelin.

Agnes looked up at him over her shoulder and turned. "I am the only woman here, Messire de Lusignan."

"Messire de Lusignan?" he said. "Is that all I am to you now, *ma dama*—a simple knight?"

She offered him a demure smile, but no more than what was proper in this place. "The days of finding comfort and consolation with you in my bed have long gone by. I am married now, as are you. Or does Eschiva no longer keep your interest?"

"She keeps my interest well enough," he said, glancing around, "even when others do not."

"What brings you to Court?" she asked, trying not to look into the depth of his dark gaze. Suddenly, he seemed uncomfortable which only made her all the more curious for Amalric de Lusignan never seemed anything less than self-assured.

"My lord of Ibelin is abed with a fever. He bid me come in his stead to offer his greeting at the king's return."

Their eyes locked. She felt her heart beat faster. "You weren't present on the campaign?"

"Regrettably, my lady, I was not, for I would have liked very much to have witnessed our young king hand the Sarrazins such a humbling defeat."

"Ah, spoken like a true Defender of the Holy Sepulcher. Be careful, Messire. With such talk my son may think to make you Constable one day."

"To serve my king in such a way would be a great honor," he said softly, touching the hilt of his sword.

"Such lofty words of praise for a knight who has yet to fight for his king," she said, mocking him with a smile. Her voice grew suddenly cold. Women heard many rumors at Court and she wondered at the darkest of them. "But I wonder, *sirrah*: Whom would you really be serving—my son, or your own interests and those of Sion?"

Amalric bristled at her use of the derogatory form of address for a knight—but more so at her mention of the secret cabal whose existence he thought her ignorant. It was a familiar game: she would make an insult and shoulder past him in flight; he would pursue.

Only this time, she froze when Amalric discreetly took hold of her arm. Baldwin stood not five paces behind them, staring, seeming to form out of the very shadows of the hall. His presence was unmistakable. He wore a gold and purple cotte—longer than what was in current fashion, but expensively embroidered as befitted a king— bloused trousers, plain, white, and foreign for a king of the Franks, but no more foreign than the purple silk kaffiyeh he wore around his head, bound across the brow with his father's slender gold crown. A long length of the silk cloth swept down across his face, shadowing his large, dark eyes. Those eyes flickered now with amusement or anger. It was never easy to tell with him.

Agnes glanced uncomfortably at her former lover. The king, her son, saw the brief, involuntary exchange. Her breath caught in her throat. If he heard or suspected anything of them, he kept it to himself. Amalric had the good sense to make his obeisance to Baldwin.

Curse you, Amalric, she thought to herself. He had known that her son had been nearby all the time. He had marked Baldwin's entrance and used her ignorance to his advantage. Moreover, he had done so simply to gain an introduction to the king using his mother.

"My son, have you met Messire Amalric de Lusignan," she said, finding her voice.

The knight sketched a bow. "Your Highness."

"Lusignan?" Baldwin whispered, his bright, dark eyes narrowing in the shadow of his kaffiyeh. "You fought with my father."

"About nine years ago in Egypt. I was a knight, then, in the service of Hugh of Caesarea. His Majesty ransomed me when I was captured."

Baldwin stared at the man before him. He paused, weighing his words carefully. Agnes tried to move discreetly away, drawing closer to her son. "My father... my father must have esteemed you highly, then, Messire."

"Your majesty is generous with his compliments," Amalric said, inclining his head. "I am but a simple knight of Outremer, without land or title. My brother, Hughes, was made Lord of Lusignan in Poitou, while my brothers and I were left to make whatever fortune we could in the world."

"And yet, you won the hand of the Lady Eschiva d'Ibelin," Agnes interjected, curtly reminding the knight of his wife.

"A simple knight, indeed," Baldwin laughed. "The hand of the Lady d'Ibelin is no small accomplishment. Ibelin's fief is one of the most important in the south of the kingdom."

The Poitevin knight smiled obsequiously. "My lord of Ibelin is a generous man."

Baldwin laughed heartily. Agnes felt a sigh of relief escape her. "And a man who obviously knows the quality of men who serve him. You intrigue me, sir knight. I would like to hear more of you sometime, but alas, I am afraid more pressing matters occupy my attentions, just now. If... if you don't mind, I need to steal my mother away from you for a short time."

It was a dismissal of the subtlest degree. Caught between the willful designs of both men, Agnes yielded to the authority of her son, if only reluctantly. Taking his arm, she allowed him to lead her away. As for Messire Amalric de Lusignan, she dared not give him even the briefest glance of a parting for fear of what her action might betray.

It was a long time before Baldwin finally spoke, but when he did, he was a firestorm of emotion.

"God's bones, mother. Given the rumors floating around Court, do you think it was wise to be huddled away in a corner with Lusignan without any of your ladies about; especially with your husband in such close proximity?"

"If you must know, it's true that we were... intimate for a time. But—"

"Mother, p-p-please... spare me the sordid details of your *amours*," he said, shaking his head.

Her eyes fell; Baldwin perceived it as shame. He apologized immediately like a child seeing that he had brought his mother grief. "I'm sorry, mother," he said, trying to control his stammering tongue. His father had stammered as well. "Whatever you have done in the past is past. I'm sure you would do nothing to bring dishonor to you or myself."

Relief washed over her: she had avoided the subject of her past indiscretions without further explanation. Her eyes found his across the small solar. It was hard to remember he was only fifteen. She wanted to touch him, give him assurance of her forgiveness, but he was up again, prowling the room like a caged beast.

Suddenly, he stood before her. He towered over her by a good hand. When had he grown so tall? A mother should have noticed such things. He was not a boy any longer, but a man nearly grown and a king. Her anger flared anew, briefly, at the politics of the High Court that had kept her from her only son. They would pay—all of them—for what she had lost to time, particularly the Church and its self-righteous, backbiting servants of God.

Agnes put on a sweet face and smiled at Baldwin. She would do whatever it took to protect him from such men. What kind of mother would do anything less? She would be his shield, his haven against the long night of his illness.

She knew what the whispers at Court said behind her back— that God had cursed her son with disease because she had married within a forbidden degree. For that, she saw Amaury put her aside, her marriage annulled, her children taken away. Of course, no one ever blamed Amaury. He was a man; and everyone knew that women were the origin of sin.

Baldwin brushed her brow with a veiled kiss and knelt before her. He set a gloved hand on her knee. Reluctantly she took his hand. "I don't want to argue with you, mother," he said softly. "I need your advice."

He gave her no chance to reply; he was up again, pacing. The room was small and confined—a mere corner chamber of the palace with a narrow slit of a window for light. The space served only to restrict Baldwin's pacing, making him more frustrated. Agnes rose and stopped him in the middle of the room with a gentle hand.

"I just received word from Acre," he said. "Emperor Barbarossa was decisively defeated by the forces of the Lombards. With Frederick's loss, his war with the Pope and the King of Sicily will be prolonged all the more." He paused, looking at her. "The aid we thought to gain with an alliance with the Emperor through a Montferrat marriage will now become more of a liability than an asset. No new relief will come any time soon. By the time it does, all could be lost to the Sarrazins. Once the Court hears of this, they will be clamoring for me to break off Sibylla's wedding with Longsword in hopes of gaining help from some other quarter. I need a man at Sibylla's side now who can lead the kingdom if I fall."

"Then do not allow them to force you into a decision you do not want as your father did. Stephen of Sancerre rejected your sister once. If her engagement with William is broken, she may not ever make another suitable match."

"You think I don't know that."

In a sudden fit of despair the crown and kaffiyeh fell in a heap at Baldwin's feet; the gold coronet went clattering across the floor. "I can't do this, mother—I want to, but I just can't."

Her hand touched his arm and squeezed it. "You will because you must until you can no longer. You are king. The people—your people depend on you."

"Look at me, mother. How long do you think I will live? Already the disease begins to take its toll."

It was true and terribly so. What she saw horrified her, though she tried to ignore it. The leprosy was beyond hope of cure now. It had grown strong in him while he was away on campaign. It ravaged his handsome face; the beautiful arch of his aquiline nose had ulcerated with the disease, his lips were dry and cracked. Despite the distortions, though, the dark luminous eyes of his great-grandmother, Morphia of Melitene, remained clear and unchanged. They drew in her gaze, capturing her attention and, for a moment, letting the hideousness of his illness blur into nothingness. It was a gift he had, to distract the eye from all else but his bright gaze.

She wanted to reach up and stroke back the wheat-gold locks from his brow, to comfort him with a touch, but dared not. Death stalked him, biding its time, eager to take from her what she had only recently reclaimed.

She bent and retrieved the crown from the floor. She handed it him. Her mind raced, searching for words of comfort—how she might help him. Inexplicably, she thought of Amalric de Lusignan and their earlier conversation, of the aid he might lend, if only for his own dark purposes.

"I still have friends about the kingdom despite what the lords of Jherusalem may believe. For now, do nothing. Only be the king you were born to be—the one your people believe you to be. Let me handle this issue of William of Montferrat. Perhaps, someone can still persuade your lords to see the wisdom of his marriage with Sibylla; if for no other reason, than to produce an heir to the throne."

It might prove an empty promise she knew, but the response it prompted in her son was worth any disappointment that could result. Baldwin embraced her tightly and whispered his thanks. It was the first embrace he had given her since her return to Court. Her eyes welled with tears. Perhaps true affection would blossom in time between them after all. It was something for which she could still have hope. She only prayed he would live long enough.

* * * * *

A tear slid down Sibylla's cheek and splashed on the surface of her embroidery. She dabbed her eyes with the corner of a cloth and cursed the weakness of her feminine emotions for the second time that day.

Certainly, it was unfair her forced betrothal, but necessary in a land surrounded by enemies and desperate for whatever allies it could find, especially, with a king more a ghost than a man. Still, she didn't want to marry a nobleman from the Piedmont in the Italies, no matter how high born he was, no matter how handsome or brave, or that he was a cousin to the Holy Roman Emperor, Frederick Barbarossa. She wanted love. Even the convent and the solace she once enjoyed in the daily routine of prayers and toil would be better than marrying a man she did not know.

She was being foolish she knew, acting like a spoiled child, wallowing in self-pity. She did not care. Her sniveling servant-girl would no doubt tell her mother, and, then, *ma dame* would once more scold her, reminding her of duty and privilege, and reiterate the many praises of William of Montferrat.

Women—particularly princesses—were born to breed heirs. They had no other purpose.

Her hand and eye found the knotted blue stitch in her needlework and worked at it to loosen it. It was not the only flaw in her work of the past half-hour. With a vigor that threatened the delicate cloth, she tore at the stitches to remove them. The needle pricked her finger. It bled terribly, adding to the ruin she had made. Flinging it aside with a whimper, she leapt towards the door to find an escape.

The king—her brother—stood there, leaning against the frame.

"You look like you could do with some mischief in the city," he said, holding up a bundle of clothing in each hand. "Which would you prefer—the blue one, or the green?"

Sibylla laughed at his suggestion. "The blue one."

Their escape was a simple enough thing to accomplish. A minor diversion for the guard at the Tower; a dash along a narrow, twisted side street into a dark alley; several quick turns; and they were in the midst of the city, lost in a stifling crush of humanity on David Street where it intersected with the Latin Exchange and the Triple Market to become

Temple Street. Baldwin drew her back, blending into the press of people along the street.

Pilgrims, newly arrived to the Holy Land and clothed in tatters of sackcloth, clotted the streets, their faces upturned in joyous rapture at being in the holiest city of Christendom. They competed with a caravan that had recently arrived, trying to move its carted goods, and with the soldiers, intent on keeping order on the busy boulevard. The pilgrims were a motley band, moving in slow procession towards the Church of the Holy Sepulcher, chanting songs and prayers, and waving the palm of Jericho. A solemn line of black-clad monastics rounded out the pious mob, clouds of incense enveloping the procession.

Baldwin led, Sibylla followed, growing ever more eager in their adventure, though she still was not completely at ease with him. She had often heard rumors from the women at Court about her brother's fondness for such ventures, but this was a scandal. That he wanted to include the sister he hardly knew made it irresistible. They were two ordinary women of Araby garbed in manifold layers of silk, their faces hidden away behind the world of the veil.

Of course, it was the perfect disguise, for Muslim women in the East were rarely, if ever, looked upon in public for the sake of propriety. It offered them freedom to do as they pleased, so long as they adhered to the rules of their assumed sex.

The only flaw to their otherwise perfect plan, however, was Baldwin's height, which, among a people not particularly known for their stature, was rather conspicuous—not that her height was any less unnoticeable. He tried to slouch down behind her as they shouldered past pilgrims and peasants, but it was no use. Curious eyes followed them everywhere. Recognition nearly clipped the wings of their newly won freedom before they could attain full flight. Once they were well away from the palace and the many eyes that might recognize them, he discarded the veil, donned his more familiar kaffiyeh, and played the part of a man.

It was a pity, too, for he made a truly handsome woman. Her comment to the fact won her a laugh and a mild threat for her indulgence.

"Next time, sister, perhaps we'll cut your beautiful hair and dress you as a man. Then we'll see which of us has the greater right to make a jest."

She laughed and ran after him.

His comment only proved what she was all too quickly discovering—he was not what she had expected him to be.

A king he was, and leper, but beneath it all, a shy, quiet boy, gentle and soft-spoken, yet always eager for mischief and laughter—and certainly, no creature of the Court as the lords of Jherusalem would have him. That she was young and beautiful and nearly his equal seemed to be of no consequence, only that she was his sister and willing partner in his exploit. What she discovered was that she liked her brother.

Not surprisingly, Baldwin knew all the places two young truants might want to visit: the markets, the shrines, the splendid Dome of the Rock with its brilliant, golden dome that blazed in the afternoon sun like fire. Holy place it may be to Islam, but the Templars were the masters here now, Christians in an unchristian place, with the great mosque of al-Aqsa as the headquarters of their Order.

They walked leisurely along the shaded portico, weaving in and out of cypress and olive trees, but with the Templars at their afternoon drills and both of them in Muslim garb, Baldwin thought it best to leave. Descending the high and holy hill through the Jehoshaphat Gate towards the Kidron, they found a fruit-seller willing to part with two oranges. He frowned, though, at the thought of two Muslims willing to pay him with Frankish coins.

"*Pullani,*" he muttered under his breath, trying to reconcile in his mind what he beheld—western faces in eastern garments.

Baldwin drew the cloth from his face and leaned close to the man, whispering a few words in Arabic. The eyes of the fruit-seller widened in wonder and more wonder still. Baldwin pressed a gold bezant into his hand and gave him a parting pat on the back.

"*Pullani?*" Sibylla asked when they had melted away into the band of travelers heading down the road towards Olivet and the cave of Gethsemane. She was quickly learning how little she knew of the land over which her brother was king. The convent had prepared her for nothing beyond its own enclosed world.

With the long hot months of summer, the dry road choked the air with dust. Her brother produced a skin of water and handed it to her.

"Colts," he said, wiping his brow. "It's a word the people of this land use for those born in conquered territories that still have a strong Muslim influence in them. He thought we were Armenians from Cilicia."

"What did you tell him?"

"The truth. And then I gave him a bezant in appreciation of his silence," Baldwin said, wrapping the long strip of his headcloth across his face. He chuckled. "By nightfall he'll be unable to keep his tongue any longer and word will spread through the quarter that *El-Mesel,* the Leper King, was seen wandering the city with his sister at his side in

Muslim garb. It will make a wonderful tale that none of his neighbors will ever believe, but by then we will be safely back in the palace. Shall we see Gethsemane now, sister?"

With the late afternoon, sunlight filtered through the ancient olive trees in slanting rays, casting long grey shadows on the ground. The cave was crowded with pilgrims waiting to pray at the sacred shrine, so Sibylla and Baldwin sat quietly among the stone presses that the natives had used since time immemorial to make their olive oil. The pilgrims paid them no mind. Voices rose in a hymn from the nearby Tomb of the Virgin. It was here, so the priests said, that Judas had betrayed the Blessed Savior with a kiss on the night before his crucifixion. Sibylla wondered if her brother was conscious of that when he asked her to accompany him to the garden.

A breeze rustled the leaves above them; a shaft of light fell between them, emphasizing the sudden tension that had sprung up between them at a word.

"I'm sorry, Sibylla" he said, sinking down beside a block wall. "I... I know you don't want to marry William."

His concern touched her. "It's none of your fault, brother," she said, sliding down beside him. "Count Raymond arranged the marriage. It is what I was bred for."

"But it's not fair for you to have to bear the burden I cannot carry. If... if I hadn't got sick, then you would have been free to choose your husband."

Without knowing why, she suddenly felt sorry for him. "That is not your fault. Your illness has robbed us both of what neither of us can ill afford to lose: my chance for love and for you, your life."

Silence fell. For that, she was thankful... until it stretched on too long. Sibylla removed her veil and combed out her long blonde hair with her fingers. She leaned closer and nudged her brother. "You are the first person who has not told me that I have to marry William out of duty."

"I need a man like William. He's a warrior—a man bred for war," he said, afraid to look at her. "But I won't make you marry a man you don't love."

Sibylla was stunned and confused. Here was the freedom she longed for, but it seemed an empty victory. "Why would you do that?"

His dark eyes swiveled towards her. "Because I know how you feel—trapped, unable to breathe. I do not want to be king, Sibylla, but as long as the kingdom insists on needing me, I have no choice to do otherwise. I won't see you do the same unless you choose to."

In that moment, Sibylla wished she had known her brother better to know if she should fully trust him. "What would you have me do?"

"Choose freely," he said wearily. "Either way, I'm dowering you with mother and father's old fiefs of Japhe and Ascalone so that you'll be taken care of should something happen to me."

Freedom and love were hers for the taking. She could not believe the betrayal of her own tongue and heart. "Then, for you, I will marry William and no other."

"But you... you don't have to."

She laughed with humor. "If I don't, the kingdom will only force Isabella to marry when her time comes. It is enough to know you have given me a choice," she said, dashing away a tear with her finger. She took his hand in hers. "Until now, I didn't really understand that duty meant more than doing something against my will—it sometimes means putting the needs of others first. I will marry William without complaint and together, you and I will bear the burden of the throne. Perhaps in that we'll both find the freedom we desire."

She only prayed that she would not live to regret her decision. "Only promise me my freedom should the man prove a terrible bore."

Baldwin glanced at her, his eyes dancing with laughter. "I promise."

† CHAPTER THREE

Behold I will send my angel, who shall go before thee, and keep thee in thy journey, and bring thee into the place that I have prepared.
—*Exodus 23:20*

Othon de Saint-Amant startled as a bloom of handfire blazed suddenly before his face. It was magic, not the alchemical trickery that he knew, but pure magic: elemental, wild, and forbidden. Such magic could only belong to one man.

He startled with an odd mixture of anger and fear. It was an intrusion. Here, beneath the splendid Muslim mosque that had become the center of Templar power, beneath stone and rubble, and the accumulated dust of countless years, lay his private place of solitude.

The first *cruscignati* had mistakenly thought they had discovered the stables of Solomon upon taking the Temple Mount in the name of God and Christ. The name had stuck and so had its use. The Templars knew better. Even before their official founding as an Order, men had come here, knowing both the truth about the stables and what they held; the storerooms in which the ancient priests of the temple of Herod had hid their most precious treasures when the city fell to the Romans. Their teachings, their vessels of worship, their records. Their secrets. Secrets that the Templars had discovered. Secrets that had become the wellspring of their fabulous wealth. Or so he had been told.

"My lord," Othon said, choking on the word. His horse, a bay gelding, shied in protest at the sudden noise of his voice; it steadied again under his hand and the soft stroke of the brush. Out of long habit, he made the sign of the cross—a mistake he knew.

"Were you expecting someone else, Othon?" Amalric de Lusignan said, drawing back the hood of his dark cloak.

"You caught me by surprise."

It was not exactly a lie, although Othon had been watching for the master of the Order of Sion for the better part of the last hour.

34

Somehow, he had missed the man's entrance to the stables. If he had not known better, he would have sworn that the master had appeared out of thin air—an impossible feat of magic, even for one reputedly born of the blood of a faerie. Or was it?

Othon was not sure when he had first become aware of it, but he feared the man he had come to call his master.

A murmur of voices—other knights, no doubt, on their way to evening prayers—echoed through the vaulted halls. The handfire that had so brilliantly illumined the stall shrank to a small, glowing pearl of light. Lusignan set a finger to his lips, commanding silence until the voices faded away.

A finger touched his brow. Othon shuddered. He felt suddenly dizzy.

"Forgive me, Othon. I had to be sure there was no treachery in you."

"You—you read my thoughts?"

Amalric's laugh was a bitter, cruel thing. "Not exactly—but close enough for what I need."

He was not a fearful man, but this... this brought a chill to his bones.

"Did you bring it, Othon?" Amalric de Lusignan inquired, his impatient eagerness putting an edge to his voice.

With a word, the fear that gnawed at Othon's belly like a worm at an apple suddenly shriveled and died; the anger that had competed for the mastery of his emotion turned the cankerous worm to fire.

Disillusioned and discouraged by the vicissitudes of secular life, he had laid aside land, title, and wealth to naïvely take up the cross of Christ and the cause of the Templars. Vowing an oath poverty, chastity, and obedience, he hoped to make a difference in the world; he had risen quietly to attain what should have been the height of his career, only to learn that he was merely a pawn in a far greater circle of power.

Othon reluctantly handed the Master a worn leather satchel. Dark eyes glinting with the light of handfire narrowed at his hesitancy. "These are the copies of all the letters the courier carried from Acre?" Amalric asked.

"All of them," said Othon, though he wished it were not true. He was growing increasingly concerned about the direction the leadership of Amalric de Lusignan was taking the Order of Sion. It smacked too much of self-service and pride, not the sworn devotion of a guardian of the *sangreal*.

"Pope Alexander's victory over the Emperor cannot bode well for Sion," he said, returning to the care of his horse.

"It is not the first time we have suffered a setback, my friend. Nor will it be the last," said the Master of Sion. "We are in a game of quiet patience; one of risk and manipulation, of chances won and lost… of sacrifice. The Pope may have won a battle, but he has not won the war. A new war will come, never fear, my good Othon. And when it does, we must be ready."

"And the princess' marriage to Montferrat—what of that?" said Othon. "An alliance with Frederick could prove troubling if the Pope should happen to prevail."

Amalric smiled. "Or it could prove a great asset if the Emperor can manage to make a reversal in this war. Either way, things have a way of happening unexpectedly. Do not forget—newcomers to this land have an unfortunate habit of dying from one disease or another. Who's to say if William of Montferrat will be any different?"

"And so we walk the sword's edge between loyalty and treachery."

"No," Lusignan sneered. The handfire pulsed white-hot. "We walk the path set before us by the Brothers of Ormus a hundred years ago. Our only loyalty is to the Way of the Baptist."

Othon began brushing his horse with more and more vigor, trying to fend off his annoyance. Amalric stepped around the other side of Othon's horse.

"Incidentally, how did our young king distinguish himself on campaign? From the embroidered stories they're telling at Court, you'd think he actually led the charge himself."

"It is no embroidery," Othon said. "He was like a young lion at his first hunt." He paused, lifting the brush his horse's flank in thought. He had been there. He had seen the valor of their young king. He let his head hang in frustration. "I think you underestimate him, my lord. For a king who is barely a man, he is remarkable—an opinion that even old Humphrey the Constable shares. And right now, he is the only thing holding this kingdom together."

"Of course he is, you fool," spat Amalric. "He is a king born of the sacred blood of Christ. And therein lays the problem you refuse to see, my dear Othon. He cannot sire an heir; therefore, he cannot be the chosen vessel of our purposes. Love him, adore him, and follow him as you will—he is king, after all. But it is to the princess Sibylla our focus must turn."

"I think you are a making a bold mistake."

"Calm yourself, my friend," said Amalric. "I did not say Baldwin would be removed from power—only that he would not be enlightened about our existence or our purposes. Nor did I say we would remove our unseen hand from his throne. In fact, we must work now to strengthen his hand for the day when Sibylla must reign in his place as queen. We must bend every power we possess towards that goal. Do not despair, Othon. Our young king's valor and abilities may be of great benefit to us after all. If he can hold the throne, even a year, or three, it will give us time to prepare Sibylla for her role in our plans."

"So, she must be told, and soon."

"To that end, however, we may have a small problem I think I can resolve, but I need your help."

"And that is?"

"The de Courtenay woman knows of us."

Othon stopped and turned. "How?"

"I'm not sure... yet, but it could prove to be one of those risks that we must chance for the good of our cause. If we can control her, then we can control the king."

"Can she be trusted?"

"Given enough reason, I think so. She has no love for the Church that annulled her marriage to King Amaury. In fact, I believe she may prove herself as great an ally for our cause as was Queen Melisende. I will handle Agnes de Courtenay. In the meantime, I want you to keep an eye on her. Find out where she goes and who she sees."

"Is that all?"

"With the king's illness now openly proclaimed, events will begin to unfold quickly. We must be ready to strike, for this chance may not come again for many long years."

The light of the handfire winked out. Between one breath and another, Othon found himself alone in a dark stable smelling of horse and hay. Only then did he realize what his heart had long known to be true: if not stopped, Amalric de Lusignan would destroy them all. And only Othon knew it.

* * * * *

The tiny chapel lay bathed in the soft glow of candlelight. The bare rock of Calvaire lay nearly hidden away beneath the care of pious devotion and the shadow of an altar. Baldwin knelt at the bench, praying. His knees hurt; the smoke of candles wrinkled his nose.

As a child, he had scarcely given thought to such rituals; as king, they had become his consolation. The altar had certainly seen its share of his anger, his bitterness, his silent pleas for strength. He gave into his newfound habit and let it lead him through his obeisance to God. There was comfort in the ritual: prayer, genuflection, more prayer. He tilted his head, gazing up at the figure of Jhesú in its mosaic frame of gold. The savior seemed to look down at him; his expression was one of understanding towards his suffering.

Finishing his prayer, he crossed himself, and rose, wandering towards the tomb beneath its high and airy dome of gold and white stone. A circle of columns rose through the haze of incense and sunlight. The hymns of pilgrims filled the choir. It was discordant and raw—angelic.

A line stood before the ornate shrine. The pilgrim season was winding down with the coming of autumn. Soon the steady streams of worshippers would slow to a trickle. Opposite the guarded shrine, a tall urn stood alone, marking the place the clerics claimed was the navel of the world. Over the years, visitors had taken to leaving small coins in token of their pilgrimage. Baldwin lingered by the urn, waiting as the line to the tomb dwindled to a few patient souls.

An old woman, small and hunched, bundled in the tattered rags of a tunic, leaned over the pilgrim's urn, fumbling in her scrip for a coin. She was nearly beside herself with frustration. Baldwin laid a gentle hand on her shoulder and deposited two coins in the urn.

"Let me pay your tithe, widow-woman," he said. "I'm sure God would not hold it against you."

Her hand clasped his arm. The grip was surprisingly strong for an old woman. "Bless you, young lord."

The last of the pilgrims were filing into the shrine, eager to descend into the empty tomb. The woman shuffled forward at the priest's gesture.

"So what do you think of our humble little church?" Baldwin asked, leaning close. He felt a small measure of pride at the renovations his family had made to the basilica in the last seventy years.

"It's not as pretty as the Hagia Sophia in the Golden City," she said.

He should have been offended—for the sake of kingly pride. Instead, he was amused. "You would compare the beauty of our Lord's tomb with the church of the Byzantines?"

"I see too much of the vanity of men," she said, looking around sharply at the dark and gloomy expanse of the church, even with all its candles and lanterns. "And too little of the humility of our Lord."

Baldwin murmured a soft chuckle. "Don't tell the priests, but I rather agree with you. All the same, it is a wonder to behold."

"Did I say it wasn't," the woman hissed. He caught a touch of humor in her breath. "Still, I would worship here as I ever have, even if it was the lowest of churches in the world."

He fell silent at her words and helped her forward as the priest guarding the tomb motioned for her turn in the crypt. Crossing herself, she gave him a thankful squeeze, and descended into the holiest of holy places.

The shrine was an elaborate affair, worked in beautiful marble by the finest imaginations and artistry of man; below, hidden beyond a low lintel of stone, the dark tomb that was the object of adoration and the center of the kingdom's being.

The old woman had barely gone down into the tomb when the priest called her out again. She regarded the fat, slow-eyed cleric with annoyance, but acquiesced to his command. Helping her out by the arm, Baldwin made the sign of the cross, and bent beneath the lintel into the cool darkness. The silence was deafening. Such holiness overwhelmed him: a simple tomb—a glorious resurrection. The stone itself whispered of its sanctity. He closed his eyes and offered up a prayer. Any moment now and the priest would call him up.

The moments lengthened, and no call came. Baldwin thought it a blessing and a courtesy of the priest. In the shadowy gloom, his hand found the chiseled wall and the curve of the low bench within it, worn smooth with the centuries of pilgrimage. Here was the center of all Christendom, of all true faith; here, where the power of Heaven had met the simplest need of earth.

Reverence, fear, and the sudden thought of his own impending death, overwhelmed him. Tears sprang to his eyes, bearing him down to the cool stone of the floor. It was an offering of sorts: of his grief and his self-pity. The release of emotion scoured his soul. It gave him an unforeseen comfort where he had had none; a new strength like the tempered steel of Damascus. When he had shed all the tears he had, he took flight from his place of sorrow, and ascended the steps of the tomb into the clear light of day.

He found her waiting in the courtyard. He almost missed her huddled against the wall in the shadow of the belfry tower. The courtyard was deserted.

"The priest should not have treated you that way," said Baldwin by way of apology. He joined her by the wall.

Her aged smile warmed him. "He is a fool and a man. He saw me only as a woman, and as an affront to his self-righteous piety. He forgets that the first visitor to his cherished tomb was a woman."

"Still," he said, dropping his eyes, "he should have treated you with more respect."

"As you did, young lord?"

Baldwin turned away, embarrassed. "I am not like other men."

"No. You are a king, with a king's compassion."

His eyes darted, curiosity aroused. "You knew who I was?"

She laughed. "It takes more than a crown and the muttering words of a priest to make a man king."

"Even if that man is a leper?" he said and turned away.

"God gives us no more than what we can bear."

The words struck him. In his mind's eye, he saw the city of Tyre and the grey-green sea spread out beyond; a tower rising above the two; himself falling and lifted by an unseen hand. He turned again on the woman who had suddenly become strange and fey.

"It... it was you who saved me from falling in Tyre."

Her gaze fell upon him. "No. Your will to live saved you," she said. Her voice had grown oddly beautiful. There was music in it: warm, rich, and sweet as honey. "I merely spoke the words that set your thoughts to reason rather than madness."

"But how..." he said, and stopped, afraid of the impossible answer to which his words were leading him. There was some small working of enchantment here; he felt it in the air, but didn't shrink from it though he knew that its touch could condemn his soul forever. "Who are you?"

"More than the simple pilgrim you see; less than what our Lord wishes me to be."

Before his eyes, the tattered rags of her cloak fell away, revealing a woman bathed in white and gold, and very beautiful. It *was* magic; the devil's handiwork, if he believed the priests and he caught in the very midst of its subtle working. He cursed it silently for what it was, and stood transfixed, his heart racing with the sheer wonder of its promise.

"*Deo Mater*," he breathed and made the sign of the cross. *Beware you do not forget to entertain strangers; for by doing so some have entertained angels unawares.* Father Aimery had spoken those very words in his sermon only a few days before.

She plucked the very words from his mind. Her laughter was high and light and wonderful. "Me—an angel? Hardly. I am somewhat less I'm afraid just as God intended all those of my kind to be."

His mind raced, searching for meaning—for understanding. Nothing came. "Your... kind?" Then, he *Saw* the peculiar cast of her features—human enough, but with a touch of an unearthly beauty so rare that it hurt the eyes to behold. Wine dark hair that shimmered with fire when struck by the sun and eyes large and bright and round in the midst of its glorious fall. It was as though scales had fallen from his eyes.

A chorus of names leapt into his mind: *faerie and elf-maid. Witch. Devil's get.*

She hissed, perceiving the direction of his thoughts. "No. That is how the Church condemns us. It condemns all things that do not fit into their careful, narrowly laid down theologies that glorify man and not God. I am no spawn of devils. You have nothing to fear from me, Baldwin of Jherusalem."

As fear gave way to curiosity, his suspicions grew. "If I have nothing to fear of you, tell me who you are. What do you want with me?"

"I am one who would be your friend and not your enemy."

"Why should I need your friendship—I have friends aplenty," his stubborn adolescence said just to prove his insolence.

Fire blazed green in her eyes. She smiled, but coldly. "And enemies to match, my young king. Not the least of which is the Lord Salehdin." She drew closer and raised a warning finger. "But, there is an enemy greater than the lord of Islam before you. An enemy whose will is to turn all to darkness and lies."

Baldwin glared at her, unsure whether he should trust her words. "How do you know this?" he said, biting off the words with his impatience.

Her response was simple and plain: unexpected. "I have fought this evil before," she said, almost in a whisper. "They will stop at nothing to gain what they seek. You and your kingdom are in grave danger."

"If you want to help, then heal me of this disease so I can fight this hidden danger. Surely you must have the power to do so."

She fell back a step, her arms hugging her frail body. He noticed suddenly how small a creature she was. "If I could, I would do so, but the leprosy that consumes you is a magic stronger than even I can heal. The kingdom and the spell are one. As you begin to weaken, so too will your kingdom. There is nothing I can do."

Despair grabbed hold of him, pulling him down. His shoulders sunk. Sweat sprang to his brow, beading thickly. He felt suddenly hot. "Then all is lost."

She touched him, light and quick. Her grip on his arm was like steel. "It isn't, yet. Trust me, king of Jherusalem. I will help you defeat this evil before it consumes us all."

"Why... why are you doing this?"

She lifted a hand; a small gold coin shone in the midst of her palm. "You are the first king of this land to show pity on an old woman since your people came from the West."

He reached and took the coin from her hand. He had dropped its twin into the pilgrim's urn in the church.

She was gone before he could reply. He felt her lingering presence, though. It was like a veil about him. Baldwin stood starring at an empty courtyard. What he had just seen was impossible; what he had just spoken with was unimaginable. He laughed, suddenly, realizing his newfound ally—whether it was real or born of his imagination or insanity—had still not given him her name. Laughter rippled through the air, mirroring his own insane humor. It whispered a name that strangled his laughter and set his heart to pounding.

—My name... is Mary Magdalen.

He felt suddenly dizzy and weak. He touched the back of his hand to his brow. It was warm. Feverishly warm. He heard voices, singing: the monks at their prayers in the monastery. He swayed, and staggered. The world spun wildly out of control into darkness.

* * * * *

"How did you know?"

The voice—a man's—came from the garden window. It was pleasant and familiar—very familiar. Its owner wandered from the window to her chair. She watched him in the large oval of her silver mirror. He set his hands on her neck and shoulders. She tensed.

"About what, Messire—Sion?" she said. "I didn't with any certainty until just now."

His strong, callused hands began to knead her neck. Her skin seemed to turn to fire. He laughed coldly. "You always were a bit too clever of a woman, Agnes."

Agnes gently set the hairbrush down and stood, turning in the loose circle of his hands. She smiled at Amalric de Lusignan. His thumb pressed against the sides of her slender throat. Her blood pounded beneath his fingers. If she felt fear, she would overcome it; if it were excitement, she would be undone.

"What will you do now? Silence me?"

He kissed her, hard and long. A direct assault was usually the best tact; this was most unfair—and most pleasant, at least for her. It was trickery she knew, but was powerless to stop him... until he spoke.

"I'm not in the habit of killing women who have shared my bed, *ma dama*."

She bit his lip, hard. "No—only kings who won't obey you. That is most chivalrous of you, *Messire*."

"Children, however, are another matter."

She raked him with her gaze. "You wouldn't dare."

"I would, and I will, if you don't answer me now, Agnes," growled Amalric. "I'm in no mood to play games. How did you know?"

Her sleeping gown slipped off her shoulder. She pushed it back on. He pushed it off again, caressing the soft, bare skin with a hand. A flush rose into her cheeks, burning.

"Are you planning to seduce me to get what you want?"

"Do I need to?"

She sighed languidly. "If you must know, Amaury told me the night his brother died. He told me all of it. And, that Sion killed his father. He feared for our children's lives."

Amalric let his hands fall and stepped back, regarding her coolly. "Fulk was a stubborn man. He cared more about his Angevin interests than Jherusalem. It was simple enough to make it appear as though his saddle had crushed his head when he fell. No one ever suspected."

"Did you kill Baldwin? Amaury?"

His eyes narrowed at her, calculating the worth of his admission. "There is more at stake here than the simple politics of kings and kingdoms, my lady. So much more."

"Then tell me what you are so poorly trying to say."

She schooled herself to patience; she was too eager, too willing to listen. He smiled. She glared.

"Come with me outside," he said, holding out a hand. Hesitantly, she took it.

In the center of the small garden lay a rectangular pool overgrown with lilies and a misshapen statue out of old Rome rising out the water. He brought her to the pool and set her upon the edge of its low wall. Moonlight touched the water with a silver sheen. "What do you know of the cup of Christ—the one used at the Last Supper?"

She had to think, sifting back through the years of learning her father had commanded for her—a training not usually given to young girls. "Legend says Joseph of Arimathea took it with him to England in the years after the crucifixion. There are other stories, though, that say that the Magdalen took it to the Languedoc. Either way, it was eventually lost and forgotten."

A faint hint of a smile played across Amalric's face. "You impress me, my lady. You are a credit to your sex. But what if I were to tell you that it was not lost, but hidden away until a new kingdom should arise in Jherusalem; a kingdom born of those who are of the blood and lineage of Christ."

"I would say that you are madder than a hare in March."

"Am I, *ma dama*," he said, withdrawing a cup of gold and dark red agate from his cloak. He dipped it in the pool and held it up, close to her face. He caught a stray beam of moonlight in its dark depths and breathed upon its surface, stirring its shimmering mirror into motion until it glowed with a soft pale light.

She startled. "What kind of deviltry is this?"

"A kind which would damn your soul to Hell, if a priest were to witness it. Would you still see it?"

The word came out unexpectedly, almost breathlessly. "Yes."

It began simply enough: a flicker of movement, a ripple of light beneath the dark surface. Images came and went, seemingly of their own accord—or of Amalric's.

The water stilled. An image appeared. A tree; eradicated; encircled with a crown. It shimmered and rose, hovering above the cup, a thing of light and mist and hauntingly wondrous in its simple beauty. She blinked and the image dissolved.

"What was that?" she asked. The sound of her voice seemed far away, detached.

He dashed the water upon the pavement and caught her hands in his. "The tree is the kingdom of Jherusalem, and the lineage of the blood of Christ. It is the end of Rome and all her lying priests. It is new beginning."

"A new beginning?" she said, bewildered, afraid. "I don't understand. I don't understand any of this."

"The Order of Sion is the guardian of an ancient secret that the Church will do anything in its power to keep from seeing the light of day. Very soon, however, we will reveal the secret and then all the wrongs of a thousand years will be set to rights. Imagine a union between Christianity and Islam: a Frankish king, a Muslim queen—a marriage of the two lands. The power of Rome will crumble and Jherusalem will become the new seat of power in the world where Jews and Christians and Muslims alike can learn the true teachings of Christ and the Baptist."

For all his lofty words, Agnes heard only one truth. "You would propose treason against my son—against your king."

"No," Amalric argued. "It is a plan for peace; a perfect, winnable peace. A peace in which your son can finally find the rest he needs and deserves. But I need your help. Only then can true peace be made with Islam."

"My help? What can I do?"

"You can listen to me and do as I say," he whispered in her ear as though it were a spell. "Do this and your children will live, I assure you."

Her body rebelled and tried to flee. He kept her there by the sheer force of his will and a word of command. "Agnes, stop."

She drew back; but spoke boldly without fear. "You are not the Amalric de Lusignan I knew, are you?"

He watched her from the edge of the pool. Shadows and darkness swirled around him. He drew them in and made them into a cloak of invisibility. His voice spoke out from the darkness. "Who do you think men say I am?"

She wrapped herself with her bare arms. "But you're not. You can't be. Amaury told me as much. He saw you die at Damietta. He warned me not to trust the man who had come up out of Egypt—that you were somehow… different."

He sighed; chuckled. "Men can be reborn—resurrected to new life. Is that not what the Church of Rome teaches?"

"This has nothing to do with Christianity," Agnes said. Her sudden anger brought her a step closer.

"It has everything to do with it, my lady."

Agnes shook her head. She had the scent of something dark and mysterious, hidden. He knew it and tried to hide it with a cunning smile. She would not let him mislead her so easily. "You must wear his face very well to have misled so many all these years. Is there truly such strong magic in the world that a man can wear the face of another for so long?"

His smile deepened. It grew feral and dangerous. Light danced in his eyes. "Not just one man, my lady, but many, many more. Shall I name them for you? Each of them I wore until they were no longer of any use, and then, I discarded them and took a new one. Ormus. Basilides. Mani. Arius. Pelagius…"

The names confused her. Words without meaning assaulted her ears like an army in battle, battering down her defenses. She wanted to run; she wanted to hide. But she listened with an ever-growing sense of fascination. There was power in his words: an enchantment. She heard him speaking, but for all his talk, he still had not answered her simplest questions. Or had he?

"Who are you?"

"I am the voice of one crying out in the wilderness."

The voice of one… His words were light cast suddenly into uttermost darkness. She had heard them before. In the Scriptures—in the Gospels. "They are the words of the Baptist."

"The words I learned long ago at the feet of my master."

"But…" she stammered, so reminiscent of her son, "but that is impossible."

"It is truth, my lady," he said, "if you will only hear it."

† CHAPTER FOUR

For he hath given his angels charge over thee; to keep thee in all thy ways.
—Psalms 90:11

The battle was a rout: swift, complete, and without mercy. The king, maneuvering behind his line of soldiers, tried to form some semblance of a defense. It was no use. His men were falling, first one, and then another. The Sarrazins hounded his every move. The line could not hold much longer.

The sultan, resplendent in black and gold, held his ground, his victory all but assured. Holding the center, he commanded his Mamluks to the right of the field in a flanking movement. It pressed inward; the line of Franks wavered, crumbled in upon itself under the force of the assault. His castles captured, his knights slain, the remainder of the Frankish army driven from the field.

A single error had led to this defeat: his delay in attacking had let his enemy choose the battleground. It was a lesson of youth and inexperience that he would not soon forget. Even in defeat, though, there was honor still he could win: live to fight another day; spare the life of a queen he would never have. Only a fool would fight a battle he had already lost. Circled and outnumbered, Baldwin yielded to his opponent and surrendered.

"Not your best game, Your Highness," said the Archbishop of Tyre as he began to arrange the pieces on the chessboard. "Another game, perhaps?"

"Maybe one more," Baldwin said, stretching in his bed. He yawned; his jaw popped. "This time, I'll let you be white. Perhaps it will give our little Frankish army a real chance of victory against the Sarrazins."

"If you insist, my lord," said William, laughing. "But remember, chess is game of patience and careful thought. Your mistake was…"

"… that I went out too quickly and with too little strength. I hesitated and lost."

47

William nodded. "A mistake you'll remember I trust. Now, shall we begin again? I believe white starts," he said, and led out with the pawn of his king's bishop. It was his favorite opening.

The game naturally moved apace with the player's separate strategies; quickly at first—a flurry of move and countermove with Baldwin doing most of the latter—then, more slowly, more thoughtful, as each tried to take control of the board's center. Baldwin was losing again before he had time to recover from a series of thoughtless blunders. It cost him his queen, his knights, and half his pawns. Only his bishops and rooks remained; and one of his stoic clerics was in danger. The end game usually gave Baldwin most of his trouble. William found his opponent infuriating. It was the usual outcome whenever his king refused to concentrate or care, or when Baldwin was simply trying to lose to escape his boredom.

As for his fever, Dawud had explained that it was part of the weakening state of his condition. There would be others; and probably, more frequent. The monks of Holy Sepulcher had found him when they had come to pray for Vespers. Stripped, bled, and cooled with compresses, the doctor put him to bed, whereupon he had lain asleep for three days, burning it seemed with the fires of Hell. William prayed endlessly over him; his mother ranted her anger at the guards for letting him slip their leash. He woke the fourth day to find Sibylla asleep in a chair at his arm. She said nothing, simply rose, giving him her most beautiful smile, and went in search of their mother. She had rarely left his side since he had taken ill at the church.

Amid the silent ebb and flow of the game, his mind had begun to wander. The sun slanting through the window lay full upon him, warm and soft, whispering of slumber. His mind ran easily to distraction. His heart was just not in the game. It wavered between the reality of his dreams and the wild imaginations of his waking mind, all of it centered on her. *She* was continuously in his thoughts.

His heart groaned. Had he imagined her in the throes of fever or had she been real? Whenever he closed his eyes, he saw her beautiful face: radiant, angelic, and impossibly real. It was a distraction far greater than the sun or slumber or boredom. It haunted him.

His mind tried to shut out the thought; but it whispered from behind the wall he set in his mind. It—she—could not be real. It was his fevered dreams, nothing more. Still…

"You're a learned man, Father William," Baldwin said, casually venturing into a conversation he might otherwise avoid.

"I'm flattered that Your Majesty takes notice of such things," said William. He leaned closer to the board, studying it intently. "But if you're trying to distract me, Sire, it won't work."

"What do you know about the Magdalen?" The words were out before Baldwin realized he had spoken them.

The archbishop gave him the briefest of glances. His gaze fell again to the board, scowling. "Your Majesty knows it is impolite to talk to an opponent while he is contemplating his move," he said, meting out his words judiciously as he touched yet another piece.

"Just as the archbishop knows that I am his king and... and that he should answer me."

Another glance met his, a look that was all defiance. "Ah, but I am only answerable to God and the Holy Father in Rome."

Baldwin opened his mouth to reply. A cautionary finger shot up above the chessboard, invoking his silence. He swallowed his less than charitable remark. With a heavy sigh, he fell back into the soft nest of pillows of his bed, waiting on his insolent Chancellor. When William's pondering stretched on indefinitely, he began to sulk. The archbishop smiled behind his blank mask of meditation. He pulled a long face, trying to hide it. His hand stretched out to a chess-piece; a knight captured a pawn setting Baldwin's king in danger. The king retreated: Baldwin tipped his black sultan and reclined back on the bed.

William frowned. "You didn't even try this time, Your Highness."

Baldwin armed himself with a smile. "And now you can answer me my questions. What do you know of the Magdalen?"

"A rather peculiar question for someone so lately risen from a fever to ask, don't you think—Sire?" said William. "Did you have dream?"

"No."

An eyebrow arched. "A vision?"

"Certainly not!"

"What, then?"

"None of them," Baldwin said, exasperated. "It was only something I thought of the other day when I was at the tomb. The day I took ill. Is it true she was the first person to see the risen Savior? Brother Heribert told me—"

"Shall I answer your questions, Majesty—or do you propose to do it for me?"

"Sorry," said Baldwin. He leaned forward in the bed. "Is it true—about her being the first apostle?"

William sat back in his chair; he fixed Baldwin with a ponderous stare. "The early Church called her, *Apostola Apostolorum*—the Apostle of the Apostles—since it was she who brought word of the Savior's resurrection to the disciples. Once the Church held her in high esteem, but I'm ashamed to admit that in the days since, that view has fallen out of use along with the Magdalen's reputation." He paused; sighed. "Her position has been relegated into insignificance and the Church has branded her a harlot—a view I don't share with my superiors."

"Why would the Church do that?" asked Baldwin, trying to reconcile what he was hearing with what he knew—and had seen.

The archbishop shook his head. "The motives of the Church are beyond yours or my understanding, Sire. I rather suspect it has to do with what the Church perceived as a threat to their theology. To them the Magdalen was a sinner, a harlot—worse, a rival to the Virgin herself. Her cult is widespread, particularly in the south of France."

"What do the scriptures say of her?"

"Only three things: she was a follower of the Lord and that he had cast seven daemons out of her; she stood at the foot of the cross; and she saw the risen savior after the resurrection. After that, she disappears from the scriptural record. The Church maintains that the sister of Lazarus and the woman who washed Jhesú's feet with her hair were both the Magdalen, but I think that that is a gross distortion of scripture meant to harmonize the identities of the woman surrounding the Lord during his earthly ministry. There is nothing to prove its validity, though. Only speculation."

"That's it? Nothing more?"

"Nothing."

"What happened to her, then? Is it true that she left the Holy Land after the resurrection and traveled to France?"

William pursed his lips, nodding. "Tradition says she did indeed travel to Gaul, as it was called then. Some say she arrived at a place near Marseilles in the company of Lazarus of Bethany, Maximin, Joseph of Arimathea, and the two other Marys, Jacobi and Salome. She died there of old age and was buried at Saint-Maximin. I have seen her tomb. It is a simple thing, but hallowed far more than any tomb should be."

Her tomb. The words made no sense. If she had died, then who was the woman who visited him at the Holy Sepulcher? Had he imagined her after all? His gaze shifted, wandering towards the window and the soft sunlight. He turned sharply, his eyes darting back to the archbishop sitting quietly, his hands folded neatly in his lap.

William smiled at him benignly, but his eyes betrayed him; he was not telling the whole truth. *Curse these priests and their penchant for talking in circles, for never giving any ground in an answer to a question,* he thought. He was surprised Father William could not hear his thoughts as loud as they echoed in his mind. He was definitely keeping something back—something important—and Baldwin was not about to be put off so easily. Dissatisfaction and impatience gave birth to irritation and frustration; it swelled, blossomed, and burst into words. The Magdalen's face loomed suddenly in his mind, smiling and deceptive.

"I've heard she was a witch," he blurted, desperate to get his Chancellor to reveal something he knew.

The said Chancellor shifted, noticeably uncomfortable in his chair. It creaked under his weight. Leaning forward, he picked up the black queen from the chessboard and held it up in the palm of his hand. "And I've heard it said that in some circles she is considered the queen of some secret kingdom. But just because I've heard, that doesn't make it true or that I believe it. And neither should you, Your Highness. There are strange forces at work in the world—ones that you would do well to avoid."

Baldwin folded his arms across his chest and lay back in his bed. "You are a very obtuse man when you want to be, Father William."

"It is my nature, Sire, and my privilege," he said, winking.

"Is there nothing more you can offer me; no myths, no legends, no traditions wrapped in mystery?"

"None, Your Majesty," said William. He rose and set the chessboard aside on a table. "Now, I think your Highness has had enough theology and history for one day. You need rest."

"What His Majesty needs is for everyone to stop treating Him as though He is a child and an invalid."

"It has been barely a week since you took ill," said William. "You need rest. Perhaps later, some fresh air and a walk about the garden."

Baldwin glared. "You are not my doctor."

"No. But Dawud is," he said. "And he says you need a few days more rest."

"Very well," said Baldwin, his anger cooling. "I'll do whatsoever you wish, but only if you answer me one last question."

William sighed, giving in to his whim. "What is your question?"

Baldwin felt a sudden surge of emotion—of mischief and a sense of hard-won victory.

"Do you believe in faeries and magic and such?"

* * * * *

51

The Compline bell found Archbishop William of Tyre alone in the chapel with only the shadows about him to help keep his vigil. An alabaster statue of an open-armed Virgin looked down upon him, her eyes round, dark, and as large as any icon's. Her sympathetic stare offered him only scant comfort. She proved a better listener than councilor. His prayer offered little more. It seemed too heavy, too mortal—too full of his sin to penetrate the enclosing roof of stone.

Pater noster, qui es in coelis, sanctificetur nomen tuum… Our Father, who art in Heaven, hallowed be Thy name…

He had come to the small chapel in the palace to pray and to think, but became lost in the endless litany of his petitions. It was his seventh—or was it the seventeenth—prayer. All he could think about was the king and his questions; questions too poignant for him to answer, at least with any truth.

He sighed wearily and removed his stole. After kissing it, he folded it neatly and set it on the altar; his hand paused, fingering the delicate embroidery of the Chi-Ro stitched in the finest gold thread. It had been a gift from the Count of Tripoli upon his elevation to the Archbishopric of Tyre—an appointment Raymond had made as Regent.

William sensed her before he ever saw her: a prickling of the senses like a cool draft through a chink in the chancellery door. Only this draft was warm and glowing, wholly alien to all he believed. Finishing his prayer, he made the sign of the cross and rose to greet her. The chapel lay dimly lit. She stood in the midst of it, all in white and gold, bathed in the soft glow of candlelight.

"When you pray, do not use vain repetitions as the heathen do: for they think they will be heard for their many words," she said, throwing the words of the Christ in his face with a sly, wicked smile.

She was often that way with him: taunting and playful, annoyingly forthright. "You told him you were the Magdalen," he said, ignoring her acerbic remark.

She laughed suddenly, musically. "You make it sound as though I were lying."

He narrowed his gaze. He was in no mood for her playfulness. "Did you tell him all of it?"

Her levity dissipated like a vapor. In her anger, she was a fearful presence, terrible to behold. Candlelight and shadows were unkind to her unnatural beauty. "He is a boy, even if he is a king," she said, taking a menacing step towards him. "I will tell him when he can best handle it—when he decides that what I've already told him is true."

William stepped back against the altar, jarring the candlestick. The light flickered; it cast grotesque shadows against the wall, and settled. She always seemed to have the power to unbalance him. In the five years he had known her, he had never quite felt at ease in her presence.

"And if he doesn't?"

"Then he will have to be made to believe—as I had to do with you. He is not some child to be mollified with simple answers and half-truths. He needs to understand why his enemies have marked him for destruction."

William shook his head. "I think you risk too much, lady."

"His father was lost to us because we risked too little," she said, turning away towards a small alcove veiled in shadow, pacing restlessly. "I won't see anything more happen to Baldwin if I can prevent it."

A pang of sorrow knifed through his heart, a sympathy born of the guilt he knew Mary bore. "You cannot continue to blame yourself, lady. What you did was necessary. You thought only to protect him."

"Hollow words cannot excuse my folly. I alone am to blame for what he has been made to suffer."

An uneasy silence fell between them, and lengthened. William could not let the matter rest, though. "Have you discovered yet who is behind the Order of Sion?"

Mary laughed coldly. "I am immortal, my friend," she said, softening her words to a more amicable tone. "Not omniscient. The Master of Sion is an old, old enemy, as subtle and elusive as the Father of Lies." Her face changed; a wild gleam brightened her eyes—a wild, *inhuman*, gleam. She drew nearer. "But he is here—in Jherusalem. I can sense him; his power is very strong. He cannot elude me for long. He will make his move on Baldwin. I am sure of it. I have only to set a trap for him. Then, it will only be a matter of time before he is revealed."

William swore under his breath, words hardly fitting for a man of God. His sudden anger made him bold, reckless. "You would use Baldwin as bait for your snare?"

His anger was no match for hers. She beat his down into submission with a level stare and calm, evenly spoken words. "What would you have me do—wait until our enemy's working completely destroys the king and all is lost?"

"Of course not."

Her hand touched his, a movement both subtle and comforting. "Trust then that I know what I must do to protect him."

† CHAPTER FIVE

Behold, I set forth in your sight this day a blessing and a curse.
—Deuteronomy 11:26

Illiam of Montferrat arrived in the Holy Land the first week of October accompanied by a Genoese fleet eager to reclaim holdings they had lost over the years; six weeks later, the church and the kingdom celebrated the royal marriage in the Church of the Holy Sepulcher.

Finally, Baldwin was free to breathe: the throne, and the succession to it, was secure. By all accounts, Sibylla was more than happy with the High Court's choice for her husband. He was tall and fair and handsome, all the qualities she considered desirous in a husband. Unfortunately, his ill temper and his liberal excesses of food and drink overshadowed the deeper qualities of his character—his strength, his courage, and his martial skill. They were qualities hardly suitable in a future king, especially in a kingdom that had more than its fair share of factious lords and self-aggrandizing clergy. For the sake of peace and prosperity, and a sick king whose days were certain to be short-lived, the Court set aside its reservations and worked diligently to make the kingdom's future as secure as possible. By all indications at least, William and the soon-to-be-appointed lord of Hebron and Oultrejourdain, Reynald de Châtillon, would work well together to hold the southern defenses of the kingdom, the most likely point of invasion by Salehdin from Egypt.

On a chilly morning in late November, Baldwin and his court set out on a royal progress from Jherusalem to see the new Count and Countess of Japhe and Ascalone safely installed in their residence. It was a splendid procession. The sun shone; the birds sang for joy. Lords and ladies, soldiers, knights, and horses, all of them decked in their finest attire, crowded the road, acknowledging the well wishes of the peasants and offering them gifts of freshly minted coins. Set amidst the progress, rode a smattering of dour-faced clerks, scribes, and clergy who thought the business of court too important to set aside even for a day or two.

The levy of forty knights owed to the crown by the new Count escorted the royal assemblage. A column of Templars rode with them, bound for their stronghold in Gaza.

Laughter and music accompanied the procession; a jongleur put hand to lute and sang them a bawdy song that set the men to laughing and the women to blushing. The clergy scowled and muttered their shock into the cowls of their less than festive colored habits.

All in all Baldwin felt better than he had in many a day. That alone was enough to put him in a high good mood as they made their long, slow way out of the Judean hills onto the rolling green Plain of Sharon, and south, along the old coastal road to Gaza and Ascalone.

A cool breeze, kissed by the sweetness of sun and water, blew gently in from the sea, setting the standards of the procession to rippling. As the progress thinned out along the road, Baldwin excused himself from his bodyguards and set his heel gently to his horse. Coming up alongside his sister, she dismissed her ladies-in-waiting and sent them chattering away.

"Is it true what the women at court are whispering—that you truly are happy with William?" he asked.

A smile dawned beneath her sheer veil, wild and winsome; her bright blue eyes shone brilliantly, deepening the emotion. "I am, Your Majesty."

Baldwin sat back in his saddle, feigning hurt. "Is that what I am to you, now, sister—Your Majesty?"

"My husband is your humble vassal," Sibylla said, bowing her head. "Should I not set a proper example as his wife?"

"So long as you don't forget that you are my sister and the future queen of this kingdom."

"I'm sure that day is still a long ways off," she said and glanced away.

"So," he said, leaning close to his quiet sister, "was your first night with him so hard to endure?"

The question had its intended effect. "Baldwin," Sibylla cried, aghast at his effrontery. Her hand went to her mouth too late to stop the word. A blush of pink crept up to her cheek. "For a king you can be so boyish at times."

Baldwin merely shrugged and whispered, "It was better, wasn't it?"

Sibylla raked him with her gaze and a demur smile. "I'm not going to tell you anything of the kind."

"Could you at least tell me if you are pregnant yet?"

"I've only been married for a week," she laughed. "Even if I was, I wouldn't know for some time."

"But you'll let me know when you are, won't you?"

"I promise, brother."

Baldwin lowered his voice, looked about at those who might overhear their conversation. "Promise me that you'll also speak with Father William about taking the throne should I decide to abdicate."

Now that he had brooked what she perceived as his true motive for speaking with her, Sibylla grew more serious. Her gaze unconsciously strayed to her husband; the serjeants of his newly acquired knights surrounded him, deep in conversation. "But I thought you already spoke with him."

"I did—and he all but refused my request unless I die."

"Don't say such things," she hissed.

"Why—it's true; unless some miracle takes me by surprise." He paused, watching her. His courage made her uneasy. Her eyes fell, staring at her hands; the reins of her horse knotted about them. "I'm not afraid, Sibylla. I have had a long time to consider it. When it comes, I will be ready."

"But I won't," she said, wiping away a tear.

He gave her a moment. "I have a gift for you," he said, leaning forward and peering under the edge of the kaffiyeh that hid her eyes.

Her face transformed from sorrow to intrigue. "But you already dowered me with Japhe and Ascalone as a wedding gift," she said, laughing softly. A tremor shook her voice.

"This is a gift, Sibylla, for you alone and none other."

Stretching out his arm, Baldwin caught three sunbeams in his hand—or so he made it seem. Not that he could not have worked real magic if he so wanted. He remembered the first time he had discovered his ability as young boy alone in the garden of the palace. He had been sitting beneath a tree with the sunlight streaming through the swaying branches, dappling the ground with shadow and gold. It was a simple enough thing to accomplish; a mere thought, a binding of will and substance. He had only to think, to touch, to hold the light in his mind, to take it in his hand, and it yielded to his desire. Only later did he learn that he could call forth fire at a word and hold it in his hand. It had served him well many a night, as he lay alone in bed, afraid of the darkness.

The sunlight streamed through his fingers, warm and bright, translucent. Pretending to twist the beams into a single strand of luminous light, he produced a golden ring that he had had made beforehand by a goldsmith, and set it in Sibylla's trembling hand.

She gasped with delight and a wary fear. "Baldwin, it's beautiful. But how... how did you do that?" she asked, whispering as though it was an accusation.

"It was a trick—a conjurer's sleight of hand," he said, chuckling softly.

"It was magic," Sibylla said, now more exited, and intrigued than afraid. "Wasn't it?"

"No," he replied, sorry now that he had revealed his secret. "The power of magic is in what you want to believe you have seen."

"But I saw you form this ring from the sunlight."

"You saw what I wanted you to see, Sibylla. Nothing more." He began to doubt the wisdom of displaying his magic. He had been so eager to share something with his sister that he had underestimated her response. He had tried to awe her with a blending of magic and substance; instead, he earned only curiosity and intrigue from her. "I shouldn't have tried to deceive you. It was a childish thought to impress you."

She shook her head. "I know what I saw," she said. "But I don't understand why you would try to share something so extraordinary, and then suddenly deny it? What are you hiding from me? This is not a secret you can keep hidden, Baldwin. Does mother know— Father William?"

"No; and no one else can know." His horse felt the tension in Baldwin's body—in the way he sat in the saddle—and danced beneath him. He settled Altair and turned the skittish stallion, coming knee to knee with his sister. "It is my secret, Sibylla," he said, all but acknowledging the truth by his admission. "It is my gift to you: a token of my trust."

"Why me, Baldwin?" she said, barely comprehending the depth of his generosity.

Baldwin looked around, careful to keep his stammering tongue from saying too much. "You... you are my sister... and my friend. And, because I needed to share my secret with someone I can trust."

* * * * *

"What was that about?"

Sibylla startled and turned to find her mother staring intently at her. Agnes had ridden up from a small circle of men and ladies-in-waiting at her back and caught her by surprise. Sibylla noticed that one of the men—courtly admirers if past conversations of this variety were any indication of their identity—the handsome Bishop of Caesarea, Heraclius, kept his eyes on her longer than the rest before turning away to talk with his companions.

Agnes dropped her gaze, glancing about furtively; she was careful to make sure no one was close enough to overhear them. She urged her mount closer.

"It was nothing," Sibylla said, stumbling over the words. She glanced towards Baldwin. "He just wanted to give me a gift. It is a small thing really—a ring."

Her mother appraised it as she held it up in the sunlight. "Hardly worthy of Jherusalem's future queen," Agnes said.

Sibylla's eyes fell to her hands; they clenched the reins of her horse so tightly the leather bit into her gloved fingers. Her mother had that effect on her of late. Agnes had changed—not that anyone would ever mistake her mother for a saint. She was different somehow—more suspicious, more to herself. She was always around, hovering, and watchful, as though she dared not let Sibylla out of her sight. If anything, her marriage to William would put her mother at a comfortable distance, if only the few leagues that separated Ascalone from Jherusalem.

Sibylla glared at her mother. "You say that as though my brother were already dead of his disease."

"You, stupid girl. Did I say I care nothing for him? He is my son. I would not see anything happen to him, but it is only a matter of time. What has befallen your brother cannot be changed." Agnes paused suddenly, collecting her calm. "He will die. You are what matters now."

Sibylla had heard it too many times in the past several months. It was always the same and she was weary of hearing it. She turned away, gazing out over the rolling Plain of Sharon.

Her mother grabbed her arm none too gently. "Whether you like it or not, you will be queen—probably sooner, than later—and you are ill prepared for it."

"What would you have me do, mother?" hissed Sibylla, turning on her. "I have already married against my will, no matter how pleasing my husband may be to me. I'm sure the kingdom will find itself with a new heir before long."

"There is more at stake here, girl, than the throne of Jherusalem. Far more; things beyond your simple grasp of understanding just now."

"I will not betray him in any way."

"I'm not asking you to," Agnes said very softly. "Only give him your loyalty and your friendship. You must begin to act as though you are queen. Gain his confidence and his trust."

Sibylla's eyes lifted from beneath her long lashes. Anger burned away what tears she might have had for the brother she was just beginning to love. A brother who called her friend. "And what—tell you everything?"

Agnes smiled deceptively. "Only what will benefit us both in helping your brother govern this troubled kingdom during what little time he has left."

* * * * *

Dawn stained the stone of Kerak castle the color of fire and blood. The sun, breaking over the desolate wastelands of Oultrejourdain—the ancient Moab—glinted off the naked weapons of the troops guarding the pilgrim caravan passing beneath the castle walls. The defenders of the Frankish castle knew the Hajj route between Damascus and Mecca very well. Too long, the followers of Islam had the freedom to travel along the narrow ancient way; too long the spies of Nureddin, and now Salehdin, had used the desert road to send messages between Egypt and Syria.

But no more.

At a command, the garrison of Kerak attacked the caravan. It was a carefully conceived plan; something akin to setting a fox loose in a yard full of hens. Only the fox was Reynald de Châtillon, the former prince of Antioch, and the hens, the plump, plunder-rich merchants coming out of Egypt.

After his long imprisonment in Aleppo at the hands of the Sarrazins, Reynald was all too eager to vent his anger on the heathen dogs of the desert. Now, he had the perfect opportunity to vent that pent-up anger. Baldwin had charged him with seeing to the southern defenses of the kingdom by doubling the garrison of Kerak with a fresh contingent of crown knights. He had also rebuilt much of the castle walls that had fallen into disuse since the death of the previous lord of Oultrejourdain, Milon de Plancy, Stephanie de Milly's late husband. God and king willing, he would have her as his wife before long. Baldwin had more than hinted as much at their last meeting.

The garrison swept down from the castle with a fury and scattered the pilgrims in a fit of terror. Hooves pounded the ground; the earth shook. An avalanche of beast and men and steel overwhelmed the caravan. There was no escape. It was over in a moment: a clash of arms, the screams of women, the body of a dead Arab guard sprawled on the guard. Reynald shouted a command and his men gathered up the stragglers at sword-point. A knight threw a man down at his horse's feet. The soldiers laughed at the panic stricken Muslims.

"This is an outrage," said the pilgrim on the ground through an interpreter. "What right have you to treat us this way?"

"Every right, Arab," Reynald said, sheathing his sword. "You trespass on my lady's land. And my king's."

The man defied his captor and stood slowly. "I am an envoy of my lord, the sultan Salah ad-Din, on a mission of peace."

Reynald shifted in his saddle; his armor creaked with the movement. He kicked the man in the head, sending him sprawling again on the ground. The interpreter stood mutely, wide-eyed and uncertain. "You are a spy and a poor one at that. Do you think it is mere coincidence we just happened to fall upon your party when so many cross this land so often."

The Muslim groaned a string of slurred words through bloody lips; the interpreter translated. "I am an envoy of my lord—no more."

Reynald's sword rasped from its scabbard. He leveled it as his captive. "Kill him."

"Wait," a second man pleaded in the Frankish tongue and stepped forward. His accent was excellent. Spears fell against his chest. "He tells the truth, my lord Frank. We are indeed envoys of our lord the sultan."

The man realized his mistake too late. Reynald raised an eyebrow. His sword swung slowly towards the Muslim envoy. "You speak our language. That is most unwise of you to admit. Serjeant, arrest these men and take them into custody."

"And the others, my lord?"

"Strip them naked and send them on their way," Reynald commanded. He pulled on the reins, turning his horse in a tight circle. "And serjeant, be sure you relieve them of their weapons and goods. I would not want to see them robbed along the way by some desert bandits. I'd hate to see word spread that these pilgrim roads are left unguarded."

* * * * *

The falcon fell like an arrow out of the clear blue sky: swift, silent, and deadly. The dove never had a chance of escape. It screamed its sudden terror and fell silent in a flurry of wings and feathers and razor-sharp talons. With a shrill whistle, the hunter came back into obeisance and the dead bird lay at the feet of its master. The falcon, beautiful and proud, danced lightly upon the Prince of Antioch's fist, the tiny silver bells of its jesses tinkling softly as it settled. Its eyes shone bright and keen with the lust for blood.

"Ha," roared Bohemond. "That's seven to your five, my lord of Tripoli."

Raymond rolled a disinterested eye towards his affable kinsman and shook his head. "Six, but whose counting," he muttered. His own falcon sat restlessly on his arm, batting him with its wings, eager to fly. Raymond calmed it with a gentle stroke.

"Quit being so surly, cousin," Bohemond said. "You're supposed to be out hunting, not fretting over the king and the politics of Jherusalem."

Count Raymond disagreed. He was not in the high good mood of his cousin. He had other concerns on his mind—and none of those had anything to do with hunting or being affable. The hunt, after all, was only a ruse. He had worked too hard and too long to see all that he had accomplished in the name of peace slowly crumble into ruin. Events were in play now that even he could not stop: letters sent; offers made—in secret and in good faith. He prayed God would forgive him if his actions proved treasonous.

They had come up out of the rolling plain about Tripoli onto the hills that buckled the land as it rose into the Lebanon. Drought had blasted the land, searing it brown in the furnace-heat of the summer sun. Still, a bit of green stubbornly clung to the rocky defiles that wandered down from the mountains. It was a cruel jest to the people of this land to live so precariously between the harsh expanse of the arid desert and the promising vastness of the green-grey sea. It was a sword's-edge existence between life and death. It made the people of greater Syria, Muslim and Christian alike, resilient to the changing patterns of the seasons and the vicissitudes of war that saw an endless stream of victors hold the land in the palm of their hand.

Raymond turned, looking back towards the city in which he had spent so little time during the past two years. Tripoli shone like a jewel on the edge of the sea; a great pearl set amidst the delicate filigree work of terraces and walls. Here was the heart and center of a county that had been his family's demesne since the first knights had come out the West to take Jherusalem from the heathen Muslims. He would not he see it given over to the enemy.

His horse danced beneath him, sidling up next to Bohemond's large rown gelding. Raymond glanced annoyingly at the Prince of Antioch, turning his horse to face him.

"That's easy for you to say, it's not your honor the king is trampling underfoot before the Sarrazins."

Bohemond grunted predictably. He handed his falcon off to a page; he took it in silence and backed away. "Is that what's bothering you—a broken truce. It's been months since Ba'albek."

"I just can't believe that Baldwin is that eager for war with Salehdin."

"Why shouldn't he," said Bohemond. "He's Amaury's son and well trained to it from birth. He probably felt that he had no choice—it was only a matter of time before Salehdin did the same. If you ask me, it sounds as though the boy has the reins of the kingdom well in hand."

"Yes: but for how long? And at what cost?" Raymond calmed himself, willing his words not to betray his actions. "Baldwin's sickness is progressing rapidly now. How long do you think he will last? The princess' wedding to Montferrat gained us nothing with the West. Now Baldwin has renewed plans for an invasion of Egypt. He's sending an embassy soon to Constantinople to negotiate a treaty with the Byzantines for naval support."

Bohemond groaned and let his head fall back. "If I know Manuel, just for spite he'll negotiate to have me married by this time next year to some fat Byzantine cow with more of an appetite for sweetmeats and marzipan than for any man. He has waited long and patiently to find some way to bring Antioch more securely under his control. Now he has it."

"It would serve you right for all the years you've spent wenching in the taverns and back-streets of Antioch." His statement clearly did not amuse Bohemond. Raymond laughed coldly. "So, do you still think Baldwin has the kingdom well in hand?"

Bohemond grumbled. Raymond moved his horse closer. "Just now, everything hinges on a truce with Salehdin: a truce the king stubbornly refuses to renew or even consider. Worse, I am certain de Courtenay is behind the king's actions. It is not the right time for this war. One misstep and we could all die a very glorious, but wholly unnecessary, death."

Bohemond glanced around. The squires had moved off a ways with the falconers, deep in conversation. No one stood close enough to overhear them; they were very much alone, the Prince of Antioch and the Count of Tripoli. "I know it's not something you want to consider, but if what you say is true, then the time may come when you may need to lay claim to the throne—by force if necessary. The barons will support you if the kingdom is threatened... well, at least most of them."

Raymond looked sidelong at his princely cousin. "What you are proposing is nothing less than civil war."

Bohemond shot him a wary glance. "Better that than certain death at the hands of the Sarrazins. If Jherusalem falls, so too, will Tripoli and Antioch."

"In the end, if it comes to it, we may well have to take that road." Raymond turned away, looking towards the hills expectantly. A signal flashed there: the sun on a polished shield. "But until then, there are other avenues we may be able to consider."

* * * * *

Hooves clattered on stone, echoing. The walls closed in, rising, shadowing the narrow passageway in darkness. The scent of so many horses in such a small, crowded place was close to overwhelming. Beyond a low arch, sunlight swelled in a golden haze.

As men and horses began filing into the courtyard of the castle, servants and grooms appeared at the doors, setting about their accustomed chores. Swinging down from his horse, Reynald gave the stallion a perfunctory pat on the neck, and handed off the reins to a groom.

She was waiting for him as he expected she would be. He turned to find her standing in a doorway, leaning against the frame, arms folded across her chest. She smiled demurely. Even at her age, she was still a beautiful woman, especially in her favorite blue and silver gown.

"So, my lord, are these the men that have occupied so much of your thoughts these past many days," said Stephanie de Milly of Kerak, nodding towards the Muslim prisoners held under heavy guard.

"They are indeed, my lady," he said, unbuckling his sword and handed it to his squire; mail coif and helmet followed. He bent forward and kissed her proffered hand, lingering with the warm smoothness of her skin against his mouth. She smelled faintly of lavender.

"Your actions will not be well received by the king when he hears of this," she said. The tone of her voice brought him to his feet.

"It was his majesty who charged me with strengthening the position of this castle against incursions by the Sarrazins. What I have done, is no more than what he asked of me. Or should I simply allow spies to continue to plot against us just to keep from offending Muslim sensitivities?"

Lady Stephanie glanced past him to the guards and their prisoners. "So what will you do with them now that you have them?"

"I will not put you in danger by keeping them here," Reynald said. "I will transfer them to Jherusalem when I leave and set them under the care of the throne."

Her sudden look of displeasure roused his passion. He touched a hand to her cheek. "I will return soon, ma dama. I swear it. My mission to the Byzantines will last only a few months. I'll be back by Easter and then Baldwin has promised me he will consent to our marriage."

Her eyes fell. "Must you truly go?"

He cupped her chin in his hand. "Yes, my love."

"But why you? You've barely been released from prison."

Reynald was growing impatient. He tried to keep it from his tone. "We've discussed this many times, my lady. I am the king's cousin—or nearly so, discounting blood. He trusts me—which is something he needs just now."

"But it could be dangerous for you," she said, lifting her dark eyes. Tears filled them. "You could be trading one prison for another."

He remembered the incident to which Stephanie alluded. Twenty years before, as the young prince of Antioch through his marriage to Princess Constance, the Byzantine emperor, Manuel Comnenus, inflamed his wrath by refusing to compensate him for expenses he had incurred in the emperor's service. Reynald took out his vengeance, perhaps unwisely, on the island of Cyprus. Peaceful and defenseless, the islanders suffered cruelly under Reynald's merciless hand. He ravaged Cyprus; Manuel was outraged. Two years later, the emperor came against Antioch at the head of a vast imperial army. Reynald had no choice but to submit in humiliation. The Emperor forced him to lead him and his horse barefoot into the city in recompense for his sins. It was a small price to pay.

"Why? —Because of what I did to Cyprus," he snorted. "I assure you, Stephanie, the emperor has long ago forgiven me the insult I committed against him. He will not jeopardize this mission to indulge an old grievance. I am an ambassador of the crown. In the interest of peace and friendship, Manuel will do me no harm. He owes me as much for the loss of my son this past summer at Myriocephalum."

"And what if you're wrong, Reynald?"

He smiled deviously. "Then, I am wrong. I'm sure there are nobles aplenty that Baldwin would be all too eager to marry you off to— for the sake of the kingdom."

She slapped him. He caught her hand when she tried it again. "You are a hard man, my love, to treat a lady so cruelly on the eve of your departure."

"Oh, I doubt you are as frail a creature as you pretend to be, my lady. Not living out in this God-forsaken land." He stepped closer and took her gently by the arm; he bent his head, letting his mouth find the soft curve of her neck. He kissed her. "Nor as virtuous," he whispered.

"My lord, we are in public," she sighed, pulling back. "This is most unseemly."

Reynald let his hands fall down her sides to find hers. "Then perhaps, we should find a place more private so that I may demonstrate to you a more proper way to treat a lady on the eve of my departure."

* * * * *

The light over Tripoli was sharp, though blunter than the razor edge that pierced the air of Damascus; still, it could cut, and deeply. It had honed Raymond's face to the same raw-boned thinness of the Syrian who had ridden up before him in the company of a fair-haired boy and a band of white-robed Mamluks. The Sarrazin's splendid Arabian stallion pranced beneath him, tossing its long, narrow head. The Mamluks sat their own horses as stolid and impassive as steel.

At a nod, the fair-haired boy—a Frankish slave, no doubt or perhaps a Circassian—nudged his chestnut mare forward a step and bowed. "The lord Semsedolus offers you his greeting on behalf of his brother, the lord Salehdin, sultan of Damascus and Syria."

"Salaam," Raymond said, molding his tongue to the Damascene dialect. "In the name of the Prophet, upon his name be peace, I greet thee."

The stern-faced emir bowed deeply in his seat, touching hand to head and heart. He smiled. "My brother told me you had a fair command of our language. I disbelieved him that any Frank could do so. It appears I was wrong. May Allah forgive my foolishness."

Raymond nodded. "Not foolishness, my lord, but a fair understanding of the arrogance of my people. Not all of us, however, are so minded. There are some—those of us that have lived all their lives in this land—that have respect for the faith of Islam and its people. We would have peace between our peoples."

"As would my brother, the sultan Salah ad-Din."

"We are of one mind, then, concerning some measure of a truce between us."

"As a measure of good faith, if your king approaches my lord for a truce, then my brother would be willing to sell your people grain at half-price."

65

"And I will allow your people to travel through my lands about Galilee without fear of harassment, so long as no troops pass that way."

"Agreed," replied the Syrian. He made a very deliberate bow and backed his horse away, letting the conversation rest on his final word.

When the dour emir and his party were gone, Bohemond let out a long, slow whistle. "If nothing else, you're at least bold. Especially knowing that come spring, Baldwin intends an all-out invasion on Salehdin in Egypt."

"You think me wrong to want peace so much?"

"Not entirely. But you must remember, my friend, peace is like a beautiful, young lover: having her is not the same as keeping her. Worse, just having her could cost you more than you are willing to lose."

Raymond drew the reins of his horse together tightly in his hand and turned the animal towards Tripoli. "That is a risk, cousin, I'm willing to take."

"For the sake of the kingdom?" said Bohemond.

"For the sake of us all."

* * * * *

Baldwin stole quietly along the torchlit corridor that led from his room; a deep spell of slumber lay upon the castle of Ascalone, softening his footsteps in the ears of those that might wake and find him. With the Christmastide festival drawing near, the servants had decked the halls with holly and mistletoe. Banners hung from the balconies. For all he knew, he was the only soul that stirred this longest and most silent night of the year. A voice, though, had called to him, whispering his name from the depths of the shadows and darkness.

Baudouin...

The chill breath of a breeze off the sea whined through the narrow slit of a window. He pulled his cloak closer about his throat.

A ripple of eldritch laughter, faint and distant, lured him cautiously beyond a turn in the hallway, and then, another, and another. The stone was different here, older, courser, with a deeper memory of a more ancient time. It spoke silently of bloodshed and war, the wholesale slaughter of thousands. Fear took hold of him at seeing how the castle's corridors were turning impossibly inwards upon themselves in a way never built into the original stonework. Always leftward, the path of power—and of magic. He clasped his iron-bladed dagger tighter, a talisman against the dark, fey spirits that haunted him. A childish belief he knew, to think iron could have any power over the unseen.

66

Abruptly, the torchlight ended. Darkness enfolded thick as night. Of all things in the world, he feared darkness the most. He cowered, unable to move. His hand shot out instinctively, reaching for the wall for guidance, for surety. The masonry changed between one turn and another. His hands scraped upon rough stone. He forced himself to return to his bed and sleep this waking dream away; he even said the words aloud that they might have power over him to act, but youthful foolishness and curiosity forced his body to an obedience all its own.

He ventured a careful, cautious step and stopped. He felt dizzy. The paved floor beneath his feet had turned to the uneven ground of a forest path. Fallen leaves and spent flower blossoms quieted his footsteps. He had crossed some ill-defined boundary, stepping from one place to another. A pearl-grey dawn filtered through the walls of mist-shrouded trees circling around him, though morning was still several hours away in the world he knew.

That she was here in its midst clothed in white and glistening pearl, waiting, surprised him little. He expected as much.

She drew close to him, almost gliding on the air. The breeze blew gently at her back, billowing out her hair like a mane. She made a fearsome specter: beautiful and wild, cloaked in the many long years of tradition and legend that surrounded all her kind.

"Your little dagger of iron has no power here, Your Highness, or against me," she said and took the blade in her hand. "It is only a wife's tale, old even as it is."

He cast his gaze abruptly from the knife to her face, his curiosity getting the better of him. "What is this place?"

"Many names it has been called: Broceliande and Avalon, Elysium and Hesperia. But of old and firstly, it was called Eden, the land cursed by Adam's sin."

"But... but that's impossible," he said, ordering his tongue to speak without its accustomed stammering. "Scripture says that... that cherubim guard the way to the Garden of Eden with a flaming sword."

"Once," she said, "that was true—a long time ago when the Tree of Life grew in the midst of the garden. The tree has long since disappeared, just as this place has faded from the world of men. This is my place now, as it once was for others of my kind before they turned away. Only those born with the gift of magic can pass through the borders of mist to find their way here."

"So, you brought me here."

She laughed. "It was none of my doing, Your Highness, which brought you here. I merely called your name. It was your own magic. It is in your blood—an inheritance of your ancient fathers."

It was true, of course. He knew it with a certainty born of an instinct he little understood. Of the how and why of the matter, he knew nothing, only that what she said was true; she had no reason to lie. It explained so much of what he had always questioned about his... abilities. Still, he feigned ignorance in the hope of gaining a greater understanding.

"Inheritance?"

"Seven hundred years ago a woman of my kind fell in love with a king of the Franks."

"You?"

"No, Your Highness. She was a halfling princess of the Sicambrians named Argotta. She gave birth to a son—Merovech, the father of Clovis and the Merovingian line that the Church made their secular right arm."

"The Sorcerer-Kings? But they died out centuries ago when... when the last of them died at the hands of assassins."

He had caught her off guard. Fire flared in her eyes, green and feral. "No," she said. "However unlikely, a scion of that ancient house survived; an unbroken line that has flourished in secret until this very day. Unfortunately, as there ever is when power seeks after power, a group of men known as the Order of Sion—at least in its present form—sought to corrupt the outcast princes with lies and empty promises of glory and power to bring them under their influence. One of those lies is that the Church betrayed the house of Clovis, so the Order promised the outcasts a chance of revenge upon the Pope and the whole of Christianity. Now their presence seeks to overshadow all that is done in the kingdom of Jherusalem."

She paused, crossing her arms over her chest. "You are an heir of that house, King Baldwin; a house in which the magic of the faerie kind still runs strong—at least in some."

Baldwin stared at her for a long while, looking for some sign of falsehood. She seemed to tell the truth, however stinting she was in doling it out. "So what is your part in this fabulous tale, if you truly are the Magdalen?"

She smiled at him in the pale moonlight—a most uncomfortable thing to behold—and laughed as much in veiled annoyance as in humor. "You are not one to believe easily are you, Your Highness," she said, her voice a cheerless sound. She grew suddenly serious and grave. "Wisely so. There are too many unscrupulous men about you that you should give your trust so easily. As for me, plainly told, the Order of Sion claims I was the wife of Jhesú and that I fled to France after his death with his child; a child who became the heir of a terrible secret—the truth behind the bloodline of Christ and the Merovingians. And they claim they can prove it."

"There is no truth in that, is there? The Scriptures never mention Jhesú as having a wife."

"O, it is a lie of the deepest blasphemy, but it suits the needs of these ruthless men to claim that the magic of the Sorcerer-Kings came from the blood of Christ, as it still does today. Think what it would mean if such a lie was openly proclaimed and believed to be true."

Baldwin did think, and he saw immediately how the Order of Sion would use the lie. Now he understood the secret about which his father had tried once to warn him.

"Christianity would suffer a severe blow; its power diminished," she continued, "The establishment of a new Holy See with its center here in Jherusalem with the King of Jherusalem superior to all the crowns of Europe."

"That cannot be allowed to happen," said Baldwin, shaking his head.

"No, Your Highness, it cannot. Nor will it," she said. "Fools they certainly are for what they seek to do. Nor will I allow them to do so. The Order of Sion is not without power and allies. It will stop at nothing to claim the throne of Jherusalem. Not when they are so close to achieving all they desire."

Baldwin fell silent and shivered. You are an heir of that house, King Baldwin. Raising his hand, he called up fire, a cold, blue luminance that grew in his palm until it overflowed like water. It took barely any thought at all to do so in this place of magic and ancient power.

His gaze lifted to the Magdalen. She stood near him, watching. "There is more, though, isn't there? Something you haven't told me yet."

Her gaze narrowed, amused. "You are a most clever boy, Your Highness. You must have driven your tutor to madness with the depth of it."

Baldwin allowed himself a recalcitrant smile. "Only a little. And then Father William would hound me without end until he found some way to put it to proper use."

"He is a wise man, the Archbishop of Tyre," she said, her eyes falling. She folded her arms across her chest. "Perhaps, wiser than I."

A thought, brief and agonizing, shot through Baldwin's confused mind. It formed on his halting tongue, blossoming into words and understanding. He spoke it aloud.

"My... my illness is... your fault." At hearing his accusation, she seemed to fade, dissolving into the air and the grey dawn of the garden. His command made her solid once more. His simple question made her answer. "Why?"

"I thought only to protect you," she said desperately. "It was a spell meant to conceal your small abilities from the enemy. The enemy, however, discovered the spell. Sion took what I did and twisted it to evil. The leprosy devouring your body is your own magic turned against you into a disease to destroy you."

Sudden emotion—anger, hatred, a sense of long-lost hope— brought him to the verge of tears. For so long he had accepted his illness as a cruel jest of nature and of God; but knowing that his belief was so far from the truth, only made him numb to the reality.

"You can remove the spell, then," he said, almost whispering, daring to hope. His knees gave out; he sunk to the ground. Her hand touched his brow, pulling back the kaffiyeh from his head. Gently, without revulsion or fear, she took his head in her hands, caressing the sores, running her fingers through the thick waves of his wheat-gold hair. It had been so long since he had felt such a caring touch. It softened the blow of her words.

"I've tried, believe me, King Baldwin" she said. "But each time it only worsens the disease, as it did the day you first saw me at the Tomb. Your fever was the result of my effort. I dare not try again for fear it may take your life."

A breeze sighing through the trees dried his tears. His fragile hope shattered. "The disease prevails, then, even against your magic?"

"Not mine alone, Your Highness," she said, clenching her hands in his hair and pulled him close against her shoulder. Your magic feeds the spell, spreading the leprosy. "Perhaps, now, you begin to see the power the enemy commands."

Baldwin stiffened. "So all is lost, then."

"Not yet," she whispered. A hint of renewed resolve brightened her voice. Taking his hand, she stood and drew him to his feet. "Together we may be able to break Sion's power—at least for a time. Will you trust me?"

"It seems I have little choice, ma dama," he said, venturing the briefest sound of laughter.

Her hand tightened on his. "There is always a choice, Your Highness. Unfortunately, because of my folly and arrogance, yours may require the life you vowed to give to defend the Holy Tomb."

A silence fell between them at her words, one filled with all the beauty the mist-shrouded forest and the magic of Eden could command.

Baldwin was not sure still what to make of the Magdalen or her startling revelations. He knew at least, though, that he must trust her. What choice did he really have?

"If you could change what happen to me, would you do so?" he said, breaking the silence.

"With my own life if I could."

"I believe you."

"Just that easily," she said, laughing suddenly. "I might have lied."

"True: but I have to start trusting you sometime. Why not now?"

She laughed merrily, dispelling the heavy gloom of their long conversation. "Why not now, indeed, Your Highness."

Baldwin laughed with her, knowing not really why, only that it felt good to do so with this beautiful creature, this angel, that surely God had seen fit to send him in his darkest hour.

MONTGISART
1177

† CHAPTER SIX

For there is nothing hid, which shall not be made manifest: neither was it made secret, but that it may come abroad.
—Mark 4:22

Mary woke with a gasp. Darkness and silence and the bitter-pungent scent of burnt incense filled the tomb. Her cheek felt cold with the stone that lay beneath it. Voices whispered about her, memories of the past. The priest that usually guarded the tomb had gone to his prayers. She was alone.

She had dreamt of music and wine and dancing. She dreamt of him, whom she had loved more than life itself: the one that had set her free from the long dark night of her imprisonment by daemons so many years ago.

She first saw him at a wedding in Cana. In Cana, where the servants of the Father of Lies that held her in darkness first saw how they might bring the Son of the Most High to ruin and sin, and she the willing instrument of their wickedness. Before that, she had only dim memories of shadow and loneliness and the howling of the desert wind at night.

She had loved him even more when her temptations had failed, for instead of wrath and condemnation, he had simply forgiven her. She had awakened that day, as though from a dream, into the light of a new day. It was an old dream, familiar, as it was comforting, even as it faded into the soft embrace of memory.

She smiled, chasing the mists of slumber from her mind. At once, she remembered with stinging eyes the reason she had come here in the dead of a summer's night, to this dark tomb in the heart of an ancient church. It was to cry out to the heavens for understanding and mercy.

William of Montferrat was dead of a fever; the king's sister was left widowed, alone, and three months pregnant. Rumors were flying of poison; worse, if the rumors were true, then the enemy was about to claim an even greater victory, for Baldwin lay sick and near death of the same fever in a bed in Ascalone. Jherusalem was without an heir and the government in the hands of the king's Regent, Reynald de Châtillon, newly returned from Constantinople with the seal of the Emperor on a treaty that insured Byzantine help in the upcoming campaign with Salehdin.

Despite the rumors of poison and treachery, though, she could detect no taint of the enemy—of magic or any other hint of human agency. All she could find about the king and the dead Count of Ascalone was the bitter sorrow of death's dark shadow. Still, the shadow of the enemy was strong, and growing, spreading like a pestilence. It clung to stone, and air, and earth with its all too human stench; and of something far, far older, and evil. An immortal shadow that gnawed at all that was fair and light.

It was a cruel day to have gained so much, and then see it drift away like mist before the rising sun. It would be far easier to shrug off the weighty semblance of her human appearance and fade into the bright sunlight of her own place—easier not to care what the evil of men brought forth in the world, even in fair and sacred Jherusalem.

Her hand, trembling, yet resolute, touched the talisman at her throat, commanding her heart against what her thoughts desired. Power flared, swelling into light amidst the darkness of the empty tomb of Christ.

If this illness of the king was no work of Sion, but wholly of nature, then perhaps, she could heal it. At the very least, she had to try, even if her gift of healing was very, very small.

Wrapping the very air of the tomb about her, she stepped *in* and... *through* the misty grey shadows of her world to Ascalone.

* * * * *

Archbishop William of Tyre knelt at the king's bedside, trying to find solace and hope in his prayers of healing. As of yet, he had found none. Dipping his finger into a silver bowl of holy oil, he anointed Baldwin's forehead, sketching the sign of the cross upon the corrupted flesh. After so long, he little feared any contact with the contagion. Of course, he knew the truth about the king's illness, and that no amount of contact would contaminate him. The magic was too specific.

He wondered still if it had been truly wise to tell Baldwin the truth. He had always displayed remarkable resolve to fight off the effects of his illness; now he believed it was only a matter of time before the enemy was defeated and he made whole once more. It drove him onward each day, sometimes with reckless abandon. It had driven him to exhaustion and illness. William had counseled him to patience and reason, but Baldwin was too determined, too resolved, to discover the identity of Sion's master.

The leprosy—or rather, the devouring effects of the Magdalen's magic—was progressing more quickly now. It had eaten away Baldwin's nose and wreaked havoc with the rest of his face, making him all but unrecognizable. Patches of snow-white disease mottled his skin; his fingers and toes had disfigured. It hurt him to sit a horse, but he stubbornly refused to yield to his discomfort. The litter he used on occasion spoke to his worsening condition.

The candles guttered, scattering the hovering shadows. A hint of incense and lavender scented the air. At a hiss of a snuffed candle flame, he glanced up to see her step out of the air as though it was a doorway between heaven and earth. Even in rags, she would have been beautiful; in a gown of softest white, she was radiant.

"My lady, you have a peculiar habit of always interrupting my prayers with your sudden appearances," he said, smiling wearily.

She ignored his remark and glided gracefully to the king's bedside. "How is he?"

William lifted a hand and set it gently on Baldwin's sweating brow. "His body still burns with fever. I fear it will only feed the magic's power."

He let his gaze fall upon the king's face. Despite the illness, it was serene, as though he was dreaming of healing and faraway places. "Is this the work of the enemy?"

Her hand touched his shoulder. "Fortunately, this time it is not, only a cruel jest of sin's curse."

"Can you do anything for him?"

"My skill with healing is small, but I may be able to draw away some of the fever's strength. The rest is up to God and prayer."

He sighed. "I'm afraid the faith of my prayers is a little lacking just now, my lady."

She smiled and laughed unexpectedly. "It is not faith you lack, Father William, only the strength of will to use it. Now pray as though the king's life depends on it, for it very well may."

Properly chastised, William obeyed and bowed his head. Closing her eyes, Magdalen stretched out her hands above the king's body and began to whisper softly. At first, the words seemed oddly familiar—the cadence of speech, the reverential tone of her voice—but at the same time, foreign. Not surprising for one schooled so long in the Latin of Mother Church. Her voice was beautifully rhythmic, the words intoxicating and powerful. It might have been a spell—or, a prayer. Then, it struck him. The words were Hebrew—no, Aramaic. The Lord's Prayer in its original language: the very words she had learned at the feet of the Master himself.

Our Father who art in Heaven, hallowed be Thy name…

Without thought or reason, he reached out and took her hand; her hand clenched on his, tightening in an iron grip. Her voice echoed in his mind.

—Pray now, William. Pray, as you have never done before.

It was a battle, not of arms and steel, but of words and will and spirit. It was glorious; it was wonderful. It tore every fiber of strength from his body. Of all the prayers he had ever sung, this was the most sincere. This *was* prayer; prayer unlike anything he had ever known before. Distractions and whispers assailed him. Shame pushed itself to the fore of his thoughts. But that was pride disguised, seeking to take the place of the one for whom he was praying. With all his will, he fought back; he concentrated on the only words that mattered in the midst of the battle.

…Thy will be done.

In the midst of it, he found joy and the quiet tranquility of God's presence. It drew him in, deepening his thoughts until only the will of the Father remained in focus. Everything else fell away into insignificance.

Mary stiffened with the strain of the battle. She was weakening. She drew on his strength, drawing him into the white-hot center of her being. Fear made him draw back; his curiosity and swelling faith pulled him deeper into her magic.

Of a sudden, the fever broke. His skin tingled with the touch of her power. Her gasp broke the spell of thoughts and words and sanctity. Her hand recoiled.

"What—what is it, my lady?"

Her eyes shifted, lifted to his, their color a strange and horrible sight. She shuddered. "I touched the enemy's mind, William. I have seen what he intends," she murmured. "I know him; and what I must do to stop him. Pray, my friend, that I am right," she said, standing back from the bed with her arms around her thin body, and was gone.

Silence fell in the room. William was alone again with the king. Spent and weary with the ordeal, he bent his head to the side of the bed and closed his eyes. The Magdalen's words of the enemy barely registered; even their prayer—so powerful, so transcendental only a moment ago—had slipped elusively away.

A bandaged hand caressed his tonsured head. The gesture smote his heart with an unexpected joy.

"How long have I lain abed?" Baldwin whispered.

"Too long, my king. Too long," William said, trying not to seem overly concerned. His hand slid around Baldwin's disfigured hand.

Baldwin squeezed his hand weakly. "How long, William?"

"A month," he said, afraid to say any more. Baldwin turned his head towards the window of his room.

"Has... has word come yet of my cousin of Flanders?"

"If the winds are favorable, his ship is due to arrive in a matter of weeks."

The young king's head rolled back towards him on the pillow. "The Count is dead?"

"Yes."

"And my sister?"

William patted the king's hand. "Your Highness, you need rest. Don't tax your strength with all these questions."

The king stared at him, reflecting his impatience.

"Your sister is worried that you'd leave her queen long before her time."

Baldwin's eyes filled with tears and closed. "You knew of the Magdalen and didn't tell me," he murmured.

The words were a knife plunged deep into his heart. The words of a boy in a body still not quite a man. William took the king's hand and laid it against his brow. "Forgive me, Your Highness. I—we—thought only to protect you."

"From what?" Baldwin shifted, trying to sit up in the nest of pillows. "The enemy? It seems a little late for that concern." He glanced at him, shaking his head. His ravaged face had recovered some of its color, but it was still gaunt and sunken with his illness. "Don't fret, Father William. I'm not angry with you, only disappointed."

William reclined back in his chair. He crossed his arms and cradled his chin in his hand. He smiled awkwardly. "Interestingly enough, I was never supposed to know about her either. Our meeting was quite by accident. Shall I tell you the story?"

The king stared at him from beneath lowered brows. That gaze could be so disconcerting: dark eyes shining in the depths of a sickness-shadowed face. "Promise me you'll keep no more secrets. The kingdom is in too sad a state for me to have my most trusted advisor keeping things from me."

His words stung, more so, because they were the words of one who trusted him and called him friend and Chancellor. Thirty years ago in a Gaul, as a young novice entering the service of the Church, he had never imagined doing the things that circumstances had forced him to do in the name of God and the crown of Jherusalem.

But no more. Baldwin deserved at least that much loyalty.

Humbly he bowed; he shook his head determinedly. "No more secrets, your Highness. I promise."

* * * * *

Agnes sighed contentedly, luxuriating in the steaming water. She slid down, immersing herself and rested her head against the age-worn stone of the steps. Sunlight slanted through the upper windows of the small bath, diffusing the circular hall with a golden haze. A minstrel plied his trade from an adjoining room. The music lured her towards slumber.

The old Romans certainly knew how to enjoy life. Unfortunately, these old-style baths left over from the days of the Empire and centuries more of Muslim domination and neglect were a rarity in Jherusalem. That it was a house built of old Roman stone with a Roman-style bath there was no doubt; the names of *Valerius* and *Legio X* were still visible on a pillar by the door. It overlooked a quiet street in the Patriarch's Quarter and a small well-kept garden that rivaled Eden itself. She felt almost guilty over her shallow covetousness. Almost. Certainly, God would expiate her for one small sin. After all, he certainly owed her for the loss of a throne, a husband, and soon, a son.

She ran her hands down the length of her body, pleased with what she found; the deep swell of breast and hip; the firm flatness of the region between. Her skin had the supple smoothness of a woman half her age. The firmness of her body she credited to her daily rides about the countryside, her youthful beauty to the men she brought to her bed. She was proud of both. It had won her four husbands and many more admirers and enemies. It had also won her a few lovers—lovers such as the man who stood watch over her, waiting for her to finish her bath.

Plunging beneath the surface of the pool, she turned and stood naked before her solitary watcher. Heraclius did not even have the decency to be shocked; only amused. With both hands, she reached up and wrung the water from her hair. He smiled appreciably. He usually did when she flaunted her body before him. The Archbishop of Caesarea was a handsome man, blond hair, aquiline nose, blue eyes. He had a tendency to forget that he was a man of the cloth, a servant of God. The vestments of his office only added to his allure: a consecrated vessel of holiness unafraid to indulge his baser appetites.

Agnes stepped out of the pool; Heraclius held open a robe for her. He hesitated a moment, letting his eyes drink in the length of her body, and wrapped her in the voluminous robe.

"It is time for your instruction, my lady," he said mildly. "Shall we begin?"

It took her a moment or three to comprehend his meaning. She stepped back from him. "*You* are a member of Sion?" She turned away, confused, but gaining understanding. She turned back to him again, realizing how he had used her. Anger and betrayal made her tighten the robe about her body as she saw beyond his words. "I see. I had no idea, my lord *Archbishop*," she managed to say imperiously, trying not to let her emotion get the best of her.

Heraclius sighed and settled on a stone bench by the wall. The summer heat and the steam from the bath made it uncomfortable for one so richly dressed. "The hand of Sion, my lady, reaches to the highest levels of the church."

"All these months sharing my bed, and you never told me," she said. "Was this Sion's way of keeping an eye on me?"

"Our Order," he said sharply, clipping his words short. He smiled benignly. "Our Order exists in the utmost secrecy—a secrecy we are bound by oath and blood to uphold. As for keeping watch over you—yes, we have done so, but for good reason. We had to be sure of your loyalties."

"Why?"

"Since our foundation our number has always remained very small; no more than nine members at a time. We are short a member just now."

She understood his meaning; it needed no explanation. "I'm flattered, my dear Heraclius. But I am curious: Why a woman?"

"Our number has always included a woman, in honor of the role the Magdalen took in founding the early Church."

"As *Apostola Apostolorum*—the first apostle. The reason Rome hates the Magdalen with such fervency and denounces her as a sinner and harlot. She was the intended leader of the Church—not Peter."

He nodded. A sparkle touched his blue eyes. She gave him her most demure look; she let the robe fall open. She smiled at his quiet reaction.

"You're testing me."

"Brother Stephen is a rather zealous teacher. I have no need to question his instruction," said Heraclius. He steepled his fingers and touched his lips. "But if you are to become a member of our Order, there is still a great deal more you must learn." He produced a small, worn book from the sleeve of his costly robe. It looked very, very old. He held it out to her.

Curiosity won out over her not so subtle game of enticement. This was a lust born of a different nature. She wrapped her damp robe about her body and sat down beside him, her eyes never leaving the book. "What is this?"

"The Book of John."

She glanced at him uncertainly. Nervousness and the heat of the bath brought sweat to her brow. She dabbed her face with her sleeve. "You mean the Gospel of John, don't you?"

"No, my dear. The Book of John. The secret teachings of the Baptist that a small brotherhood of faithful monks in Alexandria gave their lives for centuries to preserve."

"Amalric spoke of the Baptist with the same reverence, but I didn't understand him. What does the Baptist have to do with Christianity? He was beheaded by Herod long before the Church was even founded."

The archbishop chuckled. "He has everything to do with it. The doctrines of Rome are not the doctrines of all those who call themselves Christian, especially to those who lay claim to a far older tradition than that of Rome."

Once more, as with Amalric, she had a niggling of doubt—a sense that she had touched upon something terribly evil, but was unable to resist. He spoke of a great mystery—a mystery too deep to comprehend. Her curiosity was too great. "I don't understand."

Heraclius caught her gaze with his deep blue eyes. "That is because you fail to realize that as the heir to the throne of David, Jhesú was sent by John to proclaim a far greater truth than the one the Church has taught. Nor do you understand how that ancient wisdom was brought to Europe, and the true part the Magdalen had in its transmission."

Agnes drew back, nervous and excited at once. Here was power—and knowledge. Secrets the Church would rather not acknowledge. Such was the lure of Sion. Hesitantly, she reached for the small, leather-bound book. At her touch, Heraclius snatched the book away.

"There is another matter we must discuss first."

She blinked; breathed. She hadn't realized she was holding her breath. She rose and suddenly fled away from him, knowing what would follow. It was becoming an all too familiar argument.

"No."

"With the unfortunate death of your daughter's husband and the king's illness, the High Court will demand she take another husband. And soon."

"They wouldn't dare," Agnes breathed. "She's only just been widowed and with child."

She heard Heraclius rise, the whisper of his robes against the worn stone of the bath hall as he drew near. "They would. And they will, my lady. Even if a proper period of mourning is granted to her and she is not forced to marry, the question of who she'll marry will be decided one day soon."

He gently touched the edge of her face. She turned, leaning into his hand. "What do we do?"

He bent to her; he kissed her neck, her face, her lips. "There are certain factions growing within the kingdom which must not be allowed to gain control. They will try to seek out just about any man with the ability to wield a sword and the titles to prove it. As a widow, Sibylla will have some say in the matter. When the time comes, she must be ready to marry the man the Order chooses. Moreover, your son must give his assent. Everything we have worked for depends on it."

She looked up at him, helpless. "And if he resists?"

Heraclius' hand slowly slid down the gentle curve of her neck and shoulder, brushing aside the heavy robe. It fell silently to the floor. "Then, my lady, you must convince her."

* * * * *

"*Ya Allah*," cried Salah ad-Din Yusuf ibn Ayyub. "Leave me! All of you." Without hesitation, his emirs leapt up from the table and scurried out of the hall like scared mice. The last of them—an emaciated, grasping old man left over from the days of his uncle Shirkuh—turned at the arched door and made his hasty obeisance. Only his Mamluks remained, mute and impassive as stone to his mutterings.

In a fit of anger, he cleared the short dining table with the back of his arm in noisy clatter of dishes and cups, leaving only the silver *kâffe* service and a pile of parchment maps.

From the midst of the courtyard, a fountain echoed softly. Its liquid melody helped ease away his frustration. It gave him an unexpected clarity of thought. Chin on hand, Yusuf leaned over the table again and studied the largest of the maps. In the wide region between al-Qihara and Urshalim, only the desert and the Nile offered any kind of defense against an invader. Neither prevented the Ifranj from coming against Egypt in the past. His only hope lay in an offensive campaign. He needed a plan; and, he needed intelligence.

His spy network was unsurpassable, but they were not an army. His spies had recently sent him reports of unfolding events that troubled his plans for a campaign. The Ifranj had made a considerable effort to strengthen the southern border of the kingdom in the past several months. Worse, the Byzantines were widely rumored to be finally sending a fleet to assist in an attack to win Egypt and a great lord of the Ifranj with a sizable army at his back was due to arrive any day from out of the West. For the first time in many a year, al-Qihara and the whole land of the Nile was in real danger of being lost to the infidels if he could not find a way to thwart them.

With a growl, he tossed the map away. It floated through the air and settled on the pillows surrounding his divan. "Worthless councilors; they have no more brains than what Allah gave a camel."

"Perhaps, that is because you expect the impossible of them."

A lone figure swathed all in white and gold stepped from the shadows of the innumerable marble columns of the palace and strode purposefully towards him. The sunlight, slanting through the hall, set her gown ablaze as though with fire. She was achingly beautiful he discovered as she slowly shed veil and cloth and humanity.

Instantly, his Mamluks drew their swords and closed. With the slightest wave of her hand, they disappeared into the air. He made the sign against evil.

"Your men are safe I assure you, son of Ayyub. They will awake in their beds, none the wiser for their ordeal." Her voice was like the whisper of silk over steel, and just as deadly.

"*Ifritah.*" The word escaped his mouth without thought.

She smiled, as would any true daughter of Iblis. "I am one who would make a bargain with you," she said, demure and firm. "A gift for a gift."

"And what would you have of me, my beautiful lady?" he asked. Fear gnawed at the depths of his heart—fear and excitement.

"The Seal of Suleiman."

A burst of quick laughter escaped his throat. "A curious request, I think, my lady. With such you could raise the realm of the *jinn* against me."

"That is certainly not my intention," said the *ifritah* with the wine dark hair, bowing her head respectfully.

Even as child, Yusuf could be reckless, headstrong. His father had thought he could beat it out of him. All he had succeeded in doing was driving his son to be more honest. "What is the word of an *ifritah* to me?"

Her eyes shot up; anger flared in their depths. He had seen the same, wild expression in a lioness. "It is better than the word of a faithless Turk."

Amused at the slur on his heritage, he poured from the silver service on the low table before him. "*Káffe?*" he asked. She declined with a curt shake of her head. She sat gracefully opposite him at the table, staring.

"What would you give me in return?"

"Whatever is in my power to give."

Yusuf lay back on a pillow. He nervously fingered the edges of his beard. "Why should I not just keep the seal and use it to bind you to my will?"

She laughed coldly. His blood froze, but he kept the fear from his face. "You may try, my lord sultan," she hissed. "But it is only as strong as the hand that wields it. Have you the strength to wield it against one such as I? Do you even know my name?"

Almost he tried to answer her. Almost. Prudence, however, schooled him to wisdom. Instead, he asked, "Can you tell the future?"

She eyed him suspiciously. "After a fashion—yes."

"Will I drive the Ifranj from Urshalim," he asked, arching an eyebrow. He leaned closer, curiosity making him too eager. She saw the eagerness in his eyes and smiled.

"As long as you act alone and make no alliances against them, then yes, Jherusalem will fall."

He chuckled. "So, you give me what I desire most, but you place a condition on it. And yet, you would still expect a favor of me in return."

"That was our bargain, lord of Egypt. A gift for a gift."

"*Inshallah*," he sighed. "But alas, the seal is no longer in my possession."

Her arms crossed. She seemed to pout. He knew better, especially of a spirit of fire and air. "Where is it, then?"

"Gone—a gift for a gift." He sipped at his *káffe*. Unwisely, he let his gaze falter. He brought it back into obedience. "Would you hear the story, my lady?"

Her eyes narrowed; their light flared with impatience. Yusuf thought it best to proceed. "Until a year ago, I had the seal. With it, I had the command of the greatest spirits of the *jinn*, spirits that delivered into my hand the Fatimid Khalifa and the whole of Egypt. But in my arrogance, I thought to lay siege to the great fortress of Masyaf and restore the cult of the Ismailis to the true teachings of the Prophet. I was a fool. One night as I slept in my tent, the Old Man of the Mountain visited me. I have no doubt that it was he, and not one of his *fidais*. In the morning, I found a knife at my bedside with a note and the seal was gone. Twice before Sinan had tried to take it from me—twice he had failed. This time I understood his meaning: the gift of my life for the gift of the seal."

"You are a man most fortunate."

"Most fortunate, indeed," he laughed. "But if it is the seal you want, my lady, then I'm afraid you must seek out the *Sheikh al-Jebel*, though it will not be easy, even for one such as you."

With the graceful fluidity of all her kind, she stood to take her leave. She bowed deeply. He sipped again at his *káffe*. Between him and her, it was as a shield, making him bold. "What would you do with the seal?"

She lifted her head; a disconcerting gleam filled her eyes. "I intend to destroy the power of an old enemy threatening the life of a young king," she said very, very softly. "This is not the last time we shall meet, I think, noble prince of Islam."

Yusuf nearly dropped his cup. Miraculously, he was able to find his tongue and make use of it. "What is your name, my lady, that I may greet you properly the next time?"

"In the tongue of my people, I am called Mariamne."

"Maryam," he repeated softly, rendering it into Arabic. He said it as though to a lover. Even before the name escaped his lips, she was gone. Yusuf whispered a prayer to Allah and thanked him for his many blessings, not the least of which was the knowledge of the eventual deliverance of Urshalim into his hand.

Sometimes the word of an *ifritah* was worth more than a thousand treasures.

† CHAPTER SEVEN

Put not your trust in princes: in the children of men, in whom there is no salvation.
—Psalms 145:2-3

The kingdom of Jherusalem was in a state of excited, eager anticipation. The streets buzzed with news out of the north. Philip d'Alsace, the Count of Flanders, had arrived in Acre with a small, but impressive retinue of Flemish and English knights; the Byzantine fleet in accordance with the treaty Reynald de Châtillon had negotiated was expected within days. Not since the Conquest had the kingdom been so well prepared to repel the Sarrazin threat, if not break its back once and for all. Egypt was a plum ripe for the taking: Cairo first, then Damascus. It was a season of hope; it was a season of celebration.

Although he had recovered, Baldwin still suffered from the lingering effects of his malarial fever: headaches, fatigue, and dizziness. Still, when word of the Count of Flanders' arrival reached him in Ascalone, Baldwin had himself immediately carried in a litter, bumping and bouncing along the hot and dusty road, back to Jherusalem. A *curia generalis* convened; the nobility and clergy gathered at Court. Even Raymond and Bohemond responded: they escorted the Count and his retinue from Acre.

Baldwin stood quietly at a window in the Tower, watching as they rode through the Gate of David into the city, the black lion on gold of Flanders alongside the standards of Tripoli and Antioch. None of them had seen battle yet, but they rode into Jherusalem as though the enemy had already been beaten and driven back into the sands of their native desert. They made a dazzling display in their polished armor and weapons and the brilliant colors of their livery. The narrow and twisted streets echoed with cheers of the populace.

"The people hail him as though... as though he were king," Baldwin whispered. His illness made his stammer worse.

William stirred at his side, made a slight gesture with his hand towards the window. "It is the promise of hope he brings, Majesty. Nothing more. His father was well known for his warrior spirit. The people remember."

Baldwin glanced sidelong at his Chancellor, then back again out the window. "Even you are not that naïve, Father William. The people know that he has the ear of Henry of England and Louis of France."

"Having their ear is not the same as having their sword," said William and drew closer for a better view out the window. "Are you certain that offering Philip the Regency is still the wisest course?"

Baldwin stared intently on the movement of men and horses through the gate below. He was not sure if it was tears or the effects of his fever that blurred his vision. Either way, his long, slow death forced him into decisions he did not want to make. "I've discussed this with Reynald. He harbors no resentment about my decision to replace him as *bailli*. He agrees that Philip offers us the first real chance we've had at turning the tide of this long war against the Sarrazins."

"Perhaps, but at what cost?"

His gaze caught William's critical eye. "Only as much as I, or the Court, is willing to suffer. No more."

"From your mouth to God's ear, my lord," William said, making the sign of the cross over the troops issuing into the city through the gate.

Baldwin let out a short bark of laughter that seemed to break his somber mood. He set the kaffiyeh and the heavy gold crown that had belonged to his father on his head. Its weight felt like that of the whole kingdom. Drawing the long end of the white cloth across his diseased face, he turned again to his friend. "Shall we... shall we go down and meet this would-be savior of our people?"

It was high summer and the heat was close to unbearable. Servants stood about the crowded hall, doing what they could to cool the air with fans dampened with water. Baldwin's eyes darted, taking in the calculated movements of people about the crowded hall, the predictable, whispering circles that formed among the courtiers. The scene was like a dream: ethereal grey figures floating amid a hall filled with the smoke of incense-burners, the silver glint of mail and crucifixes, the rustle of gowns over the stone of the floor.

For this meeting with his royal quest and kinsman, Baldwin chose to give the impression of a kingdom armed for war. Over a padded gambeson and a long shirt of light riding mail and bloused trousers, he donned a white, knee-length eastern-style robe bearing the royal insignia of three clubbed crosses stitched in silver and gold. He looked more like a Muslim emir than the King of Jherusalem.

Baldwin watched the carefully orchestrated procession with interest and amusement from the shadowy concealment of his veil, waiting to see what impression his illness would make on the newcomers to his kingdom. It was usually predictable. There was a certain benefit to the discomfort the unsuspecting felt at seeing him for the first time. It put men ill at ease.

Philip came forward first, materializing out of the shadows, his retinue following in his wake. The steward announced each of them. Baldwin studied their faces, memorizing their names for future use. Philip brought with him an unexpected group: Robert, the Advocate of Béthune, and his two sons, Robert and William. Accompanying them were two other unexpected personages, Hugh de Lacey, the earl of Meath, and William de Mandeville, the earl of Essex, the personal representative of the English crown. Baldwin wondered what reason these men would give for their strange enlistment in this illustrious retinue. They gave none, however, nor did Baldwin inquire about one.

Of course, Baldwin had his own circle of intimates arrayed about him like a constellation of brilliant stars—for the sake of impression. He would not have these Western-bigoted nobles think the states of Outremer were nothing more than uncultured Orientals. First, there was his mother, resplendent, dominant, and overblown as usual; then there was his uncle, the Seneschal; and lastly, Sibylla, his acknowledged heir, looking elegantly beautiful in a cloth of gold gown and a veil of white silk embroidered with seed pearls. Joscelin stood behind the throne, his mother and sister sat on lesser thrones to his left and right hand. That alone—his mother occupying a throne of any sort—he meant as a reminder to the Church who was king.

Whether by a trick of fate or divine providence, a shaft of sunlight angled through the hazy smoke of the hall, illuminating the floor before the dais. Philip stepped forward into the light and knelt at Baldwin's feet. A murmur rippled through the Court and stilled.

Baldwin stretched out a gloved hand to bless his cousin, but Philip deftly averted his touch and bent his head, pressing his brow to Baldwin's foot. If the Count was in any way repulsed by his leprosy, he had cleverly managed to master any such response by his obeisance.

"We," Baldwin said softly and slowly, trying to control his stammer as Philip rose, "are honored, cousin, by your presence in our kingdom. We remember your father with fondness as a generous servant and friend. May you prove yourself an even greater defender of the Holy Sepulcher."

Philip bowed his head. "Your Highness is a most gracious man." He clapped his hands and two of the English knights brought forward a heavy, ironbound chest. "We in the West were terribly grieved to hear of your affliction, King Baldwin. And yet, you bravely persevere in ruling this kingdom. It is this concern that prompted His Majesty, King Henry, to send this gift of five hundred marks to help sustain the kingdom, as well as a gift of an equal sum as alms to the good brothers in the Hospital of Saint-John."

There was an underlying message in Philip's words that spoke of hesitancy in regards to his sickness and another delay for any hope of a new holy war.

Baldwin's eyes shifted to de Mandeville. He bowed his head a fraction of a degree. "Our brother, your king, my lord of Essex, sends a gift that is most fortuitous in this time of impending war."

De Lacey stepped forward, almost challenging; his accent was clear among so many Franks. "We understood that the kingdom has been at relative peace for most of the past year."

Baldwin glanced about at his guests, letting the uneasy quietude swell into tension. Joscelin broke the silence. "Peace? No, my lords. We are never at peace in this land. Nor will the Sarrazins ever give us rest until they drive us into the sea."

Letting his Seneschal vent his anger no longer than was appropriate, Baldwin raised a silencing hand. "Peace, uncle," he said in a rasping mockery of a voice. The Court held its collective breath, straining to hear him speak. "These men are our friends, our brothers in the name of the blessed Christ, not our enemies."

He stood slowly, drawing every eye in the hall, and stepped down from the dais; his family and officers of the kingdom fell in behind him. His two hounds leapt from their sleeping mats beside the throne and padded at his heels. Philip, he noticed, turned to walk beside him, but was careful to avoid his touch. Baldwin inclined his head towards his cousin.

"Forgive my uncle, he has seen too well the hatred the Sarrazins hold for us first-hand as a prisoner for more than sixteen years in Aleppo."

"The situation has changed, then, since I set out from France," Philip said in a softer, more conversational tone.

"The death of my sister's husband has put us in a vulnerable position." He coughed. "Our southern defenses are crumbling. Salehdin prowls just beyond the border waiting to strike. We have long planned to campaign against him and win Egypt once and for all, but I am growing sicker. You see the effects of my illness. I am dying. I can no longer… I can no longer govern this land alone," he said. Just speaking the words, Baldwin felt himself weaken as if the simple admission was draining away his will to live.

Philip paused before a tapestry depicting Godfrei de Bouillon refusing the crown in the Church of the Holy Sepulcher. "You have an heir; let her marry a lord who can help govern the kingdom."

"There are none who can marry her within a permitted degree," Baldwin said. He glanced at his cousin above the edge of his veil. The Count's eyes fell from the tapestry and found his. "We are in need of a man of proven ability to act as Regent with the power to control the affairs of the kingdom during peacetime and war. Would you do this for us?"

Philip glanced around the hall. There was little privacy amid so many courtiers and lords. "I have come as a pilgrim and knight; I had not thought to act as a king. I have people and a county of my own to consider. The situation in Flanders just now is, at best, precarious. I cannot commit myself to staying in the East but a short season."

"The people of Jherusalem have a greater need of you, my lord of Flanders," Baldwin argued. He could not believe he had heard his cousin aright. Noble men had bled and died to wrest the Holy Land from the hand of the Muslims; men had died since to protect that noble sacrifice. Ambitious men had traded their very souls to the Devil to gain what he freely offered. That Philip should dismiss such an offer in favor of his allodial lands was unbelievable.

"Make no decision now, cousin," he said, waving his hand in mild protest. "Only think on what I have asked of you." Philip recognized the finality of his words on the subject and bowed his head in submission. Baldwin held out a gloved hand towards the doors. "Would you come and pray with us at the Tomb for the defense of the kingdom?"

* * * * *

"God's bones," growled Reynald de Châtillon. He feinted with a thrust and spun; switching grips behind his back, he caught the king's parry on the hilt of his blunted sword. "The man is worse than a fool, Sire."

Baldwin pushed him back and made a savage, upward swing from the left to right with both hands. His swing went wide, throwing him off balance. He recovered agilely. "What… what was his answer this time?"

"Much the same as he gave before: he cannot commit himself to staying in Outremer with conditions at home so uncertain." Reynald grunted and swung angrily. "Nor will he consent to acting as commander in the campaign against Egypt. If you ask me, Sire, it sounds like a coward's excuse… or, a nobleman's selfish gambit."

Reynald parried a blow, lunged; both men exchanged alternate sword blows, trying to create an opening. The clanging of their steel rang in the yard; fierce laughter undercut the grunts of exhaustion. There were only a few spectators to this mock battle in the practice yard: their squires, the master-of-arms, and Reynald's ever-present serjeant working at the pell. The master-of-arms scrutinized their combat, yelling out his criticism. All four of them gave the combatants a wide berth.

For a man barely fifty, he was still quite agile and could handle a sword as well as any man half his age. All the time he was a prisoner, he had kept up his training, practicing every drill he had ever learned repeatedly in his mind. In the time since his release, he had worked hard to marry his body to his martial knowledge. His muscles often complained, even rebelled at the regiment of training, but in the end, his body complied. The king was a worthy opponent, despite his age or illness.

They had been at this for the better part of an hour. Sweat poured down Reynald's face from beneath his mail coif. Even in the shade of the palace wall, the summer heat made an oven of his armor. The king fared little better. His recent illness tired him easily and made him careless.

Baldwin stumbled backwards and fell to his knee. Reynald pressed his advantage. He lunged with an overhead blow. The master-of-arms shouted a warning. Baldwin escaped, dropping to his left, sword raised to deflect the blow on his shoulder. He twisted, driving Reynald's sword sideways to the ground. Reversing his grip, Reynald struck back, slicing at the king's legs with a backward, whirling attack. Baldwin swung again with an overhead chop. The heavy blow jarred his arm; pain shot through his shoulder. Reynald let Baldwin's weight bear him down, creating an opening. He reached instinctively and drew his dagger. He pressed it against the king's exposed ribs.

"Will you yield, Highness?"

Baldwin pulled off his coif wearily and withdrew. Even beneath the mail, a veil bound his face to protect his sores from chaffing. "You cheated, my lord of Kerak," he panted, his eyes smiling above the edge of the veil.

"No, Your Highness," Reynald said. "I improvised. There are no rules in battle. Remember that—it could save your life."

The king nodded and sheathed his sword, handing the master-of-arms his coif. He fixed Reynald with a hard gaze. "Now, about Philip d'Alsace."

Reynald snorted his disdain. He made no apologies about his opinion about the Count of Flanders. Bloodshed and the fierceness of battle had taught him the meaning of hatred; sixteen years in an Aleppan jail had honed his hatred to a sword's edge. He had little tolerance for those who did not share his hostility towards the Muslims. Just as he had little patience for those who refused to back up their words with the point of their swords.

Baldwin sighed and set his hands on his hips. "If… if he won't accept the Regency or the command of the army in the campaign against Egypt, what *will* he accept?"

"I'm afraid he wants nothing less than Egypt as his own territory," Reynald said, slamming his sword into its sheath. He glanced around the practice yard. He lowered his voice. "It isn't a new issue, Your Highness. Nor is it the first time a lord of Flanders has disputed a claim to conquered territory. What Philip refuses is to shoulder the blame if the campaign fails or to be robbed of Egypt if he succeeds."

"A rather convenient stand, don't you think?"

"Not to mention self-serving."

Baldwin stood staring, licking his dry, cracked lips. "Something is amiss, Reynald. He can't be that contrary," he said, wiping his arm across his forehead. "Have you learned anything else?"

Reynald crossed his arms and leaned against a column supporting the upper arcade of the palace. "He and the Advocate of Béthune are constantly huddled together discussing God knows what between them. Not only that, the man has the audacity to protest you making me Regent again." He smirked, shifted his weight from one foot to the other. "He is certainly not making many friends at Court. Only the Hospitallers along with Tripoli and Antioch seem willing to give him any kind of support."

Baldwin swore under his breath. "I'm not surprised. Raymond and Bohemond have made their views about the Egyptian campaign quite clear—at least in private." He let his head fall back, thinking for several long moments. With a guttural growl of frustration, he pulled off the veil and threw it on a bench.

Reynald had seen the horror war could inflict upon a man's body, but the ruin he saw in Baldwin's face was hideous. Ulcers and the slow decay of disease ate away the gift of beauty and grace that once existed within him. Only the large dark eyes remained of his youthful handsomeness. An uncharacteristic sense of pity went out to his sworn king. That the petty bickering and squabbling among the nobles had forced this boy of sixteen to keep his throne instead of retiring appalled him. No man—and certainly, no boy—deserved to have to rule under such conditions.

"We need Egypte if we are to break the back of Salehdin's ambition for empire," Baldwin breathed heavily in exasperation.

Reynald pushed himself away from the column. "You're not seriously considering giving Philip what he wants?"

"I'm not a fool, Reynald," Baldwin said. His eyes flashed with anger. "But neither... but neither will I see some scheming noble jeopardize all we have worked so hard to accomplish. If the Greeks catch wind of Philip's protestations, they could withdraw their fleet. We must provide a united front for the campaign."

"What would you have me do, Sire?"

"Where is Philip, now?"

"Supposedly, he's visiting the pilgrim sites with the Advocate and the English earls. I believe he mentioned Bethlehem."

Baldwin withdrew his sword and hefted it in his hand, weighing it thoughtfully. He glanced towards the practice yard. "Do nothing for now—only keep a close eye on our fickle Count and see that he causes no more trouble. Something tells me that it won't be long before Philip finally shows his hand."

Reynald touched hilt and blade to his face, saluting the king with his sword and left. Baldwin joined the master-of-arms and began working at the pell with his sword. Within moments, the sound of steel on wood echoed through the yard.

As he exited the yard, Reynald motioned to his serjeant with a gloved hand.

"My lord," Hughes said, clipping the word short in his usual fashion as he closed the distance between them.

Reynald crooked a finger, urging his serjeant nearer; he lowered his voice. "I want you to find the Count of Flanders and have him watched—but do it discreetly, Hughes. I want to know everything he says and who he says it to."

Hughes was not a man to question his lord's orders. He made a stiff nod and went about his business without a word. It made what Reynald planned to do all the easier. The king himself had suggested the idea. *If the Greeks catch wind of Philip's protestations...* No, Egypte would not fall into the hand of the Count of Flanders, not as long as he had breath to prevent it. Even if it meant sabotaging the very treaty that he had negotiated with the Emperor.

* * * * *

Sparrows chattered incessantly as the last few breadcrumbs fell from Sibylla's hand. They sounded too much like the barons in Court who were arguing her fate. She giggled softly at the thought, and burst into sudden tears.

Her insides churned; her emotions and the strength of her will turned to water. She felt like Queen Penelope from Homer's *Odyssey*, waiting for her husband's lords to burst in on her and finally demand that she marry one of them. Her hand moved to the swollen mound of her abdomen and caressed it protectively. Her baby would save her, but only for a while. There would be no heroic return of a beloved Odysseus to clear out the rebellious suitors from her Court. Eventually, the Court would force her to marry against her wishes. Not even her brother could delay the decision for long.

It was those not so pleasant deliberations that brought her to the quietude of a rose covered bower in the garden. A fountain would have been nice for the sake of distraction and tranquility. This, however, was the palace of the kings of Jherusalem; such luxuries did not exist in what was nothing more than a camp armed for war. Tucked in a shadowed corner between the palace and the imposing Tower of David, the courtyard of the Citadel was a jumble of ancient, crumbling stone and the riotous scent of citrus trees and sun-drenched flowers. In the late August sunlight, the stone walls turned to the color of polished gold.

For Sibylla, the palace was a prison that held her hopes and dreams captive to the whim of a divided Court bent on pursuing its own ambitions.

Her thoughts strayed to her dead husband William. In the short six months they had been married, she had begun to love him. She had been… happy, she realized—happier, perhaps, than she had ever been growing up at the convent of Saint-Lazare. William could be ill tempered and crass to his men, but never with her. He treated her with kindness and genuine affection, even doting on her in what some would consider as an unmasculine manner when he discovered she was with child. He had brought her flowers. They would have made a good king and queen when her brother finally passed. That had ended with William's death.

She would not be so fortunate again if her brother permitted the barons of Jherusalem to choose her next husband. She had done her duty to the kingdom. For the sake of her love for William, she would resist, even her brother if necessary.

Her hand balled into a fist on her belly as she fought to control another wave of tears. Angrily, she tore off the jeweled veil that marked her inferior sex and shook out the golden tresses of her hair. "I will not be made to marry against my will," she growled.

Her sudden outburst startled the sparrows, setting them to wing; the reply to her impassioned plea startled her.

"Nor should any woman who is as beautiful as you," said a deep and masculine voice.

She stifled an outcry with a whimper and an admonishment. "You caught me by surprise, Messire—you are knight, are you not?"

"I am, *ma dama*."

The stranger stepped around the corner of the bower and she could see that he was indeed a nobleman, and very handsome, almost pretty with his long, wavy locks of wheat gold hair framing a ruddy face not used to the Eastern sun. Piercing blue eyes lay astride a strong, aquiline nose that bore a slight scar where it had once been broken. Silver mail sheathed the rest of his tall, lean body. It accentuated the black and gold tabard of Count Philip's house.

"I marked your entrance along the portico and waited to make my introduction," he said, plucking a rose and handing it to her with a flourish.

Sibylla looked at him demurely. She glanced at the offered rose and took it, holding it close to her nose. "I think you presume too much of me, Messire."

"Forgive me, Countess, that was not my intention," he said, bowing.

Sibylla leaned back against the lattice of the bower and studied her unexpected guest. He amused her; she laughed. "So, you admit knowing who We are, and yet, you dare to approach Our Majesty," she said, slipping into the formal speech of royalty. "You are bold, if nothing else, sir knight. We are alone. Your actions could be misconstrued as less than honorable."

"I assure you they are not," he said. "I am but a humble knight from Poitou, of the house of Lusignan."

The name was certainly familiar. Her mother had often sung the praises of the knights of Lusignan—or, at least one of them. This man bore little resemblance, though, to the knight her mother praised. "Lusignan," she said slowly, purposefully rendering the name with a particular Eastern accent. It seemed to amuse him.

"My brother is Amalric de Lusignan, Your Grace," he said. "Perhaps, you know of him."

She coyly held the fragrant rose again and smelled it. "We are, indeed, familiar with Messire Amalric. But tell us, good sir, what is your name?"

"Guion, my lady," he said proudly, dropping to one knee. "Guion de Lusignan."

* * * * *

August came and went and there was still no word from the Magdalen. It had been two months since she had healed him of his fever. If ever Baldwin needed her help, it was now. Twice he had stolen out and gone to the Holy Tomb, hoping to catch her by chance, but it had been a vain hope. William tried to ease his mind after his second such visit to the church.

"The Lady Magdalen comes and goes as she wills: but never when she is bidden." Baldwin was beginning to suspect his aged Chancellor was right.

He stood at his accustomed place by the window in the Tower of David, looking down upon the city. Sunlight and the grey shadows of early evening gave it an idyllic setting. In the distance, the great golden dome of the Templum Domini gleamed blood-red with the waning sun; the lesser silver dome of the Church of the Holy Sepulcher had turned to the dull color of pewter.

Baldwin leaned heavily against the window ledge. The effects of his illness were beginning to take their toll on his body, but he refused to let anyone know the extent of it. Pain had long ago ceased to be a concern. It was numbness; it made him insensitive to whatever touched him: heat or cold, or simply the caress of a human hand. If only his mind was as insensitive to the despair he felt about of losing his own self, his identity. Perfume and the shear weightlessness of his veil was becoming a mask too heavy to bear. He prayed more often now for wisdom and strength, the will to see his days through to their end.

Father William babbled at his shoulder, something having to do with the Count of Flanders. It was all anyone ever talked about anymore. Frankly, he was weary to death with hearing it. Philip was a bitter disappointment—a reflection of the prevailing opinion the West had of the kingdom of Jherusalem. *Come to Outremer; make your pilgrimage; have your sins absolved for your humble action. Perhaps you might even enhance your reputation; but do nothing that might endanger your position of standing at home.*

The Holy Land had become only a shadowy dream veiled in jewels and silks and the exotic trappings of the Orient. War was a seductive distraction, a noble cause sanctioned by the Pope to advance the cause of Christendom to the hordes of heathen Sarrazins.

The sound of William's voice trailed off into silence. He dismissed a page with a nod; the door closed quietly. "It seems we've stood here before discussing the virtues of your noble cousin, Your Highness."

Baldwin turned and regarded him with a level stare. "Only then we had thought him the bearer of so much hope; so much promise."

"Agreed, Your Highness. Agreed."

It was many long moments before either of them said anything more. He was not in a very pleasant mood and William knew it. Brushing past his friend, Baldwin went to a sideboard and poured a goblet of wine. He handed it to the Archbishop.

William sipped his wine several times and cleared his throat peremptorily. "You know he's calling for your sister to remarry now as an answer to the problem of a Regent, if it's necessary again. He thinks her need for a period of mourning is frivolous in the face of Jherusalem's greater need."

"What business is it of his?" Baldwin snapped. "If he is that concerned, he should have... he should have taken the Regency when I offered it to him. Just who does he think Sibylla should marry in such a hurry—I'm sure he must have someone in mind?"

"Not just Sibylla, Your Majesty," William said, taking a judicial sip of his wine. "Isabella, as well."

"Isabella is only seven years old. He must have someone very desperate in mind if he is willing to marry off a child. Who is he?"

William suddenly found the silver crucifix on his chest of greater importance. He fingered it thoughtfully and adjusted its lay across the breast of his ecclesiastical robe with meticulous care. "He won't say, Sire, unless the Court swears to abide by his choice, but I think I know his mind. It has been quite apparent from the start to anyone with eyes enough to see: the sons of the Advocate of Béthune."

Baldwin snorted half in disgust, half in amusement. "Philip must think me a fool, as well as a leper, if he thinks I'll agree to that union."

"You have to admit—as I'm sure even the Court would—that the unions have merit given the Count's position with the kings of England and France."

"I won't admit to any such nonsense. Neither will I see my sisters used as pawns in an elaborate scheme to steal the throne."

In a fit of anger, Baldwin turned away and limped towards the window to allow the heat of his anger to cool. Night had fallen at last; the city lay enfolded in a mantle of glittering stars and darkness. The golden dome of the Temple of the Lord glowed like a candle flame amid its circle of flickering torches. Allowing him a few moments of private introspection, William quietly made his way over to Baldwin's side.

"Do you think we can hold Jherusalem against the Sarrazins," Baldwin said. His words came out as a whisper so soft, so uncertain, that he wondered if he had actually spoken aloud.

William hesitated, glancing out the narrow window towards the city. "Only, if we are truly willing to give peace a chance."

"You sound like Count Raymond."

"That's because what he says is wisdom to those who will only listen," William mildly admonished him. "Abandon your plans of war and make an offer of truce to Salehdin—at least until a more propitious time. Rumors are circulating around Court about certain comments the Count of Flanders has made in regards to the campaign. His seeming insincerity towards the war has made the Byzantines rather… agitated. They are threatening to withdraw their fleet."

"You say that as though Raymond or Bohemond's opposition to the war have no part in this tension with the Greeks."

William sputtered incredulously. His loyalty to his patron, Raymond of Tripoli, was well known. Baldwin wanted to laugh. Instead, he turned to pace the floor of the room. He stopped suddenly, surprising even himself, and glanced furtively at his narrow-eyed Chancellor. He smiled behind his veil.

"What are you thinking, Your Highness?"

"A way of luring my illustrious cousin from Jherusalem, and thereby, being rid of him," Baldwin said. He paused and leaned against the post of his bed. "If Philip is so determined to avoid a war with Egypt, I'll send him north to Tripoli. Raymond and Bohemond have been pressuring me for some sort of organized campaign in Syria for the past year. The loss of Damascus would be a serious blow to Salehdin's plans. Philip will be all too eager to follow the example of his father in trying to win even the smallest parcel of land from the Sarrazins."

"And in doing so, you still shun a chance for peace, no matter how tentative."

"I will not waste the opportunity to wage a successful war with so many knights in the kingdom at one time," Baldwin said through clenched teeth. "This is a gift from God, no matter how much trouble Philip makes."

"I disagree, Your Highness," said William.

"That is your choice, my lord Archbishop."

Of a sudden, a knock came at the door, abruptly cutting off their conversation. A young page, liveried in the blue and gold of the palace, entered and made his way sheepishly to the Archbishop.

They talked for only a few moments. When they had finished, William patted the young lad on the shoulder and sent him, much relieved, on his way. The archbishop rejoined him once more by the window.

"What trouble now?"

William cleared his throat. "Our troublesome Count is requesting an audience with you at once."

Baldwin shook his head with a weary sigh. He closed his eyes, shutting out the night and the city and all else that sought to demand his attentions. He shook his head again, this time more vigorously, until he let out a tormented growl. He struck the wall and pushed himself away from the window.

"Make him go away, Father William. I do not want to talk with him anymore. There's nothing left to discuss."

"What am I suppose to tell him—you're tired of his ignoble demands and refuse to deal with him anymore?"

"I don't care," he spat and flung himself down on his bed. "Tell him I'm ill and can't be disturbed. It's not so far from the truth."

"Your Highness—" William began, but Baldwin cut him off.

"Tell him anything you like, so long as you do it."

William was visibly annoyed. He opened his mouth, but promptly closed it again. He took a step towards the bed. "Sometimes, Your Highness, I forget how young you are."

"But," Baldwin said, trying to hold back a burst of laughter. He never could stay mad at his former tutor for very long.

William saw no humor in his actions. "But then, you do something so childish that it reminds me of it with startling clarity."

Baldwin lay back in his bed and waved his Chancellor towards the door. He laughed to himself at seeing William's face.

Reluctantly, and none too pleased, William complied. "The Count of Flanders won't be so easily put off, Your Highness, by such simple excuses," he said at the door and closed it quietly behind him.

Baldwin lay in his bed, staring up at the ceiling long after the candles had died out and the shadows deepened into utter darkness. It had been a long day. Too long. It had started with Philip; it would end with Philip. If God was truly merciful, he would see that tomorrow dawned a little brighter and Philip would declare that he was returning home to Flanders. He doubted either would prove true.

The priory bells of Holy Sepulcher signaling Compline made him sit up abruptly in his bed. He had fallen asleep. Silence had crept through the palace. It seemed as though he lay in a grave and suddenly awoke. Only the steady rhythm of his beating heart told him he was still alive. His fear turned to near panic: darkness and silence were too closely akin to death.

Holding out his hand, it filled with a small globe of cold blue fire. The shadows fled at a thought. Calming his breath and his pounding heart, he rose and went out into the night. There was still one opinion he wanted to hear before the night had passed.

† CHAPTER EIGHT

For our wrestling is not against flesh and blood; but against principalities and powers, against the rulers of the world of this darkness, against the spirits of wickedness in the high places.
—*Ephesians 6:12*

Mary stood just inside the moonlit world of men, her hands raised towards the gate of Masyaf, the impregnable castle of the Old Man of the Mountain and his infamous Assassins. With every grain of her power, she tried to reach within the invisible wall. Her effort proved useless as it had every other time she had tried in the past few days. The wards refused to yield even to her will.

It was magic—her magic; the magic of the *jinn* and faerie and every other immortal creature denounced as a child of the devil or the demon Lilith—which barred her entrance. It was the power of the Seal of Solomon; it protected the fortress as it protected the one who wore it.

Eldritch laughter rippled through the air. Shadows flitted near; minor spirits whispered in her ear. "Did you think to find entrance to the Master's castle so easy," said one of the spirits, its hideous voice rasping like the rustling of dried leaves.

Mary ignored the taunt and raised her arms to the walls once more. The spirit passed in front of her, hovering. Moonlight flashed green in its inhuman eyes. "It is no use. The way is barred to all those who do not serve the Master al-Rashid Sinan."

"It is not barred to me, spirit."

"And yet you stand without the walls," it hissed. "Beware of pride, lady. It goes before a fall."

"Be gone, spirit," she said. "I grow weary of you."

The shadow hovered nearer. Its breath stank of fire and smoke. It whispered softly and seductively. "There are other ways; other magics you might use."

Others had offered similar promises to her long ago. She shuddered at the memory. Her gaze broke and she glanced narrowly at the shadow-daemon. It purred with delight.

"I know your name, daemon. I remember," she said and turned away from the gate of the fortress. "Leave me before I banish you to the fires whence you came."

"You wound me, lady. We were friends once."

"We were never friends. Now, be gone," she commanded, drawing in her power.

The spirit spat and laughed cruelly as it rose shrieking into the sky. "Remember me when you have need of me."

With a growl of anger and frustration, Mary wrapped her cloak about her frail, thin shoulders and faded from the mortal world.

The sun was soft in the midst of a golden haze; light angled through the silhouetted trees in a landscape washed with every hue of green. A mist rose from the dew-laden earth, mingling with the shimmering pale dawn of Eden. She slipped along a path strewn with the leafy mould of a forgotten season; blossoms swirled in the air at her passing. Time slowed to a pace no mortal sun could mark.

She paused at the tumbled stones of a small gate and looked back, a fleeting glance that stilled the phantom shadows that crept out of the wood. Shedding her cloak and the glamour of her human semblance, she came to a mound in the midst of the ancient forest and cast herself down on the ground. There had been a spring here once, long ago, where the ring of stones stood, but no more.

The whispers troubled her even here, only these were the whispers of her own memories. They accused her of using a young king's illness to accomplish her own purpose, of having little love to share with a dying boy.

Her prayers helped a little to silence the whispers; they helped more as the Spirit of God enveloped her in his embrace. She found comfort in the words she mouthed, and strength. *Lead us not into temptation, but deliver us from evil.*

The whispers lied, of course. She had loved once... and lost.

Even after a thousand years, she wondered at how little she understood the frail creatures of dust God had created for his glory. How little she understood their passing from this world to the next, or the effect they would have on her. One by one, all those whom she had loved—the two Marys, Maximum, her dearest Lazarus, even Joseph—had died; and more in the days that came after with the tribulation of Nero and the fiery destruction of Jherusalem foretold by John.

Sorrow multiplied into sorrow, and she slowly, slowly began to fade from the world. The loneliness was preferable to the loss. Her pain became a living thing; it choked her. She wandered for years out of count, keeping to the deathless lands she knew, only occasionally taking note of what passed in the world of men. Long years passed; the world changed. All the while, a darkness began to grow that she could not ignore—a familiar evil from her earliest memory. It began as a whisper among the shadows, a secret that slowly unfolded like the blossom of a flower.

The evil grew and spread like a malignancy that covered the East in a darkness that called all of Christendom to win back the Holy Land from the infidel. It became a holy cause: the Pope had called it so. Beneath it all, however, was a most unholy purpose.

She came to Jherusalem as an unseen challenge to the evil, hoping to thwart its plans, but it was elusive. It was prepared; it knew her, and knew how to conceal its presence from her. She could call it by name—Sion—but she could do nothing to expose it or reveal the one who lay at its center. Oh, she knew its true name, but not the form he had taken. For all his cunning, for all his subtlety, he had erred. He had thought to cast down a young prince using her protecting magic. In so doing, he had created a means to find him; and perhaps, bind him if she could claim what the Lord of the Assassins held in secret. The Seal of Solomon. The talisman the ancient king of the Jews had used to bind the immortal spirits of air and fire to his will.

Hunched over her bent knees, she banished the dark specter of her thoughts with a word. *Fool*, she hissed under her breath, castigating herself for her blindness. She rose, laughing softly like a child and, gathering the power of the land about her, passed along the shadow-ways towards the border of the mortal world. Flowers blossomed in her wake; the trees put forth the bright green foliage of new growth. Sun and shadow mingled. She sped along the straight ways few could see; in her absence, the mortal moon had turned a full cycle.

With each passing step, the edge of the ancient forest extended into the world of men. Masyaf loomed, its walls pale and insubstantial in the light of the overlapping worlds. She raised a hand and the wards about the castle crumbled, yielding to the greater power of Eden.

* * * * *

The back streets and alleys of Jherusalem were unnaturally quiet. Night and the heat of late summer had settled in a thick, impenetrable darkness that spoke of fear and danger and the subtle lurking of evil. It was never quite safe in the city after dark or alone.

Disguised as the leper he was, Baldwin only had to make use of the clapper once to clear a path through a small group of drunken soldiers who stumbled into the alley from a tavern along the street. Whether it was the fear of disease or the watchman that happened by, the wisest of the soldiers made the sign of the cross on his chest and pushed his boisterous companions towards the street without incident. When the soldiers were gone, the watchman urged him back into the darkened alley with the butt of his spear and a coarse, derogatory gesture.

"Get out o' here, y' stinkin' leper. We've enough trouble in 'e streets at night wit'out yer kind addin' to it."

Despite the kingdom's general acceptance of lepers, there were those who would rather see them driven from the city and condemned to the midden fields of Gehenna.

Rather than get angry, Baldwin was amused, if only slightly. He fumbled in his scrip and tossed a small gold coin towards the soldier with a grunt. It clattered on the stones and rolled. "For your kindness, gentle sir," he whispered. Perhaps the gesture would heap coals of fiery guilt on the man's head, as Father William was wont to preach.

As the watchman scrambled for the coin in disbelief of his sudden good fortune, Baldwin melted into the shadows and shuffled away. Keeping to the walls and the moon-shadowed arches that spanned the narrow passageways, he slipped from one dark pool of darkness to another, careful to avoid any cutpurses or worse. Thieves prowled the city this time of year with the pilgrim season at its zenith and the holy days near at hand.

A heavily laden cart lumbered through the crossroads, taking the wide Street of David towards the tangled knot of lanes that was the Latin Exchange. The donkeys brayed noisily beneath their burden, but plodded on, climbing the hill towards the sacred mount of the ancient temple of Solomon. He darted across the broad avenue and plunged into the blackened crevice of the adjacent alley. Sound became an eerie thing; the high walls and ancient contours of the stone twisted it, bending it into a living specter that haunted him as he crept along.

A cat cried with a pitiful, wailing mew that echoed the length of the alley. Baldwin froze and crouched against the wall. His heart leapt into his throat, pounding. A rock fell from on high with a shout and a curse. It exploded against the cobbles sending the feline daemon running.

Silence fell just as swiftly as it had been broken. Wrapping the tattered rags of his cloak about him, he ran along the shadowed alleys of the Patriarch's Quarter towards the postern gate near unto the Hospital of Saint-Lazare and Tancred's Tower. He had enough of slinking about in the city and the darkness to last him a good long while.

Small campfires burned in the courtyard of the hospital. The meager light was barely bright enough to keep the dark shadows of night at bay. Men moved in those shadows, seeking comfort and companionship for the night among the recumbent bodies that littered the ground. It was not unusual for the patients of the hospital to spill out into the courtyard during the hot summer months; it freed up bed space for those who were closer to death. An ignorant passerby might have expected to hear moans and cries of pain from the shadows of the walls. There was none: there were only the whispered conversations of men whose advancing sickness had rendered their diseased extremities insusceptible to pain.

Baldwin slipped from fire to fire offering words of encouragement and pressing gold bezants into the hand of each knight disfigured by leprosy to help pay for their care. It was not an act of charity by a king that led him to do so, but a need for a fellow soldier of Christ to help those stricken by a common affliction. The knights knew him; the men clasped his diseased hand and blessed him for his gift. Often they would ask him to stay and visit and give them some word of the kingdom, but he declined, for he had other, more pressing business among them tonight.

He found the object of his clandestine visit in the corner of the yard near to the door of the house. The flames of the nearby fire cast his bold, misshapen silhouette against the high wall. Brother Theoderic knelt over a basin filled with a mixture of water and bloody discharge, carefully washing the ulcerous feet of a patient. Taking his time, he finished bathing the man's feet and wrapped them in fresh, clean bandages in silence. Planting a kiss of blessing on the man's head, Theoderic stood, wiping his hands on the blood-smeared apron covering his habit.

Theoderic was no longer a young man, nor was caring for lepers his first calling in life. He had been a soldier once, a knight in the army of the Byzantine Emperor before he came to Jherusalem during the Second War of the Cross and took up service with the lord of Ibelin. He had won distinction at the conquest of Ascalone and fought in Egypt; he had even been a Templar briefly before leprosy had overtaken him and he had to take refuge within the cloistered walls of

Saint-Lazare. For seven years, he had managed to hide the mild, early symptoms of the disease, refusing to give in to the deleterious effects until he could no longer ignore the obvious. If he had died in battle, no one would have ever known, but God had other plans for the last years of his life. Of all the people Baldwin knew, only Theoderic understood what he was enduring or why he chose to do so.

"Theo," Baldwin called.

The brother turned, peering uncertainly through the darkness. "Baldwin? Forgive me, Your Highness, I mistook you for one of the patients," he said. "I get so busy with the men I lose sight of all else. It's a grim task I admit, but it's what our Lord expects of us."

"You're a better man than I, Brother. And a better Christian."

"Shall I tend your feet while I'm at it, Sire?"

"No, no, my friend," Baldwin said, moving to the opposite side of the fire and sat down. "Dawud saw to them this morning. It's almost an obsession with him."

"And well it should be," Theoderic said as he levered himself down next to Baldwin. "Do you know how many of these poor devils would still have the ability to walk if they had only taken the time to wash their feet more often? Perhaps then, they might have noticed how infected their sores were and been able to clean and bandage them. Instead, they worry about their once pretty faces and ignore the rest of their deteriorating bodies."

Baldwin leaned towards Theoderic, pulling back his veil. "And do you take the time to wash your own feet," he whispered. "Or do you gaze at what the leprosy has done to your own pretty Greek face?"

Theoderic sputtered, almost unable to reply, but he managed. "Why you impudent, young pup…" he began to expostulate and snapped his mouth shut at seeing Baldwin's crooked smile. He crossed his arms and propped his head on his hand. "What brings you to Saint-Lazare so late in the evening? Shouldn't you be in the palace entertaining your noble guest?"

Baldwin snorted. "Philip? I'm done with him," he said, dismissing the thought with a wave of his hand. "He won't commit to the war in Egypt in any way, but would you believe that he's been out playing pilgrim the past week. Can you imagine that—a pilgrimage at a time when we need him most."

The brother gave him an inquisitive look. "Why now?"

"Why not now? He thinks his seemingly pious acts will win him favor with the Church and the people. It's nothing more than an excuse."

"Not to mention that it allows some heads to cool within the Court while he's dallying about the countryside." Brother Theoderic shook his head and frowned. "I've always thought it best not to put much trust in princes who stand to make great gains from the spoils of battle. Such was the problem, you know, during the Second War. Too many men of noble birth squandered away opportunity after opportunity because they refused to act when they should. Instead, they squabbled about who would receive this land or that title even before it was won from the Sarrazins." He picked up a stick and stabbed the fire as savagely as if it had been a sword. It sent sparks floating into the pitch-black night. "Pilgrimage, indeed. It's an affront to all that's holy and blessed."

"Did I tell you that tomorrow he's heading north through Naples to visit Nazareth. He claims he won't rest until he gets his little metal badge from the hand of the Archbishop himself."

"Naples, you say?" Theoderic mused. Several long moments passed. "Isn't your step-mother living in Naples?"

"Maria?" Baldwin said. "You... you don't think Philip would stop there to get her advice?"

"Would he have reason to?"

Baldwin's eyes slowly tracked upwards to meet his friend's as understanding finally dawned. "She's a Byzantine. Philip is at odds with the text of the Emperor's chrysobull regarding the treaty that brought the imperial fleet. It stipulates that any land captured by the campaign will fall under imperial suzerainty."

Theoderic whistled through his rotten teeth. "We Byzantines are certainly a crafty lot. The Emperor has assured himself of compensation for his alliance. And he has effectively frustrated our fickle Count." He tapped a finger against his lips, musing. "I expect the Queen will council him to agree to take part in the Egyptian campaign, just as I'm sure the Byzantine ambassadors will require some sort of oath of good faith from him to insure his sincerity."

"Philip will never agree to an oath that might cast doubt on his honor."

"Then your long planned campaign might be in danger of failure before it ever starts. What will you do?"

Baldwin sighed deeply. "I've already decided to send Philip with Raymond to campaign in Syria for the time being. At least we may gain some benefit from his presence in the kingdom," he said and fell into silence. Theoderic allowed him his peace. It was the first time in a very long while that he had been given the opportunity to just sit and think without the members of the Court hounding his every thought.

His hands clenched and he brought his fist to his mouth, tapping his lips, thinking on all that had transpired in the past two months. None of it made any sense.

"Something is still not right in all of this. Philip is acting as though he has some other purpose in being here—and it's not fighting or marriage brokering."

Theoderic stiffened and sat straight. "You don't think he's plotting a coup? I've heard he and Raymond have been supportive of each through this whole ordeal."

Baldwin shook his head. "No. Raymond and I have disagreed on some things for certes, but he is loyal. He'd never plot to take the throne from me by force."

"At least, not knowingly."

"At least, not knowingly," Baldwin admitted reluctantly. It was not the first time someone warned him of danger within his kingdom of late. *You and your kingdom are in grave danger.* The words of the Magdalen shot through his mind. It was as though she had whispered them in his ear. Words she had spoken in reference to the order of Sion. A shiver of cold fear crept slowly up his spine.

Theoderic set his hand on his shoulder. "Watch your back, Your Highness. We Knights of Saint-Lazare are not the army of the Count of Flanders, but if you need arms, call upon us and we will answer. We may be lepers, but still hale enough to fight. We'll defend you with our swords and our lives, even to the last man, if necessary." He winked and smiled crookedly. "Imagine an army of lepers armed with only clappers and our disfigured faces set loose among the hordes of marauding Sarrazins. We'd set them running for their heathen lives."

Baldwin grinned and laughed. He hoped his sudden humor would dispel his fears. "Of course, we could hope that our long-awaited savior, King Prester John, will finally march out of the East and help crush the Sarrazins once and for all. They say he's conquered nearly all of the East."

A snort erupted from Theoderic's nose. "I shouldn't count on it, Your Highness. That old rumor has persisted since the Second War and has amounted to nothing more than false hope. I doubt if he exists or if he ever did."

"But the Holy Father has sent his personal secretary as an emissary to gain his support."

"And where is he to find this great king clad all in white who is to be our savior—India, Ch'in, Abyssinia? No one knows for certes where he is." Theoderic shook his head vigorously. "No, Sire, he is a myth. Our hands alone will defeat the Sarrazins. We cannot look to some mystical legend from out of the East. Now," he said, giving him a curious look, "have you learned anything new about this mysterious Order of Sion you spoke of the last time I saw you?"

Baldwin's eyes darted upwards, looking askance at Brother Theoderic. The question was innocuous enough—he had indeed questioned him about it shortly after his first meeting with the Magdalen—but the suddenness of it surprised him. For a moment, he almost grew suspicious, but Theoderic's look of genuine concern won back his trust. The warrior-monk had proven himself too good a friend for him to judge him so unfairly.

"No," he said. "For all my trying, I've learned nothing."

"Perhaps, then, the question you should ask is whether or not you can truly trust the warning you were given—whatever its source."

* * * * *

Othon de Saint-Amant sat in the narrow window of his office above the refectory. The room was spacious enough, filled with a desk and chairs, a tapestry or three, an eastern-style carpet, and bookshelf, which was a treasure in itself, and all of it illumined by a heavy lampstand that stood by the window. It cast a soft ruddy glow throughout the room. By his own choice, he had kept to himself as they waited the fourth member of their conspiracy. Yet even in his office, set in the midst of all Templar power and authority, he felt somehow... overlooked, insignificant in the presence of Amalric de Lusignan, as though his presence was of no consequence here. He knew what made him feel as he did: Lusignan had appropriated to himself, and therefore, the Order of Sion, too much power, too much authority in the affairs of the kingdom and in the Templar Order.

The night was quiet and deep outside the window. The faint chant of the brothers singing the prayers of the nightly offices echoed from the chapel on the air. It was the duty of every Templar to recite the paternoster one hundred and forty-eight times each day as prescribed in the Rule set down for their Order by the sainted Bernard de Clairvaux. For some, the monotony of words proved too tedious a chore that served only to dull the mind with its repetition. For Othon, though, it was a comfort; a rhythm that provided a meditative focus that centered his thoughts and actions on the divine.

He should have—would rather have—been with his brothers in the faith, but other, more pressing business took him from the observations of the evening offices this night; the Seneschal had taken his place while he was otherwise detained. Slipping the knotted prayer cord between his fingers, he found the last knot and silently repeated the last of his prayers just as the Count of Flanders entered through the warded door.

"You have done well, Philippe, in deflecting the king's requests," said the Master of the Order of Sion.

Philip d'Alsace went down on one knee in homage before Amalric de Lusignan. He kissed the master's ring and stood with a wolfish smile. "At no small cost to my pride and my reputation, Master."

The older man chuckled darkly. "Your sacrifice will not go unnoticed, I promise you. With Montferrat's untimely death and the Egyptian campaign in disarray, the only thing keeping us from our goal now is the life of a dying king."

"Did Ascalone die of natural causes... or was he poisoned?" Othon said from his overlooked perch in the window. It was more an accusation than a question.

The dark eyes of the master swung slowly towards him. His was the look of a serpent eyeing his prey: a look as old as the Garden of Eden. "No, my good Othon," said the malevolent voice. "His death was not by my hand or any other of Sion. Rather, it was the result of a most propitious turn-of-events."

"Even if we had poisoned him, what would it matter?" said Heraclius, the Archbishop of Caesarea.

Othon glanced at the self-important cleric. Heraclius pulled a frown and looked down at an outstretched hand, examining his carefully manicured nails as if the death of a man meant absolutely nothing. Othon feared and mistrusted de Lusignan, but the archbishop he detested to an appreciable degree. He was grasping and vain, but more than that, he was a learned man, trained in theology and law in Bologna by no less of a personage than Pope Alexander, and that made him very dangerous.

Othon slipped from his seat in the window and strolled casually up to the archbishop. Heraclius regarded him with a beatific smile. "It matters," he said, "because we're supposed to be the guardians of the bloodline. If Montferrat was poisoned, then someone came very close to killing the king as well. It's only by a miracle that Baldwin survived his illness."

"A miracle... or an unfortunate recovery," Philip said as he dropped heavily into a chair. "I've seen the effects of my cousin's disease. If God was indeed merciful, then he would have let Baldwin die."

Othon turned towards Philip, eyeing him narrowly. He laughed coldly. "And then what, my lord of Flanders? Who would you propose to take the throne—you? You wouldn't even take the Regency when you could have, nor would you commit to the campaign against Egypt."

"Enough," Amalric de Lusignan commanded. At the sound of his voice, a tremor rumbled through the room like a moan; the candles guttered, calling down a darkness that settled briefly and lifted. "Philippe's purpose in coming to Jherusalem was never to lead the king's war against Salehdin." He glanced furtively at the archbishop of Caesarea. "His purpose was to bring a new sacred king to Jherusalem."

"I assume, then," Othon spat sarcastically to Philip, "that your friend, the Advocate of Béthune, won't be too pleased since he seems to think you're trying to broker a marriage for his two sons to the king's sisters."

"That was meant only as a ruse to keep the king frustrated and unaware of our true motives," said Philip. "Béthune will have to learn to live with disappointment."

"I see. So where is this... sacred king, now?"

"Acquainting himself with the kingdom and its people," remarked Lusignan.

Othon looked around the room, taking in the faces gathered. There were conspiracies within conspiracies here. Decisions made without his knowledge. "I thought we agreed that we would wait on crowning a new a sacred king," he said, weighing his words carefully. "Baldwin is the rightful king and heir of the *sangreal*."

"The House of Anjou is not the only claimant to the bloodline," Heraclius said, sipping his glass of wine. He set the glass down on a sideboard. "There are others with an equal, if not better, claim to the throne."

"You plan to remove Baldwin from the throne, then?"

"As long as Baldwin can keep the growing factions of the kingdom in check, he will remain so."

Othon leveled his gaze towards the archbishop. "That sounds, Your Grace, like a fancy way of saying that Baldwin will be spared only as long as he remains useful to us."

The Master of Sion raised a conciliatory hand. "I know you have reservations, Othon, about crowning a king while another still lives, but Baldwin is a leper and incapable of performing the sacred duties of a king. Montferrat is dead. We have the opportunity to accelerate our plans if the princess can be persuaded to marry the man we crown."

"Nevertheless," Othon said, "your ceremonial king will have no power or authority to act on behalf of the kingdom. A secure Egypt would better serve our plans just now. Leper or not, Baldwin has a real chance to defeat Salehdin."

"I agree," Lusignan said. He walked over to the sideboard near to Heraclius and poured two glasses of wine. He turned back to him. "But a campaign into Egypte would be suicide."

"Why?"

Amalric answered him far more plainly than he expected. "Egypte is warded by magic far older than the Flood. No army can conquer it, except by treachery or by the betrayal of its people. This war cannot proceed, nor will it. Too many have tried before and failed."

"So *you* have decided," Othon said. "But then, it seems a great many things have been decided without my knowledge. Fortunately, it is the king who will make the decision, not Sion."

The room suddenly grew darker; the light fled as if before a storm. The shadows seemed to take living form. "You would defy us?"

Othon's hand strayed to the hilt of his sword. The light seemed to return, pushing back the shadows again. "The Rule of the Templars commands that we defend this land from the Sarrazins, not to run from battle."

"No, my friend," said Amalric de Lusignan, his voice deceptively calm; his dark eyes glittered like shards of black glass. He closed the distance between them with a few casual steps. "Your Order was created to serve as the military arm of Sion. Either you will obey my orders, or another will be found who can. Do you understand?"

Of that, Othon had no doubt. His hands clenched. He glared at the Master, almost willing him to abuse his magic. He doubted that he would, though, in front of the count and the archbishop.

"I will obey, *Master*," he said through clenched teeth.

Lusignan drew back and smiled before pulling the hood of his black cloak up over his head. "Come, my friends. I think we've given the Master of the Templars enough to think about for one evening."

When his guests had gone, Othon stood, staring for a long while at the back of the heavy oaken door. His anger seethed. Whipping his sword from its scabbard, he spun around, slashing the air with a growl. He stared at the blade for a moment and flung the sword onto the desk. It clattered noisily and fell to the floor with a crash. He set his hands on the edge of the desk and leaned heavily against it. A deep sigh of regret escaped him in a moan. He tried to pray, to find some solace in the simplest act of devotion, but he felt nothing, only remorse. His hatred and anger had burned away all his delusions.

He was wrong to trust Lusignan; he saw that now. For so long he had thought that the ideals of Sion were noble, a necessity to right the supposed wrongs of a faith gone astray. Instead, it had become only a bitter disappointment. There was some evil design at work beyond the normal subterfuge of the Order, something cold and calculating that he felt each time that he was in the presence of the Master. Amalric de Lusignan had other thoughts in mind—other motives. None of them revolved around restoring a lost bloodline to its rightful place or the restoration of a purer form of Christianity.

He dared not resign for fear of whom the Order of Sion would choose as his successor or what they might still try to accomplish through the Templars. No, he would have to continue, paying lip service to the very Order he now despised, all the while seeking a way to destroy it, and, if need be, the Templars themselves.

His hand went to his collar and drew out the small oval pendant of polished silver hidden within. Snapping the delicate chain with a jerk, he held it away from his face, letting it dangle from his hand. It spun freely, catching the meager light of the candles playing on the intricately etched symbols and writing on its face and rear. Watching it spin, this way, then that, he considered carefully what he would do—what he must do.

In the end, it was a simple thing really, turning from soldier to betrayer. He needed only to remember his vows. *I will suffer all that is pleasing to God.*

Setting the pendant on the desk in a neat, deliberate pile, he took out pen and parchment, and sat down to write out a short message. He could not reveal to the king his own part in Sion's treachery, but he could give him a warning, even if anonymously.

* * * * *

The walls of air and magic had not fallen as Mary thought; rather, they yielded to the bounds of Faërie that spread out before her with each step. She passed through as though the walls had never been. Flowers sprang up at her feet; the fragrance of honeysuckle clung to her as she stepped from forest to fortress.

Walls of stone rose before her eyes in the deep shadows, a crumbled arch, and stairs descending into darkness. Mary crept down the fractured steps into a vaulted corridor. She paused, looking about, and ran silently into the dark depths of the castle.

Masyaf was a vast fortress, she discovered, and old. The very air reeked of death and decay, of dust accumulated through many long years of neglect. The stones whispered of fear for their master. No living thing seemed to be about this night, only the darkness that deepened with every turn. In the midst of the maze of corridors and walls and stairs, she found a garden bathed in the glow of silvery moonlight. A tower rose above it, looming against the starry sky.

Guards stood at intervals about the courtyard swathed in voluminous folds of shadow and white cloth bound with a red sash: the *fidaïs*, the dreaded servants of Rashid ad-Din Sinan. True to their name, they bore only the famed daggers of their Order for arms. Even in his own castle warded by magic stronger than steel, the Master of the Assassins took no chances.

She whispered a song into the air, weaving an enchantment that spoke of dreams and the soft embrace of sleep. Slipping from shadow to shadow along the edge of the garden, she lightly touched each Assassin on the shoulder. They went limp in her arms and she gently laid them on the ground, bound by a spell that held them more firmly than the drug-induced fog of their accustomed hashish. Voices guided her towards the center of the garden. She edged closer, concealing herself in a mantle of woven air and magic.

She found the Master of Masyaf sitting in a tent beneath an ancient almond tree. A small bird of fabulous beauty sat perched on his shoulder. It shimmered, glowing with a greenish, magical light. It whispered briefly in Sinan's ear. He smiled and held up a handful of seed.

Sinan was not what she had expected: handsome and dark, with black, wide-set eyes, a man of middling height. Like his fidaïs, he wore the simple white robe of his Order.

Another man knelt on the ground at his feet, a Christian by his look and his arguments: the master and his student. They spoke at length for a time, debating the Resurrection and the end of days. It was a curious discussion—not one that dwelled on the differences of their beliefs, but one that found common ground in the many similarities of their separate faiths. All the while, Mary watched the little green bird that glowed with such eerie luminescence.

Only when the younger man stood to leave did she notice the blood-red cross of the Templars emblazoned on the front of his white habit. A curiosity, certainly, though not surprising, given the constantly shifting alliances between the House of Islam and the servants of Christ. Nor was it surprising given the enmity between Sinan and Salehdin. Baldwin's father, Amaury, had pursued an alliance once, only to see it destroyed by the avarice of the Templars. The politics of Jherusalem was an ever-changing thing.

Making his obeisance to the Assassin leader, the knight disappeared into the night. The bird chattered, nibbling at Sinan's ear. The master stoked his long grey-black beard.

"You needn't hide in the shadows, my dear. My guest has gone," he said, turning in her direction, peering into the darkness. His voice was melodious and tranquil: powerful. She felt a sudden constriction of the air about her, a compulsion of thought that sought to bind her to its will. It moved her to respond to his words without question.

Mary let the veils of shadow fall away from her and warily stepped into the scant torchlight, drawing closer to Sinan. "You keep rather strange company, my lord *Sheikh al-Jebel.*"

His dark eyes twinkled, amused at her use of his native tongue. "The Templar?" he said, chuckling, eager to amuse her curiosity. "We are old friends, he and I. He often comes in times of peace that we may debate the deeper things of our faiths."

"Still, he is a Christian and an enemy at a time of war."

"I welcome all those who seek me, regardless of their faith."

Mary circled around in front of the revered master and drew back the hood of her cloak. "Even those who come by stealth in the midst of the night?"

Words leapt to the fore of his thoughts as if they were pictures for all to see: *ifritah* and *houris*, the virgins of Heaven. Beautiful. She plucked the words from his thoughts and threw them at him. It seemed that even the famed master of Assassins was not beyond the slightest thought of lust for a woman.

"What did you expect?" she laughed. "Sharp fangs and horns protruding from my brow?"

"Something of the like," he said in a voice that mocked his feigned insouciance. His words were more guarded now, the impressions of his thoughts unreadable. Fear reminded him of what stood before him.

The luminous green bird danced upon Sinan's shoulder, chattering quietly at his ear. Sinan gave her a long, reflective look. "Who are you, my lady of the *ifrit*—a thief, or some dream of my waking eyes?"

"I am one who would speak with you."

"Tell me your name, then, that we may speak with each other as civilized people."

"Forgive me if I refuse," she said, bowing her head in reverence. She glanced at him from beneath her lowered brows. "Names have power, especially against those of my kind; more to the point, for those who have the means to command me against my will."

Sinan smiled unexpectedly. "So, we come to the point of it already. You want the Seal of Solomon."

She smiled ever so slightly. "I see the *Sheikh al-Jebel* is indeed as wise as he is powerful."

Sinan ignored her. The bird chattered. "Why should I simply give the seal to you? What need would an *ifritah* have with a talisman of such peculiar power?"

"So that I may destroy an enemy older than both our religions; an enemy that would see Islam and Christianity destroyed—or worse yet, used as pawns in a battle not quite of this world."

He studied her for several long moments, weighing her words in his mind. "And if I refuse—what then? Will you take the seal by force?" He leaned back on a small worn bolster and spread his hands wide in surrender. "I am unarmed, unprotected. No one will stop you."

It was a lie, of course, or rather a kernel of truth wrapped in layers of lies and deceit; something he meant to keep back in secret. For a moment, she was almost able to tease the elusive strand from the ordered chaos of his thoughts, but then it faded, retreating into the dark morass of intelligence he kept hidden. She could still sense it, hovering just behind the outer edges of his mind. His subtle game of deception, though, revealed more than it hid.

"I doubt you would be so confident of your safety if you truly possessed the seal," she said caustically. "Where is it, Sinan?"

He smiled deceptively. "In the hand of one who has the most need of it."

Without warning, Mary flung the full force of her power against Sinan's mind, hoping to pluck an unguarded thought. Power surged around him, shielding his body in a wall of magical fire. Within the protective shell, Sinan's whispering green companion transformed with a hideous shriek into a writhing mass of fangs and shadow and glowing red eyes. Spreading leathery black wings, the daemon hissed and spat venomous blasphemies against the Most High. All the while, a smile of smug satisfaction spread across Sinan's face.

Mary's power recoiled at the unexpected reaction to her touch; the magic fell away. The bird returned to its luminous green self. A thin tendril of her power, though, clung weakly to a single word that had strayed from Sinan's firm control. Gently she pulled at the slender strand of Sinan's thought. It unraveled from the tightly wound knot of deception. He was unaware of her intrusion, but the thought held firm, refusing to betray its master. The one word was enough: *Syun—Sion.*

At once, she understood her error. Whether by accident or by design, she had been deceived. The seal was not here, but the working of its power bound every creature within the walls of Masyaf to its will.

"I am bound to the seal," Sinan said as though he had read her mind, "As are the very walls of this fortress. The one who commands the seal, commands me."

"Then you are a fool, my lord Rashid ad-Din," she hissed, "if you think the Order of Sion will protect the religious freedom of your people as they promised for your alliance and friendship. It is an old promise they have broken many times. The same promise they made to the early Christians, until they twisted its truths beyond recognition. The same promise they made to your prophet when he was little more than a desert bandit proclaiming his visions to the tribes of Araby."

"That is blasphemy."

"No, it is truth," she said, stepping closer. "But Mohammed spurned their false promises to bring your people back to the worship of a single god. More so, he might have done so had he not listened to those who counseled him to bloodshed and war, all in the name of Allah. Now Sion would make the same promise to the followers of Islam again. Would you see all that Mohammed taught destroyed? If this enemy succeeds, it will not tolerate any religion other than its own."

Sinan held up the bird on a finger, admiring it fondly. He glanced at her, a gleam of penultimate triumph dancing in his eyes. "Perhaps, my lady of the *ifrit*, your words might once have had some meaning, but my master, Hasan, has given me a vision. The time has come to make peace with all men under the banner of one faith. Ever since Hasan proclaimed the Resurrection I have awaited the return of the Lost Imam, the Mahdi."

Mary tilted her chin imperiously. She chuckled briefly and cruelly. "The Mahdi is a myth; a dream."

"No, my lady," said Sinan. "The Chosen One will restore justice and the true faith of God. He will bring Jews, Christians, and Muslims together as one. Not divide them."

His words amazed her. It was hard, listening to this man, to remember that he was the dreaded mystic who commanded the Assassins of Masyaf.

"The one you seek is the servant of Iblis," she said.

Anger burned suddenly in the eyes of the Master of Assassins. He stood abruptly, closing the distance between them. He stood close enough to smell his thinly veiled fear; his jaw clenched noticeably. The daemon bird flew from his hand to the highest branches of the almond tree. "You have overstayed your welcome, lady. Leave me."

He stood shorter by half a head. She stared down at him and smiled. Stepping back, she wrapped the shadows of night about her like a cloak and called forth the boundaries of Eden to take her from the death-tainted walls of Masyaf. The air filled with the sudden-sweet scents of honey-suckle and a dew-drenched forest. The sun slanted through the rising mists of dawn. Sinan was certainly no stranger to magic, but even this was beyond his experience. Still, he bore it well.

"Tell your new master I look forward to meeting him once more," she said and faded from the mortal world.

† CHAPTER NINE

Am I then become your enemy, because I tell you the truth?
—*Galatians 4:16*

The breeze blew gently through the delicate white columns of the Dome of the Winds; it brought with it a hint of sea and salt that swirled about the hill of al-Armah and down, down into the streets and souks of the old city of al-Qihara. A thin pall of dust hung in the air, mingling with the sunlight that slowly softened with the changing season, obscuring all but the tops of the tallest minarets and date palms.

Al-Armah was a holy place, sanctified by the scattered and forgotten graves of Jews and Nasrani that once graced the ancient hill. Amid so much sanctity, the builder of Qubbat al-Hawa had thought the inclusion of a small house of quiet rest and the simpler pleasures of life, however magnificent, was only fitting, a haven of solitude that transcended the affairs of a turbulent world. Perhaps, even, heaven on earth.

Salah ad-Din Yusuf had no use for such pleasure pavilions or the decadence of a long dead Abbasid governor three hundred years in his grave. The private retreat Hatim ibn Harthama had built on the sprawling spur of limestone overlooking the eastern city was only one example of the excesses that had made al-Qihara a treasure whose depths he had yet to plumb. Such waste and extravagance had made the city vulnerable; and so it would again, even with the supposed magical wards that protected it. Salah ad-Din was wise enough not to put too much trust in the invisible things of the world, save Allah alone. Only a fortress guarded by impregnable walls of stone would ever keep an enemy from ravaging the city again.

Yusuf stood on the pavilioned hill of al-Armah, looking out over the work that had progressed thus far. His oldest son, al-Afdal, stood beside him. Large hazel-brown eyes looked up at him from beneath long black lashes, blinking in quiet admiration. Only the fondness of a seven-year-old son for his father could look at a man in such a way. Yusuf squeezed his shoulder.

The din of construction rose above the noise of the city's daily activity. Of the fortress' proposed eleven towers, one was near completion. Its solid, imposing bulk stood starkly against the airy architecture of the Dome of the Winds. Baha ad-Din, Yusuf's thin, camel-faced palace controller pointed his finger at the surveyor's map on the table while he directed Yusuf's gaze towards the work that would connect the Citadel with the older mud-brick walls of the old Fatimid palace-city of al-Qihara. Both men, veterans of the intricacies of war, stood over the plans quietly discussing the slow progress of construction.

"When the work is complete, my lord, the walls will encompass a city ten times its present size and an impregnable fortress," said Baha ad-Din.

Yusuf nodded appreciably. "Impressive."

A sudden commotion at the door—the brief exchange of murmured words and the bow of a white-turbaned head behind a wall of Mamluk swords—interrupted their deliberations. Yusuf recognized the white-turbaned visitor: Abu Musa—Maimonides, in the tongue of the Jews—his trusted doctor and the rabbi of the Jewish community in al-Qihara. The Mamluk guard knew well their duty to their master. An enemy could force a friend, however dear and trusted, to do its will. The Old Man of the Mountain had taught him that lesson too well. The guards escorted the physician towards the cluttered table and made their obeisance at his dismissive nod.

"My good doctor, come, tell me what you think of my new fortress," Yusuf said.

"It is not my place to comment on the actions of my lord," said the Jew.

"It is when your lord asks it of you," Yusuf growled.

Abu Musa frowned. He fingered the heavily jeweled pendant at his breast. "I would rather know why you are not still abed with the ague that has afflicted you the better part of the last week, as I ordered."

Yusuf snorted. "The ague has passed thanks be to Allah. You worry too much, my friend."

"Is that not why you pay me, Your Excellency—to worry about your health when you will not?"

The Jew's servile tone put a hard edge to Yusuf's smile. "I can pay for your council as well, if our friendship is not enough to loosen your tongue. Now answer me."

Maimonides bowed reverently. "As you will. You would have made an admirable Egyptian," he said. "Not since my ancestors were forced to build the great cities of the Pharaohs has this land seen such wonder and such strength."

The Jew's words were careful and measured: a proper response. His words were also a subtle reminder that they were both strangers in a strange land. It was also a rebuke: a rebuke for using Ifranj slave labor to build his fortress.

"But—" Yusuf said.

Abu Musa turned away, glancing out over the city and the great work going on around it. "But, you weaken yourself with your constant preparations for war. You need rest. Hunt; play at polo; spend some time with your beautiful wife—anything. Only leave the troubles of building your Citadel to your commanders."

Yusuf laughed. He shook his head. "So, you do not approve. You Jews have a peculiar skill for speaking your mind without ever saying what you truly mean."

"I would rather see you pursue peace. Instead, you build a house of war. Is that plain enough for you?"

"Sometimes peace can only be found through war."

Abu Musa glanced at him narrowly. "Not for those who set themselves squarely in the will of God."

Yusuf snorted. "*Jihad* is the will of God.

"I suppose that depends on your definition of God."

He glanced at the doctor, frowning. "Your family traveled from Cordoba to Urshalim, and now al-Qihara, to find peace. Would you not see them protected at last by strong walls and a people who accept them? Or, would you see the Ifranj take this city and slaughter your people as they once did when Urshalim fell."

"Persecution is the allotted portion of my people. It is… *kismet*. And that will not be changed by any war of your making or anyone else's."

"And yet, you fled persecution in Spain."

Maimonides smiled slyly, ignoring his remark. "My only concern, just now, is for my patient. You worry yourself too much with thoughts of the Ifranj."

"The Ifranj are hardly my only concern," Yusuf spat. He set his hands protectively on al-Afdal's thin shoulders and held him close. "I have lived long enough in this land to know that war is as certain as the rising of the Nile each summer. I have as many enemies within this city as I do without. Six years and three rebellions have taught me the meaning of precaution. I will not see al-Qihara fall prey to petty thieves and vindictive Shi'a clerics bent on restoring the Fatimids to power."

The rabbi raised an eyebrow. "Does this mean you plan to stay on in Egypt, then?"

"I mean to see that all I have accomplished will last beyond my meager span of years."

"Even at the expense of your health?"

"If Allah wills it."

Abu Musa moved slowly, drawing himself closer within Yusuf's hard gaze. "And what, my lord Salah ad-Din, if Allah wills that you should forsake your *jihad*?"

"*Jihad* is not a choice, my friend," Yusuf said softly and coolly. "It is the duty of every Muslim as commanded in holy Qur'an to make war on the infidel."

"But only in defense of Islam."

"And who do you think made war upon my people and took Urshalim in the name God? It was the Nasrani."

"Just as Islam took it from them in times past."

Yusuf snorted. "They defile the holy place with their mummeries of faith."

"A holy place that belonged to my people long before it was any of yours or the Nasrani."

Yusuf glanced at him narrowly. He swallowed his pride and his folly. He laughed softly. "Your words are like a fine steel blade; they cut sharply and rather deeply. I wonder sometimes if Allah has sent you to torment me with your incessant arguments, or if it is Iblis who does so."

The rabbi from Cordoba bowed. "I assure you, my friend, I am no servant of Shaitan. I simply offer you the wisdom of my few short years."

A sudden, uneasy silence fell between them, and in its midst, a guard drew near and bowed deeply. "My lord, a rider approaches from the north with much haste."

Al-Afdal broke loose from Yusuf's embrace and ran to the edge of the hill, pointing excitedly. "Father, look, look."

It was indeed a rider. A cloud of dust rose above the road with a beautiful white beast of a stallion riding before the billowing tempest. Sunlight shone brilliantly off his golden mail like fire amidst the desert sands. Yusuf recognized his nephew even at a distance. No man ever sat a horse like Taqi ad-Din, his brother's son.

Man and horse galloped along the unfinished walls, the native workers rising and shouting their curses as they thundered past. Taqi ad-Din bent to his horse's ear; the horse dropped its small head and leapt over a shallow ditch. Rounding a broken outcrop of stone, they disappeared behind the rise of the hill. A few moments later, the young emir strode hurriedly across the pavilioned hill, brushing the dust from his robes, and went down on one knee. He touched his head to the ground and extended a small scrap of parchment in his hand. "A message has arrived from the border, uncle. It comes all the way from Urshalim."

Yusuf snatched up the tiny scroll and paused, unsure what message it might contain. Glancing at Taqi ad-Din, he tore it open and scanned its contents. His heart raced. It was not what he had expected—actually, it was, only not so soon, surely. War with the Ifranj was inevitable, but this—this was a gift from Heaven. *So long as you act alone and make no alliances against them... Urshalim will fall.* So had the beautiful *ifritah* that visited him all those months ago had said. He smiled wolfishly and handed the scroll back to Taqi ad-Din.

"Have your commanders gather the army north of the city at once. Have them ready to march within the week." His nephew made his obeisance and turned on his heel, waving over a Mamluk to give his command. Yusuf called him back with a word. "Inform my brother as well to hold back a force large enough to keep the peace in al-Qihara."

"As you wish, uncle," Taqi ad-Din said and was gone.

Yusuf turned slowly to the rabbi, taking his time to measure his words carefully. "You speak of the will of God, my friend, as if it is a changeable thing," he said, smiling. "I tell you it is not."

Abu Musa glanced at him uncertainly. "What message have you received, my lord, that it has emboldened your opinion so firmly?"

"A gift from Allah," he said. "The Ifranj in their zeal to pacify a visiting lord from the West have extended their hand too far. They have all but emptied Urshalim of its knights and marched north to harass Suriya rather than Egypt. The leper king has no one to defend his city, but a handful of soldiers. Tell me now that Allah has not ordained that the infidels should finally be driven from these shores."

Maimonides boldly set a hand to Yusuf's shoulder. It was the action of a friend, not an enemy. "If this is the will of Allah as you say, then be careful, my lord Salah ad-Din, that you do not act with over confidence. Your own holy book commands that you should fight against those who persecute you, but to commit no aggression."

Yusuf clasped his friend's arm and squeezed it fondly. "It was not I who started this war with the Nasrani, but neither will I take my rest until I see it finished once and for all."

* * * * *

Darkness lay heavily upon the city. The clamor of church bells rang with alarm. Fear swept through the city like an unseen presence that threatened to destroy them all. In the palace courtyard, several hundred knights of Jherusalem were mustering in response to the king's anxious summons. A pitiful few to stand against the massed thousands of Salehdin's advancing might.

Baldwin shared in the fears of his people. Not since Godfrei de Bouillon had breached the north wall and taken the city in the name of the blessed Savior, had Jherusalem seen an attack by an enemy. Years of neglect, though, and the foolish pride of kings, had left the walls in a sad state of disrepair. They were crumbling, victims of sun and cold, and the slow assault of time. They would never withstand a protracted bombardment by the Muslim siege engines. Only the Tower of David offered any real hope of defense against the Sarrazin hordes. Even that, however, would take a small miracle. He needed to stop Salehdin before he ever reached the city.

Pacing the battlements of the Tower, he prayed for the wisdom to know how he might defend his kingdom against so great an enemy as the Sultan of Egypt. The words, however, would not come. The only prayer he could remember was the Shepherd's Psalm. *The Lord ruleth me: and I shall want nothing...*

The slightest whisper of sound made him turn with a startle. His sword rasped smoothly from its scabbard to fall level at the breast of the Magdalen. A sudden wave of dizziness caused him to sway. He stretched out his hand to steady himself against the parapet. Fear and disease were beginning to take their toll on his mind and body, but he refused to let either have their way. The sword wavered ever so slightly in his heavily bandaged hand.

Mary brushed aside the sword with the back of her hand. "You must make peace with Salah ad-Din."

"Peace? For five months, you leave me without word. Now you return on the eve of war and tell me to make peace with an enemy only four days away from threatening the gates of this city."

"You need not have any fear of the sultan. His time has not yet come."

"No fear?" He slammed his sword back into its scabbard. "Where have you been?" he blurted. His words were more than a question; they were an accusation. "Do you know how often I've called upon you these last few months and you never came?"

Magdalen's eyes blazed with green fire. "Forgive me, Your Highness, if I cannot come whenever you beckon," she replied; a subtle harshness edged her voice.

"It has been five months!"

"I know," she said suddenly, more softly, more apologetically. "But the sun I walk beneath keeps time in its own fashion. It is not bound to the same laws of the mortal world."

"But you... you promised you would help me whenever I needed you."

"And so I have," she said. "Although you may not think so when you hear what I have come to tell you."

Baldwin stared at her, silent and unyielding. His hostile gaze forced her to continue, if only reluctantly. She pressed hands together as though in prayer and touched them to her lips. Her gaze faltered. "I am sorry, Baldwin, but in my pride I thought I could protect you. Instead, I've put you in even greater danger."

"What have you done, my lady?"

"When you were ill and I prayed over you to relieve your fever, I caught a glimpse of the enemy's thoughts and what he intends to do. He is looking for an ancient talisman called the Seal of Solomon that has the power to bind the spirits of the air to one's command. I thought that if I could find it first, perhaps I could thwart Sion's plans."

Baldwin shrugged, trying to lift the great weight of his armor from his shoulders, however briefly. It settled all the more heavily again upon him. "You failed," he said softly, evenly, knowing the answer even before it came.

"I was too late," she said. "And now the enemy knows that I am aware of his plans. He has allied himself with the Master of the Assassins. He will only grow stronger now. The enemy has only to call upon the spirits of the air with a word and you and your kingdom will be at his mercy."

"So you have continually warned me," he said, turning away, "and yet, Salehdin has proven himself the greater concern to me."

Magdalen drew closer, almost touching him. For a moment, he could feel the aura of her power. "Do not underestimate the Order of Sion, Your Highness, or their purposes as your father did."

"My father?" Baldwin turned slowly back to her, the meaning of her words dawning in his mind. "What did he have to do with Sion?"

"He brought them to within a hair's breadth of the throne and then he defied them. He paid for that betrayal with his life."

Baldwin suddenly felt as though he was walking the sword's edge between two unknown fates, both of which were determined to destroy him. He did not know whom or what he could trust any more—not even the sainted woman before him who had promised him her help.

"What do you want of me?" he said, throwing up his hands in exasperation.

Magdalen stepped towards him; she cupped his face in her hands. The November night air felt suddenly very cold. It cut through the heavy mail and padded under-tunic of his armor. Mary's touch on his face, however, felt warm and comforting; it touched the depths of his tortured soul. "I am your friend, Baldwin," she said. "I want you to trust me as you once did."

Baldwin looked at her anew, suspicion growing as his heart pulsed with each pounding beat. She was still as beautiful as ever, clad all in white and gold, but the shadows and darkness lent a particularly unsettling cast to her face that was anything but alluring. He shivered and stepped back. He wanted so desperately to believe her, to put his faith blindly in all she said. It only made his next words all the harder to say.

"Trust you, my lady? How can you speak to me of trust?" he cried. "You continually warn me about the Order of Sion, and yet, you withhold the truth from me. How do I know *you* are not the enemy I should fear—some witch trying to use me for your own purposes?"

"Why do you suddenly fear and mistrust me so much after all this time? What truth have I kept from you?"

Baldwin clenched his bandaged hand into a fist, almost squeezing the small silver medallion in his palm out of shape. It had come to him quite unexpectedly not three days ago, yet already, the peculiar design of its image lay deeply burned into his memory. On the one side it was stamped with a large, scrolling letter M—the astronomical symbol of Virgo, the heavenly Virgin—interwoven with smaller letters to form the word, *Ormus*; on the obverse side, it bore the severed head of a bearded man and inscribed with the name, *John*. He knew it at once. Knowledge called to knowledge: magic to magic, power to power. It haunted his every thought, his every waking moment. He had only to touch the medallion with a finger for a moment and the shadowy images of faces familiar, yet somehow, unfamiliar, of soldiers, horses, and blood-red crosses, flashed within his mind.

"If you would have me trust you once more, then perhaps you might tell me the meaning of this," he said and held out his hand, letting the silver medallion fall from his fingers, dangling on a frail, thin chain.

* * * * *

Mary glanced at the young king and reached hesitantly towards the gently swaying medallion in his hand. Her outstretched finger grazed the smooth edge, knowing well what he held. At her touch, images flashed before her eyes, vague and insubstantial. A shadowy face lifted among the many, its eyes focusing clear and bright upon her in recognition.

The taint of the enemy's presence was strong upon him: dark, malevolent, and painfully familiar, though the face was not his own. Her heart leapt to feel that power once more. It had been so long. Pain knifed through her heart. Almost she yielded, letting the magic draw her to its hidden source. With an agonized mental scream, her hand recoiled.

"I, too, can sense the spirit of the knight that once held this dear," Baldwin said, and snatched the medallion back into his bandaged hand again. "When were you going to tell me, my lady, the enemy you seek is in league with the Templars?"

She ignored him, but eventually he would press her for answer. It had been a mistake not to tell him, but other matters were of greater concern now. Her eyes cleared and she gazed up at him. "This is blood-silver. Where did you get it?"

"It was put into the hand of a brother in the palace chapel not three days ago with a simple written message: *Beware all those who call themselves friend—Trust no one.*"

Mary stepped closer, eager. "Did he say by whom?"

"He says he has no memory of when or how or who gave it to him. Only that he was instructed to give it to me."

Mary shook her head. "No doubt his memory has been wiped clean with magic." She glanced towards the courtyard below, crowding with soldiers and horses preparing to ride to battle. "Where are the Templars now?"

"Almost all of them rode north with Philip and the Count of Tripoli three weeks ago," Baldwin said, waving his hand towards the Japhe Gate. "The remaining eighty left only yesterday for Gaza with Saint-Amant to protect the roads to Jherusalem. What does it matter," he asked, all thought of his former anger and mistrust replaced by his new, single concern. "What is blood-silver?"

"It is magic, Your Highness, of the darkest kind," she said, her mind racing excitedly with questions too many to answer at once. In the midst of her sudden excitement, a sense of hope blossomed, a chance to undo a great evil. "It binds the life of a servant to the will of his master. Whoever sent this to you is one of the Templars that rode to Gaza and a servant of the Order of Sion. This is an unexpected gift. While the connection is still strong, I can find him. We have a chance at last to strike a blow at the enemy and expose him."

Baldwin fell suddenly very quiet and turned away. He set his hands on the parapet and leaned heavily against it. She followed him to the wall of the ancient Tower and set a hand to his, feeling the power of the magic that was destroying his body. The gate of his mind, however, stood barred to her. In the past few months, he had somehow learned to shut his mind to the most casual of touches. With the eyes of one born to magic, she could see his power burning within him like a candle flame in the darkness. His focus on his troops below only made it blaze all the brighter. With age, he was growing stronger. So, too, was his illness. She wondered if he even knew.

When Baldwin finally spoke, his voice came so soft she almost did not hear him. "Are you in danger of falling under the enemy's power if he calls upon the seal?"

"So long as he never learns my true name, he can do nothing against me," she lied.

Baldwin turned, his large, dark eyes taking in her gaze. "And what... what if it is a trap laid for you? You said yourself that the enemy knows that you have discovered his plans."

"I must do this, Baldwin. Or at least try. We may never have this chance again."

"But I need you," he said with some difficulty. "I... I can't chance losing you now."

Mary smiled, warming at his words. It was a concession of sorts on his part, an unspoken declaration of his forgiveness and newfound trust. "I have known this enemy, King Baldwin, for years out of count," she said lightly. She squeezed his arm. "He would not make so subtle an attack against me. It is not his way."

Baldwin grasped the hilt of his sword and drew himself up to his full height. He lifted his chin a fraction. The flame of his power flared suddenly white-hot. For a moment, his defenses cracked, letting her sense the war of his competing emotions within him. Despair and fear wrestled with his fierce determination to be a good and proper king. Out of the turmoil, anger, much like a child who does not get his way, emerged. He trusted her once more for no other reason than he must, but his duty to his crown and to his kingdom opposed anything she hoped to accomplish. It reminded her painfully that he was nothing more than a boy forced to play the part of a king.

"Do what you will, but I must defend my people against Salehdin. Anything else... and I will betray them," he said and handed her the medallion. He brushed past her, but paused before taking a step back towards her. He stopped beside her and leaned close. "Whatever you decide, make sure, my lady, that your judgment is not affected solely by your thoughts of revenge against your enemy."

* * * * *

The small chapel of the Virgin in the Tower of David was an ugly affair when compared to the great cathedral of the Church of the Holy Sepulcher. Here, surrounded by rows upon rows of glowing candlestands and a cruciform window set high in the wall with the most beautiful stained glass that blazed with dazzling color in the sun, Baldwin felt more at peace, more at one, with God than in any other place in Jherusalem. Only the stained glass stood blackened now with the dark shadows of night, but the cross still had the power to comfort and to encourage, lifting even the most downtrodden of souls.

He knelt before the cross and the altar with its snow-white cloth and golden cup of the Eucharist, absorbed by the meditations of his heart. He prayed now with purpose and confidence, knowing not whether he spoke the words aloud or in the quiet recesses of his mind. His encounter with the Magdalen had burned away his doubts and fears; it had given him an unwavering determination of what he must do to defend his people.

The sword lay across his upraised hands; it felt light, insubstantial. It was a banner of faith rather than a weapon of war. For him, this was true worship—simple and plain, unencumbered by the emotionless ritual and pageantry of Mother Rome; it was the heart of a penitent sinner laid bare before a sovereign and omnipotent God.

...Defend Your people—not the king, nor the lords and ladies in their high places—but the innocents, the simple and ordinary folk of this land who worship still with pure and upright hearts.

Defend the helpless, the widows and the children, the young and the old, who had no part in the politics of this kingdom that have brought us to war. Grant courage and honor, not for the sake of victory, but that Your name may be glorified among the nations.

But if by Your hand this kingdom must fall, I pray that You ease the suffering of those who will fall by the sword and bring them swiftly into Your presence that they might find peace...

In the midst of his prayer, a single, discordant thought kept nagging at his him, demanding his consideration, until it finally set his mind to wandering.

...The politics of this kingdom that have brought us to war...

There were other forces, besides the Muslims, that conspired against the throne—against him, the anointed of God. It was no secret: his court was slowly dividing. Factions were forming, aligning themselves along familial and ideological lines, and he was powerless to prevent it. Well, almost powerless. With illness keeping the Constable, Old Humphrey of Toron, from his duties, the leadership of the army fell to him. The battle was his to lose or to win, and by that victory, gain immortal fame for its wondrous miracle. Such a victory would give him the power to keep the kingdom firmly in his hand, and the conspirators at bay—even the elusive Order of Sion.

"Did you know that they had a hand in the building of this chapel," she said nearly at his side. "It was a subtle reminder of the Order's power to control the throne. It is protected by the strongest of magic."

He did know, he realized. Perhaps, he always had. It was the magic in his blood: like called to like.

Baldwin brought the sword down and laid it across his thighs. "Have you returned from Gaza so soon?" he said, focusing his eyes on the golden cup glowing with candlelight on the altar.

"I will not forsake you in the hour of your need," she said so softly he barely heard her voice. "There will be time enough to uncover the traitor when the army joins up with the Templars at Ascalone."

Baldwin inclined his head and smiled as well as his disease-ruined mouth would allow. It was a victory of another sort, but it was a start. He looked askance at her. "Would you stay a little while, my lady, and pray with me?"

† CHAPTER TEN

The king is not saved by a great army: nor shall the giant be saved by his own great strength...
—*Psalms 32:16*

The earth shook with the pounding of hooves. It began as a rumbling, soft and low, like thunder echoing through the rolling Judean hills and grew, building into a reverberating wave of shuddering noise that descended into the coastal plain towards Ascalone and war.

It was a wild ride they made in the wan light of that early dawn. Reynald de Châtillon rode knee to knee beside the king at the head of the army. Banners snapped in the cold morning breeze beneath skies dark with lowering grey clouds. Behind them rode Baldwin's uncle with the standard of Jherusalem, and the Bishop of Bethlehem holding aloft the True Cross glittering with rubies and diamonds and gold. The brothers Ibelin and the stepsons of Raymond of Tripoli, Hugh and William of Saint-Omer, followed at their backs with the whole of their small army, two thousand strong. Onward they raced, through hills shadowed with olive orchards and fields lying fallow, waiting for the first of the winter rains.

Reynald glanced sidelong at the king. He was amazed at Baldwin's incredible determination to lead the army despite his consuming illness; lesser men would have consigned themselves to a litter or simply stayed at home and left the fighting to others more capable. God only knew how much pain he was in, his hands and legs and feet so eaten away with disease beneath his armor, and he sitting atop his fiery Arabian courser like a hero from an ancient Greek legend.

He thought of his only son, another Baldwin, who had died more than a year ago in the service of the Emperor at the Battle of Myriocephalum. Even now, the white-hot pain of that loss was too raw to set aside. It focused his anger, his grief, into blinding hatred for all things that touched upon the Muslims and their faith. He glanced at

Baldwin again out of the corner of his eye and wound his fist tighter about the horse's reins. He felt almost a fatherly pride for the young king who was so much like a son. He curled his lip into a smile inside his helmet. Finally, someone understood how precarious a situation the kingdom lay in with the Sarrazins hounding ever at their heels, a king willing to bring war to the enemy at any cost, at any odds. Before they left the field of battle, the sons of Satan would certainly know the courage of a Frankish king.

The army stopped by a small stream in a wooded portion of the valley of Sorek to water their thirsty horses and to let Baldwin change mounts after his horse threw a shoe. It was well past dawn, but the sun stayed hidden behind the thick blanket of clouds.

The air was thick with tension; even the horses were restless and skittish. Despite the knights' accustomed bold bravado, Reynald could sense their underlying fears. It was palpable. They were riding to their fated doom.

This was an ancient land; it had deep memories of war and bloodshed... memories that seemed to linger in the autumn air.

The men kept to themselves, finding different ways to cope with the nervous tension of inevitable battle. Not a few of them cast an uncertain eye to the darkening grey skies and the shadowed woods, and made the sign against evil. Advance scouts were reporting that Salehdin's army numbered well over twenty-five thousand to their meager two. They were advancing rapidly on Ascalone. With no word from the Templars, Reynald wondered how the knights had fared in Gaza: had they fallen or had the Sarrazins shut them up within the city? Either way, it would be a race to Ascalone with the future of the city, and the kingdom itself, hanging in the balance.

At present, Reynald had more concern for the king. Despite his objections to the contrary, the ride had visibly exhausted Baldwin. It had been more than a year since he rode to battle; less than six months ago, a fever had kept him abed in the very city towards which they were riding.

Assisted by his squire, Baldwin slid stiffly from the saddle and nearly fell into Reynald's arms. Reynald grabbed a skin of wine, poured a cup, and handed it to the king. "Drink this, Your Highness," he said, helping Baldwin to sit on the trunk of a fallen tree.

"I am not a child, Reynald."

"No, Your Highness, but you are ill and weak." He sat down beside the king and pulled off his helmet and mail coif. Baldwin did the same. "The situation is quickly turning against us," he said, glancing around at the assembled knights—anything to avoid looking at that disease-eaten face. "We cannot hope to outlast the Sarrazins with so few men. Before we are too far from Jherusalem, issue the *arrière-ban* and call every able-bodied man who can bear arms, to Ascalone."

The king took very little time to consider his plea. Baldwin drained the last of his wine, put on his coif and helmet again. In that one small action, he was the image of a warrior king once more. "Issue the summons," he said, his voice rasping and calm. "But send a summons to the lepers of Saint-Lazare as well. They promised to respond if I ever had need of them. God knows we could use every available sword right now." He chuckled unexpectedly through his helmet. "Although, I think the sight of a few lepers will instill far more fear into the Muslims than their swords."

Reynald laughed with the king and stood, holding out his hand to him. "Well said, Your Majesty. Well said. Now, shall we ride on to meet our Muslim friends?"

The coastal Plain of Sharon offered a faster and less exhaustive ride for the king; but it was certainly not without peril. Less than five leagues from Ascalone, they encountered the enemy. Cresting the rise of a low hill, the semi-circular walls of Ascalone lay huddled in the distance near unto white beaches washed by the waves of the grey-green sea. Beyond the city, a pall of dust stirred up by the march of an approaching army rose to mingle with the grey of clouds driven by winds off the sea towards the mountainous spine of the Judean highlands.

Only a chance break in the clouds, at the very moment that they were racing towards the city, let a stray beam of sunlight through to glint off the helmet of a Sarrazin rider. It was too late for the man to slip away unnoticed. If Reynald had been a religious man, he might have thought it was divine providence.

A second rider, and then a third, joined the scout from the cover of the orchard spreading out from the city towards the hills. In one swift movement, they drew arrows and fitted them to their small, wickedly curved bows.

Baldwin made a gesture. Reynald kicked his heel into his horse's sweaty flanks with a curse and sent the horse flying after the Muslim scout. Hugh de Saint-Omer raced after him in close support.

The first volley hit wildly off its target; the second nearly found its mark. Reynald had to deflect an arrow with his shield and bat another away with the flat of his sword. A third volley penetrated his defenses and bit into the thick muscle of his upper thigh. Hugh spun his horse protectively in front of him and took an arrow in the saddle horn.

Pain exploded like fire in Reynald's leg. He broke off the shaft of the arrow with a grunt and angrily wheeled his horse, waving Hugh back towards the column of the army. "Get the king out of here, now.

Ride for the city," he screamed, and spun his horse around again, keeping himself between the Frankish knights and the enemy scouts.

Kicking his mount into a run, he lay low over the animal's neck and angled his retreat to intercept the king at the foot of the hill. Arrows whistled over his head. The Muslim scouts gave chase, but broke off as he neared the protection of the army. It was a show of intimidation, nothing more.

Rejoining the column, they entered Ascalone in a whirlwind of steel and dust and sweaty horseflesh. The gate closed behind them with a shuddering thud, shutting them within the city. They had barely beaten the sultan to the city, but now he had them trapped within their own walls.

* * * * *

"The Ifranj are safely within the city, my lord," reported Ahmad ad-Din.

Yusuf glanced away from his nephew's younger son towards the city the Muslims called, the *Virgin of the Desert*, because it alone had stood inviolate against the infidels' advances when all others had fallen after the first War of the Cross.

Companies of mounted soldiers rode up behind him to the clamor of skirling pipes and beating drums, filling the plain with the vastness of their number. He had given them freedom to range afield throughout the region, burning and pillaging as they willed among the local peasantry. He seldom gave such an order; but this was to be a new beginning, a purging of the land to rid it of the foul taint of the Nasrani. *Jihad* demanded nothing less.

"Do you think they suspect our deception?" he asked, folding his hands neatly about the pommel of his saddle.

Ahmad smiled. "We harried them only enough to make them think we came upon them by chance. Before long they'll realize their mistake."

Yusuf reached up, smoothing the corners of his beard with a hand. "How many men do you estimate the Leper King commands?"

"No more than two thousand horses, uncle."

"Two thousand," he mused. "You have done well, Ahmad. See that your father finds me when you find him," he said, dismissing the scout. "We'll camp here for the night," he ordered his emirs. He cast an uncertain glance towards the lowering grey skies. He did not like this sudden change in weather. It meant too many uncertainties if it turned to rain. "Set a guard out of bowshot around the city every fifty paces," he said over his shoulder. "Make sure no one enters or leaves this city."

Isa al-Hakkari, one of his senior commanders, rode up alongside him and bowed his head. He spoke softly. "What are we to do now with the Ifranj, Your Excellency?"

Yusuf drew rein, turning his horse in a tight circle to face the aged emir. "I'll give them until sunset to think over their present situation; perhaps by then they will be more willing to consider surrender."

* * * * *

The banners of the army of Jherusalem snapped briskly in the wind above the gate of Ascalone. Reynald escorted the king to the wall to view the massing forces of the Muslims. The lords of the kingdom—the few that were actually on campaign with them—had already gathered atop the battlements to discuss their predicament. Balian of Ibelin stepped forward and handed the king a written estimation of the sultan's troop movements. It was not an encouraging report. As Baldwin debated tactics and stratagems with his lords, Reynald stepped aside to assess for himself the situation forming below the walls.

The plain swarmed with soldiers like ants about a hill. Column after column of men filled the plain: archers, lancers, and swift, light cavalry. In the midst of the sea of horses and steel, Salehdin's personal guard of yellow-clad Mamluks, a thousand strong, gathered around a single, palatial tent of white and gold.

Reynald had endured sieges before. He hated the waiting. It was worse than prison. He felt more comfortable with a sword in his hand and the pounding of hooves beneath him. He was a knight, a soldier of Christ. He wanted battle: the clash of steel and the warm spray of blood on his face. A siege was nothing more than a prolonged death. Watching the Sarrazin companies assemble before the gates, he saw an army meant for the swiftness of battle. It was not an occupying force.

"Ascalone is not the prize Salehdin seeks, Your Highness," he said, turning towards the king. "This is not a siege, my lords. Salehdin certainly means to keep us here, but he plans to march on Jherusalem itself unopposed."

"You must summon the Templars from Gaza, Your Majesty," urged Joscelin de Courtenay, the king's uncle.

"A fool's suggestion," muttered Albert, the Bishop of Bethlehem, under his breath. Joscelin glared at him, but said nothing.

Balian grunted and shook his head. "Eighty Templars will hardly be enough to drive off the Sarrazins."

"They don't need to," Reynald argued.

The king held up a gloved hand, silencing the elder Ibelin before he could press his brother's argument. "What do you suggest, my lord of Kerak?"

Silently, he agreed with the bishop: it *was* a fool's suggestion. It was also the only suggestion that might actually offer them any real chance of success. Better to die by the sword, than by starvation, if he could at least take a handful of the Muslims with him.

"Summon Saint-Amant from Gaza, Your Majesty," Reynald said. "If we time our charge right, we can break through the enemy lines to rendezvous with Templars, and then ride like Hell itself was at our backs for Japhe. Perhaps there, we can regroup and come up with a plan of attack."

* * * * *

Thrice that long cold day the plaintive call of the *muezzin* sounded across the plain of Asqalan. It sounded eerie to hear the *azan*—the Muslim call to prayer—echoing across a land that had been Nasrani for so very long. For Salah ad-Din Yusuf, it was a dream he saw come true.

Urshalim will fall, the voice of his own thoughts whispered in his ear. *Urshalim will fall*. In the midst of preparing for the ritual prayer, he found himself repeating the words as though they were a *dhikr*. It gave him hope; a hope he clung to as a dying man clings to life.

Urshalim will fall. Urshalim will fall…

Setting aside his armor and his finery of war, he donned a simple tunic and prayer shawl of rough black homespun. Turning his back to the city, and the Ifranj, the whole of the army of Islam turned with him to the southeast and lay prostrate on the ground towards beloved, holy Mecca. This was war of another fashion, a war against fear and pride and all the invisible forces of nature.

The ancient imam, who always traveled with the army, lifted his voice and led them in prayer to Allah. In that moment, the sudden silence of twenty-five thousand servants, slaves, and soldiers was utter and complete. He could hear the breeze sighing softly through the trees of the citrus orchards. Then, those same twenty-five thousand voices lifted as one, each focused on a single, unwavering declaration of faith.

In the name of God, the Most Gracious, the Most Merciful:

All praise is due to God, Lord of the Universe.
The Most Gracious, the Most Merciful,
Sovereign of the Day of Judgment.
You alone we worship, and You alone we ask for help.
Guide us to the straight path;
The path of those on whom You have bestowed your grace,
Not of those who have earned Your anger, nor of those who go astray.
Amin…

* * * * *

The castle of Gaza was a picture of ordered chaos. The brothers of the Temple had just finished singing the prayers for Compline when a commotion erupted at the gate. Earlier that day, the Muslim army had passed them by without a challenge. Salehdin had simply left a small detachment of soldiers camped outside the walls and moved north towards Ascalone.

Othon de Saint-Amant stood on the stairs of the castle chapel, waiting for a report on the supposed rider at the gate. The flames of the torches cast eerie shadows along the walls. The yard was a sea of activity; serjeants and servants ran about on various errands, each of them focused on the commotion at the gatehouse. A serjeant ran towards him, helmet tucked under his arm, and saluted, his fist touching the breast of his black habit.

"My lord, there is a rider. He says he is from the king."

"Did the king make it to Ascalone, then?" Othon asked.

"I don't know, my lord," the serjeant replied. "The guards are bringing the rider through the gate now." Othon ran his hand over his thick, bushy beard, thinking. With a detachment of the Sarrazin army keeping watch outside their gates, whispers had already began to circulate about how a rider could have gotten through unnoticed, even at night.

"Bring him to me at once, Thibaut," he said.

He sighed and leaned back against the wall, his eyes closed. How had things come to this so quickly? He was supposed to be leading the way against the lies and heresy of a Church that had lost its moorings of truth, even if it was in secret. He was supposed to be restoring a lost line of kings to its rightful place in the world. Now the kingdom of Heaven was in jeopardy of being lost, and he was defenseless against it. This was not what he imagined his life would come to—trapped within a fortress with the enemy encompassed about and he a traitor to the king he swore to protect. A king he loved. The sacred heir of the *sangreal.* He shook his head. He was not even sure if he believed that was true anymore.

God, what have I done? What lies have led me to believe in a cause I no longer see?

If he truly wanted an answer, he did not receive it; a few moments later, the serjeant returned. He escorted a man cloaked with a voluminous black hood. Once the serjeant had departed, the man drew back the hood and stepped into the light of the flickering torch, revealing his face. It was Amalric de Lusignan.

"My lord," Othon greeted tersely with a slight nod.

The Master of Sion took his arm and pulled him inside the chapel door. A hint of candle-wax scented the air. "The king has great need of you and your Templars at Ascalone."

His anger flared unexpectedly. It usually did anymore in the man's presence. "This is so typical of you. You simply appear and expect me to act," he said. "If the need is so great, then why not simply whisk us away by magic?"

"That would be rather obvious, would it not?" Lusignan replied. "No. There is time yet for you to act, if you leave tonight. The city is loosely besieged, but I suspect Salehdin will move the bulk of his army on to Jherusalem in the morning."

Othon shook his head. He spun away from the Master and turned back again. "This is the outcome of your scheming. We may lose the kingdom even before we had a chance to gain it."

"It is only a minor setback, that is all," said Amalric de Lusignan. "But it is also an opportunity for us to get closer to the king. He expects you to rescue his army. He will be so grateful, he will refuse you nothing."

Othon ground his teeth. "This is a little more than a minor setback, my lord," he growled. "With only two thousand men, we are outnumbered by more than twelve to one."

"Calm yourself, Messire," the Master of Sion said. "Half of the sultan's army is nothing more than common Cairene rabble. They are no match for fully armed and mounted knights. If we ride now, we can reach Ascalone by morning."

Othon balled his hands into fists. He hated to admit that Amalric de Lusignan was right. He had to ride to the king's summons. It was the Templars' sacred duty to protect the king as well as obey the Master of their Order. It did not mean he had to like it, though.

"If the king requests our service, then I will obey."

"Don't despair, my friend. We have allies other than you know."

"What allies?"

Amalric de Lusignan smiled at him. It sent an icy chill down his spine. "When the time comes, they will be revealed."

* * * * *

It was well after sunset when they made their way towards the gate of Asqalan to sue for the city's surrender; the only evidence the sun had set was the sudden darkening of the skies from grey to the black of night.

Yusuf spurred his black stallion towards the imposing walls. Four large Mamluks, each bearing guttering torches in one hand and the poles of a small canopy in the other, moved slowly forward around him. A blue-eyed Ifranj slave walked beside him beneath the canopy, dressed in a long black robe of silk with words from the Qur'an worked in flowing gold script on the sleeves. His hand rested nervously upon his foot. Yusuf gazed up at the banners snapping in the breeze. He had dreamt even as a small boy living with his father in distant Ba'albek, of the day when the armies of Islam would stand at the gate of the once great cities of their people and demand retribution of the infidels. This was the day.

Urshalim will fall.

When they reached a safe distant from the gate, Yusuf raised a hand and they stopped. The blue-eyed slave stepped out from just beneath the ornate awning and addressed the Ifranj lord who had come out to speak with them under the white banner of truce.

"You are not *Al-Abras* of Urshalim."

"No," said the dark man, crossing his arms. "I am Reynald de Châtillon, the lord of Montréal and Kerak. I speak for the Leper King."

Yusuf bristled at the name of the Nasrani knight. In the last two years, he had become quite familiar with Brins Arnat of Shaubak and al-Karak. He had cost him dearly in terms of men and arms and goods between Egypt and Suriya. But he would pay for his impertinence. Once Urshalim had fallen, he would deal with the former lord of Antikiyyah who had raided one too many of his caravans.

"My master, the sultan Salah ad-Din, has a simple message," the slave said. "He gives you but one chance to accept terms of surrender."

"Surrender?" Brins Arnat chuckled. "Why should we surrender when the greater part of our army is even now marching here to protect Jherusalem?"

Yusuf smiled deceptively. He spoke directly to the arrogant knight; the slave interpreted. "I think you put a great deal of faith, my friend, in the ability of an army that is closer to Aleppo than it is to Urshalim, to give you aid."

The Nasrani curled his lip with a sneer. His dark eyes flared with hatred in the torchlight. "I think you will find our army more difficult to defeat than you imagine. But what terms do you offer my king?"

"Surrender and the lives of your people will be spared. Refuse and I promise you there will be no mercy." The slave hesitated to interpret the message. His blue eyes turned to him as though he was afraid to repeat the words. "Tell him," he commanded. The slave glared at him, thinking of defiance. He turned back to the Ifranj lord and relayed the terms.

The knight of Urshalim spat at the slave. "Tell your master we would rather die in Hell, than surrender to a Sarrazin dog."

"So you have chosen," Yusuf said in the language of the Ifranj. The surprise registered in the knight's arrogant smile. "But remember, it is you who have sealed your own fate. May Allah have mercy on your infidel self, for I will have none."

Yusuf turned his horse and rode back through the deepening night, leaving his escort and the Ifranj lord behind. He had nothing more to say.

His emirs rose nearly as one as he rode back into camp. Dismounting his horse, a servant took his horse and his helmet. He ran a hand over his head, ruffling his hair. The youngest of his emirs stepped forward: a gleam of fire set his eyes aflame. They were all like this one, young lions eager for the prospect of war and the thrill of the hunt. "We march on Jherusalem with the dawn," he said and entered his tent alone to pray.

* * * * *

The army of Jherusalem made a valiant, glorious charge the next morning from the gates of Ascalone. At the sound of a distant horn, the armed camp of the Muslims mobilized their forces and formed a hasty line of defense to the seaward side of the city. The Templars charged; a brief skirmish ensued; Muslim and Christian bodies lay strewn on the sandy shore washed by the sea. The trumpeting of a second horn from within the city gates threw the Sarrazins into a panicked retreat from which almost none survived. It was over within a few heartbeats.

Baldwin rallied his knights before the gates of the city. He raised his blood-spattered sword and commanded them to silence. After even such a brief battle, his arm felt heavy and trembling. He had to direct all his will just to keep his weakened arm aloft. It was a struggle. Then, suddenly, a tingling sensation coursed through his disease-stricken arm, giving him strength.

—I am with you, Your Highness, whispered the voice of the Magdalen into his thoughts. I will be your strength, even if yours should fail you.

His men looked to him, drawing confidence and hope where none had existed only the night before. He wheeled his horse, letting it dance and fret beneath him. He felt the Magdalen's presence about him, even if no one else could see her. She was his guardian angel.

"The sultan of Egypt thinks us weak and afraid to face him in battle; now he shall pay for his mistake. You are knights, defenders of the Holy Sepulcher," he shouted in his halting, raspy voice. They heard him, though. They brandished their swords, beating them against their shields. "You have nothing to fear, save only the shame of cowardice. Vows you have taken, each of you; oaths you have sworn to your king. Now, give yourselves wholly into the service of God and He will not forsake you. Ride, now, soldiers of Christ and defend your honor. Ride, and defend the kingdom of Jherusalem from the Sarrazins."

Their response was unanimous, a deafening roar of acclamation. *Deus lo volt... Deus lo volt... Deus lo volt!*

* * * * *

The army of the Muslims scattered throughout the undefended kingdom of the Ifranj like the fingers of a hand. The vanguard rode northwards, ravaging the countryside by burning the small hilltop village of Mijdal Yaba and laying siege first to al-Ramla, and then to the Nasrani stronghold of al-Ludd. By nightfall, the black smoke of a dozen villages or more would smudge the western skyline of Urshalim. All Salah ad-Din had to do now was close the fingers of his army around the walls of Urshalim and the city would be firmly within his grasp.

By midday, bands of disorganized Nasrani peasants—little more than boys and aged men, some of them lepers—armed with nothing more than clubs and knives or sticks, began to filter out of the surrounding hills, streaming towards Asqalan. The Muslim soldiers snatched them up quickly and bound them. Yusuf cursed them for the nuisance they were. The lepers he ordered slain for fear they might spread contagion.

He brought the hardiest of the lot before his emirs to be made an example of; a stout, gap-toothed man with a wooden bucket for a helmet, a boiled leather tunic for armor, and a rusty sword with a broken tip and jagged nicks along its hastily sharpened edge.

At a nod, Taqi ad-Din knocked the man to the ground and forced him to kneel. Yusuf bent his gaze to the man and then to his army. He shook his head. "This is the mighty army the Ifranj threatened would defend against us: men with sticks and clubs instead of swords or spears. It is a wonder we have not driven them from this land long before now. Surely, Allah has brought us to such shame. Take him away."

"What should we do with them, Excellency?" his nephew asked. "Kill them?"

"No, Umar. We will show them mercy. Our grievance is not against such men as these; it is with Al-Abras and his lords. Bind them for now to the camels in the baggage train. We can sell them later as slaves. The profit will help defray some of the cost of this campaign."

* * * * *

"They have burned everything between here and Ibelin, Your Highness," Reynald said as he rode up to the king. He had ridden north towards Ibelin and Ramlah with the Master of the Temple and the lords of those esteemed seigneuries, while the king waited with the rest of the army. What he had seen would dishearten any lord or knight who had pledged his life to the defense of the Holy Sepulcher; more, it angered him with an unquenchable fury.

"Mirabel is in flames and two detachments of the Sarrazins are encamped around Ramlah and Lydda," said Balian of Ibelin.

"The sultan has relaxed discipline among his army and let them scatter," the lord of Ramlah said, patting the neck of his horse. "This may be to our advantage."

The wind had picked up throughout the day, bringing with it a hint of winter rain. A gust caught the king's blue cloak; it billowed out behind him like a rolling sea wave. Baldwin nudged his horse forward knee to knee with him. He narrowed his gaze, trying to catch some unspoken message in the set of Reynald's face, even behind the mask of his helmet. "What haven't you told me, Reynald?"

Reynald lifted a hand above his shoulder and made a motion, signaling his knights to form ranks with the rest of the army. He wound the reins tightly around his hand and glanced away. Guilt kept him from looking directly at his king. "Many of the men summoned by the *arrière-ban* have been captured by Salehdin. God knows what he'll do with them."

"If God is merciful, he will kill them."

Reynald turned slowly back to Baldwin, amazed at his indifference. He knew better, though. Baldwin felt every bit of the responsibility of having sent innocent men to certain death. "Not if we can take the sultan by surprise," he said. "His troops are scattered and too far afield to be called to any sort of order on short notice. If we can hit at the center of Salehdin's forces, we can break them."

Baldwin rubbed his chin with a glove. "Do you know where the sultan is at this very moment?"

"No," Reynald said. "But God has delivered a Muslim soldier into our hands."

Baldwin's horse snorted and stamped its hooves as a knight threw the Muslim to the ground. He calmed the animal with a hand. "Does... does he know where his sultan is hiding?"

"I'm sure, Your Highness, that I can persuade him to tell us," Reynald said. "Then we can plan our attack."

* * * * *

Baldwin cleared the chessboard of pieces and placed the white king in its place; the black king—the sultan—he set in the middle of the board just behind a line of pawns angling diagonally across the checkered squares. He glanced up, searching the faces of the lords who had assembled in his tent to listen to his plan of attack on Salehdin. He had discussed the plan earlier that night with the Master of the Temple, Othon de Saint-Amant, and Reynald de Châtillon, two men whose opinions he valued highly; now he presented it to all his vassals. He expected little opposition to his plan.

"The main force of the sultan's army"—he pointed to the black sultan on the chessboard—"is positioned near the creek just south of the castle of Montgisart. We will split our army in three: Othon will lead his Templars; Reynald will lead his troops along with those of Japhe and Ascalone—and, if my lord of Sidon does not object, you will ride with them." His stepfather nodded his assent. "My uncle and I will lead the rest of the royal troops along with the Ibelins, the Bishop of Bethlehem, and the brothers Saint-Omer. We cannot hope for reinforcements; the Sarrazins captured many of those summoned by the *arrière-ban*. We must act alone with the forces we have."

Baldwin picked up the two white knights and coughed. The spasm wracked his chest, stealing his breath. Reynald took the knights from him and set them at opposite ends of the pawn-line, on the sultan's side of the board. "The wings will cross the creek upstream and down, and take up their positions. When the signal is given, both will charge the Sarrazin position; at the same time, the king will charge the Sarrazins on this side of the creek and drive them back into Salehdin's face."

"If... if God is merciful," Baldwin said, "we will prevail against the enemy."

"Masterfully planned, Your Majesty. But how do we know what the sultan intends?" Balian of Ibelin asked. "We risk a great deal if we don't know for certain."

Baldwin glanced at Othon and Reynald above the edge of his veil and cleared his throat. "A Sarrazin scout was captured earlier today and questioned. Have no fear, my lord of Ibelin, Salehdin will be there when we attack. He will pay for your brother's loss of Mirabel."

"And where is this unlooked for blessing whom God has given us," asked Hugh of Saint-Omer, "in case he should prove himself a liar?"

"He did not survive his questioning," said de Châtillon.

Reynald's bluntness outraged the Bishop of Bethlehem; his face turned bright red. He complained to Baldwin without hesitation. "Is this how we treat prisoners now, Your Highness—like the heathen Muslims?"

Reynald slammed his fist down on the camp table. "Dead men can't betray us, Your Grace. Besides, does not the Church and the Pope teach that killing Muslims is an act of service to God?"

"You are little more than a brigand, my lord Kerak," replied the Bishop. "Worse, you abrogate the mercy of God with your own lust for Sarrazin blood."

Baldwin held up a gloved hand, gesturing for restraint. "We are at war. If this plan is to have any chance of success, my lord Bishop, it must be unexpected."

The calm after the storm of their council of war overwhelmed him. Baldwin pulled off his turbaned helmet and leather gloves and threw them aside. He stared at his hands. Ulcers covered the back of his right hand, raw and weeping; the two outermost fingers had healed together as one. They were twisted and stunted. His left hand was only just beginning to show the effects of his disease.

He brought his hands slowly together and sunk to his knees before the True Cross. The Bishop had brought it to his tent earlier that night so that they could pray to God for success against the Muslims. Baldwin prayed alone now simply for the strength to lead his knights into battle. If he could win even one significant battle against Salehdin, it might be enough to give his people a chance for peace, if only for a few seasons. Provided his lords did not sabotage their efforts with their petty differences.

* * * * *

Four Templars stood in a circle marking the cardinal points of the compass; Othon de Saint-Amant took up the fourth position, guarding the South, the place of Michael the Archangel. In one hand, they held their swords against their chests, in the other hand, each held an emblem of the sacred elements: a cup of baptismal water, a chest of consecrated earth, a feather, fire atop a white candle. In their midst lay a small piece of yellowed parchment covered front and back with a verse of scripture to protect them against the forces of evil they were about to summon.

The master of Sion had alluded in Gaza to other allies they could call upon, if needed. Now, he understood his meaning. If he thought Amalric de Lusignan was dangerous before, he knew it now for certes. All thought of his betrayal of Sion to the king fled now with the fear of what he knew the master could do to him.

Lusignan walked slowly around the tent to seal the circle of magic with words of an ancient incantation of power. The air crackled; it gathered as a faint bluish mist, drawing itself into a swirling vortex about the circle.

He took the cup of baptismal water and bowed to the West with a word of power. *Fiat, fiat, fiat voluntas mea*, he said, invoking the power of the elements. Next, he moved to the North and mixed the consecrated earth in the water. He bowed again. Moving to the East, he waved the feather signifying the power of the air over the cup, gently disturbing its contents, and bowed to its guardian. Lastly, he turned to face Othon in his place of the South. A swirling mist rose from the sacred cup.

Lusignan drew a silver athame from a scabbard at his belt and drew it slowly across his palm; blood welled dark and red from the wound. Smearing the blood across the face of the large bronze seal ring on his left hand, he crouched to the ground and set the seal to the parchment scribbled with scripture. Immediately, the blood flared red with a glowing, infernal light. Holding the parchment to the candle, the flame consumed it, turning the blood and parchment to ash. The master executed every action, every movement, meticulously without the least bit of hesitation or thought. With each step of the ritual, he murmured more words, first in Latin, and then in a tongue of a far older tradition.

Given the Order of Sion's origins, he guessed the words were Egyptian, perhaps Hebrew.

Stirring the ashes of the parchment in the cup, Amalric de Lusignan drank the potent mixture. The cup fell from his hand and he grasped his throat before falling to his knees with a strangled cry.

The air in the tent went suddenly cold; the torches guttered as if blown, but there was no wind. Othon had known fear only a few times in his life; now, he knew a fear far deeper than any he had ever imagined before. He drew his sword and fell back from the circle, ready to defend against any power that threatened them. The other Templars did the same with equal fear.

The fit lasted but only a few moments and then, Amalric smiled coldly, knowing the spell had worked successfully. He stood and held up his hands. Closing his eyes, he began the final incantation and spat out a vile, hideous name, calling forth a black daemon of fear and despair to his will. Just the sound of the name alone sent a shiver of fear down Othon's spine. He tried to close his eyes against what was to come, but could not.

"Come, thou servant of Hell, spirit of air and darkness and the power of fear," Amalric de Lusignan said, making sure he intoned the ritualistic formula of summoning correctly. "By the Seal that was Solomon's which hath power over all thy kind, I bind thee to my command and bid thee come. Bear thou no hatred and bring thou no allied servants of Hell to give thee aid against my will. In the Name of God, Jehovah, Elohim, Sophia, and his servant John, I command thee, come."

Thunder gathered; a gust of wind shook the tent, extinguishing all but the flame of the white candle in Othon's hand. Darkness descended. In that darkness, shadows gathered and took form; in its writhing midst, two red eyes glowing like embers of fire glared at the Master of Sion. Othon let out a strangled cry.

"I have come as thou hast bidden," the daemon hissed, spreading its great black wings. "What would thou will of me, son of man?"

* * * * *

Mary wrapped herself in her cloak and stepped between the worlds. She found herself in a darkened tent; a man snored unevenly. Even in the darkness, she could make out his white habit with its distinctive blood-red cross of the Templars. Power, wild and raw, had shaken the very foundations of the realms of magic. She had grasped hold of its rapidly scattering threads and traced them backward towards its source. A hint of it lingered still in the tent: the acrid scent of burnt blood and the bitter stench of Hell.

The enemy had used the Seal of Solomon; he had summoned a daemon. It had been a heavily warded working of power; else, she would have felt it long before its completion. She knew at once the author of the working; it had been the Master of the Order of Sion. She shuddered for fear of what that might portend.

She glanced around. Her enemy had fled from this place of the black art, but his fellow conspirator had not. Gently, but hesitantly, she bent to the sleeping, snoring man and touched him. He stirred and rolled over, but did not awake. Images flashed in her mind, reminiscent of those she had seen before through the medallion of blood-silver that Baldwin had given her only a few nights before.

She stood and backed away in revulsion, recognizing the man as Othon de Saint-Amant, the Master of the Templars. He had sent the warning and the medallion to the king. A man Baldwin trusted with his life.

She bent to him again and touched his brow. His sleeping thoughts revealed all that had occurred earlier that night, but not the face or name of the Master of Sion. Too well he had warded his servants against her.

Mary withdrew the medallion of Sion from her belt and wound the chain about the fingers of the man's open hand. *Let him wonder how and why this has returned to him*, she thought. Perhaps, it will give him pause to consider the consequences of his betrayal against the king, and against God.

Wrapping herself in shadows and in the knowledge of a traitor found, she stepped in and through the veil of night, into the sunlight of her own world.

† CHAPTER ELEVEN

The sword shall devour, and shall be filled and shall be drunk with their blood....
—Jeremias 46:10

Horses pawed the ground; they snorted and tossed their heads, eager for the coming battle. Baldwin hefted his lance, weighing it in his hand. He glanced up at its iron point and the streaming blue pennon snapping in the breeze. All around him a forest of bristling lances stood at deadly attention. His muscles were as taut as a bowstring, ready to snap. It would begin in a matter of moments, the defense of Jherusalem and the kingdom of Outremer.

His uncle, Joscelin de Courtenay, count of fallen Edessa, sat to his right, knee to knee, on a matching black charger; he carried the standard of the kingdom with its potent crosses of gold on white, rippling in the breeze. The Bishop of Bethlehem sat on his left atop a large roan gelding, the sliver of the True Cross fastened securely to a standard in its crucifix of glittering gold, ready to lead them all to victory for the cause of Christ, armored only in his ecclesiastical robes. His hatred of all things unholy would sustain him as certainly as any weapon of war.

The marshal blew the horn, signaling their readiness. A few tense moments later, two other horns blew north and south of the hill, signaling that the wings of the army under the command of Reynald and Othon had taken up their positions as well. He hoped the trumpet blasts would have their desired effect: throw the Muslims into a panic by informing them that the Christians surrounded them on all sides. There would be no time for Salehdin to set a defense. He could only retreat, or fight.

Joscelin set a hand to his shoulder and leaned closer. "Are you ready, Sire?"

Baldwin looked forward and down the hill towards the distant line of trees where the Muslims had been crossing the dry creek bed. At the sound of the trumpets, the army of Islam took flight with nowhere to retreat.

The moment had come; the moment the whole of the kingdom had long waited, and feared. "How could I be anything less, uncle? It is what I have been trained and bred for since I was a child."

He raised a hand to signal the Marshal to sound the charge. His war-horse, Bellerophon tensed beneath him, ready for the charge. His hand trembled…

And fell. The horn winded. In that space between thought and action, before the army of Christ plunged headlong down the hill of Montgisart into the waiting battle, the rain began to fall from the ominous grey skies above. The sound of the charge rent the fabric of the clouds from one end of the dark heavens to the other. A sudden torrent fell, pounding the earth in cadence with the hooves of two thousand horses.

* * * * *

Othon slowly wound the reins of his horse tightly around his palm. Feeling the nervous tension in his seat, the destrier snorted and shook his massive black head; the muscles of its flanks tensed beneath him. Crowded so close together with other horses, with the scent of steel and fear in the air, it fidgeted, stamping its hind legs. Othon calmed his mount with a gentle caress.

The eighty knights that rode with him formed up into four columns with the mounted serjeants arrayed behind. No one spoke lest he give away their position to the Muslims scavenging the countryside. The *gonfalon baucent*, the black on white war-banner of the Templars, snapped in the gusting breezes. The menacing grey clouds threatened with the promise of rain. Thunder rumbled overhead.

The plan was simple: at the signal, the knights would charge. Just before they engaged the enemy, the columns would split into two prongs and drive into the heathen dogs with all the savage force of a cavalry unit could muster. With any luck, Reynald's charge from the south would drive a wedge through the gap and not collide with their horses. It could prove a bloody ordeal, indeed.

Anxiously, his hand crept up the length of his lance to touch the medallion of blood-silver he had knotted to the shaft. He feared how it had come back to him, so unexpectedly, so close on the heels of their summoning of the daemon. He wondered what it might mean, what else the master had commanded of the spirit of fire.

He had sold his soul to the Order of Sion. And in so doing, he had played the part of traitor against his will to two kings; first, as King Amaury's Marshall and Butler, and later, as the Master of the Temple and a chief councilor of the Court under Amaury and Baldwin. But no more.

He was done with betrayal and magic, the intrigues of Sion. This was what he had come to Outremer to do. It was for this that he had trained and lived. If God were truly good, merciful, and kind, he would fall in battle defending the kingdom founded in His name. Beyond that, he cared less whether his soul found forgiveness or God condemned him to the everlasting flames of Hell. He deserved Hell.

His hand closed tightly over the medallion. The trumpet sounded across the vale, calling them to battle. With one voice, the Templars raised their weapons, and shouted their battle cry, hurling it towards their enemy as they rode. *Baucent! Baucent!*

Their hooves churned up the earth and as they gathered speed for the charge. Even with so few, they were a terrifying sight, clad in chainmail and their long white tunics. With a final cry and a blast of the horn, their lances fell and they broke upon the scattering Muslim horde. There was a moment when every sound fell away into sudden silence, and then, it lifted in a deafening roar as the hammer of the Franks struck heavily against the anvil.

* * * * *

The trumpet sounded the call to war and bloodshed. His pulse surged, beating rapidly; blood pounded in his ears, echoing in the hollow of his helmet. Reynald de Châtillon was a warrior first, a lord and prince of men thereafter.

The Muslim line held only long enough to be trampled under by the crushing impact of the charge; those that were unfortunate enough to survive fell back upon their companions trying desperately to form up some sort of defense.

Reynald's sword rang from its scabbard, taking off the heads of the first two Muslims that crossed his path. Blood sprayed in a wide arc across his chest and face. Its taste was warm and salty on his tongue, the sweet nectar of battle. The Sarrazin devils flung themselves wildly at the Franks. For their dolorous effort, the knights sent them shrieking and screaming into Paradise.

The bodies of the fallen slowed the momentum of the charge. Reynald finally came to a stop and turned his horse into the line of mounted Sarrazin troops. Two of the sons of Satan rode at him; he ducked and swung desperately at the left man. He lost his shield on impact, but the screaming daemon fell to the ground clutching his severed arm. The other soldier wheeled away, and came at him again from behind.

A backhand stroke split the man cleanly from shoulder to waist. The blade stuck fast, however, in the man's pelvis; the sudden weight of the dead body pulled him from the saddle. Reynald fell and rolled. Horses and soldiers crowded him. He dodged both and dropped onto the bloody body of the Sarrazin. He yanked the sword loose and swung upwards just in time to slash through the armor and chest of a grinning soldier. Blood spurted from the gaping wound. He pulled off his helmet and threw it angrily at a Muslim who leapt on the back of his horse and rode off. Sheathing his sword, he grabbed a battle-standard from the hand of a dead serjeant. He hefted the standard in his hand and threw it at the fleeing Muslim.

"Come on, you Muslim dogs," he screamed in a rage. "Fight me; fight me, you cowards."

Laughter at his back caught him off guard. He turned. Another of the slant-eyed Turkish daemons stood there holding a knife. Reynald feigned surrender, and then backhanded the leering soldier and ran him through with his sword. A gurgling sound rose in his throat; bloody foam oozed from his lips. The man grabbed hold of Reynald's tabard and tried to pull him down. Reynald shoved him back with his foot, freeing his blade. His son had died in much the same fashion: a knife in the back from a dying Turk. He would not die the same way.

Fighting his way across the body-littered battlefield, he joined with several other unhorsed knights in a loose circle. Again and again, Reynald lifted his sword, the blade singing with joy as it swung through the air. Bodies began to pile. Injured men cried with pain, moaning; a horse screamed. The fighting was no longer a battle; it was a rout.

The rain turned the ground into a slick quagmire of blood and gore. He slipped in the mud and fell. Another Muslim ran at him, scimitar held aloft, screaming his guttural war cry. Reynald rolled to his right, and kicked the Muslim in the face as he brought the scimitar down towards his head. The blow sent the soldier sprawling to the ground. Reynald was on him in a moment, running his sword into the man's belly.

Just then, a horn sounded, long and clear from the trees, halting the battle for only a moment: the king's charge had broken through. With a growl of renewed vigor, Reynald lifted his sword and lunged at the line of soldiers running at him.

* * * * *

The Muslim cavalry troops were no match against the infidels. The heavy Ifranj destriers broke over the lighter Arabian horses like so much flotsam before a flood, washing them up upon the hither banks of the dry streambed. Salah ad-Din Yusuf cursed his own arrogance for thinking that *Al-Abras*, the Leper King, would ever cower behind the walls of Asqalan, licking his wounds while he marched on Urshalim.

The hired soldiers he had taken on in al-Qihara to swell his numbers, fell like sheaves before the scythe; it was a massacre. He had no choice but to gather his ranks as best he could and hope they held against the Ifranj assault.

If he was to have any chance of saving the remnants of his army, he needed to slow the advance. The lack of discipline divided the army; Isa al-Hakkari was with the rear-guard, setting fire throughout the countryside; Taqi ad-Din was in the van besieging the Ifranj fortresses in the north. While his Mamluks took up their defensive position, he ordered Ahmad ad-Din to form up his ranks of archers and set them in a line before the charging Ifranj. At a command, they emptied their quivers into the thundering line of armored knights and horses, and drew their swords.

With the collapse of the second charge, the Mamluks marched forward to the noise of beating drums, clattering nakers, and skirling pipes. If they could hold the Ifranj army, they could break the assault. A horn sounded in the distance; the Ifranj pig that they called king, had rallied his knights, and made a renewed charge across the dry streambed.

Of a sudden, as though it held back a force it could no longer subdue, the center collapsed. Only, the Ifranj did not cause the collapse; they washed over the might of his Mamluks like waves breaking gently upon the shore. An unseen presence spread fear like a pestilence—not the fear of battle or of an overwhelming enemy—but the fear of never seeing one's home or family again, a fear that whispered of death and destruction and the denial of Paradise for one's sacrifice in battle.

He knew at once the power of the enemy they faced. He had possessed the Seal of Suleiman long enough to recognize its potency. This was dark and malevolent. A spirit stronger than any *ifrit* he had ever dared to summon. Even he, who seldom knew the weakness of fear, was not immune to its terror. It came upon them as a darkness that clouded the mind, and numbed the senses to all else but fear and despair. It moved throughout their ranks, bringing men to their knees or causing them to run like frightened children. His trained Mamluks, who knew naught but the strength of their skills in battle, cowered in the shadows of their former selves.

Al Nasir Salah ad-Din Yusuf, the King, the Rectifier of the Faith of Islam, drew his sword and screamed his defiance at the unknown enemy. Glowing red eyes laughed in his face and threatened him with defeat and the utter humiliation of his house. It spoke again, whispering images into his shaken thoughts. He saw his wife, his children, naked and mutilated, lying in the burning ruins of his mighty citadel. He could do nothing but tremble at his words, no matter how much he tried to disbelieve their truth. The daemon breathed death, and it was so.

Yusuf refused to bow to his fear and despair. He focused his mind, his thoughts, his whole being on the name of Allah. Again and again, he repeated the phrases of the *shahadah*, the declaration of Islam. His voice rose in the familiar ululation of the faithful.

Allahu akhbar; Allahu akhbar; Allahu akhbar... God is greater; God is greater; God is greater...

With each repeated word, his strength grew and multiplied, casting down the dark images of his mind. His faith became a shield behind which he fought off the terror that besieged them.

Then, in a sudden blaze of sunlight that rent the lowering clouds in the northern sky, the darkness rolled back and fled away. In its place, a new working of deviltry unfolded: a golden cruciform of light that overspread the lurid heavens, drawing every eye to its glorious sight. In that moment, the grand army of Islam was undone.

* * * * *

Othon did not die—not yet. Slashing their way through the wall of Sarrazin infantry, the Templars found themselves circled about with swords and the fierce hatred of all things Christian. His marshal sounded the horn, trying to regroup for a second charge.

Wheeling out towards the edge of the battle in a tight circle, the horses found their pace and charged the Muslim center. In the time it took to regroup for the charge, Salehdin had ordered the archers to form ranks and awaited the attack. All at once, volley after volley of arrows bristled the air around them, too many finding their mark.

Othon's horse went down with a scream. He fell forward with a bone-wrenching jolt. He had no time to check for injury. Muslim infantry poured through the gaps of archers and hacked their way through the crumpling line of their charge. In the mêlée, he found himself nearly alone with the whole of the army of Islam at his sword.

The fighting fell quickly to the ugly business of hand-to-hand combat. He clashed with a charging emir in a gold and green coat, exchanging ringing blows, before he finally split the man's skull with a jarring overhand cut. He stopped and caught his breath. All around him men were dying, their blood saturating the ground with their life force. It was a battle the likes of which he had rarely seen before. There was no time to rest, beyond catching his breath.

At the heart of the Muslim forces, stood Salehdin's seasoned troops, the Mamluks in their glittering scale armor and brilliant yellow coats. They held their masters' position, while all else fell into chaos and ever-widening ruin.

A sudden dark shadow fell across the battlefield, visibly filling the Sarrazins with overwhelming dread. Men threw down their arms and ran; others fell to the ground, writhing with fear and despair. Othon knew at once the author of the panic: the daemon Amalric de Lusignan had called up the night before. It began with the charge of the king and the Ibelin household, and moved through the army of Islam to spread its shadow of horror and fear.

By the time he fought his way towards Salehdin's position, his white habit was drenched with blood and gore, the scarlet cross nearly indistinguishable. He could not guess how much of it was his blood— nor did he want to.

A Muslim swung wildly at his head and missed. Othon parried a second blow and ducked under the man's arm; he came up with the hilt of his sword and smashed it into the soldier's face. The nose bone crunched with a sickening sound as it pushed up into his brain, killing him instantly. The body slumped to the ground as Othon swung his shield up, blocking another attack from a huge black Mamluk in a golden coat. The force of the overhead blow shattered the shield and sent a numbing shudder through his arm; pain shot through the bone like a searing fire. The shattered shield fell from his broken arm. It was the mud, however, that saved his life.

He slipped and fell; the momentum of the Mamluk's blow threw him off balance and down onto Othon's chest. Othon was able to raise his sword just in time for the soldier to fall upon it.

* * * * *

As quickly as the torrent of rain began, it subsided into drizzle. Rain and blood mingled in a crimson stream. It flowed to the height of a horse's bridle. The battle was going well enough; the wings of the army had closed and circled the Sarrazins. A line of Turkish archers, though, had managed to bring down most of the Templar vanguard in their last charge; Reynald's forces were scattered throughout the field, but were holding their own.

The Muslims were nearly in chaos. Salehdin, however, was not ready to admit defeat just yet. His Mamluks held their position, only now just beginning to join the fray. They had caught the sultan off his guard, but he was still a wily and dangerous adversary. He was waiting for the full force of the Frankish assault to wash over him and then he would command his counter-attack. The army of Jherusalem was in danger. The charge had thinned them out. Baldwin had to regroup, before the Sarrazins stretched their lines to the breaking point. Their only hope was to force Salehdin into a disorganized retreat before he attacked.

Baldwin screamed an order to the Marshal to sound the horn and rally the knights to his position. *To me, to me,* the horn cried. *To me.*

Other horns took up the summons, echoing the command down the line. If they failed, they were all dead men. At once, the tide began to turn as the army mustered around the banner of Jherusalem.

Just then, the Bishop of Bethlehem's horse stumbled and went down, an arrow through the shoulder of the defenseless cleric. With the bishop, fell the True Cross, the soul and heart of the Christian army.

In a horrifying moment, an immense dark shadow surrounded the fallen cross, hideous black shapes with what looked like wings and fangs, and the burning fire of red eyes. Time seemed to slow to an infinitesimal crawl. Silence enveloped him. Horses and soldiers moved past Baldwin in a blur of light and shadow. A spear lanced up at him, slow and slowing, towards his chest. He raised his sword to deflect the thrust. It shattered in a noiseless sundering of steel and splintering wood.

Nearby, the banner of Ibelin wavered and fell amid the collecting darkness; it rose again in the hand of a knight on horseback. For a moment that lingered on into eternity, the war, the battle, even the kingdom itself, seemed to fade away into ever-quieting silence and peace. Baldwin thought of release and surrender to the place between the worlds where magic held sway and the cares of men faded into oblivion. But he couldn't—at least, not until the battle was won.

The cross, devoured in shadow and darkness, flared suddenly to glorious life, rending the darkness into a thousand shards of night. The daemons fled, scattering towards the Muslim forces. It rose from the ground and grew, its overspreading arms stretching across the sky and into the heights of Heaven.

A figure appeared amidst the lowering clouds and falling rain, a knight with a sword of fire and armor glowing with a golden light.

With a deafening roar of noise, then the silence lifted with a cry as the battle deepened around him. Shouts rose among the knights who saw the vision of the cross, screaming their war-chant. *Saint George! Saint George! Saint George!*

Baldwin gasped, gulping air into his depleted lungs. "To me," he croaked. "To me."

All around him, knights flocked to his call, taking up his call to arms. *"To the king; to the king. Holy Sepulcher! Holy Sepulcher!"*

In a surging juggernaut of steel and men and horses, the army of Jherusalem sped over the battlefield, gaining speed for the charge, St. George and the True Cross with them. In the center of the field, the Muslim army collapsed under the threat of the charge and fell back in a confused retreat. Baldwin gave the word and they gave them chase into the quickly fading light of day.

* * * * *

Mary threw off her dark cloak and stepped from her world of shadows and sunlight into the white-hot heat of battle. For the better part of the day, she had hunted the daemon through the twisted maze of shadow-paths and the swiftly shifting currents of the air that joined the world of men to that other place of dreams and tilting time to no avail.

She had watched the Templar master, knowing that he had had a part in the daemon's summoning, but she found nothing; the acrid stench of Hell was not upon him. She sensed the daemon's elusive presence, lingering, waiting for the moment of its command; it seemed to know she hunted it and took great care to avoid her.

It was the king's horn sounding the charge, which unleashed the fiend. Too late, she realized that the foul spirit of the air had hid itself in the vanguard of the army, disguised as a knight of Jherusalem.

At the sound of the horn, the daemon shed its human disguise and spread its wings, darting towards the ranks of the Muslim army with a shriek of malicious glee. In its wake, it spread darkness and fear. Other dark shadows followed in its path; companion daemons of lesser power and strength. At once, the Sarrazin advance began to waver and crumble. Its power was immense, but not infinite. A niggling of doubt crept into her mind; a fear that the enemy she had for so long tried to defeat might accomplish its purpose. It was deception, a lie of the father of lies.

An arrow through the shoulder of the Bishop of Bethlehem brought the daemon raging back upon the army of Jherusalem and upon the True Cross that had fallen to the ground. It had broken the restraint of its summoning. It gloried in the desecration of the holy relic and in the betrayal of its master. Falling upon the cross, snarling and hissing, it whispered lies and devoured the courage of the brave knights that defended the holy relic. Darkness spread; the balance of battle began to shift in favor of the Sarrazin horde.

Above the din and confusion of war, and the cries of men giving in to their fears, she heard the desperate pleas of the king to save them from the destruction. He cried out to her, calling her name with ever-growing despair.

Shedding her dark cloak, she revealed herself in all the wondrous glamour of her much maligned kind. The semblance she wore before the eyes of men was of a great warrior-knight vanquishing the beast of darkness with a sword of flame. Light glowed around her like the sun in its strength. Cries of hope and salvation rose from the soldiers, shouts that sang the praise of St. George and the Cross.

—*These are mine*, the daemon spat at her, trying to rake her shield arm with its talons. **Or did you truly think all these were believers of our God.**

—*You disobey the command of your master, spirit,"* she cried.
—**He is a weak fool who thinks himself an equal of Solomon.**

Mary glanced around at the tide of battle that was swiftly turning against the Franks. Men moved all around them, hacking at each other with swords and spears, vaporous shadows of life and ever-present death. There was no time to banter with the servants of darkness.

—**Tell me his name**, she commanded, trying not to raise suspicion in the daemon's mind.

The spirit sneered, its eyes glowing with fire. The stench of Hell rose from its beating wings. **Give me these as prey**, it said, reaching out to the knights beneath its wings, **and I will tell you all you want to know.**

Slowly Mary raised her slender, silver sword. The names of God, chased in a flowing gilded script along its blade, glowed with white-hot fire. **Begone, spirit of fear, or I will send you back to Hell.**

The daemon hissed, laughing. **You have no power here, Magdalen.**

I have all the power I need, she said and raised the sword above her head. **In the name of Jhesú, and by his shed blood, I command you to return to the place whence you came.**

She struck the daemon with the edge of the sword, banishing it to the nethermost region of Hell with a piercing wail that rose above the raging tumult of battle. She did not need the seal to bind the minions of Hell; she needed only the name of the Lord of Heaven.

* * * * *

Reynald de Châtillon waded through the gore and ruin of battle. The Muslim army was wavering, about to collapse; many of the heathen were already in flight—at least those who had turned coward and run. Only the Mamluks remained behind to fight and defend their sultan.

Reynald was drenched in blood, and yet his thirst for revenge and bloodshed was far from slaked. He wanted more.

The Lord of Sidon, the king's stepfather, had joined him midway through the battle. He stood with him, a brother in arms, surveying the field; he was only slightly less spattered with the blood of their sworn enemy, two soldiers fighting their enemy after the fashion of the true warriors of old. Hand to hand, sword to sword. His muscles ached with fatigue, his lungs burned. He was not a young man anymore with the limitless energy of a knight half his age. Only the bloodlust of battle kept him moving and fighting, trying not to lose his life to an ill-fated blow.

Guilt drove him: guilt over talking Baldwin into issuing the *arrière-ban* and guilt over the subsequent capture of those poor souls who had responded with such blind loyalty. He had fought his way towards the rear of Salehdin's army, and the baggage-train that he had brought up from Ascalone. It was there that they would find the prisoners.

Before he could get to the baggage-train, though, they had to break the Mamluks. They would not be as easy to put to flight as the common rabble Salehdin had employed to swell his numbers. They were fresh and rested, having hung back in wait as the rest of the Sarrazin army surged to the front of the battle lines. The fastest route between his position and the prisoners was a charge on horseback. The battle had been a killing field of men and beasts; several horses—destriers and the smaller Arabian mounts—wandered the field without a rider.

Hanging back as the knights pressed their brief advantage following the partial Muslim retreat, Reynald fought his way closer towards a chestnut gelding that was trying to revive his dead master. The horse had taken an arrow in its hindquarters, but still looked strong enough to ride. Catching hold of the reins, he calmed the animal, and climbed atop the saddle using the dead knight as a step. He swung up in time to see an archer who had broken through the line on horseback, swinging his viciously curved bow towards him with a drawn arrow.

Reynald recognized the Muslim scout by his garish attire. He belonged to the same party that had harassed them on their way to Ascalone only two days before. He wore a mail shirt of small brass plates sewn onto the leather, a turbaned helmet, and loose trousers of brilliant red and yellow silk. This was no common soldier; the revered yellow sash across his chest marked his as a member of Salehdin's family— perhaps a nephew, or maybe even a son of the wily old fox. He seemed no older than a boy. So many of the Muslim devils looked like ageless children.

He was too slow to deflect the arrows. He twisted in the saddle enough for it to pierce the fleshy part of his shoulder. It was not fatal, but it burned like the fires of Hell itself. He pulled it out with an agonized scream and stabbed it into the archer's underarm as he tried to run him through with a spear. The blood welled bright red from Reynald's shoulder. He slumped in the saddle. The archer came back at him, scimitar drawn, screaming his war cry. *Allah-il-allah! Allahu akbar!*

Reynald lifted his sword, blocking a jarring blow. The swords rang out, echoing above their grunts. He made a backhand cut; it swung wide. The horses danced, circling. A thrust narrowly missed. A backhand slap brought the tang of salt and copper to his mouth. Neither could gain the advantage.

Reynald swung two handed; he turned his horse, striking a blow that cut upwards, catching his opponent on the chest. The blow glanced off the armored cuirass and cut across the archer's throat. Blood sprayed horse and soldier. It pumped from the gash in a red fountain. The scimitar fell to the ground. Reynald stood up in the stirrups and kicked the wounded Sarrazin in the face. He fell back across the horse and slowly rolled off. Reynald was on him in a moment. He pulled him up by the collar and drove his sword into the man's heart with a vile curse against all Muslims. It brought him a moment of pure satisfaction to see the dead Muslim. He let out a labored breath and wiped the blood from his mouth. He spit on the man's face and swung up on his horse. The prisoners in the baggage-train needed rescuing.

Racing along the crumbling Muslim line, Reynald fought past the Mamluks and ran down two fleeing guards. The train was in chaos. The rain made a swamp of the ground. Animals strained against the tether line; men ran in circles, unsure what to do. Weapons and armor lay on the ground where deserters had abandoned them as they ran off. Reynald leapt from his horse behind a line of camels that the guards were cutting loose from their heavy burden of plunder so they could use them to escape.

Seeing a knight in the blue and gold tabard of Jherusalem, the prisoners lifted their voices, shouting for release. Reynald cut their bonds and set them loose. They gathered up the abandoned weapons and fell upon the rear of the Muslim army with the savage fury of their recent captivity.

* * * * *

The battle was a massacre. A thousand men fell in the first charge of the Ifranj; another thousand were ushered into the arms of the waiting virgins of Paradise on the second pass, despite Yusuf's best effort of a defense. Taqi ad-Din knelt weeping over the broken body of his son, oblivious to the slaughter around him. A scout had brought him and the vanguard of the army racing from the north into the heat of battle, only to see his beloved son fall beneath the sword of the accursed lord of al-Karak. This was not the dream Yusuf had long held of the infidel's defeat, nor was it the fulfillment of the *ifritah's* promise.

The commander of his Mamluks fought his way towards him and fell to his knee with a salute. He had lost his turbaned helmet and shield. A deep cut creased his forehead, dripping blood; his golden yellow coat was torn and spattered with mud and gore.

"We cannot hold the line much longer, my lord Salah ad-Din," he said. "We must pull back, or we are lost."

Yusuf gave his assent. The trumpet relayed the command. Slowly, the great horde of Islam gave ground to the enemy as it fought its way towards a more easily defensible position. It was an agonizingly slow crawl yielding the field without giving in to fear and the urge for outright retreat.

He stood proud and resolute, surrounded by his few remaining Mamluks. One by one they were falling, though, to the swords of the Ifranj. The whole of the day now hinged upon this moment. The left wing of the line wavered and fell back. It crumbled beneath the charge of the Nasrani. A knight broke through the faltering line and came at him. His sword rang free in one fluid, graceful motion; the man's head fell at his feet, dark eyes staring vacantly to Heaven. Blood sprayed across his gilded armor.

Two more knights both wearing the accursed blood-red cross of the Dawiyya hewed their way through the guard. Yusuf dispatched the closer man with a knife to the neck. The second man reared up before him, sword poised to deliver the fatal blow. He fell forward to his knees mid-stroke, a spearhead sprouting from his chest. Taqi ad-Din was on the knight with a leap, straddling him from behind, and slit his throat.

"Rot in Hell, infidel pig," he whispered in the knight's ear. Blood spurted from the wound, soaking the ground. He looked to

Yusuf. "The Leper has won the day, uncle. Save yourself. Too many have died already. Your death will not serve us here."

Yusuf growled with frustration and sheathed his sword. "Sound the retreat, Umar. Save as many as you can."

It was late in the afternoon when the battle had joined. The day was slipping towards nightfall now. If Allah was indeed merciful, they could escape under the cover of darkness. He turned his face skyward, letting the rain wash away the spattered blood. He wondered if the heavens wept for the fall of Islam, or for the destruction of so many because of one man's arrogant belief that the pursuit of *jihad* would make them invincible.

* * * * *

The tide of battle had finally turned. The Sarrazins were in flight; the victory won. It was the twenty-fifth day of November, the feast day of St. Catherine. It was to her and St. George that the army and the whole of the kingdom of Jherusalem gave praise and thanksgiving.

It would be several days before the army finished hunting down the last stragglers of Salehdin's defeated thousands and collect the spoils of their battle. The next day, the winter rains came in force, slowing the hunt and the Sarrazin retreat towards the Sinai. Those who escaped the Frankish pursuit found another threat in the Bedouin of the desert who guarded the southern frontier of Outremer. The last anyone saw of the sultan, he was riding a camel towards Egypt under the cover of darkness.

Baldwin called his vassals together and rode out from the hastily built camp they had set up to tend the wounded. Eleven hundred brave souls died in the battle; more than seven hundred lay wounded in the temporary hospital. It was a particularly difficult loss to bear for him personally. Among the dead, they had found his dear and devoted friend, Brother Theoderic of Saint-Lazare. He had died with his fellow Lazarites, fighting among the other prisoners of the *arrière-ban* who had given their lives to break the back of the Sarrazin army.

It was a somber ride they made to Lydda, even with so much for which they needed to thank God. The Bishop of Bethlehem led them out on the pilgrimage, riding before them with the reliquary of the True Cross, his arm in a sling. As was their right in their own seigneuries, the brothers Ibelin rode beside him as an escort, bearing the banners of Ibelin and Ramlah and Jherusalem. They followed the winding, muddy road in a long line, the Cross before them shining gloriously even in the steady rain as if with some heavenly light; the battle and all its bloodshed and death, they left behind on the slopes of Montgisart. They had come for prayer and reflection, nothing more.

The people of Lydda and Ramlah who had so recently fled for their lives towards Japhe, greeted them even before they entered the smoldering city with such gratitude that it moved Baldwin to what few tears his diseased eyes would allow him to shed. They lined the road, many of them holding palm branches; the women pressed in upon him as he rode by, just for the chance to touch the hem of his cloak. That he wore the veil of a leper never entered their minds; he was their king, the savior of their all too recent terror.

Outside the burnt shrine of the saint, they dismounted and took their turn praying before the fire-blackened tomb of St. George. While his city had burned, George had come to the rescue of his people in their battle to save Christendom. The celebrated saint of soldiers and warriors, he had appeared on many occasions since the First War of the Cross, particularly in defense of Lydda and Ramlah. Many of the knights, and especially the great lords that rode with him, had made this pilgrimage before. As a token of that pilgrimage, most had purchased a small badge or medallion as proof of the journey. It was the custom. They left them hanging on the tomb as offerings to the saint for the lives he had saved. Baldwin himself had also made the pilgrimage only a few years before. He stood holding his small pilgrim's medallion in his bandaged hand, waiting for his turn to pray.

He came lastly to the tomb to pay his respects. He alone knew that the Magdalen had saved them from the terrible specter of darkness and ruin, not St. George. It was to her that he owed his thanks. She had proven herself a true and loyal friend. He would not easily mistrust her again. He knew how hard it must be for her to see the sword lifted once more in defense of the city that, in all truth, had turned its back on God. Despite its claim as a light and a haven for all those who believe in God, it was the same den of iniquity the blessed Jhesú had cursed. For all its churches and its pilgrims, for all its priests and all their prayers, for all its supposed sanctity among the three religions that claimed it for its own, it was still a place of greed and malice, a dark place where the glory of God had long ago departed. Jherusalem was a stumbling block, a once great city that had seen far more blood shed in the name of God, than all the sacrifices He had required of the Jews in their day. God had destroyed it once before in fulfillment of prophecy. When might He do so again?

Baldwin took the pilgrim's medallion and draped it with care from the edge of the battered tomb. It hung inconspicuously among the others that had been left, twisting and turning on its thin chain of silver;

before a saint, even a king was accounted as the most common of men—even the king of once holy Jherusalem.

He paused, his hand upon the medal, thinking about the knights who had died defending the dream that was supposed to be the kingdom of Heaven on earth. He wondered if the sacrifice had been truly worth the loss of so much life. He wondered if it would have been far better if the kingdom had simply fallen to the enemy.

Tomorrow, or the next day, he would go to the Holy Sepulcher and pray publicly and openly with all humility as a good king ought, giving thanks for the deliverance of his people and his kingdom. Today, however, he would pray as a simple man who had seen the miraculous. A man who knew God had blessed him. He owed God, and the Magdalen, that much devotion.

* * * * *

The winter rains came, soaking the dry desert ground with much needed water. It washed away the gore of battle. The blood of Muslim and Nasrani alike mingled in muddy pools and seeped into the soil, insuring that the presence of Islam would endure in the land long after the memory of the fallen had faded. Salah ad-Din had envisioned this manner of presence for his people when he set out to conquer beloved Urshalim. Of course, he did not expect to be fleeing for his very life on the back of a recalcitrant camel towards the border of Egypt.

His army lay destroyed, broken like shards of cheap pottery by the swords of the worthless Ifranj. Making it back to his camp at al-Arish was a small miracle. Only a fraction of the army he had set out with a week ago returned. The Bedouin harassed them every step of the way and plundered their train, leaving them without food, water, or provisions of any kind. Of the men that remained, many died of starvation.

Twenty-six thousand men wasted on a fruitless campaign from which it would take more than a season or two to recover. It was certainly a stunning defeat, but he would live it down, as difficult as it would be to face humiliation and ridicule from those who resented his leadership. War sometimes took these unexpected turns. Besides, he could always find men who were eager to give their lives to see the infidels finally destroyed.

What he could not abide was the shame brought down on the house of Islam by his defeat—by his own stubbornness and foolish arrogance. He had made a grave error in judgment—no, two errors. He had trusted the word of an *ifritah* that Urshalim would fall. Worse, he had believed in an ancient Arab proverb that said that an army of sheep led by a lion would defeat an army of lions led by a sheep. The proverb embodied all he believed about warfare and leadership; that a leader needed only to be strong and faithful to the will of Allah, and he could lead even the weakest of men to victory in battle. Only the Leper had proven himself a lion of equal ability rather than a lamb. He had underestimated *Al-Abras*, the leper of Urshalim. He would not make that same mistake again.

At the border of the Sinai, he was unexpectedly met by a search party sent by al-Qadi al-Fadil who had set out from al-Qihara to bring a relief column into what he expected would be a conquered land. He sent messages by pigeon-post to his brother Saif ad-Din al-Adil, announcing his soon return, provided any rebels thought the rumors of his demise were true. Privately, however, he wrote to his brother that Allah had punished all Muslims for their schismatic squabbling and for their refusal to join as one in the cause of *jihad*. If they were to retake Urshalim from the Nasrani, they would have to unite. Islam was to be one faith, one people, and one land under the banner of the crescent. Only then, would they drive the Nasrani back into the sea. He prayed that day would come and vowed he would not rest until it did.

* * * * *

The breeze sighed softly through the mist-laden trees, whispering of dreams and the quiet rest of slumber. Mary shed her glamour and her cloak as she stepped back into her own world and fell into a gentle stride that barely disturbed the leafy mold of the forest path. The moon had risen large and round just as the sun had set in all its wondrous beauty. The forest was alive with shadows that danced in the mingled light of Eden's dusk.

She came at last to the ancient tree that was the center of her power and her very being. She set the sword against the trunk with care and hung the shield among the lower branches. She bowed to them, whispering a prayer of thanks and stepped away. They were not hers to keep, but ancient weapons that she had borrowed more than once in the past thousand years. She would no doubt need to use them again before too long.

A stream of cool, clear water ran nearby and a place where she could rest her head. The magic had taken more from her than she had wanted. Without it, though, the army of Jherusalem would have fallen into darkness and ruin. She needed only to rest her body to rekindle its fire. She dared not think about how long her absence would be in the world of men. She prayed it would not be long. Baldwin needed to know where the loyalties of the Master of the Templars lay, but she was too weary to go to him now.

"That, my lady, was most unwise, your interference on the battlefield."

Her hand was on the hilt of the sword even before he finished speaking. She lifted it dangerously close to his throat. The gilded script on the blade burst into illusory fire.

"No less unwise than your trespass into this place, from which your race has long been expelled," she said.

A mild chuckle of laughter escaped the hood of the enemy's dark cloak. She caught a brief glimpse of a strong, aquiline nose and the shadow of a beard, but nothing more. "You forget whose power I possess—how closely akin it is to your own."

The sword lifted a fraction in her hand. "A power you stole through treachery and murder."

He pushed aside the tip of the sword with the back of his hand. "Murder is such a strong word, my lady. Besides, Salome is not dead, only asleep. And so she will remain unless you break the bond that exists between us."

"What do you want of me, Simon?" she said, stepping back from her ancient enemy, and dropped her sword.

"You were warned before not to interfere in the affairs of Sion. Or have you learned nothing from the price the king has paid for your protection?" he said, lifting his chin. "Surrender Jherusalem to me, and I will spare Baldwin's suffering."

"I made a promise I will not break, not even to save his life."

"The boy's death is on your head, then—not mine."

She raised the sword again, threatening. "I will not rest until Sion is no more than a memory and a whisper of a myth."

"Your time has passed, Mariamne, while I have grown only stronger," he said. "I have nothing to fear from you."

She glared at him, trying to imagine the features of the face hidden beneath his cloak. She tried to see if she had ever seen anything about him that seemed familiar; some turn of his head or movement of his body; some quality of his voice she had heard before; anything that would clue her in to his identity. There was nothing. He was a stranger, a mystery without answer.

"If you have nothing to fear from me, then show me whose face you hide behind now, Simon."

He laughed at her. The sound was cold, icy. "And ruin this delightful little game we've played for so long. I couldn't do that to you; surely you know that by now."

"I had to try—you understand."

The Master of Sion stepped closer. A tremor of fear, of unexpected weakness, twisted through her shifting memories. She shuddered. He touched her face. Power reached out to power; memory burned like fire, consuming her anger, her hatred, and the grief of too many years.

"Tell me where she is, Simon?"

"In a place where you'll never find her," he said and then he was gone.

She fell, weeping to the ground, and pulled the sword close to her body. It was a poor excuse for comfort, but it did so all the same. Her heart groaned. *Forgive me, Salome*, she whispered. *Forgive me, my dearest daughter.*

LE CHASTELLET
1179

† CHAPTER TWELVE

His truth shall compass thee with a shield: thou shalt not be afraid of the terror of the night.
—*Psalms 90:5*

The bishop of Rome was in an ill-humored mood. Nor were the findings of the Third Lateran Council likely to improve that foul mood, either. Four days of discussion, partisan arguments, finger pointing, and what, at times, had nearly come to fist-a-cuffs among the more outspoken clerics, had resolved nothing more than a few issues on papal elections, the repression of heresy, and a rather heated decision to bring the Templars back into the observation of canonical regulations. The most important issue of sending much needed help to the Kingdom of Jherusalem had gone unaddressed. There would be no new war in the Holy Land.

Given the pontiff's mood, it was a little surprising that he requested a private audience with Archbishop William of Tyre. The evening bell came and with it the singing of Compline. A gaggle of rain-soaked monks hurried through the Lateran doors, late for their prayers. A great gust of a draft, given life by the sudden opening of the doors set the shadows and the candle-flames of the cathedral to dancing; it snuffed out half the flames, casting the hall into a dim light. In their absence, the shadows advanced eager to claim more for the darkness. Outside, wind and rain drenched the ancient stonework of Rome. A damp chill crept into the narrowest of crevices and into the candlelit nave of the *Archbasilica Sanctissimi Salvatoris*, the Basilica of the Most Holy Savior. Thunder rumbled in the distance.

William walked the length of the nave, escorted by a young wide-eyed novice who tried his desperate best not to badger him with too many questions about the great kingdom of Jherusalem in Outremer.

A glimmer of gold winked at them from every angle. The wide eyes of saints and angels, and even the blessed Savior himself, looked down on them from the heights of the shadowed ceiling, their penetrating gaze piercing his soul, questioning the depth of his professed faith and the strength of his devotion to God.

The palace and its architecture breathed sacredness, its airy lightness whispering of unseen spirits and the immortality of the soul. Every stone, every arch and molded column, every surface decorated with exquisite frescoes whose colors seemed to shine with some inner luminance, drew the mind's eye to the mysteries of the eternal Godhead.

A millennium of bishops had each added their own touch to the growing majesty of the Lateran. From the familial manor of a pagan Roman consul, it had risen to the splendor of a palace built up to house the Vicar of Christ on earth. Layer upon layer of history had anointed the halls with its memories, the flesh and bone of its buried saints adding to its holiness. Men aspired to the thrones of kingdoms and nations by the strength of the swords and the right of royal blood; but the chair of Peter devolved upon simple men by the depth of their self-sacrifice and the manifold acclaim of their humility among men.

The Holy Father received him without ceremony, and alone, in the ornate apse of the basilica. A dark-robed, cherub-faced young scribe dismissed himself as soon as William approached the papal throne. There would be no interruptions to their conversation.

Five days ago, Pope Alexander had sat enthroned on his raised dais, surrounded by his cardinals and the prefects, senators, and consuls of Rome in all their ecclesiastical panoply. He sat now, alone, attended only—or so one hoped and prayed—by the invisible angels of Heaven.

The council had ended, the delegates dismissed. Still, voices aplenty echoed through the corridors of the Lateran Palace, spiraling aloft into the upper airs of the basilica's spacious dome. The voices mingled with others he had heard during his time in Rome, rumors that whispered of heresies long held secret. Rome was a city built on secrets; the Lateran was at the center of them all.

Despite cope and miter, crosier and crown, Pope Alexander III, formerly Rolando Bandinelli of Tuscany and chief papal negotiator with Emperor Frederick Barbarossa seemed a man far older than his seventy-four years. White-haired and wrinkled, he sat huddled in his overly large white throne with the weight of all Christendom laid upon his thin, frail shoulders. Neither age, nor the weight of his solemn office, however, could bend his will to the whims of men. He was not a man easily bullied or cowed for the sake of simple expediency. His word came from God. He was the Vicar of Christ.

Only this evening, the Vicar of Christ chose to set aside the splendid regalia of his divine calling and meet with him as an equal, servant-to-servant, man to man, with a man without equal.

William knelt at the bottom of the stairs as the Holy Father descended. Alexander extended his hand, holding out his bishop's ring; William kissed it. He wiped a hand across his wet tonsure, and cleared his throat. "Forgive my appearance, Your Holiness," he said, "but I was just about to begin my evening prayers when your summons came. I wasn't expecting to be called out in the midst of a storm."

Alexander extended a hand, gesturing towards the stairs of the dais and an invitation to sit. "I am sorry about the hour, my son—and the rain," said the Bishop of Rome. "But it was necessary that I speak with you alone—tonight."

The Pope seemed to pause, hesitating over some inner conflict of his thoughts. He glanced around the papal *cathedra*, easing his mind that they were alone. Whatever the Holy Father needed to say, it would no doubt be best if a casual onlooker—or anyone else for that matter—did not overhear it. "I am troubled by certain rumors of late concerning the Templar Knights that have found their way to my door."

William had hoped that the Papal Father had summoned him to discuss a possible new expedition—he was wrong. Now he lost all sense of propriety towards the man who was speaking to him. He could not contain his impulse to question when he should have been listening. "What sort of rumors?"

Thunder pealed outside the basilica windows. The noise rumbled, echoing through the hall. It was a great noise, a commotion like an arming for war; and then sudden silence, with only the voice of an old man in its midst to keep it from drowning out all memory of sound.

The pontiff glanced at him. His hand clenched the staff of his crosier. His rheumy eyes dropped to the ring on his finger that was the symbol of his office as Bishop of Rome. He turned it with his thumb, weighing his words carefully. "Have you ever had occasion to call into question the actions of the Knights Templar—their motives or reasons, perhaps, for existence?"

"It is certainly no secret that I have no love for the military orders," William said, "but I know nothing that would suggest anything... suspicious or untoward, if that is what you mean—except, perhaps, once."

It was a lie, of course—not an outright falsehood, but certainly a misrepresentation of the truth. He was reluctant to trust the papal father too quickly, nor without reason to do so. Too many popes of late were far more concerned with the temporal than the spiritual. Men far more concerned with the politics of their actions than the Vicar of Christ ought to be.

One of Alexander's bushy white eyebrows rose in a curious arch. William looked at him narrowly, his bewilderment growing. Alexander's face seemed to shadow over with concern. He was hedging, almost afraid to say too much.

Alexander suspected something—of that, he was certain. If he gave him nothing now on which to set his sights, then suspicion could just as well end up falling on him. At the very least, it would be better to push the suspicion off to where it actually belonged, regardless of how that suspicion arose. He was walking the sword's edge now between innocence and excommunication. He prayed God would forgive him if he made a grave error in judgment.

"Once, not many years ago, now," William began, hesitantly, "when he lay abed with a fever, King Amaury questioned me about the truth of the resurrection of the body. At the time, I thought it only typical of the fears that men have of death, especially when they are so close to it—now I wonder if he had been influenced by someone who gave him cause to question his faith, perhaps, even encouraged it—someone like a Templar. It was no secret that Amaury and the Templars were of like minds—at least until Saint-Amant destroyed any chance of peace with the Assassins. In fact, His Highness, King Baldwin, has on several occasions, made mention to me of his concerns over whether the Templars, at least in part, have cause to hide something of their affairs from the eyes of the Church."

Alexander let out a deep sigh that seemed to take far more from him than a simple exhalation of breath. He reached out a frail, vein-knotted hand and touched William's knee. "You can see, then, my concern over the Templars," he said. "They are a problem that continues to unfold. They have grown too strong I fear; and so has their pride, if not their ambition. I have decided to appoint a man to oversee them during this time while the Order is brought back under the observation of canonical rule. It is certainly not something they will take easily or without rancor." He looked at William; he patted his knee and squeezed it. "They are powerful, and have allies even more powerful. Perhaps, the Holy See was unwise to have given them so much authority. Nor was it wise to make them accountable only to the Pope. We seduced ourselves with the prospect of an army of monks whose sole purpose was to see the cause of Christ advanced against the enemies of the Church at any cost. We were wrong. For that reason, my son, I need you to be my eyes and ears in Jherusalem."

"You want *me* to spy against the Templars for you? —Why not one of the other delegates?"

"You alone among the Jherusalem delegates supported our call for the Templars to be brought to heel—the others all opposed us."

"I see," William started to say with suspicion, but bit his tongue, schooling it to a more trusting tone towards the representative of Christ on earth.

"I have it on good authority that a heresy has found its way into the Order of the Templars; a deliberate and calculated plot to use the Church against itself—a plot stretching back three or four generations for sure, perhaps many, many more. They have taken on the guise of fellow servants of Christ—they pray our prayers, worship in our churches, yet all the while secretly dedicating their lives to the worship of the great god and goddess of the ancient pagans. If this is true, I cannot permit it to go unchecked. They are nothing less than wolves in sheep's clothing. They must be rooted out and destroyed before they infect the rest of Christendom."

The very mention of heresy in Outremer, in a land that bred religion and heresy and sectarianism with each new day, was like accusing the sea of crashing with waves. It was only natural that it did so. This land of shifting sands and the fiery blast of the desert wind was a crucible that purged the human spirit of the weight of its mortality and left only the spark that sought the infinite, the divine. All the same, it set William on edge; it made him suspicious, if not alarmed.

Lightning flashed through the arched windows above the aged pontiff's throne. Thunder cracked, seeming to split the heavens with its deafening noise. William startled at the sound. The candlelight shrank in fear of the storm's gathering fury.

Alexander leaned closer, almost whispering. "What if I could show you evidence of a conspiracy; one with the lies of a heresy firmly set within its center; one which advocates nothing less than the destruction of the Church of Rome and the creation of a new one in Jherusalem? What if I told you that an enemy walks among them, doing the bidding of his master Satan?"

"I would think that there is, indeed, an enemy we would do well to fear," William said.

"You are young enough still I fear, my son," said Alexander, rising to his feet, "that you may yet see the signs of the enemy's deepest held ambition before all is said and done. When you hear the cry for the

Holy See to be moved from Rome to Jherusalem, then you'll know that the plans of the enemy are very near their fulfillment."

"Then we must pray, Your Holiness," William said, "that that day never dawns."

* * * * *

The weather had turned yet again in this season of ever-constant change. The promised warmth of spring turned overnight to that which usually followed so closely on the heels of Christmastide and Candlemas. The wind blew out of the north, a cold breeze laden with the chill of snow that lay upon the heights of Hermon. It set the bright green foliage of new growth to sudden dormancy. The weather boded ill for the days ahead, and the imminent campaign of war that crept closer with each passing day.

Despite the cold that bit into the raw open sores of his disease, Baldwin rubbed his gloved hands together to give them a spark of warmth. Then, with a rare and sudden burst of laughter, he set his heels to his fiery Arab mount, urging it away into a gallop. Ri'jl stamped his hooves and set off at a run. It was a race to the bare, skeletal oak brooding over the crossing with the constant care of an aged grandparent.

The crossing at Jacob's Ford lay upon an ancient road that rose in the hot desert sands of distant Egypt and wound its long slow way northwards through the lands of the Bible to sun-girt Damascus which the Arabs claimed was the oldest city in the world. It was the olden Way of the Philistines which led by the sea—the Via Maris of the Romans who had made of all roads, one, and twin to the King's Highway leading up the winding caravan route from fabled Araby. For long seasons out of count, a large and solitary oak tree commanded the banks of the ancient crossing of the Jordan where Jacob had wrestled with the angel of God. It stood as a silent sentinel that had seen its share of the continual movements of the local tribesmen with their flocks from one green pasturage on the heights of the Golan to another.

The ford lay upon a road hoary with age amidst a strip of frontier nigh unto the Sea of Tiberias that neither Christian nor Muslim controlled, but both had claimed. It was for that reason that Baldwin's new castle at the ford, overlooking the only approach to the north and to Damascus, only one day's travel distant, had caused the Sarrazins and their ever-wily sultan so much consternation.

Reynald's heavier palfrey was no match for Baldwin's lighter and faster Arabian. Baldwin reined Ri'jl in beneath the oak and held out a gloved hand, waiting for his cousin to fill it with the winner's coin. The prince of Oultrejourdain was a gracious loser, but not a quiet one.

"Had I a lighter horse and half a length's lead, I might have bested you, Your Highness," said Reynald de Châtillon.

"That and a few stones less weight, and you might have very well, my lord of Kerak," Baldwin replied in his halting voice. He swept off his helmet with a gloved hand and grinned crookedly, the best he could offer with a face palsied with disease. The illness had grown worse in recent months, keeping pace with a body that had grown leaner with his passing from adolescence to manhood. "Excuses, however, are nothing more than that—excuses."

Reynald spurred his horse as it danced sideways, urging it shoulder to shoulder with Ri'jl, and likewise removed his helmet. "Excuses they are, indeed. I am afraid age creates that disadvantage, Sire. It takes a toll on body and mind, and gives nothing in return. When I had your years, I was a trim, fit young knight with ceaseless energy. I could fight in a battle and my arm seldom tired. I fought once for two days with an arrow in my ribs. Now... now, I am"—he held up a hand; let it drop—"what you see." He chuckled. "Still, it was a pleasure to see you laugh and smile again, Your Highness, even if it was at the expense of my pride, as well as my purse. It has been too long since anyone has seen that from our king."

Baldwin glanced away, watching a small band of shepherds leading their flocks over a bald, green hill on the far side of the Jordan. A bleating rose on the breeze. Clouds came, and passed, blotting the sun for a moment, before they blew off towards the east, chasing the broken, hill-strewn horizon. He picked at a stem of dried grass from his cloak and tossed it aside. He looked at Reynald.

"You're right, cousin," he said, drawing a deep breath. "It has been far, far too long."

"Your heart weighs heavily for the kingdom. You've had far too much to consider in the face of your illness."

It was true, all that Reynald said. Despite his success against Salehdin at Montgisart more than a year before, it was fear that urged him to such haste in the building of a fortress on the edge of the kingdom and the edge of Muslim forbearance. It was fear that led him to give in to the Templars in their request to garrison the castle despite the suspicions the Magdalen had against them and their traitorous master. *Watch him closely, Your Highness. Trust nothing the Templars do or ask*, she had warned him. He had heeded her words, except now he needed their strength of arms to hold the castle against the Sarrazins. It was fear that made him cautious, that made him want to cower behind stout walls and locked doors, hidden away from the storm of war that threatened always to break upon them with sudden fury. Fear of the doom he felt laid upon him; fear of what his illness was doing to him, mind and body; and fear of the horrible, agonizing torment that would await his people if the kingdom fell because of his actions—or his inaction. It drove him to constant distraction and worry; it rendered him impotent to make even the simplest decision.

"You've only done what was necessary, Your Highness, for the good of our kingdom and for the chance of peace, if your heart is still set on that course," Reynald said, seeming to read his mind and mood. "Those damned Sarrazins will think twice before mounting any attack on Jherusalem from Damascus."

He glanced at his Regent doubtfully. For Reynald de Châtillon to offer such council, when war was so much more to his thinking, was a sure sign of his allegiance—at least as far as he could impress upon him an alternative worth supporting. He had no doubt that the war-mongering lord of Kerak would act on his own impulses if he felt it necessary, despite his loyalty to his king.

"They've complained already that it's a breach of truce," Baldwin said. His gaze fell to his gloved hand clasped stiffly about the reins. "Salehdin has raised his offer from sixty thousand to one hundred thousand dinars, if I demolish Le Chastellet."

Reynald snorted his disdain. His horse capered a step or two; he brought the spirited animal back under control with a sharp snap of the reins. "They complain of the breach, Sire, only because you were clever enough to beat them to it. You know as well as I, that any truce between us, will only delay the inevitable. It is breathing space, Your Highness, and nothing more. Let us not be fools. Salehdin's offer of coin to buy your compliance is a diversion. He is too busy bringing the rebels at Ba'albek into submission. Once that small problem is settled, he'll turn to arms rather than coin to deal with Le Chastellet." Reynald jutted his chin towards the half-built castle crowning the hill to the west of the Jordan. "He knows the importance of our control of this crossing. He fears what we may do to him."

The construction of Le Chastellet was a bold move. It would be the cornerstone of the kingdom's defenses in the north, just as Kerak and Montreal were in the south with the caravan route through the desert so close. It would be a constant thorn in Salehdin's plans to unify the lands of Islam: he would have to garrison an army large enough to defend Damascus. A brilliant move—so said the Old Knight himself. Humphrey praised him for his foresight in deciding to fortify such a strategic position. *A masterful stroke, Your Highness*, he had laughed. *You will catch the old fox completely off his guard. Damascus is the shining jewel in his crown. Between Le Chastellet and the Assassins, you have given him very little wiggle room to insure the safety of his precious city.*

Since Montgisart, Humphrey had entrusted a good many decisions of war to him, as he had this one. So why was he so fearful, if a personage no less the great Constable himself had seen the merit of his strategies?

"And what if I have misstepped and brought ruin upon our people and the kingdom?" Baldwin said.

Reynald's pale gaze caught him like a bolt of steel. "Building Le Chastellet will not set us on the path to war, Your Majesty, any more than praying the rosary will make me Pope—but the promise of doing nothing surely will."

"I gave my word, Reynald."

"As did the sultan. And many times more than this. This is not about honor, cousin: it is about our survival against an enemy who has sworn to see us driven from this land by any means possible. You gave Salehdin enough to think about and fear at Montgisart. But if we do not take war to the Muslims, they will surely bring it to us."

Baldwin laughed sourly. "Spoken like a true knight of Outremer."

Reynald slapped his helmet on his head. "No, Your Majesty," he said tersely. "Spoken like a lord of Jherusalem and the High Court. Now, shall we race back to the castle? Double or nothing?"

* * * * *

Darkness fell about Yusuf like a heavy cloak. It stole his breath, squeezing ever tighter as he struggled desperately against its hold. All around him echoed the clash of steel upon steel and the sound of men crying in the agony of pain and the stark, sheer terror of their fears. A wind blew, driving the shadows against them. In the midst of the deepening blackness, two eyes glowed red like burning embers of fire.

Images flashed before his eyes, familiar, as they were fearful; his wive, his sons, his daughters, cast into the desert sands to be meat for the vultures circling overhead. Al-Qihara was in flames; the banners of his enemies flew above his Citadel. The piercing wail of a scream rose above the deafening tumult and terror of war. The scream was his, crying out to Allah to protect him from the daemon that raged against them with all the fury of Hell.

Salah ad-Din Yusuf awoke, gasping and sweating, clinging to the bedding as though it was a shield. A small, wickedly curved dagger had found its way into his hand. He never slept anywhere without one—not since the day the Old Man of the Mountain had taught him the meaning of disloyalty and betrayal.

A hand reached out to him, warm and gentle, feminine. It touched his shoulder, caressed the contour of his scarred back with the tip of a finger. Ismat's voice whispered to him from the depths of their pillowed bed. "It was only a dream, my lord. You are safe here. Nothing can come against you within the walls of the harem of Dimasq."

He had returned to his beloved city less than a week ago after dealing with a minor revolt in Ba'albek that occupied more of the spring season than he had anticipated or liked. The people of Ba'albek were a troublesome lot, just as they were in the days when his father had governed the ancient city. He would rather have turned his attention to the Ifranj and the troublesome fortress they were building only a day's journey from Dimasq.

"Wards and hedge-magics will hardly protect against the fears that rise in a man's sleep," he complained and immediately regretted his sharp words. He drew up his knees into the tight circle of his arms.

Ismat shifted in the bed; her chin came to rest on his knees. Large, round eyes, which, in the light of day were as dark and shimmering as a summer's night, looked up at him from a dusky face, filling his sight with their gaze. Her hand stroked his beard. "What is it you fear, my lord, my love?"

He thought on her words for a moment, and found that she had seen straight through the heart of the dream he tried to brush aside with such false bravado.

"Having done all I can and it not mattering. That is what I fear, my beauty of the desert," he said. "I hold Suriya and Dimasq in one hand, Egypt and al-Qihara in the other. And yet, in between, the Ifranj remain, firm and resolute. No matter what I do, Al-Abras withholds Urshalim from me. Worse, he thumbs his nose at me and spits defiance at every turn." His head fell, hanging between his knees. His voice turned to a faint whisper. "I fear that Allah has forsaken me for my pride."

Ismat kissed him tenderly and pulled on his hand, lying back amidst the pillows. "Come back to sleep, my heart. Forget the Ifranj and your thoughts of war for one night."

"How can I forget the Ifranj," he said, pulling his hand free of hers. "They are a constant plague on my every waking thought."

"You need sleep, my lord," she purred. "I can help you forget, if you'll only let me."

"Is that what you think the king of the Ifranj is doing right now—worrying about whether or not he is having a good night's rest? I doubt it, my lady," Yusuf said sourly. "I sincerely doubt it."

In one fluid motion, he was up and out of their comfortable nest of pillows and bed linens, making his escape towards the balcony and freedom. Mercifully, Ismat allowed him his privacy.

Her words, however, did not. They followed him, denying him any thought of peace or comfort. He fled the harem, beating a retreat through a winding maze of delicately carved lattice screens and filmy gauze curtains. Just as in his dreams, the shadows and the darkness assailed him, choking the breath from him, until he stumbled onto a delicately pillared balcony crowded with potted trees and sleeping blossoms, overlooking a thin, gurgling finger of the Barada.

The air, soft and luminous with the rising of the crescent moon, and stirred by a gentle breeze, clung to him with the fragrances of the night. Even as he caught his breath, his heart pounding within the hollow cavity of his chest, Ismat's words found him again, whispering.

What is it you fear, my lord?

He growled and bowed his head. A fist came up; it pounded the rail of the balcony, slowly and gently. He feared far too many things concerning the godless Ifranj of late. Ever since that fateful day at Montgisart, where he had suffered a defeat greater than any he had had before, where the swords of the Ifranj had spilled far too much Muslim blood, he had grown ever more afraid to make war directly against the Leper King, or his kingdom. It was more than that, though.

How could he confront what he had trouble admitting even to himself—that he was afraid of the magic used against him, the very magic he had used to bring Egypt into his hand? Such was the magic of the Seal of Suleiman that could command the *jinn* and *afrit* alike, and all the other invisible spirits of the air. He was not a cowardly man, only one who understood the power such spirits could give to those who commanded them.

A blur of grey and a beating of wings startled him from his musings and his fears, or rather, his dozing. He had fallen asleep briefly, it seemed, curled against the balustrade. A pigeon settled on his knee, blinking innocently, cooing gladness for the nearness of its master. He swept up the cooing creature and the message bound tightly to its leg, and held them to his chest. The bird and the message were from his nephew, Farrukh-Shah, the governor of that same Ba'albek that had caused him so much trouble of late.

The message was simple, yet troubling for the words it relayed.

175

Most gracious and illustrious uncle, greetings. As you commanded, I have kept watch over the Ifranj at Jisr Ya'kub. As you feared, they have finished construction of a tower and the outer ring of the wall. Al-Abras seems determined to keep his army in the field to protect the work. Advise me what I should do against the infidels...

Having read the message a third time—or was it a fourth—Yusuf passed a hand over his eyes with a sigh and let the small piece of parchment fall from his hand. Darkness quickly swallowed it as it floated down and down on the fragrant breeze, drifting towards the gurgling Barada. Fate, or Allah, was forcing his hand now to react to a situation he had already tried more than once to resolve without war and bloodshed.

No matter what fears or terrors he harbored of magic and the spirits of the invisible realms, he knew he had to confront the Ifranj. He needed to ride out against them and destroy the offending fortress they sought so eagerly to build as a threat to Dimasq and the northern roads into Suriya. A fortress that breached the oath of peace that Nasrani and Muslim alike vowed repeatedly to keep between them.

The choice was simple—particularly since the Nasrani king made it for him. He could not rest until he saw the Ifranj driven back for the last time or he lay dead on a field of battle. Before he rode out, however, to face the Ifranj and his newfound fate, or his fears, he would arm himself with the humility of his prayers and the firm hope that Allah—may his name be praised forever—would smile favorably upon his servant once more. He only prayed that Allah would not demand his blood as a sacrifice for the black sins of his arrogance.

Even before he could gird himself in the armor of his prayers and faith, Ismat had decided on a far different course of action, though it had nothing to do with war or leaving him to his privacy. She came, and wrapping her arms gently about his waist, led him back through the twisting, shadowed maze of the harem into the waiting nest of pillows and linens, and a hot, steaming bath, fragrant with attar of roses that his lady had seen fit to ready in his absence.

* * * * *

Sunlight pierced the ornate hall, slanting across the floor, gilding the thin haze of incense hanging in the air. The room grew warm with the sun's soft touch. The slave girl had an equally soft and gentle touch. She dipped the reed into the small inkpot at her feet and dabbed the dark henna on Sibylla's milk-white hand, adding to the intricate pattern of dots and whorls she had been painting for the better part of the last hour.

In her brother's absence, Sibylla stood in his place at Court as she often had in the past year, hearing what minor grievances petitioners brought before the crown that could not wait for Baldwin's return. This last hour, though, she set aside for her own pleasure. She made herself a promise to take a moment or two to enjoy a simple, if only brief, pause in the proceedings her brother had left for her, a chance to find even the smallest bit of silence amidst the chaos of the Court.

Her mother sat with her by the narrow, latticed windows of the solar, her hands busy with the tiny stitches of the needlework that lay in her lap. Their conversation was sporadic, a sort meant for women's ears alone; they exchanged the idle gossip of Court and the whispered secrets of affairs among the more flamboyant courtiers. One particularly delicious scandal making the rounds at present was the rumored liaisons between Heraclius, the profligate Archbishop of Caesarea, and the beautiful widow of a merchant of Naples, Pascua de Riveri. Sibylla and Agnes felt no fear or threat from the small, dark Muslim slave who sat at their feet. Shahdi was a young and pretty thing, but she was deaf and mute, a prisoner of a world of silence who heard nothing of their conversations. She would only smile and bow her head, content with her silence and in her art of dabbing her mistress' hands and feet with henna.

It was a lovely scene they made in the women's quarter of the palace; one of family and devotion; of the quiet pursuits of womanhood. Her son of fifteen months, Baudinouet—named for her brother the king—sat on the floor. He laughed happily, striking his wooden toy camelopard repeatedly against the floor. It had been a gift from his great-uncle, the Seneschal, a miniature of the strange and exotic, long-necked, spotted animal that had passed through Jherusalem not long ago in a caravan bound for the East and the fabled menagerie of the Caliph of Baghdad.

A musician struck up a song on a lute beyond the layers of veiling curtains and finely carved lattices that gathered the shifting shadows of the room and made them one with the dark silhouettes of ferns and trees and the hanging tapestries that covered the walls. It was a troubadour's song—a female's no less, a trobairitz: one Azalaïs de Porcairagues by name. It was one of many songs of high chivalry and forbidden romance—a *chanson d'amour*—making their way lately from Provençe and the Languedoc of France.

In the somber, haunting song, Sibylla's heartfelt the cold sadness of a husband lost. The same loneliness Azalaïs portrayed in her lament over the death of her friend, another troubadour. She would have given a year or more of her life to put aside all the cares of the palace and the court, and exchange them for a chance at real and lasting happiness. What she had now was an... existence—a life dictated by duty and responsibility to a people who knew nothing of her plight or her fears, of her deep longing for a life that was hers alone.

She longed to have nothing more than her son and a loving husband in a simple manor house like Aqua Bella, with servants who thought of them as something all together different and wonderful in a world not so wonderful. Perhaps, her mother and brother—her dear brother, whom she loved—released from his illness at long last, to enjoy the life and simple joys of an ordinary man.

It would not be so, though—it could never be so—so long as the cursed blood of kings pulsed in her veins and Jherusalem stood with the cross emblazoned upon her battlements.

A tear slid down Sibylla's cheek. She dashed it away discreetly with a finger. "I've made up my mind, mother," she said softly; then more boldly, as she pulled off her silken veil trimmed with a golden ribbon and folded it neatly in her lap. "If I am to marry, then it will be a man of my own choosing. A man I love—not some grey-haired lord with one foot in the grave and the other in his mistress' doorway every time my brother calls him off to war."

She glanced from her son, playing so quietly on the floor, to her mother who took her time in answering. She usually did. Her answer, though, was not what she expected. Agnes leaned over from her chair and tousled her grandson's head of unruly golden curls. "Men are men, Sibylla. They will do as they please, whether they love you or not. The man you choose must command the respect of the High Court," she said without hint of rebuke. "He will not be just your husband, Sibylla, but king in his own right after your brother. He must be able to lead, if you wish Baldwin and the Court to give its consent. Can he do so?"

Sibylla did not mention her lover by name. She did not need to. Her mother knew; they had spoken of Guion de Lusignan often enough of late. He had virtues she thought, if anyone chose to see them: beauty, strength, and courage—charisma. At least he was not one of the lords of Jherusalem. Still, she found herself defending him.

"As king, Guion can almost assuredly guarantee help from our cousin, King Henry of England, against the Sarrazins," she said. "He was Henry's vassal once."

"King Henry, indeed! Henry the priest-killer you mean," Agnes sneered. "Henry cares more about his privileges than making any expedition to Jherusalem."

"Guion has a bond with Henry, mother—a bond of blood... and the bond of magic that is the heritage of the House of Anjou and Lusignan."

Agnes smiled deceptively. Sibylla had never thought of her mother as anything other than beautiful. Suddenly, in that arresting smile, she saw the woman that rumor and innuendo spoke of as cunning and dissolute in getting what she wanted in a world ruled by men. Agnes knew how to use her beauty—however fading—to bend the weak wills of men to her need or whim. Sibylla was just now learning to use a certain measure of that same power to her own advantage.

"You are certainly your mother's daughter, Sibylla," said Agnes, snipping the thread of her needlework with her teeth. "What do you know of that bond of magic?"

For a moment, Sibylla thought she had said too much. Her mother's voice had taken on a peculiar tone—one that warned her not to give away too much more. Still, she had spoken her mind. She could only see now what it would gain. Her momentary pause gave her mother the answer she sought.

"Guion," Agnes said with a wistful sigh.

"He spoke without thinking once in a fit of anger. A remark a knight made about his family being descended from a faerie—that he had the right to be king," she said quickly—too quickly. "He would say nothing else, however much I pressed him."

Her mother laughed; it was a throaty, unsettling sound. Her gaze widened, and then narrowed, the light in her eyes dancing wildly. "And now you fear what he told you. You don't understand."

"No," she whispered.

Agnes let an uncomfortable silence settle between them. Sibylla glanced away, letting her eyes fall to her son. He crawled over to her, holding up his chubby hands. The thought of magic gave her a shiver. It reminded her of her brother and the tiny golden ring he had made for her from rays of woven sunlight as a token of her trust. She twisted the shiny band on her smallest finger, remembering the promise of secrecy with which he had bound her. Now she knew her mother was equally aware of the magic that seemed to hover so close around them, hidden and unknown, but there for any with eyes enough to know what to seek.

"What do you fear, Sibylla?"

"You know of the magic of which I speak," she said. She reached over and picked up her son. His touch and the solid presence of his innocence comforted her in the midst of uncertainty and doubt.

Her mother glanced at her. She reached a hand out to little Baudinouet and chucked him under his chin. He delighted her with laughter. "Yes, Sibylla, I do," Agnes said. "And I think the time has come for you to know something of that magic as well."

† CHAPTER THIRTEEN

O God, my God, look upon me: why hast thou forsaken me?
—Psalms 21:1

W hat is all this commotion?" asked the Master of the
Order of Sion. He looked up at Othon from beneath
black eyebrows that drew together like the ominous
dark clouds of a gathering storm. Amalric de Lusignan and his brother,
the foppish, golden-haired Guion, had been at arms, practicing their
sword-work amidst the other knights of Ibelin, keeping their skills
honed, as did so many others during the long months of construction at
Le Chastellet. The master's face was sweaty, unshaven, and flushed; his
mood and temper were as dark and dismal as the overcast skies.

Othon de Saint-Amant handed his helmet and shield off to
Gilbert d'Erail, the Templar Commander of the City of Jherusalem, who
rode with him at the head of the Templar column. Both men had ridden
in from the unfinished castle to meet with the king. Baldwin's request
was simple: the Templars were to ride out with the royal army within the
hour to show the Muslims something of Frankish gall.

Word spread throughout the camp. Knights shouted orders to
their squires; the poor, wide-eyed boys ran about frantically, gathering
armor and arms for their masters.

Othon spoke quietly with Gilbert d'Erail, giving him the
command of the knights. With a sharp nod, Gilbert kicked his heels into
his horse and led the column out to meet up with the king and the rest
of the royal army. Only when he was alone with Amalric de Lusignan
and his brother did Othon finally answer the man who secretly held rank
over him within the Order of Sion.

The vast melee of knights and horses in various stages of
preparedness provided the perfect cover for Othon and his despised
master to converse without any untoward notice. Othon touched a hand
to his throat and the medallion hidden beneath his armor. In the
eighteen months since that heroic day when Baldwin had proven himself

worthy of the confidence that lay upon him, Othon had grown suspicious and fearful; his guilt made him reckless. Despite his prayers for absolution and forgiveness, he felt drawn irresistibly towards the shadow of death. It beckoned to him like a release from bondage. He prayed silently that the dark spirit of the unseen that had returned the medallion to him on the eve of Montgisart watched him closely, waiting to expose his wretched sins at long last; sins that tormented him anew with each passing day. Only time would tell if those sins would found him out.

Othon swung down from the saddle, glancing around the field; he looked from the face of one brother to another. "The king has ordered the army to assemble. We ride within the hour to deprive the sultan of his precious flocks."

"That is a bold move, even for Baldwin," Amalric said, glancing at Guion. "And a foolish one."

Othon snorted. "Why—because he dares to take war to the Sarrazins on his own terms, rather than sitting back, waiting for them to bring it against us when we are most vulnerable?"

"No, my good Othon," said Amalric. "Because he is a boy, playing at being king, with no more understanding of what he does by provoking Salehdin with his banditry than a boy swatting at a beehive with a stick." Amalric stepped closer, threatening; his brother's blue eyes darted nervously around the field. "He should be focusing his attentions on the defense of the castle. Instead, he risks open war for a few flocks of sheep at a time when we can ill afford one."

"That *boy*, as you are so fond of calling him," Othon snapped— he pointed towards Baldwin's tent billowing in the breeze on the far side of the field—"has far more wisdom and strength of leadership than the whole of the High Court. What you claim as banditry, is Baldwin's good sense to keep Salehdin from gaining the provisions he so desperately needs to keep his hungry army in the field through the remainder of the season."

"He risks too much. He is as arrogant as his father."

Othon laughed; the sound burst out of him unexpectedly. The angry reaction on the master's face was unmistakable. "You've lost control over him, haven't you? For all your threats and scheming, you cannot bring the young pup to heel. Even his mother has proven herself unable to force him to do as you wish. He defies your every whim. It must gall you terribly to know that a boy all of eighteen, a stinking leper, is all that stands between you and control of the throne."

Irritation played itself out across the master's face. He controlled it well enough, but it was visible all the same. Guion opened his mouth to say something coarse or stupid no doubt, but Amalric cut him short with a chuckle of pure malice. "Do not mistake your sudden loyalty to the king as some kind of redeeming virtue, my friend. Or, that it will cleanse your soul of treachery—against Baldwin, or against Sion." He closed with him, circling; his narrow gaze took in a quiet, unsettling measure of him.

Othon felt suddenly very uncomfortable beneath that cold, calculating gaze; a chill crept up his spine. A Templar knight prided himself for his lack of fear in the midst of battle. His fear now was overwhelming. It threatened to swallow him in its dark maw. It whispered to him. *He knows. Your sins* have *found you out at last.* Sweat beaded across his brow. Amalric de Lusignan's sword flashed upwards in an arc through a stray beam of slanting sunlight. The point of the blade pressed against the hollow of his throat.

A shocked Guion stepped between them, pushing his brother's sword down. His eyes darted, afraid that someone saw Amalric's act of aggression against the Templar Master. "This is neither the time nor place for this, brother. Deal with this in private."

Amalric shrugged Guion's hand from his sword and pushed him aside with an elbow. To Othon he said, "Did you truly think I was unaware of your treachery against us?"

The memory of de Lusignan's skill in the art of magic turned traitor against him. His tongue cleaved to the roof of his mouth; a tremor of fear twisted itself about the inward parts of his abdomen. He could feign ignorance, but he knew it would be pointless. "Why haven't you done something before now to rid yourself of me, then?"

"Because you have been of more use to me alive than dead," Amalric de Lusignan said. His smile was anything but a comfort. "Your treachery has turned Baldwin's eye to a place where he will find nothing but loyalty to the crown and devotion to the will of the Church. If he knows or even suspects anything of your particular involvement, he will think you have acted alone. The Templar Order will escape condemnation by the king and its true function as an arm of Sion will remain secret."

"I could name you as the master of all this treachery," Othon said, and realized his folly at once.

"I doubt any one would believe you. My brother and I are but humble knights of the realm—the least of our father's sons. We have no holdings of our own—no castle, no lands, only two much needed swords to defend this kingdom with our very lives if needed. Who are we that we could command the great lords of Jherusalem—or the Master of the Knights Templar." Amalric lifted a hand towards the king's tent. "Go; tell the king of our guilt. I'm sure he would believe you—a traitor and a friend of traitors." He set the point his sword to the scabbard and slammed the blade home. "Come, brother. Our young king has need of our services."

Othon de Saint-Amant stood glaring at the man he had come to hate far more than any other man he had ever known, as he and his equally detestable brother, called for their squires to arm them for the raid. A deep sense of foreboding and fear came upon him. He had felt the same strange sensation once before—the night that Amalric de Lusignan had called up the spirit of Hell on the eve of Montgisart. *Deliver me from the powers of darkness*, he prayed, afraid of the dark presence that stalked him unseen.

Climbing into the saddle, he looked around the field warily, before setting his heels to his horse, urging the animal into a gallop towards the Templar column forming up near the newly built castle of Le Chastellet.

* * * * *

The raid on the flocks of Damascus turned quickly to a battle, the battle to a bloody rout. By chance, they ran afoul of a small Muslim contingent near the wooded vale leading up out of the Belinas plain into the high hills. The heathen caught them between the thickening line of trees and the rolling plain that was the granary of Damascus. The Muslims had spied them from a vantage that gave them all the room to maneuver and the Templars and Baldwin's mounted knights no room to turn and form up a charge. They were caught off-guard and their horses flat-footed.

"It's the sultan's nephew," cried Humphrey, the old Constable, galloping up beside him, the brothers Ibelin close on his heels. "The main force of the Muslim dogs lies just beyond the far hill."

"Is this a diversion from Le Chastellet, Humphrey? Or did we actually happen upon them by plain bad misfortune?" Baldwin asked.

"I think it more the latter, Sire. The Sarrazins seem just as surprised to come upon us."

Baldwin swore under his breath. He ordered Saint-Amant to form up the Templars in a line against the Sarrazin charge. Humphrey signaled half the royal forces to break for the forest and turn to take the enemy as they came through the Templar defense. Baldwin hoped they might have a chance to turn the tide, but his hope was very, very small.

Reynald turned his horse at Baldwin's side, barking out last minute changes to the command. The Muslims were closing fast. He reined his mount too tightly, turning the black charger into Baldwin's red Bellerophon. For a moment, it seemed a disaster; but Baldwin backed Bellerophon with a touch of his knee, giving him a subtle command to rear up. Reynald slapped the reins against his horse's flanks. Its ears flattened; a round white eye rolled wide with fear in its socket. With startling clarity, he recalled the tortuous hours of training with his Muslim riding master, and reacted. The simple tactic accomplished its goal. Neither man fell.

"Skillfully done, Baldwin," Reynald said by way of an apology. There was no time for courtly niceties. "We need to set the reserves back or the line will become entangled."

Baldwin surveyed the field and the looming forest, the charging line of Sarrazin light horse, and made his decision. "Pull back Ibelin, Sidon, and Caesarea, and take your own knights back into the trees. Wait for my signal."

Reynald eyed him narrowly through the slit of his helmet. "I'll wait with the Constable," Baldwin said. He saw Reynald begin to protest; he stopped him with a command. "Ride for the trees, my lord of Kerak. And by all that's holy, hold those reserves until I give the signal."

Madness ensued. The Muslims, with their light, swift stallions, overran the heavy Templar line and passed through like so much water through a sieve. It was enough, though, to slow their pace, and bring them to hand-to-hand fighting on horseback. Sunlight glinted on sword-blades on both sides as they flicked out between the riders. Blows echoed off shields; a man cried out. A horse screamed in agony and went down. Above the din and chaos of battle, the steady drone of the Muslim battle-chant rose clear enough to hear its dreadful words. Words that were supposed to be cries of devotion and faith to God offered up in the name of war. *Allahu-akhbar! Allahu-akhbar! Allahu-akhbar!* Its sound struck fear into Baldwin's quaking heart. They were all about to die. God and His holy angels had abandoned them in the hour of their greatest need.

The Frankish line began to waver with the crumbling Templars. It fell back on itself and buckled. The Muslims broke through in a surge of clashing swords and a sickening crumble of bodies and horseflesh. Blood turned the field red. A warm arc of fluid sprayed across Baldwin's helmet as a knight fell beside him with a groan. The smell of death began to thicken the humid air.

His short lance struck again and again, until his arm grew too tired to keep his grasp and the body of a fallen Sarrazin wrenched it from his hand. A wave of sudden nausea rose on his throat; his stomach heaved and twisted into an ever-tightening knot of fear that choked the air from him. Darkness swelled up behind his eyes, drawing him down into its depths. Baldwin did not know what to do: whether to turn left or right, or surrender to an enemy that would not give them the right to do so. In his uncertainty, he gave the signal for the charge from the forest. The horn challenged the chant of the Sarrazins advance. The charge saved his life, but for Humphrey and the rest of his guard it was too late.

The whisper of a sword cutting through the air drew him back from the brink of that overwhelming black shadow. His sword flashed up, and fell back with an arm-numbing shudder. In the confusion, Bellerophon took an arrow in the flank. It was not a lethal hit, but his bit slipped and he bolted, charging towards the onslaught of the Sarrazin line.

Seeing the danger of his predicament, the Constable shouted at his men and kicked his horse into a run to cut off his charge. The leader of the Muslim horse recognized the king of Jherusalem and saw his chance for fame and glory by capturing the despised leader of the Franks.

At the last moment, Humphrey turned Bellerophon away, but his momentum carried him into the razor edge of the Muslim swords. Baldwin gained control of his horse using his knees; he screamed a curse at the enemy. It went unheeded, lost in the tumult of clashing arms.

The Frankish charge came thundering around him like a breaking storm. It crashed into them with a fury and drove the Muslims back in confusion; but it was not enough to break them. They advanced to the sound of beating drums and skirling pipes.

A horn sounded, signaling a retreat. The Frankish army rallied around a single man who held the shattered center. Reynald de Châtillon. Baldwin recognized the banners of Ibelin and Sidon circling around him, forming a protective ring. They began to fall back slowly, fighting their way towards escape.

Out of the corner of his eye, Baldwin saw Humphrey go down in a hail of arrows that suddenly fell out of the sky with deadly effect. The soldiers of Toron rushed to his side and stood their ground about their fallen lord, swords raised. It was a valiant stand. The brightly clad Mamluks swarmed around them, though, cutting down the Constable's guard with lethal precision.

A strangled cry escaped Baldwin's disease-riddled throat, echoing inside his helmet in a deafening sound. "*Humphrey!*"

A hand reached out, grabbing him in the chaos, and led him away from the slaughter and the darkness that fell about them.

* * * * *

Candle flames flickered in the night-darkened halls of Chastelneuf; fire-shadows played along the walls, grotesque silhouettes twisting sinuously along the contours of stone and wood with the floating silence of a terrible dream. A draft was most to blame, a whispering moan of air that assailed the chinks and faulty masonry work of the newly rebuilt castle in a hideous, wailing keen for the dead. The pitiful wail gave voice to the grief in Baldwin's heart that swelled to nearly bursting.

Humphrey was dead; he had fallen victim to an unfortunate ambush and a badly infected arrow wound that gnawed relentlessly at the tattered shreds of his strength until he had nothing left to spare. He fell victim to Baldwin's youthful folly to demonstrate, yet again, the willingness of Frankish steel—and thereby, *his* willingness—to challenge Muslim autonomy in Damascus. His eyes grew red and rheumy with the tears that he could not shed. The leprosy had robbed him of even that much release from his pain.

The venerable old Constable lay on the oak table in the center of his own grand hall, surrounded by tapestries and the many trophies of his long and distinguished career as a knight and lord of Toron. For twenty-seven years, he had served as Constable of Jherusalem, a valiant and honorable man seen by Christian and Muslim alike as an affliction sent of God to punish the enemy. He was a noble man who did not deserve such an inglorious death. He lay alone and unmourned, except by his young king and a few lords who knew the depth of loss his death would cause. His wife and son were long dead, those of his household slain in the same ill-fated skirmish that had claimed their lord. Only a grandson remained, a mere boy of fourteen, another Humphrey, the fourth of the name, as was Baldwin, the shy and gentle heir of Toron and Kerak alike.

Outside the door, Humphrey's chamberlain, butler, and a handful of servants waited to clean and dress their lord for burial. It was only out of respect for the king that they left him to grieve for the Constable alone. Baldwin lifted a deformed hand and removed his glove; he brushed back the long grey hair from Humphrey's brow. The fetid, putrefying stench of decayed flesh filled the air. Although his disease-numb hand caused him no pain, it was painful to know that a dead man carried fewer odors than the living corpse of his body. Fortunately, for Humphrey, he was beyond concern or worry now of what his king's touch could do to him.

Flecks of dried brown blood lay spattered across the Constable's face. Muslim blood. Angrily, Baldwin put aside all kingly dignity; he took towel and basin, and began gently to wash away the grime of war with his own hand. He owed the great man that much service—a man who was more like a second father to him after his own had fallen suddenly to illness and death.

Now death had claimed yet another father from him. He chased that thought through the intricately embroidered pattern of Humphrey's torn sleeve and the darker recesses of his mind until it formed, as though of its own will, into a question fraught with dire uncertainty.

How much more would he be required to sacrifice to hold his kingdom from the enemy? How many more would die in his defense for a kingdom he no longer thought worthy of saving?

—Magdalen, do you hear me? he whispered in this world, and in that other, immortal place that had long ago faded from the world into the realm of myth and shadow and the power of magic; that other, nearly forgotten place where the Magdalen hid herself from the affairs of men.

—I need you, lady, he cried, wiping the blood from a deep cut across the Constable's seamed brow. He closed his eyes, sending his thought outwards toward that other place in search of her.

Ever since Montgisart, Baldwin could almost sense Mary's presence and communicate with her without being near her. As he bent his will on her, a sense of her surroundings, her mood, her thoughts, began to form in his mind. Trees rose around her as she bent over a stone near a stream, praying; sunlight slanted through the leaves, cloaking her in gold and brilliant shades of green. Her thoughts strayed, wavering between the broken words of a prayer and the image of a young beautiful woman who bore a striking resemblance to her. He felt her sadness, her anger, and the raging turmoil of her emotions. She was weeping.

—Magdalen, he whispered again, calling to her. Pain shot through his eyes, exploding in a blinding light that seared through his mind. He gasped. Dizziness and a sudden weakness overwhelmed him as his power throbbed, burning like fire. Mary glanced up as he winced with the pain, turning her face to his, her gaze penetrating to the dark depths of his soul.

*—Humphrey is dead, he said, stammering. **My army is defeated and scattered. I do not know what to do. The kingdom is defenseless.***

Sorrow and anguish swept over him, quenching the burning fire of his pain, leaving only an inconsolable guilt. His hand clenched tightly in the fabric of Humphrey's torn and bloodstained tunic. His eyes snapped open. The image of the Magdalen faded, blurring into the shadows of the candlelit hall. The room closed in around him, suffocating his breath.

—Do you hear me, lady? Humphrey is dead. He is dead and it is my fault. My foolishness killed him, as surely as if I had held the blade. What am I to do? Magdalen, help me.

* * * * *

A wind rose in the garden. It strengthened, stiffening into a gale through trees that had never known more than the gentlest breeze. It stirred into motion rustling dried leaves and spent flower blossoms in a swirling tempest that raged through the forest to settle around Mary and fall at once to her command. Shadow and light were disturbed out of place, upsetting the delicate, long-held balance of peace and solemn quiescence. In the raging, indomitable midst of wind and noise, a voice called: young and desperate, its blind, fragile innocence melting away even as it cried out to her in grief.

—Magdalen...

She stood abruptly, gracefully, troubled by the deep urgency of its cry. Only one born to the power of magic could call to her in this place outside the realm of the mortal sun. His need, and his sorrow alone, would have been enough to beckon her, great as it was. The growing ember of his power, burgeoning at last into a flame of white-hot fire with his advance into manhood, was an unlooked for hope that compelled her to rise and heed his call.

She saw him, humbled and worn, bent over the lifeless body of a man, surrounded by shadow and the flickering candlelight of a dark hall. She heard the desperation of his summons and the urgency of his plight, but even that paled before the deep-seated fear that lay behind all his guilt.

—Do you hear me, lady? Humphrey is dead. He is dead and it is my fault. My foolishness killed him as surely as if I had held the blade. What am I to do? Magdalen, help me.

His troubling words sent a shuddering wave through the fabric of time. They whispered of what had been and what could be, weaving into existence a thread of uncertain reality into the tapestry of destiny. Shadows and the ethereal grey edge of the dark void of chaos hovered ever nearer, pressing in upon the shifting boundary of the world of men. Something unforeseen and unplanned had broken through the tapestry. The hand of the enemy was at work.

Wrapping her dark cloak around her shoulders, she whispered a word of hope and comfort into the heart of the hapless king, and stepped from her world into his.

† CHAPTER FOURTEEN

O sword, O sword, come out of the scabbard to kill, be furbished to destroy, and to glitter...
—Ezechiel 21:28

Humphrey of Toron was buried in the same castle he had been born in and governed for more than forty years. When the people of Toron heard of his death and the procession making its long, winding way towards the castle, they gathered alongside the road beneath the steep, brooding hill of Toron to pay their respects and mourn the passing of their beloved lord. Finally, the cortège continue on, slowly making its way up the narrow incline along a path strewn with flowers petals and through the castle gate. After a lifetime of service to his king and people, Humphrey had come home for a final time to rest.

The ceremony was as Humphrey would have wanted; simple and informal, attended only by a small contingent of nobles, including Raymond of Tripoli and the Constable's young grandson and heir who had ridden north with his mother from Kerak. A priest sang the mass and Baldwin said a few awkward words of comfort to the boy who was only a few years his junior as they stood over the great man's grave beneath the floor of the castle chapel. He confirmed the younger Humphrey in his new title as lord of Toron and accepted his oath of fealty.

Having set the affairs of Toron in good order for the time being, Baldwin rode out with Raymond at his side and half the royal army. He had given up any hope of the Magdalen's council. At Chastelneuf, they rendezvoused with the Templars and the rest of the army now under the command of Reynald de Châtillon acting temporarily as Constable in Humphrey's place, and rode south for Jacob's Ford.

Four weeks later, Salehdin forced them to march back towards Toron to defend against Muslim incursions yet again in upper Galilee and the Lebanon.

While the Franks had tarried with Humphrey's death and the fortification of Le Chastellet, the sultan had not been idle. He made several forays against Le Chastellet to test its defenses, but he withdrew only after one of his chief emirs died in a minor skirmish. To vent his frustration, he sent his nephew's troops ranging far afield, marauding and terrorizing the interior countryside between Sidon and Beirut; the sole target of his raids, the grain harvest which had just been brought in. His men were tired and starving, and they needed food desperately if they were to survive the long months of the summer campaign. What they could not steal, the bandits put to the flame. Each day, billowing black smoke smudged the horizon, darkening the northern skies of the Lebanon. Emboldened by his victory at Belinas, Salehdin had grown arrogant, thinking his army could ride at will through Frankish lands, flaunting Frankish patience.

By the first of June, as though in answer to prayer, word from his stepfather, Reynald Grenier of Sidon, reached Baldwin by rider that the Muslims were on the move again. This time, they were heading straight for the southern passes through the mountains. The message read simply: *The harvest is lost; the fields are aflame. The enemy rides for the Litani and Damascus.*

Baldwin took its veiled meaning to heart. The Litani was a long river with many crossings. The Christians of Jherusalem guarded only one. Four days later, the army was encamped at Beaufort, the rear-guard castle of Sidon high above the west bank of the Litani just a few leagues south of the famed springs of Marj Ayun.

After the humiliating rout at Belinas, tensions were running high with the prospect of another battle. Baldwin sent out scouts each day to report on the Muslim troop movements. The reports, though, were not encouraging. The raiders, a mixed assemblage of mounted soldiers and camels heavily laden with sheaves of wheat, moved slowly southwards; Salehdin waited with his larger force encamped before Belinas. It was a game now of waiting, and of wits, seeing who would make the first move against the other. Baldwin refused to take the field and hunt down the enemy too soon for fear that they would move beyond range of Beaufort castle and lose the advantage of safety should they need to retreat.

The waiting, however, only soured Baldwin's already foul and pensive temper. Even Reynald recognized his mood; he recommended practicing at arms. It was a welcome distraction his prayers could not provide, however much he pleaded with God. It gave him a release for his pent up emotions, as well as an opportunity to stab something with his sword. He would have preferred a Muslim soldier rather than a wooden post covered with armor. With each blow he struck, the festering tatters of his guilt over Humphrey's pointless death burned away, replaced by a fierce anger against the Muslims, and, to some small degree, against God for deserting them in the hour of their greatest need at Belinas.

Sweaty and worn, his lesioned hands crusted with dried blood, Baldwin retired alone to the quietude of his appropriated room in one of the towers of Beaufort castle. Abu Dawud, his Christian-Arab doctor, accosted him at the bottom of the stairs; he protested bitterly that his sores needed cleaned and bandaged to prevent infection. Baldwin dismissed him curtly with a word and a wave, and quietly ascended the tower stairs to his room and shut the heavy oak door behind him.

The steward had prepared the room earlier in the day for his leisure; he wanted nothing more than a few simple comforts. The steward had complied with his wishes. A single candle burned softly on a sideboard, barely bright enough to keep the thick shadows at bay. A pitcher and basin of fresh water sat on a table for him to wash; a clean tunic lay in a press in the corner.

Despite the fortress' solid construction, a draft continually crept through the dark halls, gusting under doors and whistling through unseen cracks in the thick walls. It only added to the already dismal atmosphere of the castle. The lords of Sidon built the fortress of Beaufort for war, not for the idyllic pleasures of life during a time of peace. With his mother at Court with his sister, and his stepfather in Sidon or on campaign with the army, only a handful of servants and soldiers kept residence at Beaufort. Many of the rooms had scarcely seen a human presence in the past few years. As a boy, he would have found the castle a wonder and an adventure; as a king and a dying man, the dark and shadow-bound halls only made his mood that much darker.

Stripping off his studded gambeson and belt, he slumped down to sit on the edge of the great bed. His eyes fell to his battered hands and closed. He felt no pain in the sores lacerated by the hilt of his sword. He had purposely wrecked such havoc on them in atonement for Humphrey's death. No amount of personal suffering would bring the man back, but he did not care. Nor did he stop the abuse until that guilt had worked its way out through his sword and the hilt of the blade was slick with blood. When the tears of guilt and anger refused to come at his bidding, he hurled the sword that had been his father's at the wooden practice mannequin in the yard, and stormed away.

He found no more relief, though, in the quiet solitude of his room than he had in the repetitive words of his prayers. The reason for both was simple. God had abandoned him. The priest who heard his confessions assured him of the contrary. He was king of the holy city of Jherusalem; anointed and blessed of God. He was also a leper; a king condemned and unclean, accursed by the most grievous affliction of Heaven. He was a sinner unworthy of God's favor.

His eye caught his reflection in a mirror in the near corner; he stood and walking over to it. He removed the veil from his face. The corpse that stared back at him through vacant, red-rimmed eyes horrified him. He saw a nose eaten away by disease into a misshapen void of bone and rotten flesh, a mouth distorted out of shape by lips that curled in a cruel and twisted smile that mocked the beauty it once held. He tried to hide the sickly, snow-white patches of skin that mottled his ruined face beneath a beard, but it was far too thin to do anything more than add to its hideousness. His face no longer resembled a man, but more like a lump of molded clay cast to the ground and forgotten. Only the clay lived and breathed, enduring the terrible ridicule of those who looked upon him without pity or compassion. Who but a mother or a sister could love such a face as his? For truly God had abandoned him.

"God has not abandoned you, Baldwin," she said, stepping from the shadows of the room.

He saw her reflection in the mirror: she had beauty and grace far too great for any mortal to own. She appeared more shadow than light as though she had not fully stepped into the world.

"Hasn't he, my lady," he said, glaring at her in the mirror. "Look around you and tell me how he has helped me. Humphrey is dead and now I must let Salehdin lead me around by the nose at his will or risk losing my kingdom through inaction. It would seem that God has, indeed, chosen not to care whether this kingdom survives or not."

"Pursue peace with the Muslims and then work to keep it. Be the king of Jherusalem that no other has yet dared to be."

"So you have continually said again and again. Tell me, then, how I am to accomplish that when war threatens our existence. I called for you because I needed your council—not your condemnation."

"You called for me and I have come," she said. "But for what—to give you my blessing on your continued folly? No, you do not want my council, King Baldwin. You want me to win you this war you have provoked against Salehdin by choosing to break the truce."

"Can you promise me that Salehdin will abide by a truce if I pursue it?"

"No," she said, stepping closer. "But I can promise you that your kingdom will not survive a sustained war with the Muslims. Your devotion to duty and the growing power of your magic are playing into the hand of the enemy. Sion wants you to make war on Salehdin."

"Why?"

"I don't know, Your Highness."

"And what if you are wrong?"

Her hand rose, entreating his trust, and fell. "I pray that I am; but either way, your actions have upset the balance of what will be, and what could be."

He turned finally from the mirror to face the Magdalen. It was the first time he had seen her with his eyes since that rain-soaked day in November a year and a half before where she had appeared as a glorious vision in the heavens at Montgisart and battled the black daemon of Hell. He understood her long absence, how time turned more slowly in her world than his; he understood the cost that her magic must have exacted from her, just as the magic took from him every time he used it, and how she needed time to regain her strength. He no longer blamed her for not being there, even when he needed her most. What he could not understand was her constant council to pursue peace with an enemy sworn to a holy war, who would never agree to a lasting peace. Unless… unless, she knew more than she revealed. The thought struck him like a blinding light.

"You can tell the future," he said, knowing that he had hit upon the truth even as he said it. He watched her face, seeing what effect his words had on her.

"Not in the manner you think," she said. Then added: "But yes, I can see some things after a fashion."

His breath quickened, along with the racing pulse of his beating heart. "Will Jherusalem fall to the Muslims?"

She looked at him curiously. "Wouldn't you rather know when you will die?"

"I will die when this miserable disease born of magic finally decides to claim me. I want to know about Jherusalem—will it fall to Salehdin?"

She hesitated, closing her eyes as though looking into the future. With a deep breath, she opened her eyes, the piercing depth of her gaze watered with tears. "Jherusalem will fall through violence and bloodshed to Salehdin, just as it fell of old to the Romans legions in the last days spoken of by the prophets."

"When?" he whispered. "When will this happen?"

"When you have passed from this world into the next."

194

Baldwin turned back to the mirror and stared at his own reflection in the silvered glass. It was easier to argue with the hideous reflection of a monster than the face of an angel. "Then there is no reason to pursue peace with the enemy."

"There is every reason, Your Highness," she spat with far more venom than he had ever heard her speak. Hands clenched at her sides. She scolded him as though he were a stubborn, spoiled child. "Peace will save far more of your people, even if it eventually fails. But if you choose to pursue this war now to its end, Salehdin's wrath will be poured out on Jherusalem ten-fold."

"I'm sorry, my lady," he said. "But I see little difference between the two."

Mary moved closer, her arms wrapped tightly across her chest. She looked small and frail, hardly threatening. He could see her white gown just out of the corner of his eye. He fought the impulse to meet her steady gaze. "You think so only because you have experienced so little of warfare. You forget, Baldwin, I saw the carnage, the terrible bloodshed that Christians—men who professed Christ as their Savior—were all too eager to visit upon their enemies when they took Jherusalem during the First War of the Cross."

She fell suddenly silent. He glanced at her; her eyes had closed. He stretched out a thin tendril of power, sensing the black horror of her memories. Her voice changed, turning soft and distant, choked with raw emotion. "They gloried in shedding the blood of Muslims and Jews alike, and sought only to shed more. Blood flowed through the streets of the city to the height of a horse's bridle. In their greed, they cut open the bodies of men and women in the belief that they had swallowed their gold and silver and precious jewels. They raped women and young girls; slaughtered innocent children and babies at their mother's breasts, all in the name of God. After such atrocities, how much more do you think the Muslims will exact their revenge when the city falls?"

Of a sudden, with the talk of war and bloodshed and death, the image of Humphrey falling beneath a ring of Muslim swords and arrows rose before his eyes with blinding clarity and reality. It played itself out repeatedly in agonizingly slow motion in his mind. His hands clenched, his anger flared, rising in a blood-red mist of rage against the enemy.

Her voice at his back cut through the mist; she had drawn closer again, almost in reach of him. He refused to look at her. In his anger, he gave her reason and opportunity to intrude on his thoughts. Her words cut like a knife to the depths of his heart.

"Ask yourself, King Baldwin, who is really to blame for Humphrey's death? Salehdin—or your own actions?"

"Salehdin has sworn to drench this land with our blood—either now or later makes no difference to him. At this very moment, there is a Muslim raiding party setting fire to the grain harvest between Beirut and Sidon, and yet, you want me to make peace with this same enemy while my people starve this winter from a lack of food."

"You caused this crisis by provoking war with Salehdin."

"What I do, I do to defend my people."

"How long will it be, Your Highness, before you learn to trust me without question?"

"When I know for a certainty that trusting you will not come at the expense of my kingdom," he said. He wanted to trust her—had promised himself that he would after Montgisart—and yet, he felt that despite her claims and actions to the contrary, she was still keeping something very important from him. He needed desperately to know that *she* trusted *him* enough to tell him everything that she kept from him. "Why did you help me, then, at Montgisart?"

"Because you only thought to defend your people, not to make war with Salehdin." Mary stepped back from him, her dark gaze shadowed by the fall of her mane of hair. Candlelight fell about her in a soft and golden glow. "It is not God's will for you to prevent Jherusalem from falling into the hands of the Muslims; it is for you to live long enough to frustrate the plans of Sion so that they destroy themselves. You need to pursue a plan for peace. Think of your people now and forsake this war while you still can. I cannot help you unless you do."

His anger flared, hardening his resolve to iron. "Can't, my lady—or won't?"

Mary pulled the hood of her cloak over her head and backed away into the shadows. "Haven't you lost enough, King Baldwin? I will not contribute to the wholesale slaughter of innocent blood when peace is possible."

"Nor will I ignore the needs of my people. I am still king of Jherusalem," he said, closing his eyes, and fell silent. He prayed that she would soften her stance—that she would yield to his will. When he opened his eyes again, she had gone.

* * * * *

"The Ifranj are on the move at last," said the sultan of Egypt and Suriya to his waiting emirs with a satisfied smile. For several days now, he had sent out his nephew, Farrukh-Shah, and his Mamluks to harass the Ifranj countryside and destroy the summer grain harvest—at least that part they could not bring back to Dimasq. It had been a ruse, bait to lure the Ifranj king into his hand. He had done so before only two months ago, and it had turned into his great victory at Banyas. If Allah was merciful and gracious, the infidels would learn something today of Muslim courage and Muslim superiority.

He glanced back, watching the telltale sign of the Ifranj troop movement. On the green slopes of the hill opposite their position, a large flock of sheep had suddenly scattered in every direction, fleeing some unknown threat on the far side of the rise.

At once Yusuf knew what had frightened the gentle creatures enough to scatter them with such panic. The Ifranj had moved recently from protecting the construction of the fortress at Jisr Ya'kub, to encamp at their castle near Marj Ayun. The witless Ifranj were moving to intercept the bait he had laid for them. From his vantage point just north of his most recent victory, he could clearly see the path Allah had opened for his next triumph over the infidels. Of all men, God had truly blessed him.

Putting on his turbaned helmet with its camail of polished brass flashing so brilliantly in the afternoon sunlight, he mounted his white Arabian stallion caparisoned splendidly for battle and the glory of victory. In the eyes of his troops, he must have seemed like one of the shining, heroic gods his people had once worshipped in their ignorance before the coming of Islam to the mountainlands of Turkey and northern Suriya.

Before the setting of the sun and the pearl-grey of dusk cast its shadow upon the world, his men would ride with him this day into the golden legend of Salah ad-Din and the glorious *jihad* spreading its way like fire across the breadth and width of Islam.

Al-Abras will wish he had died at Banyas rather than the great lord of Tibnin, he thought. *He will pray to his God that the disease that afflicts him will take his life before this day has passed.*

Drawing his sword, he raised its finely curved blade to the heavens as an offering, giving a shout to his army, urging them to fight for the glory of their God. *Allahu-akhbar! Allahu-akhbar! Allahu-akhbar!*

* * * * *

The heavy Frankish horse crashed through the thin line of Muslim auxiliaries; the impact splintered lances and shattered bones and shields in a deafening clash of noise that rose above the screams of men and horses. The Sarrazins were unaware of the danger bearing down on them until the rumbling echo of thundering hooves hit them with the force of a thousand battering rams. By then, it was too late.

At the last moment, a lone scout raised an alarm cut short by an arrow through his throat. Within moments of the enjoined battle, the Litani ran red with Muslim blood. The camels bolted with their burdens of grain.

Baldwin rode in the vanguard of his knights, his bright sword slashing at one screaming Muslim after another. Reynald rode at his side; both of them cut a terrible swath of blood and ruin through the enemy's center. Baldwin's anger and hatred gave him strength long after his arm had lost the strength to kill anymore. His knights buoyed him along the path of destruction they made; his knights and his anger, and the knowledge that his kingdom would not fall to Salehdin before his death. The knowledge made him reckless and fearless. He would make peace with the Muslims as the Magdalen had counseled, but only after he had made them see the wisdom of pursuing peace with him.

It was not a battle, or the heroic feat of Montgisart; it was a slaughter as bloody as the rout at Belinas. Muslim blood, bright and red, watered the drought-stricken land.

The Muslims fell before them like wheat before the scythe of Frankish hooves. A bloodlust overcame him and he began to sing. His knights picked up the war-song and lifted it higher than his mutilated throat would allow, matching it to the music of their clashing swords.

With voice and mind, he stretched out his power, calling to the Magdalen. She did not answer; her mind remained closed to him. All he could sense of her was a scent of incense mixed with the deep reverence of a place as ancient as stone. He called to her, sending his voice into the grey void that separated her world from the world of men.

—*Do you hear me, Magdalen? Do you see the havoc we have wrought upon the Muslims,* he cried. *You wanted me to pursue peace. Now Salehdin can come to me seeking a truce from the slaughter.*

He was certain that she heard him, for he felt her displeasure, her annoyance.

—*Fool, whispered a voice, dark and malevolent, masculine, not at all like the Magdalen. Baldwin tried to retreat from his thoughts and the connection his magic had formed to the grey void. A chilling blackness held him in its iron grip, refusing to let him see the face of its owner. This is only a prelude to a greater battle about to begin.*

Gathering all his strength of will and might, he hurled it at the shadow, and fell back; the ground rushed up to meet him as he fell. Pain exploded in his mind; stars circled before his swimming eyes. One moment found him locked in battle, hacking at a Sarrazin soldier, the next, knocked from his horse. He rolled to the right, drawing his knife as he did so. His sword was lost. His knife flew from his hand with the flick of a boot; a soldier stood over him. A sword point fell, leveled at his throat. It was his father's sword, held in the hand of a heathen Sarrazin.

A whisper came to him and passed aside, leaving an echo of its voice in his ear. **Now, Your Highness, you begin to understand the folly of your actions. You have brought death upon us all.**

* * * * *

The yellow banner of his honored household snapped in the gusting breeze above his head. Yusuf glanced at the plain banner as bright and glorious as the sun in summer, thinking of his warrior father and uncle. The sons of Shahdi ibn-Marwan were simple soldiers from Tikrit born of a family whose clan of Rawadi had close ties with the Shaddadid dynasty of Dvin, and who could trace their ancestors back through the ancient Kurdish tribe of al-Hadaniya. Ayyub and Shirkuh had gone on to claim honors in their own right as the friends of sultans and commanders of the governors of Mosul, Ba'albek, and Dimasq, all in a time of great political and military upheaval and constantly shifting alliances.

Both his father and uncle had had their heavy hand in bringing him to this particular place. His star was truly in its ascendancy. He did not need some aged astrologer in the gates of Dimasq to read his future in the natal charts. He had come a long way from the boy who was smaller than most his age; the dirty little street urchin who had ran wildly through the alleys of Ba'albek with his brothers, until their father had caught them in some minor mischief, and beat them to within a hair's breadth of their lives. From then on, his father had him watched and instructed in the ways of men and the greater lessons of Islam. Aside from a few months as a prisoner among the infidels as a child, from the day of his birth, his star had risen steadily into the heights of the heavens, drawing ever closer towards the radiant glory of Allah.

Yusuf lifted his eyes towards the brilliant sapphirine sky, searching and waiting for a sign. He smiled when it came. He held up his arm, and the falcon, falling from the clouds like bolt, opened its great wings to settle gently on his outstretched fist. It was a magnificent bird, and most unusual, an albino, or nearly so, all white above with a faint mottling of tan and gold amidst the white beneath. The falcon was his favorite among the dozen or so he owned. Farrukh-Shah had released it as a signal the first moment the Ifranj enjoined the battle.

He brought it close and caressed it with his cheek, murmuring a word of affection. His men waited behind him, quietly and patiently, but growing quickly restless. Victory and glory awaited him as well, equally impatient for him to embrace them.

The breeze stirred, carrying on its gentle currents of air the faint echoes of battle. He prayed silently for the lives of his nephew's Mamluks that he had sacrificed for the sake of victory. He prayed they would die a martyr's death and taste the pleasures of Paradise as a reward.

"Fly, my beauty; fly and hunt," he said, and heaved the magnificent bird into the air. It soared upwards, rising upon the thermals, away towards the east and the gathering feast of war. He raised his sword above his head and let it fall, signaling for his troops to attack.

The son of Najm ad-Din, the star of the faith, had a claim to his own legacy. Islam was on the march. It began again at Banyas; it would continue until the cries of Urshalim's fall echoed westward across the earth and into the halls and courts of al-Ifranj.

* * * * *

At the sounding of the Muslim trumpets, Othon de Saint-Amant and Raymond of Tripoli led out their combined knights against the sultan's troops to provide a protective wall for the king before the Sarrazin could trap them in the narrow defile between the river and the advancing horde. The footing proved uneven among the slanting rock faces and shattered stone. A bit too tricky for knights fighting on horseback. They needed to reach the wider space that lay between the hills and the springs of Marj Ayun. If they could keep the Muslims occupied, the king could regroup and guard them from the rear.

Othon swore. Salehdin kept the larger force of his army in reserve, waiting to spring his carefully laid trap. The filthy heathen heavily outnumbered and outmaneuvered them. The king needed time if he was to be of any use. Holding the Muslims at the entrance of the defile would not be enough. They needed to engage the enemy before he could form up his attack. They needed a miracle.

Othon signaled to Raymond to advance; the Count of Tripoli ordered a countermand to hold the line. Behind them, the echoing horns of the royal army blared, giving the order to form ranks. There was no time. Salehdin's light horse was closing ground too fast. There was only one choice; and it was suicide. He gave the order for his Templars to charge. Raymond's horns trumpeted to him to hold. Othon ignored him.

The Templars were answerable to only one man and he sat enthroned in distant Rome.

The next few moments were a confusing explosion of noise as the thundering hooves of eighty knights rolled over the Sarrazin charge and the white and red of Templar robes plunged into the crumbling line of garish Muslim colors. The red of rage and the spray of spilt blood, though, quickly became the common bond that drew them all together into the shadows of death. Christian and Muslim alike fell at each other's feet as they fought through a gauntlet of clashing swords and spears. The Muslims fell quickly beneath the grinding millstone of Templar ferocity; but the knights of Christ were falling as well, and their dwindling numbers were quickly lessening the ability to hold off the assault.

Othon knew that he would die. He thanked God that at least it was in the service to the king, and not Sion. He swung his sword repeatedly; left, then right, then left again, waiting and praying for the blow that would take his life. Men fell on every side, cut down by the sword; their cries called out, and then, suddenly, fell silent in death. The summer heat rose from the rocks; the horses kicked up a choking dust that burned their lungs along with the heat.

With all his might he blew his horn, calling for help; the sound echoed like a clap of thunder in the midst of a storm. Another horn answered, giving a command to hold. There would be no charge from the coward of Tripoli to relieve them: they were eighty knights against more than a thousand. The Templars were alone to bring honor or dishonor to the kingdom, and to Baldwin.

Of a sudden, Othon's charger screamed in agony and stumbled beneath a volley of spears. The force threw Othon forward over his horse's head in a tangle of reins and armor. He fell amidst a pile of dead bodies, faces he recognized as his companions of the Temple; his sword went spinning away over the rocks. He reached for it, but a spear point pricked the side of his throat, forcing him to yield. He did not need to understand Arabic to know the command to surrender. He prayed his death had given his king time to mount an advance. The kingdom needed Baldwin far more than it needed a traitor knight of the Templars.

* * * * *

A horn blared, screaming above the deafening noise of battle the command to rally behind the lord of Kerak. Reynald de Châtillon swung his sword, decapitating an enemy soldier; it swung again, plunging into the neck of another Muslim. God only knew where the king was in all the chaos. The rout of the Sarrazins had turned suddenly against them. Horns were echoing behind them to the east near the springs of Marj Ayun. Trumpets betrayed the position of another, and probably larger, Muslim army.

Reynald saw it at once, for what it portended. Salehdin had outwitted them and taken advantage of Baldwin's revenge on Humphrey's death. It had made them careless. He could appreciate the brilliant strategy of the sultan to lure them into a trap; he did not have to hate the Muslims any less to respect him. He would have done the same, given the opportunity.

The forces of Jherusalem became the anvil upon which the hammer of Salehdin's army fell from the east. Only the Templars and Raymond's troops from Tripoli stood between them. The army was rallying, but slowly, having to fight and yield ground while trying to gain a more favorable position.

The infantry caused him the most concern. Pressed back upon the mounted knights, they gave him very little room to maneuver the horses. Worse, to make an effective charge, he needed to break out from the confining ring of foot soldiers and leave them unprotected. It would be an acceptable risk only if it worked out to their benefit—a disaster if the heavy horse failed to smash the Sarrazin lines.

Forward of their position, a sudden change in the battle was causing havoc. Horns sounded, relaying conflicting commands. The Muslims swarmed through the narrow defile ending any hope to push the enemy back. The sun had become its own hammer, beating down on the armies of both faiths.

With the uneven ground and the slow, heavily armed might of the Frankish horse, the light, quick horsemen of the Muslims had the advantage, and pressed that advantage to their best use of the field. Even once he had the knights rallied for a charge, Reynald had difficulty turning the line to challenge the swiftly circling enemy. They were dead men, all of them, if he could not rally the army and make a firm stand.

The battlefield had become an open graveyard; bodies littered the ground, the mingled blood of Christians and Muslims alike staining the rocks and soil the same sickening color of death. Reynald had long ago stopped being concerned about how much of the blood soaking his tunic and tabard was his or those he had killed. In the heat of summer, some of the bodies were already beginning to bloat. He had seen many a battle, but the stench of blood and spilt entrails always nauseated him. Excrement and other bodily fluids made the ground slick and unsure. Vultures circled overhead, drawn by the same stinking odor that repulsed him. They were always the first impatient guests at the feast of every battle.

Those who had been at Montgisart and witnessed its miracle prayed to St. George and St. Denis to defend them. The younger men cried out to the Blessed Virgin, the Mother of God, and their own mothers, to save them. Fear reduced grown men to weeping. Cast-off blood flew from the edges of blades as knights lifted their swords to strike repeatedly at a never-ending line of enemy reserves. One poor knight's intestines spilt out into his own hands. He tried desperately to hold them in, but to no avail. He died where he fell; the stench of his innards rose into the heavens as a sacrifice to the Muslim god. Blood baptized young men who had never before known the horror of battle into the brotherhood of holy war.

The sound of his echoing horn became a bastion of hope to all that rallied to its cry. The banner of Jherusalem, its potent crosses gleaming gold upon its white field lifted in the hand of the Marshal, shining like the True Cross itself, gave men something to look to beyond the slaughter around them. Other banners of the kingdom found new bearers to rally the broken army of Christ: Ibelin and Ramlah, Kerak, Japhe, Ascalone, Caesarea, Hebron, and Naples. The call to Sidon had gone out before the battle. He prayed that call would be answered and soon.

With a shout, a war-song broke out amidst the advancing line as fear gave way to hope for the first time in a long, long while. As men sang with the joy of renewed battle as they moved forward giving the enemy something more to think about than their assured victory, the Muslims unleashed Hell itself, and they were undone.

* * * * *

The strength of the Templars shattered; a few were captured, the rest slaughtered. Saint-Amant had foolishly charged at first sight of the enemy, as was his usual wont. With their resolve strengthened by their early success against the Christians, the Sarrazins swarmed the field against them. Raymond tried to mount an attack, but there was too little room to maneuver.

A horn sounded and the Muslim center divided cleanly, peeling away to join the wings of the advance; the two mounted wings circled, driving into the softer underbelly of the infantry holding the entrance to the narrow valley.

Raymond cursed the circumstances that forced him to forsake the truce he had so recently agreed to between Tripoli and Salehdin. He swore again, this time taking the king's name in vain for summoning him to war with the Muslims. All his hard work, all his carefully forged alliances, however weak and tentative, and his desire to pursue peace and preserve something of the kingdom his father and grandfather had died to create, unraveled with alarming speed. The very things he had spent his life chasing after were bleeding away into the sand along with the blood of his knights who had sworn themselves to the defenses of Tripoli—not Jherusalem.

The force of the Muslim counter-attack overwhelmed their lines. It broke the back of the Frankish defense with devastating fury. Within moments, the attack forced Raymond to sound a full retreat. He realized his mistake at once. Rather than an ordered retreat, only giving ground as they could afford, the army panicked and broke into a dead run. Between the clash of arms and the screaming wails of the injured and dying, it was as though the gate of Hell itself had opened beneath them and unleashed all the terrible horrors of its darkest depths. It was a scene from the Apocalypse of Saint-John.

Men groaned around them, succumbing to their wounds and the knowledge that as captives they were at the mercy of the Muslims to do with them as they willed. Sadly, though, only those who were highborn and had a standing worthy of a ransom would be imprisoned; the rest, the Sarrazins would slay or sell as slaves in the markets of Damascus.

The Muslims pushed them into the narrow defile leading up from the river. The front line turned suddenly to a rear-guard. Men discarded their weapons and simply ran, falling over their dead comrades, even as they fell to the sword. Raymond was able to keep some semblance of order around him by the sheer force of his will and the trust his knights felt towards him. On the outer fringes of his troops, men were falling, slaughtered to a man. Only the piling bodies slowed the Sarrazin advance.

It was not long before the retreating vanguard collided with the rallying line of the king's force. Chaos ensued. It was every man for himself. He found the lord of Kerak in the midst of that surging throng of slashing swords and dying men. Reynald's own sword cast off blood as he swung it tirelessly like some hero out of the ancient Greek myths. He was Achilles, battling the indomitable soldiers of Troy.

Defeat forced Raymond yet again to make a difficult decision: sacrifice his infantry and save his valued mounted knights, or die for a cause long since lost. He chose to live and fight another day. Running down a screaming Turkoman beneath the slashing hooves of his charger, he leapt past a knot of dead Franks in the blue tabards of Jherusalem and made his escape with those he could save. The sun lingered, hanging brightly in the sky as it slowly slipped towards the west. He looked towards it, weeping as he rode, and never looked back.

* * * * *

"Al-Malik Bardawil," the turbaned Sarrazin sneered, recognizing him as the Christian king. The point of the sword pressed tighter against his throat; another sword-point pulled down the veil from his face, exposing the hideous distortions of his disease. "Al-Khinzir," he hissed, calling him *pig* in his native tongue. Baldwin knew the Arabic curse quite well.

He refused to cower now at the moment of his death. He glared at his captor. The Sarrazin spit on him and raised his sword for the fatal blow with a growl. He died where he stood. Baldwin kicked him hard in the groin and he went down on one knee. The Mamluk's head followed, falling to the ground, and rolled away among the rocks. Blood sprayed from the severed neck. The body fell backwards, revealing a pair of knights in the battle-smeared colors of Ibelin.

Both knights removed their blood-spattered helmets; the one was dark-haired, the other fair and golden. Guion de Lusignan handed Baldwin his lost sword, while Amalric gave him a hand up. "My lord of Ramlah has been taken, Sire, along with the Master of the Temple," said the darker of the Lusignan brothers.

"The battle is lost, then," Baldwin said. For all its loss, though, the fighting still raged around them; his army was desperately trying to extricate itself in a retreat. Pain shot like fire through his ankle. It had caught in the stirrup when he fell from his horse. He had not noticed the pain until now.

"I've taken command of my lord's knights," Amalric said. "De Châtillon has rallied what's left of the army to hold the Sarrazins back as long as he can. We have to get you away. Can you ride, Your Highness?"

"My ankle is twisted," Baldwin said with a painful grimace. He looked around for Bellerophon and found him among the rocks, a spear sunk deep through his chest. "My... my horse is dead."

"We'll have to escape on foot," Guion said. Other unhorsed knights of various lordships were gathering; most had seen the heaviest and bloodiest action in the battle. A small group of Sarrazins broke through the lines and rushed at them briefly before a volley of arrows cut them down.

Baldwin wiped his sword on the hem of his tunic and sheathed it. "Where is the Count of Tripoli?" he asked, raising his voice above the continuing clamor of battle.

The noise of fighting rose and fell as the capricious tide of the battle shifted away from them for the moment. The vicissitudes of battle were never certain. Amalric sheathed his sword and slapped on his helmet. "When the forward lines collapsed under Salehdin's counterattack, my lord of Tripoli retreated with his knights across the river," he said without trying to hide his contempt. "Given his actions of late, Sire, I imagine he is probably half way to Tyre by now. He even left his wife's son in the hands of the Muslims."

"How many others have been captured?"

"Too many, Sire," Amalric replied. "And more if we don't escape and make for Beaufort soon."

"Then I put myself in your care, Messire," Baldwin said, limping towards him. He grimaced again with the pain. "I'm afraid, though, I'm going to need help."

A tall knight wearing the blue and white of the army of Jherusalem tossed aside his heavy mace and stepped forward. His nose had been broken; blood caked his mouth and swollen left eye. He had lost his helmet and shield. He made a bow. "I'll carry you, Your Highness."

"That's not necessary, Messire," Baldwin protested. For the second time in as many months, he had suffered a humiliating defeat at the hands of his enemy; now, a knight offered to carry him from the field on his back. The indignity was beyond humiliation. "Just find me a new mount."

Amalric and Guion caught him by the arm as he tried to take a painful step and held him up. "It is necessary. There is not time to debate this, Your Highness. Or to find a fresh mount," Guion said. "Or would you rather die simply because of pride?"

The remark stung, more so for the truth of it and because it was a knight who had to tell him so. Baldwin bit back an unsavory response. These were his knights, each of them sworn to the defense of the Holy Sepulcher and the protection of the anointed king of Jherusalem. Without them, he would have died at the end of his father's own sword. He owed them the right to serve him as necessary.

A breeze lifted, softening into a voice that whispered in his mind. A shadow moved, hovering just beyond the boundary of his conscious perception.

—Pride goes before a fall. Do you see now what your arrogance and anger has wrought this day?

—*Who are you?* Baldwin demanded, reaching into the edges of the shadow. *Tell me who you are. What do you want of me?*

—*Your throne and your kingdom, King Baldwin. I will have them. Either now, or when you are dead. It matters little to me.*

† CHAPTER FIFTEEN

I to my beloved, and his turning is towards me.
—*Canticles 7:10*

After a long and hectic morning of hearing a backlog of grievances that Sibylla could not adjudicate in his absence, Baldwin sat back upon his cushioned throne. He removed his crown from the white turban wound about his head and rubbed his brow to ease the pain behind his eyes that had plagued him for the better part of the last hour.

Despite his many bruises and half-healed injuries from the battle now nearly three weeks old, it felt good once more to wear the finery of court rather than the armor he had worn for more than nine months. The steward in his wisdom and in his kindness had laid out the softest attire he could find. Blousy Arabian trousers of white silk under a velvet cotehardie of dark blue with the crosses of Jherusalem stitched in gold crewelwork along the edges of the sleeves and on the collar.

The Patriarch had opened the session with a prayer and a blessing over the full assembly of the High Court; a few formalities of court followed, and then the long, overdue promotions of several squires to knighthood who had shown great valor at the debacles of Belinas and Marj Ayun. After three hours of listening to complaints, the throne room had finally emptied, leaving Sibylla and Baldwin alone in the dimly lit hall of the Tower of David. Unfortunately, there was still one more complaint he had yet to hear.

Sibylla strolled leisurely towards him down the length of the hall, her long silver dress and blue surcoat swaying against her legs. An incredibly beautiful woman she was, even he could see it. As princess and heir to the Christian kingdom of Jherusalem, there were lords and princes aplenty who would want her hand; her beauty alone was enough to ensnare such highborn suitors. In the wake of the loss of her beloved husband, though, a little known knight from Poitou had ensnared her heart. She had done her duty: married according to her father's wishes;

produced an heir; and stood by her brother in association with the throne. She wanted something now for herself—nothing more.

She knelt down beside the throne, her hands and chin resting on his arm. Of all people, beside Father William, she was not afraid to touch him. His own mother, though she would touch him at times, was always fearful and timid to do so. Sibylla's smoky, dark shadowed blue eyes gazed up at him from beneath lowered brows. She smiled fondly at him. Her show of affection did not fool him.

It was an attitude she often employed when she wanted something of him. In the few short years they had been together as brother and sister, Sibylla had formed an attachment to him, a male bond that she had lacked while in the care of the nuns at Saint-Lazare. It made her vulnerable, but only to him. Perhaps, it was because of all the men she knew, he alone saw her as more than a beautiful woman raised to play the part of a pawn in the game of thrones, offering her up to whatever lord was most advantageous to the kingdom.

"Whatever you want of me, Sibylla, the answer is no," he said, patting her hand gently with a gloved hand. They were new gloves of the softest calfskin dyed an exquisite shade of blue and studded with tiny seed pearls. They were a gift from Sibylla to celebrate the commemoration of his five years as king a few weeks hence.

"You don't even know what I'm going to ask," Sibylla said.

"Don't I, sister?" He let his head fall back against the throne, staring up at the ceiling concealed in shadows. "Guion," he said breathlessly and turned his eyes to her.

Sibylla pushed herself away from him and stood back a pace. "In all your eighteen years, brother, how many times have I asked anything of you?"

"Before my coronation I saw you only a handful of times, and we almost never spoke," he laughed. "I knew little Isabella better than you. What would you have asked of a brother you barely knew?"

"And since then, I have given you loyalty and friendship, and I have given you an alliance with my dead husband's house of Montferrat. All I want is to marry Guion."

"You are already betrothed to Hugh of Burgundy."

"Am I? Sibylla said, wrapping her long blue cloak around her body. "And when exactly is my betrothed supposed to arrive in Jherusalem to finally claim his prize—six months… a year? He has the opportunity to wear the crown of the kingdom of Heaven, and yet, he dithers in Europe, fretting more about his ancestral lands in Burgundy rather than the plight of Jherusalem."

She came forward and fell on her knees again before him, pleading. Reluctant as he was to touch her thoughts, he sensed no hint of treachery or deceit in her, only love and devotion to him and to the man she desired to marry.

"For once in my life, let me do something that I want to do. Let me marry Guion. He is here. Now. Ready to take my hand. Who knows when Hugh will finally choose to leave Burgundy, if ever?"

Baldwin's heart went out to her. Where he could never marry, she had done so once for the kingdom and lost, all in the self-same year. What she wanted, and asked, was so simple, so purely unselfish from her point of view. It hurt him to deny her. "I can't, Sibylla," he said. "I'm sorry."

Her hand dropped; and lifted. She wiped her eye and pulled her arms tighter around herself. No doubt, she had rehearsed this argument to herself a thousand times; she knew all the questions and all the answers. "You were almost killed, Baldwin. And you would have been if Guion's brother, Amalric, hadn't taken charge of Ibelin's knights and rescued you from the Sarrazins."

He sighed, tortured by having to pierce the heart of his sister. "And for that, Sibylla, I... I am most grateful to Messire de Lusignan."

"But not so grateful that you will allow his brother to marry me," she said. "If you had died, who would have inherited the throne?"

"You have a legitimate son. No one will dispute his claim."

"No, but if you die before he reaches a lawful age to rule alone, almost certain civil war will break out over who should be his Regent."

Baldwin narrowed his gaze and set his hands on the arms of the throne. "Your concern for my delicate health is touching, sister, but don't be so quick to put me in the grave. I may yet live longer than you think."

"Don't say such things. You know that I pray every day that you will live, little brother," she said and squeezed his arm. "But you may not. Nothing in life is certain, not the least of which, the number of days that God has given us. Allow me to marry Guion and he can stand as Regent for my son if necessary. Mother knows Guion. She knows the value that a match with him would bring."

He could not help but laugh. He apologized immediately. "That is hardly a vote of confidence for Guion, no matter what his qualities may be, Sibylla. We both know that mother's choice of men sometimes leaves something to be desired, if the rumors I hear of her have any truth to them."

"She saw qualities in our father, and I'm sure you'll agree he was a man worth marrying."

Baldwin sighed, exasperated by her argument. "Sibylla, you make all this seem so simple, but it's not. Otherwise, I would do it, if I knew it would make you happy."

"Baldwin, please," she begged. "Don't force me to marry a man I don't love."

"It is not just my decision. You know that the Court must agree to Guion as well. If you want to marry Guion, he will have to prove his worth if he is to wed the princess of Jherusalem. I will not let my sister marry a man who is a fool, or worse."

* * * * *

Agnes sat beneath an almond tree in the shadowed corner of the palace garden; birds sang in the high branches above her head, the dulcet tones of their voices like the singing of angels in the heavenlies. A small book gorgeously bound in red leather and gold lay open on her lap, a gift from the Archbishop of Caesarea, a treasured selection from his own private library. Sunlight angled through the tree. It danced upon the pages, illuminating the fine black lettering and colorful illustrations.

She read the small book twice during her sitting—it consisted of only little over a hundred verses. She found its story interesting, but somewhat confusing for the hidden message it supposedly contained. Its wording had a particular flow to it, eloquent and poetic. She could see the words, and feel the cadence of their assembled order as they descended the page. There was more, however, to what she saw and heard in the words; a subtle turning of phrase or metaphor that lay hidden just beneath the surface, waiting for her to understand. Twice she had read it; twice she had come to its end without comprehending its deeper meaning.

With a sigh of frustration, she tossed the book aside and turned away.

"Such despair is most unbecoming a woman of your standing and rank," said a familiar and masculine voice.

Agnes startled from the bench and backed away. "Amalric," she gasped. "This is an unexpected pleasure."

He glanced at her and smiled faintly as he stooped to the bench and picked up the red leather bound book she had abandoned in her sudden surprise. His dark features matched the surcoat of soft black glove leather covering his mail shirt; his features and his attire were a reflection of her former lover's dark and subversive nature. Amalric turned the book to read its cover and handed it to her.

"I didn't mean to disturb your studies, my lady de Courtenay."

Agnes smiled coyly and slid gracefully onto the bench again beneath the tree. She laid the book in her lap, her hands curled around its spine. "You are familiar with these verses, I presume."

"It is called, *The Hymn of the Pearl*," Amalric said sitting down beside her.

"A poetic title," she said. "But I'm not sure I understand its deeper meaning."

"There are few who do, my lady. Only those who seek a greater understanding of our place in the world will find its true meaning."

She opened the book to the passage she had read and glanced up at him. "And what is that true meaning, Messire? What is the pearl?"

Amalric reclined back against the trunk of the tree and pulled his knee up into his laced fingers. "Did not the Christ speak of it in a parable, referring to the kingdom of Heaven as a pearl of great price? The pearl is truth and understanding. It is the path to enlightenment. Seek it, and you will find that the kingdom of God is within you. The hymn speaks of our separation from the divine and of our union with it again through the knowledge of our true selves. It is that spark of the divine that is within all men."

She arched an eyebrow. "And all... *women*, Messire?"

"Yes, my lady—and all women," he laughed.

It had been many years since she had heard that rich, deep sound. She also remembered that he was not the same man she had taken to her bed as a lover. He bore the face of Amalric de Lusignan, but he was not the man she knew—and yet, he was. That knowledge made her feel suddenly very uncomfortable where it almost never had before. She closed the book and set it aside, out of sight.

"I thank you for your lesson, Messire, but I doubt you sought me out simply to discuss verses of ancient wisdom," she purred.

"No, my lady Agnes, I did not," he said, rising, studying the blossoms on the jasmine climbing the garden wall. "I need your help."

"What kind of help, Amalric?"

"Your son," he replied, turning to her, his dark gaze penetrating her defenses. "I need to get closer to him if I am to protect him as I promised. It is only by chance and misfortune that I was able to rescue him at Marj Ayun. As long as he insists on riding in the vanguard of the army into battle, he will be at risk from far more than just the enemies of flesh and blood. I cannot protect him—and neither can Sion."

Agnes found that she could not sit anymore; she needed to move, to pace, anything to keep her jittery nerves under control. She prayed the tension did not reach her voice. "Just what sort of enemies do you suspect threaten my son?"

He paused, hesitating to answer her outright. She glared at him. "The spirits of air and fire—those whom the Muslims call *jinn* and *afrit*, creatures of pure magic. I fear that one of these spirits may be shadowing the king, waiting for the chance to strike at him when we are least vigilant. They came close, my lady, at Marj Ayun. The allies of the Church will stop at nothing, even magic, to destroy us; even the kingdom of Jherusalem is at risk. They fear what they cannot control."

"I thought the Church condemned all forms of magic as of the Devil.

Amalric laughed darkly. "Officially, yes; but the Church has ever played the part of a hypocrite when it suits their needs. Two hundred years ago, the Lateran actually elected a pope who secretly practiced magic in order to allay its own growing fears about the turning of the millennium. If the Church would go to such lengths to somehow prevent the ending of the world, do you think they would stop at anything less to confront the Order of Sion? That is why I need your help."

Agnes' blood ran cold, even in the midst of summer's heat. She had seen many a display of magic in the past year since becoming a member of Sion, but it still made her feel wary. "But what do you think I can do?"

"You can talk to your son," said Amalric. "The death of the Constable has given us the opportunity to get closer to Baldwin than we could ever hope." He smiled at her, touched her cheek with a caress. "You are his mother. He listens to you. As a knight of Ibelin, and even as my lord of Ramlah's son by marriage, I am at a distance from the king. I don't always know what trouble hunts him." His hand fell away; he turned and sat on the bench, looking up at her. "But if you can persuade him to promote me to Constable, I will have the privilege of being a member of his private council. And, I can protect him."

For the first time since she had heard of the Order of Sion, or learned of Amalric de Lusignan's association as its master, she mistrusted him. Worse, she felt that he was using her for purposes far beyond what he claimed. She felt trapped and alone, uncertain of what she should do. Her son's life hung in the balance of her obedience and her disbelief. Whatever the balance, however, it was she who needed to protect her son. She could only do that if she helped Amalric de Lusignan become Constable of Jherusalem.

She sat, sliding closer to him on the bench and smiled. Her hand rose and came to rest on his chest. Her eyes glanced up into his. "I will do what I can," she said hesitantly. She hated herself for every word she spoke. "After saving his life at Marj Ayun, I'm certain my son will be more than glad to reward you for your bravery. You proved your worth as my constable when I was still Countess of Japhe and Ascalone. Baldwin will trust my opinion if I give it. Never fear, he will see the wisdom of what I ask."

* * * * *

"My brother won't let us marry," Sibylla complained. Her head rested on Guion's bare chest, her hand gently brushing the soft curls of golden hair that graced the solid musculature of his abdomen. She wanted to cry, but found her mood was more conducive to breaking things and shouting.

Guion stroked her long blonde hair as it fell over her shoulder and down her back. He bent his head and kissed the top of her brow. She arched and molded her body to his. His mouth found hers; she melted at the taste of his kisses. It was difficult, but she pulled away. "Guion, I said my brother won't let us marry."

"I know," he whispered, bending his mouth to the curve of her neck and shoulder. Her skin turned to fire and goose flesh at his touch. She giggled. He certainly knew how to distract her. He rolled her over onto her back and pinned her arms to the bed. She shrieked with delight.

Sibylla bit his lip when he swooped in for a kiss and sprang from the bed, grabbing the sheet as she fled. "You're certainly in a passionate mood, *ami*."

He watched her as she wrapped the sheet about her body; he smiled, seeing how little the sheet covered the ample curves of her breast and hips. "How could any man see such beauty and not want to be with you body and soul. To a man who has been away on campaign for so many months, you are like the very goddess to me, Sibylla."

"You speak blasphemy using my name. How flattering."

"I speak the truth, my heart. And nothing more," Guion said. "You are like light to a man in darkness. And now your brother summons us again to ride forth to Le Chastellet."

"Le Chastellet? So soon—why?" Sibylla complained. "You've barely been back in Jherusalem two months. I've hardly seen you."

Guion rose and pulled on his hose. She turned to the window and the stars outside beckoning silently for adoration. Her heart, though, could only adore the man who came and stood behind her, caressing the gentle curves of her shoulders.

"Salehdin is sure to lay siege to Le Chastellet before too long. It can withstand a lengthy siege, but the king will not risk letting it fall into Muslim hands."

"And what of us, Guion de Lusignan?" she said softly, trying not to weep. "Do you not fear that I will fall into another man's hands? Baldwin says you must prove yourself worthy of my hand to him and to the lords of the Court, if we are to wed. I've pleaded with him several times now and he still intends to give me to Hugh of Burgundy."

Guion embraced her from behind, enclosing her lithe body within his strong arms. He whispered in her ear. "You underestimate your own standing within the High Court; or the allies I can summon to my aid."

Sibylla shivered within the tight circle of her lover's arms. The memory of the conversation she had with her mother gave her reason to pause and consider the importance of that which they talked about so lightly. "The powers of magic will not avail us against the opinions of the Court."

"Is that all the support you think I command?" Guion laughed softly. "The kingdom is sorely in need of knights. King Henry will certainly favor a king of Jherusalem who has ties with the crown of England, rather than with France, or the Holy Roman Empire. In light of Henry's promise of a pilgrimage and a holy war, and the substantial sum he has set aside in trust with the Church, I think the High Court will recognize that fact if someone close to your brother's throne is bold enough to remind him."

Sibylla turned in his arms. The sheet fell from her body. He pulled her closer. "I don't care about alliances or holy wars anymore, or even this kingdom," she said. "I will not marry anyone but you."

"Nor will you have to, *ami*," he said, picking her up and cradling her in his arms. "I promise you."

She wrapped her arms around his neck and kissed him passionately. "How long before you leave with my brother?" she murmured between kisses.

"A day or so; no more than three," he managed in broken words as he carried her towards the rumpled bed. Sweeping back the sheer muslin curtains, he laid her gently among the nest of pillows.

Sibylla suddenly pulled away, gazing deeply into Guion's blue eyes shining darkly in the dim candlelight. "Will you stay with me tonight?"

Guion bent to her mouth and kissed her gently, his ardor growing as his hand found the curve of her shoulder and caressed it, confirming his answer without the need for words.

* * * * *

The waxing moon glowed through the clerestory windows with a pale supernal glow; it illumined the stained glass in a manner never seen in the greater light of day. There was magic here of a different kind than hers. This was born of the elements and the alchemical properties of color and light mingling with ancient lines of power and magic hidden deep within the memory of the stones. The architecture had changed with the long and many years—a wall here; a doorway there—but the lines remained, subtle and dormant, waiting only for a touch of power to awaken them.

There was beauty in the simplicity of the *Archbasilica Sanctissimi Salvatoris*; its lines and contours, its delicate arches and fragile columns built up layer upon layer into a house of God imbued with the slightest scent of incense or the softest whisper of a prayer.

Mary slipped from shadow to shadow, searching for her friend, the Archbishop of Tyre. She could sense William's very mortal presence, but the mingled powers of the earthly and the divine distorted her bearings, making him seem to be in one place and then another in the space of a single breath. There was, indeed, more than sanctity and the power of lines laid out in stone that confronted her.

The shadowy taint of an unseen evil insinuated itself in every dark corner of the Lateran, lurking and preying upon the fears of men who wondered if all their pious acts towards a God that was ever unseen had been done in vain. Shadows whispered in the darkness that there were other gods; powers older than the newer God of Christianity whom their people had worshipped with equal or greater devotion before the Church had forced its religion upon them. Here, older powers disguised now by sainted names that every villager, from the eldest grandmother to the youngest babe, were worshipped in whispers under their ancient, more pagan names.

Here, in the midst of all that pious men had tried to make of Christianity, lay the darkest heart of evil, surrounded by the trappings of religion. The evil one had found his place in the fallen world, a throne upon which he could rule with anonymity. Mary was certainly no stranger to the conflict between the light and the darkness in the world; she had had her share of the battles in the age-long struggle. A struggle that had long ago been fought and won by one man's death; and yet, it had yet to be realized by those who continued the war. Mary sensed that lurking evil, and hurried on through the twisting maze of corridors and darkened halls.

The Compline bell rang, calling the servants of Christ to prayer in the cathedral. Monks and priests suddenly erupted from unseen doorways, drawn by the ringing bells and their vows of obedience. The ringing of Compline sent a shiver of disquiet through the ordered ranks of shadow. The bells had power to touch the heart of their magic and dampen it. The shadows scattered and hid amidst the darkness.

Mary hid among the shifting, less fearful shadows that hovered about the meager light of the sacred candles; rather than making it shine all the brighter, the shadows only seemed to challenge the candlelight, forcing it to pale before its greater darkness.

Mary watched and waited, knowing that William's resolute commitment to prayer would eventually bring him to the basilica to join his fellow brothers of the cloth. By the time they sang the opening words of their prayers, he came in alone, bedraggled and care-worn, quietly nondescript in his habit of coarse brown homespun.

She took a place among the various and numerous statues of saints along the choir, unseen and unmoving, an angelic being carved in exquisite white marble. It was a glorious sound she joined, a song of prayers and psalms lifting ever heavenward.

The melodic chant of the Compline liturgy filled her with a longing, a quiet sense of desire to sit once more at the feet of the one she had once loved as merely a man. These were prayers born of a different time; they had power and comfort, a richness of expression that surpassed all human understanding. Her people had sung these words once as they worshipped in the temple of Solomon. They were words that had power to bring Jews and Christians together in a common bond. Instead, it brought only hatred and bloodshed.

Mary cast the thought from her mind and focused on the flow of the liturgy, letting it wash over her like cool, cleansing water. The words took substance and shape, moving in her and around her; they were power—a magic of the infinite and the divine—an essence of spiritual thought that knit her body and soul.

With the intensity of her prayer, she almost missed the ending of Compline. The brothers murmured a unanimous *Amen* and silently went there way to find sleep and rest before the ringing of the morning hour of prayer. If William had not lingered to speak with the clerk of the Holy Father, she might have missed his exit amidst so many other brown habits and bobbing tonsures.

She waited to reveal herself until he had made his way from the nave into the candlelit halls of the cathedral. The clerics had broken off into quiet whispering knots of conversation. William alone, his tonsured head bowed, hurrying towards the great doors of the cathedral.

Descending through the darkness, Mary gathered the shadows about her shoulders as a cloak and walked with him. Rain began to fall during the last hour. It had lessened to a drizzle, spitting in their faces, lending a little coolness to the stifling heat and humidity of the Roman summer.

Mary pulled the hood of her habit down over her face. "Good evening to you, Brother William," she said, adding a deeper tone to her voice.

He glanced up, in no way deceived by her poor disguise; he looked around discreetly, wishing not to be overheard. "Not here. You risk much, my lady, by being here. This is not the place, or the time. The city has eyes and ears everywhere."

"Where, then, do you suggest we meet?"

He grabbed her by the arm and hurried them along through the rain. "Come with me, *brother*. There is a place not so far ahead."

William was a fastidious man and a creature of uncommon habit. Even after an hour of prayer before the altar of God, he knelt before a simple cross of woven palms on the wall of his room and spent a few moments in silent prayer. She followed the thoughts of his mind: he was weary with worry for the young king that he had left alone in Jherusalem. Word had reached Rome through the Venetian merchants out of Acre of the terrible defeat at Belinas and the loss of the Constable. That truly was a blow to his spirit, and to his hope for the pursuit of peace with the Muslims. All his concerns centered on Baldwin.

Finishing his prayer, William went to the table by the window and sat down. The small table was cluttered with scrolls and assorted sheets of parchment scribbled with notes. William took a seat on a stool in front of a desk he had obviously borrowed from the scriptorium. A guttering candle sat in the midst of his research; most of its wax had run out of a crevice on its side, spewing unto the top of the wooden table.

She sent out a tendril of her power and sensed the moving of his thoughts. He was purposely ignoring her, knowing she came because of Baldwin.

"While you linger in Rome, Jherusalem is threatened," she said, casting off the shadows she wore. "He has great need of you, Brother William."

"*Deo Mater*," he murmured, then, louder: "My God has need of me as well. I *am* a priest after all. What has the boy done now?"

"It is not necessarily what he has done, but what he hasn't done," she said. She moved towards the cluttered table. Her hand and eye made a cursory appraisal of the many documents. She found a smattering of Hebrew, Aramaic, and Greek, even Coptic, further down in the piles. It was enough to pique her interest. "The king will no longer listen to reason or to my council. He is determined to make war on the Muslims. He will not listen to any talk of peace."

William looked over at her. "I think he has given himself over to the inevitable conquest of Jherusalem by Salehdin."

Mary casually tossed aside a sheet of parchment onto the table and approached him. She studied the flow of his thoughts just behind his words, knowing he meant more than what he said. "It is too soon. If Baldwin dies now before his time, only Sion will gain by it. He must not throw his life away in a meaningless battle simply to ease his conscience over Humphrey's untimely death. He will listen to you, William."

Her answer distracted him. He turned his gaze away, suddenly finding the words of a yellowed scroll of infinite more importance. "I cannot return to Jherusalem now. His Holiness has asked me to go to Constantinople on an imperial mission to the Byzantines to prepare for negotiations for a possible reconciliation between the Greek and Roman churches. And even if I could, I do not think it would be wise for me to return, just yet."

He looked up at her. "I think I know who the people are behind the Order of Sion—or at least who they were a hundred years ago. Openly, many of them pledged their support to Rome as *fideles beati Petri*, the faithful of St. Peter; but secretly, some reasoned to bind themselves to their own cause under a different name. One more relevant to our inquiry."

He handed her the old and tattered scroll. She glanced down at it, scanning the brief missive. The words were in northern French.

> ...*Now, the lords of Burgundy who form the innermost circle of these conspirators seek to install a man of their own choosing into the Papacy of Rome. It is their hope and design that such a man will make a call for the capture of Jherusalem and the removal of the See of Rome to the Holy City of Sion...*

"Where did you find this document, William?" she asked. She had long known the convoluted history of the heretics who had founded Sion, but she had lost track of them in the last few hundred years before the First War of the Cross.

"His Holiness has begun to suspect the Templars of some role in the heresies rising across Outremer and Europe, particularly the Cathars of the Languedoc. He gave me leave to search the Lateran library for any clues to the identity of the conspirators. I found this in a batch of assorted letters secreted away in the library. It is dated and addressed to His Holiness Pope Victor."

She stared at him quizzically. He answered her unspoken thought. "The man that ruled as Pope for only one year before being replaced by Urban," he said.

"Seven years later, Pope Urban made his call for the First War of the Cross at Clermont. It hardly seems a coincidence."

"Did you discover the name of these conspirators?"

"The Brothers of Ormus," William said.

"Ormus," she repeated. "A name with which we are both familiar."

"Hence, you see the Holy Father's concern about the Templars. He has also shown me other evidence that suggests the Sionist conspiracy may have reached into the halls of the Lateran Palace as far back as Pope Gregory; perhaps, further. The Church has long been in possession of various and numerous codices of questionable content. Whether it has done so for the sake of study, or for some other reason, I cannot say. The words of this hidden letter prove the existence of Sion,—or whatever they called themselves—before Pope Urban's call. But I suspect you knew that already, didn't you?"

She glanced up from the table at him, seeing his expression. She realized he was waiting for this moment to catch her off guard by admitting her knowledge of all he had revealed of his research.

"Not in such detail," she said carefully, not wanting to reveal too much. "Nor that the conspirators had found a haven among the people of northern France. You must remember that the Order of Sion is only the most recent incarnation of the enemy's plans to destroy the Church and the Gospel of Christ." She glanced away. Her hand found a curious book in ancient Aramaic—the language of her people in the days when the Christ walked the earth. "It is why Alexander was chosen to sit on the throne of Peter and why continued requests for a new holy war have fallen on deaf ears. Nor will he make a call while he knows a threat to the kingdom of God exists. I am sorry, William, I know you have worked tirelessly to call for an expedition to help Baldwin. But it would be better for Jherusalem to fall to the Muslims, rather than see it in the hands of an enemy that seeks to destroy the Church."

He shook his head slowly and passed a hand across his brow. "These are powerful men, indeed, if they can influence the election of Popes and command them to do their bidding."

Mary smiled deceptively. "Very powerful men, indeed."

"And yet, you say Alexander was chosen as well. By whom? He certainly cannot be seen as any kind of friend to Sion."

"I am not without my own influences, Father William," she said. She glanced up at him again. "Not all men would see the Church so easily led astray."

His hand came up, fingers steepling under his chin. He blinked slowly. As her words began to sink into his thoughts, the curiosity of the scholar in William grew. "How long *has* this rivalry or heresy persisted, my lady? Certainly it must be older than the Kingdom of Jherusalem or the Order of Sion."

Mary laughed. The sound startled William. "*Much* older, my friend. Much older, indeed. It began with a rivalry that certain early Gnostic believers in the Church claimed existed between the disciples of the Baptist and the blessed Jhesú. One particular disciple of John claimed that Jhesú had also been a disciple of John and that he stole the leadership from him while Herod imprisoned their master. During this time, the disciples split into two factions as the struggle for leadership grew. When Antipas killed John, the same disciple took up the mantle of his master and began teaching that John was the true Messiah, not Jhesú. It was all a lie of course, but the damage was done; many believers were seduced into following a false doctrine—a doctrine that has continued to this day in opposition to the Gospel of Christ and the Church."

William stared at her, his gaze distant and thought-filled. "Simon Magus."

"An arrogant man filled with all manner of powers by the Evil One to lead astray many from the truths of God. Simon spread the lie that Jhesú and I married and had a daughter. After him, and since, the leadership of the disciples of Ormus—that is what they came to call themselves—fell to different men of varying Gnostic traditions. All of them, however, were of the same mind in their desire to destroy the foundations of the Church and remold it to their own purposes."

Mary picked up a handful of his notes and held them towards William. "This evidence—does it suggest any particular place as the center of the conspiracy?"

William sat up straight on the stool and set his quill carefully in the inkwell. "There is some indication by the constant reference to one particular city in Champagne, along with the references in the letter to Pope Victor, that hint that the center of the conspirators' activities was, and may still be, in Troyes. I pray I am wrong, but there is still one other possible connection woven through this dark fabric of conspiracy like a bright, glowing thread: St. Bernard of Clairvaux and the Cistercian Order. He wrote the Rule which the Pope recognized when the Templars became an official order under the Church."

Mary felt a chill foreboding tingle up her spine. "If any part of what you say is true, William, then it gives us a possible place of origin to begin searching for the earliest members of the Order of Sion; and, who they may be now," she said. After so many years of secrecy, she finally had a place to search out the enemy—her enemy. All of it coming about by a chance discovery in a place least expected. She offered up a simple prayer of thanksgiving, knowing that divine providence had led William to the cache of hidden documents. The enemy had certainly done its best to keep themselves hidden from the suspecting eyes of the Church, and from her.

"I wonder how many other Popes the Order's influence has managed to control?"

William paused and sighed. "Several," he said. He looked through the pile of documents and scrolls, pulling out a sheet of scribbled parchment paper, glanced at it, and handed it to her. He rubbed his hand across his tonsure. "I compiled a list of names of eight popes who reigned successively between Gregory VII and Honorius II. Sion—or its previous incarnation—in some way or another, most likely influenced each of them, either directly, or indirectly. However, if this letter is any indication of truth, of the eight, only Pope Victor seems not to have had any part in the Lateran plot, which may also explain why he was in office for less than a year.

"Likewise, in the same period of these eight popes, there were also an equal number of anti-popes that reigned in opposition at the behest of the Roman Emperor. Without a doubt, something beyond what Pope Victor's letter records seems to have been going on behind closed doors in Troyes and Rome—perhaps, some rivalry between the Holy Roman Emperors and the lords and nobles of Burgundy. There is even evidence that Papal influence may extend back to Sylvester II whom legend claims practiced magic. Of course, it was only with Pope Gregory's reign that the dissension between the Lateran and the Emperor began over the election of popes."

Mary studied the list, matching the names against her knowledge of events in the Kingdom of Jherusalem. Her knowledge yielded up one particularly important fact. "The last two names on this list were both instrumental in having the Templar Knights recognized as an official religious order, answerable only to the Pope."

"Not only that, my lady, but the first nine members of the Templar Order were from the region of Burgundy and Champagne—the same region the anonymous letter to Pope Victor warns was the center of the Troyes conspiracy. What's more than just a little passing strange, the first new member the Templars admitted after their formation was the Lord of Champagne, Hughes de Payens' own liege-lord. Perhaps, we should be concerned with more of the Templars than simply the Master of the Order."

Mary smiled. She came and set a kiss lightly in the center of his tonsure. "Father William, you are, indeed, a wonder and a treasure without price," she said to his mild embarrassment. "Continue searching for whatever information you can find on the Brothers of Ormus or Sion, while I see what I can do to ease the unrest in Jherusalem that Baldwin is so determined to incite. And please, William, be careful. The city has eyes and ears everywhere."

† CHAPTER SIXTEEN

The wise man hath scaled the city of the strong, and hath cast down the strength of the confidence thereof.
—*Proverbs 21:22*

W hy do you continue to hesitate, uncle, trying to buy the favor of the Ifranj, when you should be buying men and weapons and supplies," was Taqi ad-Din's opening plaint. The shrewd and keen-eyed emir paced the floor of the tent like a caged beast; his eyes darted, the fire of their glare flashing with the dark glitter of polished obsidian. "While you bargain with the infidels, uncle, they fortify their position, threatening the security of Dimasq. Is this the extent of your great *jihad*—offering the godless Ifranj gold?"

The call for the evening prayer had passed: a slave girl came and set the *káffe* service on the table and made her quiet retreat so as not to interfere with the lord Taqi ad-Din's tirade. The slaves of Dimasq were a submissive people. Salah ad-Din Yusuf sipped his hot *káffe* and set the small silver cup down beside the Qur'an. He glanced up at his brother's son. "Wisdom is the friend of the old, nephew," he said without rancor. "Folly and impatience is the province of the young. You are young yet in years, and in your faith. Why should I buy the destruction of Jisr Ya'kub with the lives of good Muslims, when gold will do the same? The Ifranj are much in need of gold. If I can supply their need and still gain what I desire, why should I not seek to do so and save precious Muslim blood?"

"The Ifranj refuse your gold, uncle," said Taqi ad-Din. "How much will you offer them before you finally decide to fight?"

"You are under the impression that the Ifranj can be bribed, my brother's son. But the Ifranj will never agree to destroy their castle," Yusuf said. He smiled and picked up his steaming *káffe*. Before taking a sip, he paused with the cup at his mouth. "The Nasrani will defend their fortress with their very lives if need be. This continual game of bribe and refusal only buys us more time to prepare. While we have kept them on the defensive these past many months, the threat to Dimasq has remained minimal. You wish me to attack; and we will. And when the mighty fortress of Jisr Ya'kub finally falls to us, it will send fear into the hearts of the infidels and they will tremble before the greatness of Allah."

Yusuf and his restless nephew were not the only two men in the tent arguing the strategy of their successful summer campaign and the troublesome thorn of Jisr Ya'kub. A third man, Izz ad-Din Chauli, the senior Mamluk of the Dimasq slave-soldiers, stood by the tent door at attention, his allegiance to the House of Ayyub quietly declared by the wide yellow silk sash he wore over his breastplate. He was a large, dark-featured Circassian with piercing blue eyes who had made his way up the ranks of his caste by virtue of his leadership quality and his ability to outlive his fellow soldiers in battle. If nothing else, he was a survivor. Of all the Mamluks in the service of the sultan, only Izz ad-Din Chauli had the privilege of speaking to his master without permission. He used that privilege now, pressing the bounds of even his master's forbearance.

"You should attack the Ifranj, now then, my lord Salah ad-Din, before they have time to muster," the Mamluk commander said in his broken Arabic. "The Leper King has returned to Urshalim. Do not lay a siege. Attack them now, and the walls of Jisr Ya'kub can be overran before the infidels can even march to their aid."

His nephew and the senior Mamluk had both spoken their minds to him; they waited now to see what reply would take root in their master's mind and words. Yusuf let the silence deepen and spread with the uncertainty of his displeasure of their unasked for advice. Out of the corner of his eye, he saw Taqi ad-Din glance nervously at the Mamluk standing motionless and mute by the door of the tent. Yusuf sipped his *káffe* without hurry and studied the latest reports from his commanders in the field. The reports confirmed the words of his would-be advisors. Only a fool would turn away a gift from Allah.

"Go, and prepare your men, nephew," he said, picking up the Qur'an for his evening devotions. "We will ride for the Nasrani fortress in the morning."

"Are we to lay siege to Jisr Ya'kub, my lord?"

Yusuf declined to acknowledge either man with a glance, not while his eyes beheld the glorious words of the Qur'an. He turned a page, finding the passage he was reading before his commanders interrupted him—the blessed Prophet's teaching concerning the nature of *jihad.*

Fight in the cause of Allah those who fight you, but do not transgress limits; for Allah loveth not transgressors. And slay them wherever ye catch them, and turn them out from where they have turned you out; for tumult and oppression are worse than slaughter...

His gaze lifted briefly from the words of the *Sura al-Baqara*, dismissing his commanders. "No. We will attack and may Allah bless us with a swift victory."

* * * * *

It was not the miracle of God for which he had long held out hope; but for Baldwin, it was enough, and a beginning. On the eve of their march northwards again to Tiberias and Le Chastellet, a distinguished group of French lords arrived in the kingdom with a substantial number of knights.

Their ship weighed anchor in Acre, and they no more had their feet beneath them, and they were off, accompanied by Raymond of Tripoli to rendezvous with the royal army at the great city of Tiberias. Among the contingent rode the illustrious trio of Henri, the Count of Champagne, Peter de Courtenay, and Philip, the bishop-elect of Cambrai. All three were of the family of the French king and kin to Baldwin through his mother and uncle, though several generations removed; worthy allies in a time of such great need.

Despite the small miracle of their timely arrival, Henri bore with him tidings that would have an even greater and more far-reaching impact on the kingdom. Sibylla's betrothed, Hugh of Burgundy, sent his greetings and a small token of his devotion, with a rather bland apology for his delay, yet again, by affairs in Burgundy. He would not arrive until after Eastertide eight months hence. Sibylla had predicted his delay. Still, she would be outraged, and yet, vindicated by the disappointed delay. Of course, her fury would only be a show for the Court. She would hound him now for a marriage with Guion de Lusignan even more. Henri's tidings were not what Baldwin wanted to hear.

Further complications awaited them in Tiberias. Word had come that Salehdin had laid siege to Le Chastellet, possibly an all-out assault. The news had come four days ago.

Baldwin rode into Tiberias ahead of his army to the loud acclamations of the people on white Ri'jl, his Arabian stallion that had been a gift from his riding master, Abul Khair, on his recent eighteenth birthday. Raymond led them into the courtyard where his wife, Eschiva de Bures, the Princess of Galilee, awaited them alone on the steps of the keep. Even from the first, an unspoken concern seamed her face with a weak smile that diminished the usual sparkle of her eyes.

At a quiet word in Arabic, Ri'jl shifted his weight and slowly knelt down on all fours, allowing him to dismount easily from the saddle. The rest of his assembled lords rode in behind them through the inner gate, crowding the small yard with men and horses. The main of the army remained outside the walls to set up camp.

Baldwin swung his leg over the high pommel of his saddle and stood beside Raymond as his lady made her way down the steps. Bowing deeply, she greeted Baldwin before her own husband, as a proper lady should. He bowed his head and took her hand lightly. He gave a chance for her to withdrawal that elegant appendage on account of his disease, even with the riding gloves he wore. He seldom gave men such an opportunity. Surprisingly, she slipped off his glove before he could kiss her hand, and kissed his disfigured hand instead and bowed deeply. Even her husband, the well-respected Raymond of Tripoli, rarely accorded him such an honor. Her devotion touched him. He set a hand to his head and his heart after the fashion of the Arabs.

"I am deeply touched, my lady Eschiva, by your greeting," he rasped. "I am seldom honored these days, even in my own Court."

Eschiva bowed her head in acknowledgment of his compliment. "I only wish, Your Highness, that I had better news to report," she said and handed him a Templar dispatch envelope with a broken seal.

News of Salehdin's actions forced them to hasten their initially slow response. There had been no need not to tire the army by rushing to Tiberias: the impregnable stronghold of Le Chastellet could withstand a lengthy siege. Now, while Salehdin harried the Templars in their newly built fortress, the army refused to go further without the Life-Giving Cross of their beloved Savior. Their faith, and their superstition, had grown with their victory at Montgisart. The army feared to face Salehdin without the Cross. Worse, it would take several days to fetch the sacred relic from Jherusalem. Hardly the picture Baldwin wished his distinguished guests of the French crown to see of his kingdom. It made him seem incompetent and overwhelmed by the duties of his office.

The Constable was four months dead and the position still needed an appointment, as did that of a new Marshal; the Templars themselves were having their own problems without a master. Saint-Amant languished in a Damascene jail and God only knew when another would replace the critical position temporarily filled by Gilbert d'Erail, the Commander of the City of Jherusalem. Oh, Reynald had tried, and admirably so, but it was too much for one man with his own lordship to govern to fill the office of Constable and Marshal.

Those were problems, though, that would have to wait. Baldwin prayed his strength would hold out, and that the strength of Le Chastellet could hold out against Salehdin's determined assault. The defense of the kingdom depended on it.

* * * * *

Tiberias, the seat of the Principality of Galilee, was a city with very little privacy. Explaining a meeting at night between the Count of Champagne and the brothers of Lusignan would draw unwanted suspicions.

Guion was as nervous and twitchy as a cat while he and his brother waited for the Count on the shore of Tiberias' wide, dark sea. He never did well in these secret, clandestine situations; Amalric was the leader, Guion the handsome follower, the little boy who was always chasing after his older brothers, pleading to join in whatever adventure they were devising.

Too often, though, the company of his brothers brought trouble. Such as the time when he and his brothers managed to incur the wrath of their liege-lord, King Henry of England, and his son, Richard of Aquitaine. Quite by accident, they had ambushed Henry's wife and Richard's mother, Eleanor, and killed her escort, the Earl of Salisbury outside the deep forest leading into Poitiers as they were returning from a pilgrimage.

The consequences of that fateful day changed the fortunes of the House of Lusignan forever. Henry and Richard expelled Guion from Poitou for killing the earl; Godfrei found refuge with their older brother, the heir of Lusignan. Amalric meanwhile, followed the example of their noble father, Hugh. He sought his fortunes in the East, in Jherusalem. It was only natural then that Guion would follow his brother to Outremer when he had nothing left to gain in Poitou. It proved a wise decision, indeed, for Guion. There were no crowns in France to be won, nor were there women to wed half as beautiful as Sibylla d'Anjou. Amalric, it seemed, was still looking out for him.

Not that he needed Amalric to look after him, or that he did not have ambitions or a sense of greed. He had ambition and greed, and he could be ruthless, if necessary. He had killed the Earl of Salisbury, after all. It was only that he lacked confidence and courage to make his ambitions a reality, to make them his own. He lacked nerve. Such lack made him twitchy.

That single, deficient quality he lacked in an otherwise, perfect and much lauded, mind and body. Many regarded him as a paragon of chivalry and beauty—and he knew it. He needed no one to watch over him, or do for him what he could not. It was just nice to have his brother close as hand—just in case.

Cloaked and hooded against prying eyes and the moonless night, they huddled near the lapping waters of the Galilee; two hulking boulders of shadow scattered among the many that dotted the gentle slopes leading down unto the sea. They bore no torches or lamps, only the starlight that glistened on the gentle waves. Other lights lent them aid: candles and torches burned all about the city and citadel of Tiberias. None burned so brightly, though, as those that lit the hall looming above the edge of the sea where the king met with his closest advisors to discuss their next course of action against Salehdin while they waited on the precious Cross of the Lord to arrive from Jherusalem.

Amalric and Guion conversed quietly for a time about the ever-changing affairs of the kingdom and the greater events happening beyond their shores that touched so deeply upon the interests of Sion. They were the same interests that brought Henri of Champagne to Outremer under the guise of a pilgrimage and a knight. Guion half drew his sword and spun with a muffled cry when the Count caught them unawares in the pitch-blackness of the Galilee night.

"Put up your sword, Messire," Henri said. "If I truly was a threat, you'd already be dead."

Guion caught a glimpse of the Count's face within the hood of his cloak as he turned to greet his brother with the kiss of friendship. Henri was a man cast in the same mold as Amalric: dark-eyed and dark-haired, with a quietly unsettling demeanor that left Guion only a little more than on edge about their secret meeting.

"I began to wonder if you forgot our meeting, my lord," said Amalric.

Henri pulled his hood down over his face. He seemed to disappear, becoming one with the darkness. Guion felt that subtle tingle of magic he often felt around his brother of late. He did not remember Amalric having that gift when they were younger.

"We have certain issues that need discussing, now, while we are far from those who might detect us together," said the Count as he sat down on a large boulder jutting out of the water. "What has become of the Master of the Temple? I hear from the king he is rotting in a jail in Damascus."

"And so will he stay until he dies. As long as he is in the hands of the Sarrazins, his betrayal is no longer a threat to us," Amalric said.

He pulled his cloak aside and straddled a rock to sit. Guion chose to stand; he was too nervous to sit for very long. "His absence gives us time to reassess the value of the Templars to our long-laid plans. I think the time has come to decide whether we should even continue our association with them. They were created as the Pope's private army; perhaps it is the time for them to become that vision, and that alone.

"I will take up the debate with the other members of the Brotherhood, when I return to Champagne, but we have other problems at present, besides the Templars." Henri tilted his head towards a sudden noise in the night: it was nothing more than the boisterous outbursts of soldiers dicing in the camp, their voices carrying on the water. Henri turned back to them. "During his time in Rome for the Lateran Council, Pope Alexander gave permission to the Archbishop of Tyre to dig through the library to find what he could about the Brotherhood."

"Has he found anything?"

Guion felt rather than saw the Count's gaze fall upon him. "Only the odd reference or two, but nothing incriminating," said Henri. "Even with our secrecy, though, there are those who have betrayed us over the years. There could be some written evidence, however slight, of the existence of Ormus or Sion. It is no secret that in the years before Urban's call for a holy war, numerous lords throughout Western Europe bound themselves to the papacy—first to Gregory, then to Urban, to do the Lateran's bidding and to support reform within the Church. Gregory called these followers *fidelis beati Petri*, the faithful of St. Peter. It was from these faithful the earliest members of the Brotherhood came. It is only a matter of time before Troyes or Champagne figures in his search."

"We must make sure, then, that he finds nothing else. If he continues to be a problem, other measures will have to be taken," Amalric said.

"How much of a threat is he?" Guion asked, cutting to the heart of the matter. He, too, had a stake in the affairs of Sion and the kingdom.

"We crossed paths briefly in Brindesi before we sailed," Henri said, standing suddenly as if to make a predetermined exit. Amalric followed suit. Guion continued to pace nervously. He felt an uneasy bond between the two men that went beyond the use of magic. He suspected that more passed between them than simple words—a sharing of thoughts and minds and will—and he was privy to none of what they shared. Still, the Count of Champagne said much that he could hear and understand. "The Archbishop was on his way to Constantinople on a diplomatic mission for the Pope, while the rest of his ecclesiastic companions returned to Jherusalem with us from the Lateran Council. He will no doubt be distracted for a time—possibly several months to a year—but whatever he learned in Rome, he will certainly share it with King Baldwin when he returns."

"Then we need to move quickly before we are exposed," Amalric said. "Once Guion is finally crowned as sacred king and married to Princess Sibylla, it won't matter what the nosy Archbishop of Tyre discovers. He won't dare to move against us openly for fear of what we can do."

Guion was not a member of the vastly secretive order of conspirators, nor did he understand all that it tried to do. That they wanted to challenge the Church and remake it in the image of an older, truer tradition of belief made no difference to him. The Church had many sins for which it needed to atone, not the least of which, its abuse of power and the secret condemnation it made against his family's house simply because they bore the stamp of the devil through the blood and seed of the water-faerie, Melusine. It would pay, though. By the very magic which it condemned the House of Lusignan, the power of the Church would be undone.

Even if he did not completely comprehend all the ramifications of Sion's actions, Guion was a central pawn in the plans they had worked towards in a century long plot to gain control of the Church universal—first, through the control of the Papal Father in Rome; second, through the creation of the ever strengthening ranks of the Knights Templar, the papacy's own private army. There remained only the last play on the chessboard; the critical placement of the king into a position of power and importance as the queen drew him into the sphere of her loving influence.

* * * * *

It took only a mere handful of days—five to be exact; the number of faith and prayer and duty, as proscribed in the pillars of Islam— for the Turkish sappers to breach the impregnable walls of the Nasrani stronghold. The outer defensive wall fell by the end of the first day; the inner fortifications were another matter. The Leper King refused to come forth to challenge him, and in his hesitation, Jisr Ya'kub waited only for Yusuf to pluck it from the infidel's hand.

The assault on the citadel began with wave after wave of arrows Yusuf had ordered to rain down from the heavens from the east and the west. Meanwhile, the sappers dug a long tunnel beneath the northeastern corner of the thick walls with shovels and fire to collapse the massive fortifications of stone. Day and night, the miners worked expanding the siege tunnel. For five days, the Nasrani waited, preparing to die in a fruitless battle.

Salah ad-Din Yusuf sat atop his stallion, motionless and silent, in the slanting shade of a wall, watching as work progressed. His administrator, the Qadi al-Fadil, sat beside him, notebook in hand, recording all that he saw. Yusuf accorded him a few thoughts on the matter, but nothing beyond a passing comment or observation on the size or strength of the fortress. What Yusuf left unsaid was the contempt he felt towards the arrogant unbelievers in the hour of their defeat. He had offered them gold to withdraw from the construction; he had extended his mercy if they would surrender. Instead, they ignored his words and rebuffed his actions with coarse slanders against his honor and dignity and with vague references to the questionable character of his mother and the circumstances of his birth. He glanced upwards, finding the white and red standard fluttering in the breeze, its offending cross so boldly emblazoned upon it. When morning came, it would be the first thing he ground into dirt beneath his heel.

Evening came, and passed in its usual, natural fashion, turning into the long hours of darkness. The sappers finished their work and the Nasrani spent the night in sleepless expectancy of early light. The army of Islam woke to the wailing cry of the *mu'adh-dhin*, calling them to prayer. Salah ad-Din Yusuf turned his face to towards Bait al-Allah, the House of God in holy Mecca, and gave praise for the deliverance of the infidels into his hand and that the Ifranj king had not answered his challenge.

As dawn began to invade upon the walls of night, the sappers lit the fires in the siege mines. The black and violet shadows of early morning melted with the intense heat of the inferno into the crimson red of fire, lighting up the over-spreading sky. A rush of flames engulfed the tunnel. It exploded into a breach that collapsed the wall above it. A shout rose from the collective throat of Islam, echoing against the walls of the fortress. Another shout replied from within, but with far less voice and confidence. The defenders were not giving up without a fight. For that, he thought them valiant and brave; he also thought them foolish. He swore to give no quarter to those who surrendered. His orders were to slay everyone wearing the accursed cross of Isa al-Masih.

Muslim soldiers poured through the immense breach in the citadel walls. Flames spread throughout the complex; smoke billowed black from fires the defenders had lit behind the gates to ward against attack through those avenues. Scrambling over stones and broken splinters of burning wood, a knot of soldiers tried to stem the tide of invaders that met them. In a bloody clash of arms, the defenders fell beneath the sword, slaughtered to a man.

Amid the noise, a horn winded, sounding a charge. A lone knight, in a desperate act to hold off the attackers, plunged himself and his war-horse into the burning gap of the wall despite the heat and the fire, and the keen, bright blades of Allah. He immediately fell into the waiting depths of Hell. Swarming over the corpses of men and horses, the soldiers spread out into the castle to find the enemy and kill them.

Walls and arches shadowed by the sun loomed above his head; darkened passageways led off in various directions. There was no beauty here, only harsh, achromous stone with blood splashed across its surface. The bodies of white and red robed knights littered the ground, screams of dying men and clashing steel echoed through the twisting corridors.

Avoiding the smoldering timbers and pools of Nasrani blood staining the stones of the fortress, Yusuf slid off his horse just as a bloodied knight ran at him and flung himself down at his feet. He babbled incessantly in the guttural, barbaric tongue of the Ifranj, pleading no doubt for mercy and for surrender. Al-Fadil leapt from his horse and hauled the man to his feet, a dagger pressed tightly against his throat for his effrontery towards the elect of Allah.

Yusuf waved the *qadi* back into a circle around the cross-emblazoned soldier along with those who had seen their master attacked by the infidel and had come to his aid. Drawing his sword, Yusuf laid the tip of the curved blade against the soldier's trembling chest and stared narrowly at him. He was young, no more than a boy, if he was any judge of age. He barely had enough whiskers to grow a proper beard, even for the Ifranj. This was no knight; he was only a serving lad who had donned his dead master's robe in the hope of defending the fortress like a man.

Yusuf spoke gently and softly to him as though to a child, knowing the Nasrani understood nothing he said. The boy pleaded, sobbing, reciting a single word repeatedly in the manner of a prayer. Yusuf knew the word. *Mercy.* The fears of one so young moved him to compassion. He smiled and sheathed his sword.

"Al-Fadil," he said, climbing back into the saddle; he sighed, collecting his thoughts and raw emotions. "Tell my nephew to set up camp outside the walls; we are not leaving here until every stone is overturned."

The *qadi* made his obeisance and pushed the prisoner towards the Mamluk guard.

Yusuf heeled his horse, and abruptly turned the magnificent black stallion back towards his respected administrator. "One more thing, my friend." Al-Fadil paused. "That boy is a prisoner. No harm is to come to him in any way. He asks mercy of us. Let us pray that Allah will grant him such mercy in the slave markets of Dimasq." He glanced up at the enemy banner still fluttering in the breeze above the smoke and charred ruin of Jisr Ya'kub. "This is no longer a stronghold of the infidels. See to it that someone takes down that Nasrani banner."

"Yes, Excellency."

* * * * *

Baldwin dreamed of horrible, nightmarish images that refused to dissolve into memory even when he woke and fell back to sleep again. The dreams grew worse each time they began anew.

He rode alone through the folded landscape of his dream world, each rise giving way to new and ever more terrible views of destruction. The carnage stretched towards the twin hills looming before him. Thousands of men had died here, butchered like animals and thrown to the birds as a feast.

He rode weaponless, shorn of armor and protective attire; his blue tunic was drenched scarlet with blood, his destrier stumbling with the many wounds he had received in this unknown battle. This was not Montgisart, Belinas, or Marj Ayun; it was not even the defense before Le Chastellet. This had the feel and air of the not yet, the future, the terrible result of a battle yet to be fought, and lost. Still, there were faces he knew, most of them, the bright flower of Jherusalem's knighthood.

Bodies of Christian and Muslim littered the field, piled in gruesome heaps, their ruined limbs entangled in the mockery of a brotherly embrace. Smoke drifted on the breeze, carrying with it the stench of decay and spilt entrails, along with the odorous waste that men release upon death. Flies buzzed in a ubiquitous dirge for the dead. Vultures descended, gathering upon the sun-bloated corpses; the scavengers tore at the raw flesh of men and horses, gorging themselves with meat, heedless of the faiths that divided the dead.

The moans of the wounded rose above the ruin of war. They pleaded for the Blessed Mother to relieve their suffering. She, however, was powerless to help them in their misery. There were others; they mumbled unknown prayers in Arabic, crying out to Allah. He slid from his dying horse and stumbled among the dead and dying. Hands reached out to him, pulling him down. Amidst the body-littered field, a knot of priestly robes lay close together. In death, even as in life, they protected the precious Revivifying Cross of the Lord. The standard bearing the treasured relic lay broken upon the ground, half of it still in the hand of a dead cleric—a bishop by his robes. The bishop's severed head had rolled against the foot of a Sarrazin, his vacant eyes staring upward towards the heavens. The cross lay beside it in the dust, spattered with the blood of Christian and Muslim alike.

Baldwin tumbled and fell before the bishop and the cross. His hand reached for the sacred relic and lifted it gently to his chest. With the hem of his tunic, he wiped the blood from its gleaming gold and precious gems. The dark eyes of the bishop suddenly blinked. Baldwin fell back with a strangled gasp and cried with fear.

The blood-crusted mouth moved, the dry, cracked lips whispering harshly. "You have done this, King Baldwin," murmured the bishop, his eyes turning to Baldwin. "Your pride and your anger have brought ruin and death upon us all. Repent of your sins while you still can."

Baldwin scrambled backwards, getting to his feet, and fell over another body. A hand grabbed him, and then another. Voices murmured to him in a babble of mixed tongues. He fought desperately, trying to free himself of the hands of the dead. He held up the cross, brandishing the relic as a weapon. It blazed like the sun. His hand burned with its heat, and he dropped the cross. A corpse pulled him down and down, dragging him into the fiery abyss that awaited all traitors.

*—**Magdalen**, he screamed, and screamed again until his throat was too raw to even whisper.*

He woke suddenly. Darkness still held sway over the early hours of morning. Dawn was just beginning to pale the skies over the eastern horizon. Sweat drenched his body and bedclothes. His heart beat rapidly in his throat. He felt disoriented waking in an unfamiliar bed in Tiberias. A loud banging startled him from the last tattered shreds of his sleep and dreams.

Someone pounded on the door of his room, and entered, bearing a lighted candlestick. It was Reynald, with Baldwin's sleepy-eyed squire at his heels, struggling to pull his tunic over his head.

"What is the meaning of this Reynald, waking me in the middle of the night?" he said, trying to calm his hammering heart.

"Sire," his Regent began and paused, hesitating uncharacteristically. Baldwin thought it odd: it certainly was not Reynald's habit to waver in such circumstances. "Forgive me, but I have dire news to report. Le Chastellet has fallen to Salehdin."

The words struck like a knife in his unprepared heart. The news was so grim it seemed he had not yet awakened from his nightmare; but he had. "How is that possible?" he mumbled. "Le Chastellet was built to withstand a siege lasting several months."

Reynald snapped his fingers, motioning towards the door. A young man entered the dim glow of candlelight, came to the side of the bed, and knelt down. He was a squire by the look of his attire, a youth no older than Baldwin, one that had ridden to Hell and back to deliver his message. His clothes were in tatters, his entire body spattered with blood and dirt; sweat streaked his face giving him a ghastly appearance. Beneath it all, dark eyes, wild and feral, filled with the dread of what he had seen, darted at the slightest sudden noise.

"What is this, my lord of Kerak?" Baldwin demanded.

"A survivor, Sire, of Le Chastellet—or what's left of it."

Reynald nudged the squire's shoulder with a hand. The squire glanced up, his eyes registering the repulsive sight of his king's diseased face. "I... I am—was—Your Highness. I was the squire of my master, the commander of Le Chastellet. He is... he is dead. All the Templars are dead. The Muslims cut off the head of all the knights and serjeants. The rest they took as slaves to sell in Damascus. Salehdin ordered the well filled with the dead bodies of the knights and the horses. My brother, Sire... my brother was a knight."

Baldwin glanced at Reynald, and then back to the boy. "When did this happen?"

"Last night, Your Highness," said the wide-eyed youth. "My master hid me in a secret passage and bid me come to Tiberias when night had fallen to report all that had happened. It was terrible, Sire, seeing the Muslims kill all the Brethren. Salehdin plans to raze the fortress and leave no stone standing."

Reynald laid a hand on the boy's shoulder again and patted him. "You've done well, lad. Go and see what Cook has in the kitchens. You have earned a bit of food and some rest. Now off with you."

Baldwin's squire led the ragged Templar from the room and closed the door. The latch had no more shut, when Reynald turned to him, arching a grey-black eyebrow. "What will you do, now, Highness?"

Baldwin threw off his sheets and climbed out of bed. Dizziness overwhelmed him. Reynald lent him a hand to steady his balance. Anger and guilt fought with the fears of his nightmares. The volatile combination ignited the fires of his burgeoning magic. It concentrated his thoughts and power into a single-minded focus of will.

Le Chastellet has fallen. It was his fault. So many lives sacrificed because of his sins of revenge and foolishness and pride. That same pride and stubbornness fought back, threatening to tear down his newfound wisdom. He beat them back with a word—a name he called out into the midst of the grey mist that separated the worlds from sight.

—Magdalen, *he cried, his heart heavy with the weight of emotion.* **Can you hear me? Le Chastellet has fallen. Forgive me for not listening to you. You were right. Peace is our only hope.**

The sainted Magdalen did not respond, though he could sense her thoughts and presence just beyond the edge of the grey void.

Instead, a shadow invaded his thoughts, a presence dark and malevolent, challenging the power of his magic. It sought to have him, to dominate his thought and will, to keep him from reaching out to her; he tried to battle it, but the darkness was too great. He fell back into the sunlit world of men.

"What will you do now, Highness?" Reynald repeated—or said for the first time. Baldwin was not sure. He blinked at him, comprehension dawning.

"Gather the army, my lord," he said. "We're marching to Jacob's Ford."

It was a half-day's journey from Tiberias to the Templar stronghold. For the sake of swiftness and surprise, Baldwin ordered only the mounted army to fly north with him from Tiberias; the foot soldiers would only slow them down. He prayed Salehdin would relax his guard or split his forces; more to the point, he prayed the sultan would make a mistake. There were fifteen hundred men garrisoned at the Le Chastellet. They needed a miracle if they were to live.

They rode at a break-neck speed, hoping to catch the Muslims unawares and drive Salehdin off from the captured castle. During those long hours, Baldwin had plenty of time—too much time—to consider his dream in light of the expected slaughter they rode towards. No matter how many times he ran the vivid nightmare through his mind, he could not connect it to the fall of Le Chastellet. The outcome of his dream, even distorted by the fantasies of his fears, did not fit reality. The dream left him with only one thought, one truth to the scene he had witnessed. It was a vision of the coming battle that would see the fall of Jherusalem after his death. His actions, whether intended or not, were leading the people of his kingdom to their destruction. It would begin here, though, at Le Chastellet.

† CHAPTER SEVENTEEN

Fear not you: for I know that you seek Jesus who was crucified. He is not here. He is risen....
—Matthew 28:5-6

Jherusalem was in ferment. Its narrow streets were crowded and ababble with the languages and dialects of every nation of Christendom. The streets were jammed in this busy season of the devout and the greedy. Merchants shouted from their stalls, hawking their wares to the wide-eyed innocents newly arrived in the extravagant, exotic East.

Since just after the Feast of the Nativity and Candlemas, the roads to Jherusalem had begun filling with eager pilgrims determined to be in the Holy City for Eastertide. The harbor of Acre had become a doorway from the West, filled with pilgrims disembarking into Outremer.

Pilgrims thronged the Church of the Resurrection to celebrate the Savior's Passion. Many of the poor souls were here in the hope of some small miracle to cure them of their infirmities; the fact that so many had made the harrowing journey alive with such physical ailments was a miracle in itself. So often, pilgrims died at the very altar of Calvaire having spent all their strength just to visit the site of their Lord's crucifixion and resurrection.

Mary stood among the crowded chapels in the church; she, just another pilgrim taking in the great drama portrayed in the numerous stations of worship throughout the great cathedral. Worshippers thronged the chapel of Calvaire; the smell of so much humanity swelled to nearly overwhelming. She made the sign of the cross upon her body like the others and closed her eyes, blocking out the distraction. She alone of the ragged mob of pilgrims had witnessed what had truly happened in this small room, the holiest place on earth. She alone understood the power the crucifixion and the glorious resurrection had unleashed in the world.

The pounding of the hammer echoed in her ears: the hammer and the silent screams of his agony only she could hear. His screams shook the foundations of all the worlds. The blows made her wince with memory of her own pain each time the pounding hammer shuddered through the cross and the ground beneath the wooden beams. The riotous crowds pressed closer, eager for a spectacle amidst the uncommon heat of the last several days. She sobbed and wailed, fighting desperately to get past the line of men that kept the jeering crowd at bay.

A shadow fell across the ground as the soldiers raised him above her; the beam slammed into the hole that held it. His silent screams of pain echoed across the void between the worlds; in the world of men, he was silent, like a sheep brought to the slaughter. Drops of blood splashed her upturned face, mingling with her tears. She had brought the ancient cup of her people, the golden vessel of the new covenant he had made that she guarded now as sacred. She held it up beneath him, letting it fill with drops of his precious blood.

Thunder rumbled over the hills, echoing from beyond Olivet and the East. The crude laughter of soldiers mocking his terrible agony only made her tears all the hotter. She wanted to unleash her anger, her power, to make the soldiers suffer for their amusement. Silently he called to her. He commanded her to restraint and forgiveness: it was for this reason that he had been born.

The ordeal stretched on towards nightfall. Time slowed, advanced, flowing at an unnatural pace. It was horrible to endure, seeing his agony, his suffering, the slow torture of his dying. She knelt at his feet, not understanding; she pleaded with him, begging him to let her save him. He refused her and hid away her power so that she could not defy him and use it to release him from his torment. He left her only the ability to sense his pain, his thoughts.

He cried out again, and again; just the effort of speaking seared through his limbs like fire. Anguish, shame, and the severed love of a father, became too great to bear at once and alone. Beaten and bruised, bloodied beyond all human comprehension, he made a final whispered cry, and died. Mary cried aloud and sunk to her knees on the ground. His mother stared silently towards the heavens, tears streaming down her face, murmuring a prayer. The earth shook violently; the sun went black as night. Man and women ran in fear for their lives. The great and terrible day of the Lord had come. The rain fell in sudden torrents, washing the earth with his blood.

The burial was less painful, knowing that his pain was over; but no less sorrowful, seeing the one she loved had passed beyond life. For all her power, all the subtle art of her immortal kind, she could not raise him from the dead. She learned that day the painful truth about the limit of power that had been set upon her kind.

Night had fallen; the preparations proceeded by torchlight. She touched him gently, fondly, as she helped to wrap his body with the strips of perfumed cloth. Her tears mingled with the costly spices. She took her time, unable to bear the thought of him sealed in a tomb with a stone. When they had finished, his mother covered his face with a cloth; Mary held the aged woman's hand. She fled before the tomb closed.

The blind madness of her anguish and her sorrow brought her to the austere house of the man who had condemned the one whom she had loved. He slept in a bed beside his wife, his slumbering thoughts a jumble of greed and indifference towards the people he governed. His dreams were untroubled by the events of the day. It was as though they had never occurred; that the Son of God had never died by his command.

She pointed the thin silver blade of her dagger over his heart. The cold tip pressed lightly against his chest. She had only to plunge it into its black depth and her revenge would begin. The next to die would be the hated king of her people. She prayed for strength and a sure hand, although she knew that such prayers were not in God's will. Instead, the Master's simple words of teaching sprang to her fevered mind and robbed her of her anger. Her vision blurred with tears. Try as she might, she could not slay the monster of a man asleep beneath her blade.

The sound of her sobbing woke her victim's wife. Their gazes locked; in her mind, the woman saw a shadow with a face more beautiful than the greatest of their household gods. The startled wife pulled the bedsheet to her mouth in a knotted ball as her eyes locked on the shining blade poised above her husband's heart. The woman shut her eyes and murmured a prayer in her native tongue. Mary fled the room, and the world, leaving the woman to her belief that a prayer to her false gods had saved her spouse's life.

It was three days before she returned to the city. She came alone to the garden outside the walls, hoping the guards would let her pray at the tomb. The soldiers that guarded it were gone and the tomb empty. She feared the worst: that those who wished to cause him further desecration had stolen his body. She fell to her knees beside the rolled away stone and wept. In the depths of her anguish, she sensed the power of the immortal, the divine, but not the one who had died. Two voices greeted her as she bent her head to the tomb; a light shone, unnatural and radiant. They hailed her as sister, those who were kin to her kind. She pleaded with them, begging to know where his body lay hidden.

The gardener answered her. She fell upon him weeping, overcome at last by her grief and sorrow, knowing not the man who spoke with her. He spoke her name; and she knew him. When he called her apostle of the news of his resurrection, the scales of uncertainty and doubt fell from her eyes. Only then, she truly understood the words of his teaching. He was indeed the Son of God, divine and eternal, but clothed in human flesh that sinful man on earth might see the holy One of Heaven revealed.

Mary stepped back and fell to her knees in worship, understanding now so much more than his words. He was God; and she, nothing more than a creation of his hands. There was no going back for either of them. She could no longer love him as she had before, at a distance and unrequited. In his mercy, he took her love and made it perfect: a newfound devotion that healed her long years of loneliness. He called her beloved and disciple. It was enough.

* * * * *

Guion de Lusignan knelt before the altar in a chapel far beneath the Abbey of Mt. Sion. Only yesterday, he had made his way to the abbey with the crowds of pilgrims and hopeful penitents who sought absolution for their sins from the Patriarch as part of the services held on Maundy Thursday. The room where the pilgrims had met with the Patriarch was not the same as the Evangels called the Upper Room. Rather, this was a smaller chamber that lay in a cave beneath the ruins of the original synagogue built by the early believers of Christ who preserved a truer form of the faith than did the followers of Paul. The Order of Sion had converted the subterranean ruins for their use as a meeting place for their rituals.

Stripped to the waist, the cool cave air blew gently across his back and shoulders with the chilling cold of winter. The pungent scent of incense hung heavily in the air, almost hiding the underlying acrid stench of burnt blood and parchment. He felt that odd sensation of power, the tingle of magic on his flesh as it surged outwards from the ring about the altar, warding the chapel against intrusion and detection by the enemy. The crumbled stone, carved out of the living rock of the mountain had a reverence of age, a hint of dust and ancient memory that had nothing to do with magic or the hidden powers of the earth and air. The stone was simply old. Incense and blood warded the chapel. That and the words of power his brother had spoken to the four quarters of the wind.

His hand throbbed where they had pierced it with a silver athame to mix his blood with the wine in the sacred grail sitting on the altar. A thrill of excitement vibrated through his body, and yet, at the same time, he felt a sense of apprehension: a sense of quilt, and of shame at what they did. It pricked his conscience. The momentary feeling, though, dissipated just as suddenly as it had come upon him; his mind filled again with the words and actions of the secret ritual. A niggling of doubt remained. It hovered just beneath the surface of his thoughts.

The shadows were dark within the hall, and inviting. He always felt most comfortable in the darkness, rather than in the light. Three candles on tall candlesticks formed a triangle around him. Within the triangle of candles, stood a circle of nine men and women—actually, there was only one woman among the nine; the *Apostola Apostolorum*— each of them clothed in robes of white and red, reminiscent of the Knights of the Temple. Their voluminous hoods hung down over their faces; only their voices gave any hint of their identity. He knew several members of the Order of Sion, but not all. His brother, of course, as the Master of the Order, he knew; but there was also Agnes de Courtenay, Renaud, the elderly Abbot of the small abbey beneath which they were meeting, and lastly, Heraclius, the Archbishop of Caesarea.

The one man, however, who was most conspicuous by his absence, was the Master of the Templars, Othon de Saint-Amant. He was still rotting in a jail in Damascus because he stubbornly refused to let the Order ransom him. In his place—or so he assumed; hooded and cloaked as they all were, it was hard to be certain—stood another of the Templar commanders, presumably Gilbert d'Erail.

As for the rest of the Order's secret members, he knew nothing, although he certainly had some guesses. Either way, the membership had gathered for this momentous occasion in their long-awaited plans: the installation of a king of their own choosing and making, even if the sacred king was to remain secret for a time until he could take the throne publicly. While the rest of Jherusalem—the King and his Court, and the ecclesiastical community, as well as the pilgrims and the citizenship of the Holy City of God—gathered in the Church of the Resurrection, listening to the Good Friday liturgy, the Order of Sion celebrated a triumph. The crowning of the *Rex Dei*, the God-king, an heir of the *sangreal*, the holy blood, upon the hallowed throne of Christendom; or rather, the Christendom that had yet to be realized by the world through Sion's efforts.

Guion bowed his head eastwards, the position of the sun at its rising, as the hooded figure in front of him began to intone a psalm in his deep baritone voice. Just the words—or was it the sound of his voice—seemed to brighten the flickering candle flames around him. The fire grew and danced, gleaming on golden vessels all about the simply adorned chapel. Magic warded their physical bodies; the psalms warded their souls and prepared them for the ceremonial rite. He closed his eyes and envisioned the words he heard spoken.

"For thy servant David's sake, turn not away the face of thy anointed. The Lord hath sworn truth to David, and he will not make it void: of the fruit of thy womb I will set upon thy throne. If thy children will keep my covenant, and these my testimonies which I shall teach them: Their children also forevermore shall sit upon thy throne. For the Lord hath chosen Sion: he hath chosen it for his dwelling. This is my rest forever and ever: here will I dwell, for I have chosen it."

The psalm ended and another began in another man's voice, this time behind him, westwards. The psalm's theme remained the same as the last: Sion and Jherusalem, and the strength and majesty of the two.

"*Behold now, bless ye the Lord, all ye servants of the Lord: Who stand in the house of the Lord, in the courts of the house of our God. In the nights lift up your hands to the holy places, and bless ye the Lord. May the Lord out of Sion bless thee, he that made heaven and earth.*"

With the second psalm sung, the pattern continued, first from the south, and then, lastly, from the north. "*They that trust in the Lord shall be as mount Sion: he shall not be moved for ever that dwelleth in Jherusalem. Mountains are round about it: so the Lord is round about his people from henceforth now and forever.*"

"*I rejoiced at the things that were said to me: We shall go into the house of the Lord,*" the northern figure sang from the position where the throne of the heavens sat. "*Our feet were standing in thy courts, O Jherusalem. Jherusalem, which is built as a city, which is compact together. For thither did the tribes go up, the tribes of Lord: the testimony of Israel, to praise the name of the Lord. Because their seats have sat in judgment, seats upon the house of David.*"

With the warding of body and soul against the evil that lurked behind every dark shadow almost complete, the ceremony turned its focus on Guion and his suitability to wear the sacred crown of Jherusalem. All this he had known would happen for he had rehearsed it before time with his brother. Now, in the midst of the ritual, he felt a change come over him, an overshadowing of confidence and boldness, a sense of his right to be king of holy Jherusalem.

"*Great is the Lord, and exceedingly to be praised in the city of our God, in his holy mountain,*" Guion sang, reciting the psalm Amalric instructed him to learn. "*With the joy of the whole earth is mount Sion founded, on the sides of the north, the city of the great king. In her houses shall God be known, when he shall protect her. Surround Sion, and encompass her: tell lye in her towers. Set your hearts on her strength; and distribute her houses, that ye may relate it in another generation.*"

A hooded figure lifted the grail, the ancient cup of the mysteries, from the altar table and held it to his lips. A hint of spices rose from its dark swirling depths: cinnamon and cloves. It veiled the pungent odor of blood and the burnt parchment. He drank slowly and deeply. Instantly, he felt dizzy and nauseous; his throat and abdomen burned as though with fire. A hand steadied his balance.

His body felt as though he looked out from the eyes of another person. He gasped and caught his breath. He had no time to think. The tall, dark figure in front of him asked a question. He responded without thinking or knowing how he knew what to answer.

"Are you the Christ—the king of the Jews?"

243

"I am the one sent from above, the innocent, the one who bears witness of the truth," he replied, lifting his head. "I am the one whom the world does not know."

"Reveal then, Son of Man, the mystery that has been hidden, but will be revealed on the Day of Judgment," commanded the deep voice of his brother, the master. "By what right do you claim the throne of thrones?"

A candle flame angled a shadow across the floor; he bowed his head. Cold scented water trickled down his bare taut back as a branch of hyssop scraped lightly on his skin, criss-crossing his back and shoulders. He shuddered. He closed his eyes.

"They flailed me with whips," he said. "But it was not I."

He opened his eyes again. A cloaked figure moved forward, and laid a gleaming sword across his upraised hands. Guion lifted it in homage. "They struck me with reeds and hit me with rods, but it was not I."

A hand set a crown of laurel and tightly woven vines upon his head; oil dripped over the golden locks of his long hair. He felt a surge of pride, of completeness, a sense of the sacred right of kingship that derived from the blood of his ancestors.

"They crowned me with thorns," he said, pausing, then continued. "But it was not me."

The dizziness returned; his vision blurred. His tongue felt thick and sluggish. It was the lingering effect of the wine. The fire had dampened, burning down to a smoldering ember that warmed the depths of his soul, but the wine and the candles and incense were having an additional effect on his mind and body. It was working its subtle way through him like a fever, infusing his wandering thoughts with amazing visions of the future. He would be the sacred king of the holy city before the night was through, but he wondered how much he would remember of the ritual with the mind-numbing haze of the cup's magic libation.

He wondered if he was supposed to remember.

Another figure stepped into the space before him, a hood falling down close to his face as the warder bent before him. He caught a hint of perfume and knew it was the Lady Agnes de Courtenay. She kissed him lightly on the brow and whispered an inaudible word before turning away. He understood its significance.

"They beat me, spat on me, and cursed me with vile names. But it was not me."

At this point in the ritual, the liturgy changed. Agnes did not move away for the last and final element of the ritual coronation. The change was not in his rehearsal. He was at a loss. A shiver of fever came over him. Agnes drew back her hood, as did the rest of his benefactors. She took the aged cup from the table and held it just above his head. "Whom does the *sangreal* serve?"

His mind raced with more questions than he had answers.

Whom does the sangreal serve?

Whom does the royal blood serve? Whom would the holy kings serve? — The kingdom? The people? The Church? The Order of Sion? No. Kings were no more kings than a servant was a servant. All men are equal, he thought. *Except those who are not equal. But why would the servants of Sion ask whom the kings of the royal blood should serve?* Fear began to gnaw away at his confidence. His brow beaded with sweat. *If he could not answer, would it disqualify him as king?*

A light struck him with sudden understanding, a revelation of the deepest truth.

A king is no greater than the least of his subjects, he thought, almost murmuring the answer. He smiled. "The *sangreal* serves those who serve it."

An unseen hand draped a robe across his shoulders, a marvelously wrought cloth of royal purple and worked with gold embroidery along its edges. He flinched instinctively at its unexpected touch. He had answered correctly. "They stripped me naked and laid a robe across my torn and bloody back. They mocked me and knelt before me, laughing at my shame," he said. "They thought I had died, but I laughed at their ignorance for it was not I, but another whom they crucified."

Amalric de Lusignan stood before him and raised his right hand. "To whom do you owe this sacred crown and throne?"

"*Deus muemque jus,*" Guion answered, "God and my right. I am the seed of David, the Chosen One."

His brother stepped closer and set his hands on his shoulders. "Then arise, Guion de Lusignan, *Rex Dei, Rex Hierosolyma*: King of God, King of Jherusalem, and the sacred king of the Holy City of God."

* * * * *

They waited in the falling darkness for the coming of the miraculous light into the Sepulcher of Christ. Pilgrims crowded every bit of floor space within the church. Baldwin and Sibylla huddled together next to a column. He pulled his cloak down over his face with a thickly bandaged hand; Sibylla held a tattered rag to her nose. The clash between the fragrant incense of the clergy and the noxious odor of the poor, itinerant pilgrims grew to overwhelming in the close, confining press of worshippers. As evening approached, the clergy extinguished all the lights in the cathedral and the expectant congregation waited with unlit candles.

The service ran late; Baldwin's lesioned feet hurt from standing. He leaned against the marble column and Sibylla's shoulder. One by one, the canons of the church stood before the Patriarch on his throne in the choir, and sang a lesson from the Old Testament that recalled the promises of a Savior to sinful man since the foundation of the world.

The pace of the service quickened after the singing of the twelve very long and very cumbersome Old Testament lessons. Two pilgrims fetched the Life-Giving Cross from its chapel. A procession made its slow way through the choir, and round about the shrine of the Sepulcher several times as it grew ever darker outside the church; the congregation waited in eager anticipation for the appearance of the miraculous light of life in the tomb. Prayers rose from the assembled into the airy galleries of the Rotunda; they echoed against its magnificent dome high above them and fell in a whisper of voices.

Suddenly, a dim light sparked to flickering life in the tomb. A cry went up from the priests and the congregation fell silent, dumbfounded by the miracle. Baldwin pulled himself up against the column, trying to get a glimpse of the resurrection light. Sibylla whispered to him, warning him to be careful. They had grown closer in the past few months; closer than he thought they would ever come. He could actually think of her as a friend. He trusted her with things he would never reveal to Reynald, his mother, or even, Father William. He squeezed Sibylla's hand, reminding her of his gratitude for coming with him undercover to the church.

A rejuvenating thrill of excitement shot through his body like a bolt of lightning. *Christ is risen*; or so, the light signified. The grave had lost its power; death had lost its sting. It was an incredible revelation, even after a thousand years. The Magdalen had been the first witness of that glorious event. He wondered if Mary had felt the same excitement, the same amazement when her eyes had finally opened to the truth of the man who had stood before her in the garden.

From a single miraculous light in the tomb, the flame of joy spread throughout the great hall, from the Patriarch to the people, until the whole cathedral was alight with the flames of thousands of shimmering candles. Amid the passing of the resurrection light, a deacon of the church stood and sang the Exultet.

Baldwin felt a sudden sense of release from his long-held guilt, a cathartic joy that rid his heart and mind of all the pent-up emotion of so many months. The glorious hymn of Christ struck a chord deep within him. For so long he had thought his motives were pure, that his desires and dreams for his people were without thought for himself—a sacrifice for the kingdom's ultimate good. He was wrong. His selfishness had blinded him from the truth. For too long, he had pretended that his leprosy, however caused, was only a minor inconvenience, an insignificant plight he could easily overlook, rather than deal with it for what it was doing to him. He had turned into a caricature of his true self; a shell of a king who thought he needed no one's advice to govern his troubled kingdom or his troubled life. He would not let anyone think him weak and simple because he was a leper.

In so doing, he had spurned the Magdalen's wisdom when it did not fit with his selfish plan to show any and every one he was more than the sores and the terrible disfigurement of his disease. He would do so no more. God in His infinite mercy and grace did not require the sacrifice of a penance—at least not in the sense the Church taught as penance—but rather, his obedience, complete and without hesitation. To that end, things would have to change. Of that, he swore to God, and to himself. No matter how many days he had left on the earth, he would pursue obedience, even to the surrender of his life or his kingdom. It was the reason he had coerced Sibylla into coming with him to the Holy Sepulcher.

It was just after the evening meal when they had slipped their ever-present guards and made their way towards the Church of the Resurrection under the guise of pilgrims. With all the travelers in the city during Lent and Holy Week, they were just two more travel-weary pilgrims making their way along the crowded streets on Holy Saturday. Beneath an arch spanning the narrow street, an elderly man cried out to them, to anyone. Baldwin stopped to help him, but Sibylla urged him towards the church before the light failed and the dangers of the streets at night awoke. Baldwin insisted; Sibylla groaned at his untimely charity.

The old man was a pilgrim and a leper. Like the poor man in the parable of the Good Samaritan, bandits had beaten him badly and left him to die. His fellow pilgrims had left him only the small crucifix of woven reeds he had brought with him from Antioch to leave in the chapel of Calvaire as penance for some sin he had committed long ago in his youth. In equal likeness to the parable, clergy and common men alike ignored the pilgrim's pleas for help. Only Baldwin had been kind enough to stop and help a dying man. He blessed Baldwin and Sibylla, and handed them his treasured cross of reeds.

"Place this for me at the shrine of Calvaire, I pray, good sir," the pilgrim asked, wincing with the pain of movement.

"Let us help you up and we'll go together to the service," Baldwin said.

Sibylla's heart had softened at the old man's story. He noticed how she had glanced more than once at the both of them, seeing how they shared the same wasting disease of the body. Her sympathy was as much for the elderly man as it was for her leper brother.

"Listen to my brother, good sir. The church is but a little distance further."

"No, no, my fair lady," he said, couching up phlegm and blood. "I am at the end of my days, children. Let me die watching the stars as they make their appearance over the holy city. Take my cross, please. It is enough for me that I have finally beheld the city of my Lord."

It was the pilgrim's last words. He died with the name of God on his lips. Shutting his eyes, they hastened on towards the church and the services of the blessed Savior.

Behind the priest singing the Mass for Easter Eve, a large fresco of Jhesú ascending into Heaven with Adam in his arms stretched across the apse of the basilica. It was an impressive and powerfully emotional scene to witness. The fresco glowed with the flames of thousands of lighted candles. Many of the pilgrims wept aloud. Sibylla dashed a tear from her swollen eyes. She squeezed his hand and held him close.

Baldwin imagined himself in Adam's place in the painting, carried aloft to Heaven in the arms of the Savior. For the first time in a very long while, he felt relief at the thought of his quickening death; a sense of relief and comfort for the fate that awaited him.

* * * * *

Agnes de Courtenay had never felt more alone than she did this night on the eve of Easter, even with so much joyous celebration of life around her. She knelt before the altar in the chapel of the Lady in the Tower of David. The small windowless room was quiet and tranquil. It held the solemn silence of a tomb. A beautifully illuminated Bible lay open on the wooden table; next to it, stood a cross. In the soft glow of candlelight, the altar cloth shimmered white with the radiance of woven beams of silver moonlight.

Lighting a candle, she sat back on her heels and prayed silently to the patron saint of the Order of Sion: John the Baptist.

She prayed for strength, for wisdom, for peace of mind amidst the turmoil of the Court. Wiping a tear, she rose stiffly and stood back from the altar. Standing back even a step, the shadows in the chapel of the Lady loomed much darker. The small soft globe of light around the candle flame glowed too timidly to have any power against the darkness. It seemed a perfect picture of her fears and concerns.

She stared at the candle flame flickering so hypnotically in the draft that breathed through the Tower. She knew that the world would hate her for what it thought she had done in the name of Sion, especially for raising a man from her lover to a knight of Ibelin, to the Constable of Jherusalem. They would never know, though, of the sacrifices she forced herself to make for the sake of her son, or her daughter. What she had done she had done to protect her children—things that others would surely claim as treachery, or greed, or even simple selfishness.

Agnes pulled her arms close about her body, trying to stave off the rising emotions within her small and increasingly frail body. Her head dropped; a tear fell. In the last year or two, the grey in her long auburn hair had begun to win the battle of age. The balance she had fought for so long had shifted; the grey was far more noticeable than the rich auburn that had been her crown of glory for the last forty-six years. Too many fears and concerns had taken their toll in the past few years.

Her children, the only two treasures that God had seen fit to leave her, were all that truly mattered now. Even her revenge against the Church had waned in importance, and with it, her regard and enthusiasm for the agenda of Sion. She was losing one of her children to the injustices of nature and of God. She would not see him cast aside simply because he was a leper, or because of some long sought after ambition of men—however grand or noble, or right. Agnes bit her lip. She held back the tears that suddenly welled once more in her eyes; and then, finally, she let them have their release.

* * * * *

The banners of the two northern lords fluttered in the breeze that blew in off the sea. Raymond and Bohemond turned inland, passing into the environs of Ramlah and Ibelin, and the green foothills of the Shephelah with an escort of mounted knights. With the full strength of troops that both could muster, the escort was nothing less than a small army. Armies made men uneasy—very uneasy—particularly a king whose two chief allies were marching with their armies against Jherusalem. By late afternoon, the escort had brought them to within a half league of the castle of Ramlah. A guard of twelve Ibelin knights rode out from the city and the castle, offering formal greetings from their lord, inviting them to lodge for the night. Delivering their message, the guard took up the vanguard ahead of them, and escorted the column to the city. They had come to the last leg of their journey, so near to the site of the miraculous battle of Montgisart. Tomorrow, they would march on Jherusalem.

It was the evening of Holy Saturday. Raymond had intended to keep the holy days in Jherusalem. At least he rode towards the holy city under that pretense. Raymond and Bohemond would not make their entrance into the city until the day of the Lord's Resurrection.

Ironically, the banner of Tripoli that went before them bore the outline of a golden cross on a blood-red field: the enemies of God besieged Jherusalem from within. Its salvation would come on the day that the cross, an emblem of shame and suffering, had found new meaning for the followers of Christ. If Raymond had his way, his *coup d'etat* would be a bloodless affair, and the Princess Sibylla would wed his choice of a husband before the royal army could react to stop either. These things, however, never seemed to go as planned.

Bohemond was not particularly pleased with the plan of the coup—he always found something to complain about—but he understood its necessity. He had enough problems of his own with the king of Jherusalem and the Church. Bohemond held up a hand and whistled. A falcon shrieked from on high and landed on his outstretched arm, its wings flapping, the tiny bells on its feet jingling frantically as it steadied its balance. The bird was his ever-present companion, a gift from a Syrian emir as part of a now defunct truce.

Raymond cantered up beside the quiescent prince to ease his cousin's conscience. Bohemond spoke first. "Is this truly the wisest course of action, cousin? Or has your hatred for the de Courtenays driven you to madness?"

Raymond held his patience in the face of his sudden anger. "Better the accusation of treachery on the lips of our people, than the sword of our enemies across our necks," he said, taking a deep calming breath. "The de Courtenays enjoy far too much influence over the crown. They are like carrion birds gathering around the living corpse of the king's body, waiting for him to die. I will not let the king hand the crown over to his mother's kin and their Poitevin lap-hounds. The only way to kill a basilisk is to cut off its head. To do that, you have to attack it in a way it least expects. This is no different."

"And does the Lord of Ramlah know that you intend to force Sibylla to marry him against her will at the point of a sword?"

Raymond glanced over at the laconic Prince of Antioch. "He knows. I would hardly say he thinks of it as forcing, though. Baldwin has wanted to marry Sibylla since she was old enough to agree to a betrothal." Bohemond started to object; Raymond cut him short with a raised hand. "Of all the men in the kingdom, Baldwin of Ramlah is one of the most respected lords in the East. There are few men in the High Court who would refuse the wisdom of seeing him marry the Princess

Sibylla, no matter how it is accomplished. The Court has only to pay the steep ransom Salehdin demanded for his release and he will be in their collective debt. Of course, then, we will have a king who is in our debt."

His cousin took his time responding, but when he did, his voice had lost its willingness to question his actions. "Remind me never to cross you, cousin," he said, stroking the feathers of the gyrfalcon's regal plumage. "You are certainly not a man I would want as an enemy. But I wonder—is there any length you wouldn't go to get what you want?"

"Don't worry, cousin," he said, turning his eyes towards the city and the castle of Ramlah looming ahead. "I stop short of regicide, if that is your concern."

* * * * *

"How could he do this to me?" Baldwin complained. Word of Raymond's advance on Jherusalem had interrupted the traditional Easter feast and set the lords and ladies at the table scurrying in every direction about the palace.

His mother took his hand and herded him towards the dimly lit office of the Constable, decorated in an oriental fashion to resemble an extension of the garden: potted plants, ornate candlesticks, birdcages, and latticed partitions. It lay just off the corner of the Tower courtyard. A peacock cried from its hidden bower high in the trees. It was a gloriously sunlit Sunday. All of the hope and joyous expectations that accompanied the Resurrection filled out the celebration. The rivalries of Court, however, dashed the day to ruin in one fell swoop.

Baldwin took a seat at the large desk in the center of the spacious room. Agnes stood beside him quietly, patiently, her hand resting attentively on his shoulder. Since the disasters at Belinas and Marj Ayun the previous summer, she seldom left his side most days. She was his shadow and ever-constant presence.

Agnes started to answer his outburst when the Constable burst into the office to join them with the new Marshal at his heels. Baldwin was never more thankful that he had filled the two vacant military posts than he was at that very moment.

For so long, Humphrey of Toron had been their guiding light in these sorts of situations, the elder statesman to which so many had come for wisdom. From what he had heard of Amalric de Lusignan from his mother, he was a capable knight who offered his advice openly and plainly, without the use of flattery to win his lord's favor, especially when it might bring harm to the army or the kingdom. Of Gerard de Ridefort, the new Marshal, he knew very little.

Both men stood around the table and bowed their heads to their king. "What have you learned of Count Raymond's movements, my lord Constable," Baldwin said in his hoarse, rasping voice.

De Lusignan turned to the Marshal and nodded; Gerard de Ridefort handed Baldwin a leather-bound scroll across the table. "He is encamped at Ramlah along with the Prince of Antioch. The Ibelin brothers are with them, Sire."

"Of course... of course they are with him. It's their fief, my lord Marshal," Baldwin said, tossing the scroll onto the polished table. His failing eyesight prevented him from reading the report. His blindness had begun to progress more rapidly in the past few months since Le Chastellet. He had told no one yet. Only his mother and sister knew. Despite his malady, he was in no mood for his officers to treat him as a simpleton who needed the most obvious detail explained to him.

His mother discreetly squeezed his shoulder. She reached for the scroll. "What do you think he hopes to accomplish by marching against Jherusalem, my lord de Lusignan? Start a civil war?"

"It is quite simple, my lady," the Constable said. "He intends to marry the Princess Sibylla to the Lord of Ramlah."

"He wouldn't," Agnes said.

"He would—and he will."

Agnes handed the scroll back to the Constable and sat down in a leather chair. "Why? What good would that do him?" she demanded, confused and outraged.

"Isn't it obvious, mother," Baldwin said. "Raymond knows that Burgundy might not ever come. Since William's death, you have seen how he continually complains about Sibylla marrying anyone who was not born in Outremer. He thinks someone from the landed families should rule the kingdom after my death. In his mind, only Baldwin of Ramlah is eligible according to the requirements drawn up by the *Haute Cour*." He hesitated a moment, thinking through the implications of the situation with his cousin, the Count of Tripoli. He laughed, shaking his head at the transparent plan laid out by his so-called advisors to make him feel in command of the situation. "The Lord of Ramlah, however, is not the only man in the kingdom who meets the Court's requirements for my sister's hand, is he?"

De Lusignan was quick to answer him: Baldwin thought he would. "My brother meets the requirements as well. He is here in the kingdom. He has rank, even if it is as the third son of the lord of Poitou. He is canonically free to marry, as the Church requires. And he is old enough to act as a Regent for your nephew should anything happen to you, Your Highness, though we pray it never does."

"Your concern for my health is duly noted, Messire," Baldwin said. The Constable's anger flared noticeably, but he held his tongue. He was a remarkable man to keep his anger under such control. It was a valuable quality in an officer of the kingdom.

"You must marry your sister to Guion before Raymond comes," Agnes said, "or he will take the throne from you and do as he wishes. The man cannot be trusted, my son. You know this."

"No," he said softly.

"You must, Your Highness," his Constable argued. "Or you risk losing all you have to a traitor."

A pain shot through Baldwin's eyes and grew. He was getting such headaches often of late; they would come upon him suddenly for no apparent reason and plagued him for hours. Dawud attributed them to the increasing symptoms of his illness: his eye sockets were desiccating, leaving his eyesight to fail. The strain caused the headaches and the growing blindness. Baldwin had his own opinion: it was the people around him. People like the good officers of his Court who stood before him now and his mother.

Gerard de Ridefort cleared his throat. Baldwin turned to him. He was a pleasant enough man: quiet, responsible, and competent to the necessity of his office. Lusignan liked him well enough. Their good relationship boded well for the kingdom's future military ventures.

De Ridefort excused his interruption. "Your Majesty, if I may be so bold to speak." Baldwin nodded his assent and leaned back in his chair. "There is more here to consider than just the actions of the Count. As you know, I was in the service of my lord of Tripoli for many years before coming to Jherusalem. I know what manner of man he is and of those who gather around him." He paused, caught his breath, and continued: "You must be wary of all those who are associated with the Count. He knows no restraint to his thirst for power—or his desire to be king in your place." Gerard paused again, watching for some reaction from Baldwin. His veil, however, covered more than just the hideous ruin of his face. It veiled any expression he might make. Only his eyes registered his emotions. Right now, the only emotion they gave away was his silent composure.

"You would also do well to watch the Chancellor, His Lordship the Archbishop of Tyre," said the Constable.

"William?" Baldwin laughed. "What does he possibly have to do with my sister?"

"Nothing; and everything, Sire," said de Lusignan. "Remember who appointed the Chancellor to his office in the first place. Since you became king, he has kept a close eye on you through the Archbishop—your every move; your every thought."

Baldwin growled with anger. His bandaged hand slammed down on the table. "How long must I act to prevent this petty, continual bickering and war-mongering among my own people," he said, running out of wind and words long before he had vented the full measure of his anger. He was tired; his mind and body far too fatigued to argue any further with this unrelenting cabal of advisors. "Isn't it enough that Salehdin wishes to drive us all into the sea?"

He had had enough. He was not sure whom he could trust anymore. Enemies surrounded him on every side, just as he had friends who were more than enemies. There was only one person he could trust. She was never around, however, when he needed her most. He called to her, but her thoughts remained closed to him. She was near; of that, he knew for certes. He sensed she continuously kept watch over him.

If he truly believed her—and he did—then his kingdom would not fall to the Sarrazins before his death. And if such was the case, then it was important that he concern himself more with the unraveling affairs of the kingdom such as keeping Raymond from his throne, or letting his sister marry whomever she chose to prevent the former. She could make worse matches than the third son of a lord who could trace his lineage from a water-faerie from Lusignan. She could make far worse choices, with far worse consequences.

What he needed was peace: peace from war, peace from the everyday turmoil within his kingdom. If anything else, his body needed rest from his labors, and that would only come through peace. He reached out to Mary once more, offering the sacrifice of himself that she so desired.

—Come to me, Magdalen. Please. It has been too long since I had your advice. Come to me and I will make peace with the Muslims, if it is still possible.

He stood abruptly and wrapped his long blue robe about his frail body. Outside the hall, the sunshine and the grey-green shadows of the courtyard garden beckoned to him with the promise of warmth and light, the quiet of peaceful solitude. The promises of Eastertide and the Resurrection were pushed aside and forgotten by the more immediate concerns of the world—or nearly so. He at least remembered something of their bright joy.

"My lord de Lusignan, do what you can to keep Raymond from entering the city with his army. If he claims he only wishes to visit the

holy sites in observance of the day, then let him—but without his army."
He turned to his mother, sitting silently by the Constable's desk. "Do
whatever else must be done, mother," he said, limping towards the door
and out into the inviting sunshine. "Tell Sibylla that she can have Guion
as a husband if she still wants him. But she must do so now—today.
And may God forgive me if have erred in my judgment."

—He will forgive you, Baldwin, Mary said softly, distantly. *I
will come to you soon and together we will pursue the peace you
desire. Only remain faithful to God and to your promise until I
come.*

—Have I done as I ought, my lady? he asked her, but she had
gone, leaving him with no answer.

* * * * *

Candlelight shone all about the cathedral. Sibylla glanced up
demurely at the man who would be king of her heart and king of
Jherusalem. Guy stood resplendent in the blue and silver of the House
of Lusignan; his crown of golden curls and bright blue eyes filled all her
sight. Her hand closed on his as the Holy Father read the words of
blessing over their marriage.

Sibylla had never been happier or more joyous. Guion squeezed
her hand in return and sealed his vows with a kiss.

† CHAPTER EIGHTEEN

Pray ye for the things that are for the peace of Jerusalem: And abundance for them that love thee.
—Psalms 121:6

Othon de Saint-Amant woke to the wail of the *muezzin*. Its piercing cry echoed from a high and distant minaret, winding its long and sinuous way through the ancient city and its maze of stone, down and down into the depths of the darkest prison of Damascus. The cry mingled with the miasma of sweat and filth and the nauseating stench of his own excrement. The combination of odors and sound overwhelmed his senses. He tore a fresh strip of cloth from his dirty tabard and held it against his nose. Even in the midst of summer in the Syrian desert, his cell was uncomfortably cool and damp; a curse of the Barada that flowed around Damascus and settled into the deep places of stone beneath the city. The cold worked its iron-strong fingers into bone and joints, into every injury of battle he had ever sustained, making him feel much older than his forty years.

Morning came again as it had for more mornings than he could remember. He had learned to hate the light dawn, just as he hated the sound of the Muslim call to prayer. Both awakened him each new day to the reality of the Hell into which his captors had thrown and forgotten him. The light and the prayer, though, he hated only half as much as hated himself. He deserved to die in this place, alone and unshriven, for his betrayal of the young king of Jherusalem.

The shadow of a rat crept along the wall, its tiny nails scratching the stone. It ignored the moldy black bread he had tossed aside in disgust a week ago. His stomach growled anew—not for the bread, but for meat. He thought to kill the rat and eat it raw and bloody, but resisted the natural urge. It was his penance: to hunger, to thirst—to die of starvation.

The intrusive rat added a simple, welcome change to the daily pattern that had become his life; a life defined by shadow, a cold stone cell, and the ethereal dim light that drifted downwards from some hidden window far away beyond some turn in the stone high above his head. He missed the simple things to which he had never given so much as a second thought: the sun, and the wind on his face; the sweat of a horse in a lathered sweat; his Templar brothers in prayer at the end of the day... the voice of another living person that knew and spoke his tongue.

"Such a pleasant, sentimental thought, my dear Othon," said Amalric de Lusignan. He stood in the opposite corner of the cell where the shadows were still darkest. At the sound of his voice, the rat scurried away into a hole in the wall. "To hear the voice of someone who speaks your tongue. I hope I'm not a terrible disappointment for you."

Othon pushed himself up from the floor and stood against the wall, the furthest he could retreat from his former master. "I wondered how long it would be before you finally came, if you came at all."

The Master of Sion stepped from the shadows into the dim light of the cell. "My dear, dear friend. How lonely you must feel, shut away from everyone and everything in the world. You have surely heard from your Sarrazin captors that we have secured the throne of Jherusalem with my brother's marriage to the Princess Sibylla. Or, that the Count of Tripoli plotted a coup against the king, but Baldwin stopped him only with the princess' wedding. No, you're right, Messire Reverend Knight," he said, holding up a hand as he paced the floor. "I suppose they wouldn't bother to tell you such."

"I am, but a simple knight and brother of the cloth, after all."

Amalric de Lusignan let out a mockery of laughter. "Such humility. God must be proud. You are certainly more than a simple knight, though, Othon de Saint-Amant. You are the Master of the Templar Knights, a servant of the Pope, and a friend to the king and lords of Jherusalem." He paused and stopped in front of Othon. "By the way, where *do* your loyalties lay, Saint-Amant?"

Othon's hand strayed to the small dagger on his belt with the sinister turn of his master's voice. His captors had allowed him the blade as a temptation to take his own life. It would be useless against a man like de Lusignan; but it gave him comfort and, perhaps, a measure of boldness just to feel its hilt. If he were about to die, he would die fighting as a knight. "My loyalties are with God."

"With God?" Amalric's gaze slid towards Othon's hand and his dagger. His head and body responded, turning to take a more defensive pose. "The Muslims were kind enough to leave you your belt and dagger, I see."

"It is all that I have of my honor," he said. "A Templar can give nothing but his belt and his dagger as a ransom—I have given them neither, nor will I. It is the Rule of our Order as St. Bernard wrote it. A man, I believe, who had some rather intimate dealings with the Order of Sion."

"A convenient excuse; and stubborn. Both of which has put us in an awkward and uncertain position," said de Lusignan. His attitude changed suddenly, as it ever did. He smiled, most unnaturally, a bizarre expression in the midst of their conversation. It gave Othon very little comfort, and little confidence that the outcome of this visit would end well. His hand closed tighter around the hilt of the dagger.

"You realize that even with your pitiful attempt at betrayal, we have progressed, if not accelerated our plan. Only history will attest to the truth in the end. The board is set; the moves made, my friend. We have but to play the game out and all will be ours." Amalric de Lusignan stepped closer, pulling off his black gloves with deliberate slowness as he spoke. "Therefore, your services to Sion are no longer needed, Messire."

Othon had barely let out a breath and blocked his thoughts, when he drew his dagger, making a backhanded lunge towards the master's face.

He moved too slowly, Amalric too quickly. The lunge threw him off balance. Othon lost his footing on the slippery muck on the floor and went down with a grunt against the wall. Filth spattered his face and hands. It reeked of death and decay.

The shadow of his attacker loomed over him, growing darker as he neared. He felt his throat suddenly constrict with an invisible hand; he choked on a weapon of the darkest magic. Other shades of daemonic power overwhelmed him. He felt their breath, warm and foul, filling his nostrils with fear and the stench of Hell. Claws of unseen bodies fell upon him.

Amalric de Lusignan's voice whispered at his ear. "Now you see, my dear, dear Othon, where your loyalties have brought you. You should not have betrayed my trust."

Othon screamed with the wounds the shadows dealt him; wounds that would leave no visible trace for the eyes of man to see. His heart beat faster, his breath more erratic. The air around him went suddenly white with a blinding light like the sun; and then darkness swallowed him up in welcome death.

* * * * *

William paced the marble floor of Blachernae Palace in Constantinople, waiting for an audience with the aged Emperor of the Byzantines. For months, he had enjoyed the generous hospitality of the Greeks while on his mission for the papal father; but now, he felt more like a prisoner of that same hospitality. His Imperial Majesty, Manuel Comnenus, was obviously stalling, forcing William to the limits of his indomitable patience.

The hall was unusually quiet; the sound of his sandals slapped the floor as he paced, echoing through the columns, adding to his already frayed nerves. The doubled guard outside the doors of the throne room offered him little comfort, though the guard paid him little heed.

For three days, Manuel kept him waiting and fuming. First, he feigned illness; then, he claimed pressing business of state confined him to his chambers. When the Protosebastus Alexius began making excuses for his uncle that were too ridiculous to believe, William despaired of ever gaining permission to leave for home.

He dared not do so without Manuel's blessing. Such actions were rude in the eyes of the manner-conscious Greeks, particularly in the case of the much-lauded Chancellor of Jherusalem, acting as a diplomatic envoy of the Pope himself to strengthen relations between East and West.

The Emperor had his reasons, of course: he was reluctant to let any emissary of Rome leave his city, no matter how unlikely a reconciliation between the two orthodoxies of the Church. Despite the tentative alliance between the Pope and the Byzantine Emperor, it was better to keep dialogue open between the two schismatic elements than letting their differences drive them to certain hostility, especially in the face of the ever-constant threat of war from Frederick Barbarossa of Germany.

It was more than just simple shattered patience and imperial prerogative that caused him such high anxiety. William worried for Baldwin. He had spent nearly a year in the ancient city of Byzantium. In that time, a virulent plague of foolishness had run rampant through Jherusalem and the kingdom. Although a truce with the Sarrazins was finally in place, it came so only at a terrible loss of life. Word had filtered through to him on the Golden Horn of the death of the Old Knight, Humphrey of Toron, of the defeats at Belinas and Marj Ayun, and the bloody debacle at Le Chastellet.

Despite the death of so many, it was still almost preferable to the sad affair of the supposed attempted coup by the Count of Tripoli and the detestable marriage of the princess Sibylla to the arrogant, coxcomb of a knight from Lusignan. Both boded ill for the kingdom. Unfortunately, Baldwin sat in the midst of the foolishness. Nor was he innocent of wrongdoing.

His young king needed him. He would make certain that Manuel understood that reality. He would make the Emperor see the need for his return to Jherusalem at once, even if he had to lie to convince him.

A noise at the doors turned William about on his heel mid-stride. His heart leapt with eager anticipation. Hesitantly, he took two steps towards the guards.

The double-doors opened a crack, and a Byzantine face, a younger version of the Emperor's, appeared; a hand motioned to William to hurry.

"The Emperor is reluctant to see anyone at present, but I've managed to convince him to give you a few moments of his time," explained the Protosebastus as he pulled William inside the hall. "But you must be quick with your request, my friend. His Majesty has very recently put down a plot to overthrow his throne. He has no cause to suspect you of any wrong-doing, so state your request plainly, and mayhap he will grant your suit."

"Was the Emperor hurt?"

Alexius took him by the sleeve of his elegant robe. "My uncle is well enough. Nothing a few days rest will not mend. He has seen battle and attempts on his life before, brother. He will not wilt before the threat of an assassin's knife, I assure you."

William narrowed his gaze. "Have you any clues as to who was behind the plot?"

"Nothing yet," Alexius answered, glancing about the empty hall. "Even with my best torturers, all we could get out of the assassin was a name: Sion."

"Sion," William repeated, all but blurting the dreaded name. Fear and an uncomfortable measure of apprehension twisted his stomach into a knot.

The Protosebastus arched an eye at his response. "Does this name hold some meaning to you, Brother William?"

"No, no, my lord Alexius," he lied. He dared not mention the Order or comment on the similarity of its name with Jherusalem's ancient appellation from the Holy Scriptures if the man was unaware of it. "It is a rather curious name, however. Has the prisoner said nothing else of importance?"

"Unfortunately, the man died of his wounds before he could tell us anymore."

William seriously doubted he heard the truth from Alexius, but neither did it matter. The less the Protosebastus or the Emperor knew of the Order of Sion, the better.

What disturbed him most was that he had not realized the extent of Sion's infernal power. So often, he had heard Magdalen's warning, but never fully comprehended the danger they presented to the kingdom and the Church. That Sion would try to assassinate the Emperor and bring the Byzantine throne under its control was terribly unsettling. The slim evidence of one man's dying word was precious little to act on; but that the unidentified assailant even knew the name of Sion spoke volumes against the order of heretics.

Now, more than ever, he needed to return to Jherusalem and warn the king of events in Constantinople.

* * * * *

The hammer of the Negev sun beat down on the desert with a merciless heat; its fierce glare on the sands burned like fire on sheets of beaten gold. In this wind-blasted land of extremes, the sun was king, its subjects, the scorpions and serpents, the hares, the falcons, and the hidden creatures that moved only by night.

On the far northern fringe of the harsh and desolate landscape where it began to climb into the Judean hill country stood Hebron, the Kirjath-arba of the Scriptures. Here, the locals claimed the Oak of Mamre still grew near the Cave of Machpelah that Abraham had bought from the sons of the desert to bury his beloved Sarah. It lay like a green oasis in the midst of a mirage, beckoning the desert dwellers to come and drink from wells that could replenish the body, as well as the soul. In the hands of the Christians, it had become a stronghold of the mighty, a vital link in the southern defenses of the beleaguered kingdom.

Reynald de Châtillon and Guion de Lusignan, the respective lords of Kerak and Ascalone set out from Castel Saint-Abraham into the south and the fierce heat of the Negev towards Beersheba to hunt, and to plot secrets where no one could overhear their intrigues; intrigues that most men would denounce as treason. Wearing the traditional garb of the East over armor more common to the light cavalry units of the Turcoploes, their hunting party would easily be mistaken for Bedouin had they ridden camels rather than their conspicuous Frankish horses.

It was the new Count of Japhe and Ascalone that had made the suggestion for their hunt; but it was the gracious Lord of Kerak who had accepted and offered the use of his castle in Hebron for a few days of lordly pursuits.

Reynald found the younger man willful, flamboyant, and unabashedly self-confident even to the point of arrogance if left unchecked. All of which were traits Reynald despised; but Guion was different. In him, the traits seemed to come together in a way that gave him a sense of boldness Reynald actually found refreshing, particularly in the future king of Jherusalem. There was more than the simple impressiveness of de Lusignan's words: he was a knight and a warrior cast from a mold shaped by long years of living by the sword. Guion was the hope—nay, the promise—of a fire that would rekindle the old spirit of such men as Godfrei de Bouillon, Tancred of Hauteville, and Bohemond of Taranto, and see it blaze to glorious new life once more.

It pleased Reynald that his support for Princess Sibylla's new husband was not ill founded, nor was it wasted on some provincial pup newly arrived from the West. By report, he was a skilled knight with a good seat on a horse and a fair competence with a sword. Given the chance, he would prove himself worthy of the crown. If Baldwin's health continued to decline at its present rate, they would learn his worth soon enough. All of which was why Reynald probably was not the least bit shocked by the Guion's proposition during the hunt.

By late afternoon, the heat had grown unbearable. Even the horses seemed to flag under the sun's relentless rays. They had brought the falcons, but decided to hunt for larger game on their return from the wells of Beersheba. The hunt for the graceful gazelle of the Negev required a slightly different, more exciting approach that appealed to their baser need to shed blood and destroy life.

Offering the local Bedouin a handful of gold bezants—far more than what they were certainly worth—Reynald procured the humble services of several young men to help with the hunt. To catch gazelles, the desert people made simple use of nets and pits, and loud horns to herd the panicked animals into their traps. While the Bedouin fanned out to track the elusive creatures to their hidden resting-places, Reynald and Guion waited nearby on their mounts for a signal from the hunters. When the time came, they would race behind the gazelles, blowing their war-horns to herd the fleeing animals towards their deaths. It was an old practice amongst the Arab tribesmen. It was also effective.

Reynald and Guion took up positions under a tree to the north of the nets while the rest of their hunting party hid near an outcrop of ancient limestone. The shade of the tree offered a welcome respite from the heat of the sun. They passed a waterskin between them. It was warm, but better than no water at all.

Despite their mutual enjoyment of the hunt, it was not war. Nor did it have the satisfaction of having a Muslim lying dead at your feet with his blood on your hands. Peace was too safe, too restless for men trained since birth to wield a sword and shield in battle. Guion seemed to sense his thoughts and to share in them. "The king wishes to seek out a formalized truce with the Muslims," Guion said rather nonchalantly.

Reynald's interest piqued. He glanced at the young new Count and arched an eyebrow. "You've certainly wasted little time getting involved with the affairs at Court."

Guion smiled smugly, triumphantly. "I've made a point of learning all that I can in the past few months. Who's to say when the king might finally succumb to his disease and leave me to assume the position of Regent for my wife's young son?"

"An admirable consideration," Reynald said, bowing his head. He neglected to remind his eager new friend that he was the current executive Regent for Baldwin when he was too ill to govern. It seemed too petty to throw it up in the man's face; besides, he wanted to keep Guion from becoming defensive. "The king has made some mention of his plans."

Guion glanced out over the desert plain, breaking eye contact. "I'm curious, my lord of Kerak—where do you stand with the king's proposal? Would you rather have peace... or war?"

Reynald followed the Count's example and glanced out towards the desert plain. There was still no indication of the hunters or the gazelles. "There is no profit in peace I've found—no caravans to raid; no Bedouin to rob; no spoils to pay your men when crops fail and grain is scarce because of drought." He turned his head, catching Guion's sharp glance. He winked. "Nor does it give us much opportunity to kill the Muslim swine without invoking the king's ire."

"With that in mind, then, my good lord..." Guion began and paused. He was baiting him, and not being very subtle about it. "Would you consider—under the guise of self-defense, of course—provoking hostilities against the Sarrazins while under the banner of truce, even at the expense of inciting the king's wrath?"

Reynald turned his head, curiously eyeing Guion de Lusignan. He was learning quickly that his first assessment of the young man, who might very well be king one day, was accurate. Guion was certainly bold. "I suppose it would depend on the nature of the hostilities," he said. "What exactly do you have in mind?"

"A strike at the very heart of Islam."

Guion de Lusignan was very bold, indeed. "Mecca?" Reynald asked.

"Medina," said the bold Count, "and the tomb of the Muslim prophet."

"What exactly do you have in mind—an armed raid through the desert at night?"

Guion smiled at the secret he was bursting to reveal. "I was thinking more of a raid by sea."

Reynald stared at him incredulously. "Do you happen to have a particular fleet at hand with which we might carry out this mad endeavor, my lord of Ascalone?"

"No," said de Lusignan. "But we could build one in the desert without anyone's knowledge. Nothing too extravagant; perhaps three to five ships—no more. We could test them on the waters of the Dead Sea. The Muslims would never suspect such a thing of us, until it was too late."

Immediately, that small, dark place in Reynald's heart that slanted towards greed and piracy, started to count the treasures he knew he would surely find in the floating caravans and gold-bedecked cities of the Islamic heartland.

* * * * *

Baldwin thought he had awakened from a dream. Darkness and silence filled his room; he stood, staring out the window and down upon the gate and the city. Jherusalem lay decked in all her ancient glory this night. Torches burned outside her most holy shrines and churches; the *Templum Domini* glowed upon its mount in the thick, heavy air of summer. It shimmered silver-gold in the moonlight; the stars burned bright in the velvet black heavens. It was a dream in every way like the one he thought he had just awakened from only a moment or two ago.

When he turned back towards his bed, though, he found that he still slept, and yet, he stood awake, staring down at himself. It was his mirror image, but the reflection he found, was not the one he knew.

Am I dead? He tried to make sense of what he saw—or what he thought he saw. A hand touched his shoulder. He almost cried in fright. Her image flashed behind his eyes as her power reached out to his. He knew her at once as friend and confidant, the truer conscience of his troubled mind.

"You are not dead, King Baldwin."

"Magdalen," he cried and turned. She put a hand to his mouth to silence the joyful noise of his excitement. They dared not rouse his squire sleeping just outside his door. His confusion and the need for his mind to understand what it could not conceive brought his senses back to the sleeping figure in his bed.

"How... how is this possible?" he said, nodding towards the bed. "How can I be asleep... and yet... awake?"

"You are awake, Your Highness, I assure you," she said. "But to all those that might happen to look in upon you, it will seem as though you are asleep in your bed as you ought to be at such an hour. No one will disturb you as you sleep. No one will know you are not here."

Baldwin turned on her. She read his thoughts before he could form the words with his tongue. Mary took the gnarled claw of his nearly fingerless hand in hers, and pulled him towards the window. Her voice took on a sudden tone of severity. "Is your heart still set on seeking peace with the Muslims?"

More than three months had passed since he had called out to her to come and help him seek a way to make peace with his enemy. In that time, he felt as though his world had begun to crumble in all around him. The only light that loomed ahead was the one that cast the shadow of death. Once he had feared that shadow, but no more.

With his admission of guilt, he exchanged his anger and his spirit of revenge for a newfound sense of fear and mistrust for those closest to him. Everyone fell under his suspicion. Only Mary, who had never spoken a word of flattery or empty praise towards him, had won through the hardened armor of his heart by telling him the hard things that a king, or a friend, must sometimes hear.

The sickness made him weak; he wanted only rest, the blessed hope of release of all his earthly duties. That would only come by seeking peace with his enemy. Such was as the Savior taught—that he should love his neighbor— even if that neighbor was his enemy and a heathen worshipper of Allah.

"It is still set, my lady, if you will lead me."

"Then we must do so now—tonight," she said. "But first you must dress, King Baldwin. And then we will seek out the sultan and see what may be done."

It took only a short time for him to change into attire that befitted his royalty. When she forbade him to wear or take anything that might suggest war, he felt unsure. She promised him he would be far safer in her care, than if he had all his royal army at his back. He believed her with unwavering and unquestionable faith. Mary had taught him that much in the few years he had known her.

Standing at the window, she bid him to take her hand and close his eyes. "Where are we going, lady?" he asked, still uncertain, though he trusted her ability and her motives.

—*Damascus*, *she said, whispering the word in his thoughts as though it was a spell.*

Her hands clenched on his in an iron grip that surprised him given her small, lithe figure. His breath caught, and everything fell into utter silence.

Suddenly he felt dizzy and unbalanced. He staggered a step. Her hand held him. His eyes opened as she bid him to do. The night air on his face felt different, warmer and drier; a trickle of water whispered on the breeze. He had never been to Damascus, but he knew it at once, as though the city was a twin to his own beloved Jherusalem.

Mary led him along a colonnade around the perimeter of a garden towards the source of the trickling water—a fountain. An outburst of laughter echoed through the garden and the columns clothed in jasmine and glowing moonlight. They slipped from column to column through the darkness and into an arch lit by torches. A pair of guards stood outside an entrance with double-doors; both guards wore the yellow sash of the sultan's personal attendants.

Magdalen held him back to the shadows while she lifted her voice in a whispered song. Taking his hand again, they walked up to the guards and the double-doors, and passed straight through as though neither of the tall and muscular Mamluks saw them.

They stood in a large and spacious hall so clearly decorated in the Eastern style, though one not used very often to receive visitors. Pillows lay piled around a small, low table in the midst of a wide circle of thin columns holding up an overspreading dome. Potted palms huddled on either side of an arched entrance leading out onto a balcony. A dark man swathed in black reclined at the table, his face bathed in the soft glow of candlelight. The rest of the room stood in restless shadow.

They approached the sultan from those shadows as he lay reclining, nestled among the pillows about the table, reading by candlelight. Mary mentioned once that Salah ad-Din was a studious man, much like himself. In another life, they might very well have made such good friends.

—*You still could be, Your Highness*, *she said to him in his thoughts.*

He ignored her, his eyes trained on the sultan Salah ad-Din.

Mary made a small, disruptive noise and bowed as they came closer. He seemed not to have noticed them at first; but then, he looked up, having eyes only for her, and smiled as though he knew of her

266

coming all along. In her deep respect for the noble sultan, she bowed her head. For Baldwin, it was a start to peace.

* * * * *

A sudden noise where there should have been none drew Yusuf's eyes to see the vision of loveliness before him. He had long hoped she would return as promised and meet with him. After so long, though, he had despaired of her ever doing so, and wondered if she existed only in some forgotten dream, an alluring figment of his imagination. She was just as beautiful as he remembered, like one of the rapturous *houris*, the lovely and wanton eternal virgins of paradise that awaited every man who died in the name of holy Islam. Her name leapt to the memory of his tongue.

"My lady Maryam," he said, bowing. He seldom did so with other women. "This is, indeed, truly an honor to have you in my humble presence once more. Have you come so that we may finally have that talk you once promised? I have so looked forward to that moment."

The Lady swept back the hood of her dark cloak, revealing her gorgeous mane of red-brown hair; it tumbled free, falling down her back and shoulders. Such an act by a woman should have outraged him, but he did not care so long as he had the opportunity to speak with her.

"*Hazrat*—honorable—Yusuf," she said, bowing, "I am afraid, my friend, that I've come again on urgent business. I have come on behalf of another who wishes desperately to meet with you about establishing a truce of peace between yourself and the Nasrani of Jherusalem."

Yusuf glanced around the circular hall at her suggestion that perhaps someone else might have come with her. Only then, did he notice the tall shadow standing just behind and to her side. His body prickled with the chilling thought that she could have brought a whole army into his presence without his knowledge, and he, powerless to do anything about it. That knowledge brought him to his senses.

His sudden anxiety dispelled the allure of his fantasies about her coming. It made him fear the power she commanded. She was not an enemy he wanted.

She smiled, offering reassurance—or perhaps a warning. "Do not be afraid, Yusuf. I am your friend, as I promised. You are safe from all harm, visible and invisible, while I am with you."

He chuckled nervously. "Who is this stranger who comes to speak with me about peace, my lady of the *ifrit?*"

The stranger pulled off the hood of his cloak and bowed deeply. He was not what Yusuf expected, the king of Urshalim. He was tall for one so young, and so accursed by illness, but then, even Ifranj women were tall by comparison with eastern men, whether they were Turkish or Arab. He certainly deserved what respect he had from his people, and more. What drew Yusuf to him above all else, was his intense gaze peering out from a slit between a deep blue kaffiyeh and golden crown that hung low over his brow and a veil that barely hid the ruin of a face eaten away by disease. His bright blue eyes stared at him without blinking, penetrating, seeming to gaze straight through him into his soul. They were the eyes that had seen far more than their fair share of pain and suffering, eyes that had seen too much sorrow and tragedy for a man his age.

"I offer my humblest greeting on the evening," said the leper king of Urshalim in a voice grown raspy with the progression of his disease. "*As-salaam u'alai kuum Al-Malik Salah ad-Din.*"

Yusuf smiled and bowed; his unexpected visitors intrigued him. "*Wa'alaikum as-Salaam Al-Malik Bardawil,*" he said with equal affability. He glanced sidelong at the *ifritah*. "What urgent business brings you into my house uninvited on so dangerous mission, my lady?"

"Those you would see the armies of Nasrani and Muslims war against each other until there is nothing left but the humble hearts of the people to claim for themselves—an enemy that commands the powers of darkness to accomplish its will." She paused, waiting to see what effect her words would have on him. He waited her out, expressionless. She continued: "There are dangerous men of the West, friend Yusuf, who have bent their knee to the hidden beliefs of the East. In so doing, they have allied themselves with the *sheikh al-Jebel* and his Assassins in Masyaf who call their own sect by the name, *al-da'wa al-jadida*, the new doctrine. The goal of these men is to destroy the Church of Christ Jhesú and the faith of Islam. They will stop at nothing to gain what they so desperately want. They would even see the great Salah ad-Din, the restorer of the faith, struck down and destroyed, simply because he is a devout follower and defender of the written Qur'an, rather than the secret teachings they claim it holds."

Her words were poignant and true, he knew it as surely as he knew his own name. He had only to think of the terrible battle he and Al-Abras had fought against each other three years ago at Madd al-Jiras to know that an even greater enemy had come close to destroying both of their armies. An enemy of shadow and fear and all things evil, who would have done so had not some unseen power intervened to drive the daemon away. A spirit called up by the power of the Seal of Suleiman to make war upon the Nasrani and Muslims alike.

Yusuf laid his forgotten Qur'an on the table with a kiss of respect and sat up amid the scattered pillows. He waived his hand towards the cushions, but they declined his hospitality. He glanced at the Leper, catching the young man's gaze. He wondered at the humility that brought a Nasrani king into his presence, taking the first step towards an uncertain chance at peace.

"Who are these men you speak of, Al-Malik Bardawil?" he said, hoping to weigh the measure of his words and wisdom.

The *ifritah* answered for him like an overprotective guardian angel. In her case, it was probably not far from the truth. "These are men most secretive, my lord Salah ad-Din," she said, cradling her thin arms together in front of her. "They claim, albeit falsely, that the origins of your Prophet's teachings lay closest to those of earlier sects of Nasrani and Jews."

His anger ignited into sudden fire, both at the effrontery of her words and her presumption to answer for the young king. "That is blasphemy. Islam is the pure teaching of Allah as given to the Prophet— upon his name be praise and blessing—by the angel Jibril. It is not some corruption of your own faith."

Maryam stepped closer and knelt before him. She smiled, but sadly. It marred the perfect beauty of her face. "So you and your brothers in the faith truly believe. There are those among the Shiites, though, that secretly teach other doctrines of mystery and falsehood: doctrines of pure heresy against God. They claim that the *Mahdi*, the guided one who is the last and hidden *imam* of the Shi'a faith who will unite all three peoples of the book, has come; he only waits now to reveal himself when peace and hope have fled from the earth. The longer we pursue war, the more we give these heretics the opportunity to deceive many, and the power to destroy all that your people and mine hold most dear."

"But what can these… conspirators, possibly hope to gain by deception?" Yusuf leaned forward, eager to hear more.

"They wish to create a new theology of God; one that embraces all beliefs whether they are Nasrani or Muslim, or even Jew," Maryam said, "so that they can all come together and worship as one at the altar of a new faith. By doing so, they lay the foundation for a kingdom ruled by one man—one king. I beg you, lord Salah ad-Din, do not let these men destroy the faiths we both love by their greed and their lies."

Yusuf pondered her words as he stroked the point of his beard. He glanced at Al-Abras, standing tall, but not proudly. The young king must have believed the *ifritah* enough for him to come here unarmed, with only a woman to help convince his enemy of the danger they faced. These things were not new that he heard. Rumors of conspiracies and heretics allying the peoples of Nasrani and Islam had persisted ever since the fall of Urshalim to the invading infidels almost a hundred years before. It was part of the call for *jihad* by such great men as Nur ad-Din and others, to protect the faith from enemies other than the Nasrani. It was part of his reason—however few men he trusted with the truth—for launching an attack not once, but twice, against the Old Man of the Mountain and his feared Hashshashin. Perhaps, it was why he gave such credence to the fears of the *ifritah* and the leper now. Leaning over the low table, he poured himself a cup of *káffe* from the silver service set he insisted on always being present when he read. He prayed that neither of his guests saw his hand shake as he poured and lifted the small cup to his lips.

Yusuf sipped thoughtfully at his cup. "I wonder, my lady Maryam, are these conspirators we speak of agents of *al-Dajjal*, the false one—what you Nasrani call antichrist?"

"No, my lord sultan,'" she said, vehement, yet calm. "But they are servants of Iblis. And if we do not pursue peace, their influence and power will grow only stronger." She held out her hands to him, pleading, entreating his mercy and support. "The enemy is both cunning and wise in the ways of the world. We cannot expect to cheat him so easily of his victory by any truce we might fashion. He will fight to break it by any means possible."

"My lord Salah ad-Din," the leper said abruptly where he had remained so quietly before. His voice, even in the harsh whisper of its ruined state, had such urgency that Yusuf found it disconcerting. It commanded him to listen and take note. "I have seen the future of my kingdom and I... I know Jherusalem will fall to you when I am dead." He paused, gazing deep into Yusuf's dark eyes. His head bobbed from weakness and some hidden emotion he could not quite control; and then, he regained his kingly composure and bearing.

"It is best that it should be so, I think, seeing that these men will not stop until they gain my throne through treachery. I would rather see my kingdom in your hands, my lord, Yusuf ibn-Ayyub, than to have it fall into the hands of liars and thieves and heretics. But between that day and now, I ask... no, I beg you," the king said, slumping to his knees, "if there is some way we can perhaps have peace between our peoples, between ourselves." He held up a gloved hand—an oddity in the midst of a terribly hot summer for anyone who was not a leper—and coughed violently. "Before you answer, I would also ask one other thing—a hard thing, given the history between our peoples. In the day that Jherusalem comes into your hands, please spare the lives of my people. For my sake—and for God's."

Yusuf rose slowly and did something in that moment pregnant with so much promise and hope for lasting peace. Humbled by the wisdom and the simple request of the young sick and dying king, he came around the table and clasped the bandaged arm of his sworn enemy in his hand, and made a promise he prayed might hold, even if for only a season. "For the sake of both our peoples, King Bardawil, I pray we might find a way towards peace and soon. Never fear. I will remember your requests in the day of my victory."

† CHAPTER NINETEEN

For there must be also heresies: that they also, who are approved may be made manifest among you.
—I Corinthians 11:19

Arnaud de Torroge seemed every bit the man Baldwin expected to meet in the grand and holy structure of the Temple of the Lord. Together they walked about the circular enclosure of the former mosque, admiring the wonder and beauty of the impressive and much revered shrine. Words could not convey the beauty of the temple: its golden capitals atop blue and white-veined pillars; the exquisite dome leafed with gold and black and red enamel in patterns that set the eye to wandering; the floating line of Arabic script that graced the inside face of the arcade in finely worked gold.

The golden dome of the *Templum Domini* soared into the air above their heads; it might have floated into the heavens if the slender columns of the arcade circling round about its base did not anchor it to the earth. Baldwin explained in his halting, whispering voice that it was too beautiful for the Christians to destroy after the First War of the Cross, although the Muslims had desecrated its beauty with their heathen declarations that denigrated the deity of the Son of God.

They paused at the *sakhra*, the foundation stone, lying beneath the dome where the Jews claimed the Ark of the Covenant once dwelt within the Holy of Holies. Arnaud paused, silent and reflective, staring up at the dome, and then down at the hallowed stone exposed beside their feet beneath the huge wooden altar that covered the stone from view. He knelt and kissed the primeval navel of the world. They both lingered for a while, praying in that sacred place caught between the heavens and the earth. It gave Baldwin time to reflect on the man who lent him a hand despite his illness and helped him kneel beside the stone.

Arnaud's name and reputation preceded him. He was a Catalan nobleman who had served his Order for the past several years in Spain and Provençe. He certainly had the dark, sharp eyes of the older race of people of Aragon. He had also devoted the better part of his life fighting in the *Reconquista* of Moorish-occupied Spain. By all accounts, he was an even-tempered man given equally to listening as he was to speaking, with enough years accounted to him to expect wisdom, rather than folly, in his actions. The new Master of the Templars was nothing like his predecessor, Othon de Saint-Amant, who had finally died in the Hell he had made of his own choosing.

Pope Alexander could not have chosen a better man than Arnaud de Torroge; and so said the scroll that Arnaud had produced for him embossed with the heavy unbroken papal seal, that when opened, explained the new master's credentials and authority over the increasingly troublesome Templars.

To that end, he could take heart in knowing that a new master, appointed by the Pope himself, would no doubt curb whatever power or influence the Order of Sion had over the soldier-monks of the Templars. With the High Court having finally settled on the language for a two-year truce between the kingdom and the Muslims, the time had come for Baldwin to turn his attentions inward to root out, once and for all, the conspirators of Sion and put a stop to their activities.

"The Holy Father has commanded me to set my Order to rights once more under the canons of Mother Rome as set forth within the writ of their original charter, as well as other matters that I need to speak about at length with you, Your Highness, at a more opportune time."

Baldwin halted, catching the Templar Master by the arm. They had moved out from under the golden dome of the *Templum Domini* and strolled through the narrow, shadow-filled ambulatory encircling the great shrine of the *al-Sakhra*. A priest entered the church and made his leisurely way passed them. He glanced up at them, struck by the sight of a Templar Knight walking in hushed conversation with the dark shade of the dying king. The priest turned away, ascended the stairs of the altar and the many rows of burning prayer candles circling the platform, and went about his duties of attending the candles.

"What other matters, Messire de Torroge?" Baldwin asked, trying to keep his much-tested and worn patience from fraying any further. "I would rather hear these matters now if they have such important bearing on my kingdom."

The master expostulated, glancing towards the busy priest at the altar. "Wouldn't, Your Majesty, rather speak about such weighty matters in private?"

"His Majesty would not."

"Well," de Torroge proceeded, obviously unsure as to whether he would not have preferred to speak behind closed doors, "His Holiness is very much concerned with certain rumors he has heard about his Templars; disturbing reports, mind you, about heresy and fraternization with the Sarrazins."

"Take heed, Messire, the trouble goes far beyond any rumors to things which I know to be true with a certainty. Dark secrets exist among your Order. An evil walks amongst your brethren."

"So His Eminence has heard and been led to believe," said Arnaud. "He knows that there is more to the Order in Jherusalem that what they pretend or claim to be. There are just too many rumors for it to be otherwise. The Pope has assigned me the task of finding out the truth and lancing it before it festers like an infected boil."

That at least, was a relief. If His Holiness, the Bishop of Rome, knew of rumors of heresy and conspiracy within the Templar Order in Jherusalem, then Sion had not been as careful with its secrets as they would have liked or thought. Saint-Amant's betrayal, however secretive, had no doubt been a genuine betrayal of the infernal Order. If there were any more daemons to find among the Templars, de Torroge would certainly exorcise them.

"Of course, there is still the matter, is there not, Messire de Torroge, of what the Pope thinks of my leprosy, and therefore, my perceived inability to rule, as the result of God's just judgment on my body," Baldwin said calmly. Too calmly, it seemed for the Templar Master's liking—or his expectation. He had turned the conversation to a far more delicate matter not often addressed with the king directly. The master's face turned as red as the cross on his breast. "It is not your fault, Brother Arnaud, what the Pope thinks. I have heard he has said much the same thing before. But I wonder, my lord Templar, exactly what sins am I supposed to have committed to warrant such just judgment by God?"

By now, the priest attending the prayer candles had taken a renewed interest in their quiet conversation in the ambulatory. Baldwin pulled his companion deeper into the shadows.

"I'm sure it is not your sins, Your Highness, the Holy Father considers as being in judgment," Arnaud answered. "It is those of the kingdom."

A spasm of coughing took hold of him as Baldwin tried to laugh. If His Holiness only knew but half the truth behind his leprosy, and how he bore in his body the ruin of a war between good and evil for the kingdom and the faith of Christianity, perhaps he would be of another mind and judgment.

The spasm and his laughter passed. "Please, Messire, don't tell me"—he coughed again—"that the new Master of the Temple is that naïve." The humor quickly melted from his words. The coughing left his voice harsher and raspier. "Please understand; I hold no resentment towards you as the Pope's representative. In fact, I pray Brother Arnaud, that we may form a lasting friendship while you are Master of the Temple, and I, the king of Outremer. But let us not mince words. His Holiness has made himself quite clear on the subject of lepers and their segregation from society. He would rather see me in a lazar house, than on the throne of Jherusalem," Baldwin said, pausing, trying to hold back the rising tide of emotions that threatened to undo his royal dignity. "I am an embarrassment to His Eminence, the abomination that causes desolation spoken of by the prophet Daniel."

For a moment, Brother Arnaud seemed visibly moved by his words; and then, that moment stretched onwards into a silence that worked on the older man's sense of honor and respect. The Templar Master fell slowly to his knee and took Baldwin's deformed hand, pressing it to his brow in homage. "I've seen great bravery and courage, Your Highness, in battle and in the horrible aftermath when men knew they are close to death. However, I have never seen such from a man in your place. You are, indeed, a king worthy of the crown of Jherusalem."

Baldwin bowed his head. "I am humbled, brother, by your kind words. But know I *am* dying, and day by day, the enemy grows bolder and more impatient," he stammered. "If you choose to confront this threat of evil, you mark yourself for their vengeance."

Arnaud winked. "You need not worry for me, King Baldwin; I am a servant of God. He will protect me and your kingdom."

*　*　*　*　*

Sibylla shrieked with pure delight; she laughed, grabbing her mother's hand and set it on the soft rounded mound of her abdomen. "Did you feel the baby, mother? Shahdi tells me it will be girl."

"Of course it's a girl. Look how high you are carrying. You didn't have Shahdi sacrifice a rabbit or any such nonsense, did you?"

"Mother!"

Agnes' fair but aging face creased with a smile that lit a joyful twinkle in her eyes. It was the first laughter she or her mother had enjoyed in more than a fortnight with another bout of her son's continual illnesses robbing them of sleep and the quieter moments of solitude.

With the height of summer passed, and the days sliding ever so gradually towards the shorter hours of autumn, the temperatures had grown milder, leaving the palace solar warm and languidly comfortable, with only the slightest hint of a breeze to stir the air. The twilight hours of dusk and dawn were the most idyllic. Baudinouet sat in a chair beside Sibylla, wrapped in a blanket. To see a child of almost three, so calm and immobile, was more than disheartening. The blue-grey eyes of his dead father were dark and sunken, his cheeks hollow; he looked as much as a living corpse as his uncle the king.

"So, are you as happy with Guion as you had hoped now that you have him?" her mother asked with a slight smirk.

"Oh, mother, he is everything that William was to me, and more. I've never been happier," Sibylla said. She could feel her face brighten with a smile; but there was still a faint shadow of sorrow clouding the great depth of her joy. She struggled to hide it.

Agnes pulled her hand back from Sibylla's belly and looked askance at her. "But…" she said, leaning over and tucking in her grandson's blanket under his chin. His head nodded in the warm sunlight and he fell asleep at her touch. "But your son's illnesses trouble you."

Sibylla sighed; she sniffled. Tears welled in her eyes and she patted the swell of her abdomen that was her unborn child asleep beneath her heart. "I know I worry too much," she said, "but I fear I might lose him. He is such a sickly boy. As much as I love Guion, my son is all I have left of William. He is my brother's heir. Baldwin worries so about the kingdom after he is gone. What if Baudinouet dies?"

The words of her concern came spilling out of her faster than her thoughts could track. She had found her happiness, but it was marred, flawed by fear and by doubt. By death. She wondered if she would ever truly be happy again. The shadow of death stalked her, as it seemed to stalk all her family.

"Baldwin will be devastated by the renewed trouble it would cause the kingdom, as well as me. Even Guion worries about him. He whispered to me one night as we lay abed about how wonderful it would be if my son would one day wed a princess of the Muslims, and bring peace between our peoples at last as Baldwin has long desired."

Her mother set her hand on Sibylla's knee and stroked it fondly. "Sickness is part of every childhood, daughter. Children get sick; children get better. You have nothing to worry about or fear. I did have two children of my own if you remember. And you, my dear, were not exactly the healthiest little girl, while your brother"—she paused, getting caught up in her own tangle of emotions—"while your brother was almost never sick until the day we learned he was a leper. Baudinouet is your brother's heir, and he will be king after him for many years to come. You have a new child on the way, Sibylla. Rest in that knowledge and take heart."

Sibylla wiped the tear that had chosen that moment to finally slide down her cheek. She dabbed her eye and chuckled softly, giving into her mother's sage advice. Her baby kicked from deep inside its protective shelter—a pleasant reminder that it would not be so easily forgotten by concerns of the day. She grabbed Agnes' hand again and set it against the tight knot moving within her womb with a beaming smile. "Mother, do you feel it? The baby moved again!"

* * * * *

Baldwin drew his sword and turned on the intruder as swiftly and silently as a whisper; the blade flashed with the chill, hoary light of the moon. He took Reynald by surprise. The lord of Kerak drew his sword with a curse and threw a folded bundle at him.

"Your mother bid me come and bring you a cloak. She fears you'll catch your death on so cold a night as this."

"My *death*? My mother worries too much, Reynald. I am not a child that needs looking after."

"No, Your Highness, you are not. Still, she is your mother, and you are an oft-time reckless son and king, who is also a leper that rarely concerns himself with such matters as sickness or health, even when he should. She does not want to lose her only son before she needs to."

Baldwin knew a reprimand, even when there were so few men that would do so boldly. He listened and kept his silence. Reynald held his peace, uncharacteristically so. That alone was intriguing, as it was troubling. Baldwin sheathed his sword and turned away, leaning upon the top of the crenellated wall of the Tower. Reynald joined him and both men gazed down from their vantage point perched atop the highest hill of the city.

Westwards the city descended sharply towards the Hinnom Valley with Montjoie opposite, the Joyous Mountain where the Christians first saw the Holy City of God. To the East, lay the ridge of Olivet above the Kidron whereupon stood the Church of the Ascension. Between the two vales twined the Tyropoeon, dividing the city and the Church of the Resurrection from the ancient Temple of the Lord, which the Muslims still claimed as their own under the name of *Qubbat al-Allah*. No greater spiritual emblem of the strife between Christianity and Islam existed than the Dome of the Rock. Despite whatever consecrations the priests made with their holy water, it was still an Islamic house of worship rising between the shrines of the Savior's death and resurrection and his glorious ascent into Heaven. It stood as a Muslim prayer of defiance and dominance raised in stone, standing as a constant reminder of the threat to the peaceful coexistence of all that lived in the Holy City of God.

Even before Reynald interrupted his solitude by his unexpected intrusion, Baldwin considered the actions he must take to mend the divisions that were tearing his High Court in two. The spiritual landscape of the city lying before him was much like the growing factions in the kingdom: divided, threatened, and eager to rend itself to pieces in war. He was helpless to remedy either situation. It was doubtful that any one man could. Before Baldwin could do anything, however, he needed to know which of his lords still stood beside him as king. Above all else, he needed to know the depth of loyalty in the man standing beside him.

"How committed are you, Reynald, to your oath of fealty to me? —And to Jherusalem? No speeches—no theatrics. Just... just an answer, cousin, plain and simple."

"What have you heard, Your Majesty? Have I offended you in some way?"

Baldwin laughed, shaking his head. "It is a simple question, my lord, and yet, you avoid answering me. Is it truly that difficult to answer?"

Reynald turned to him, his back against the wall. "I have done nothing, Sire, which you would call disloyal to you or your crown. What I do, I do in the defense of the kingdom—nothing more."

Silence fell between them. It worked its slow and uncomfortable way into Reynald's patience. He seemed almost relieved when Baldwin finally broke it with another question. "And if I asked you to lay down your arms or to give up your thoughts of war and revenge, would you do so?"

"You ask a hard thing, Sire, of a sworn knight and lord of Outremer. I would do as my king commanded me," Reynald said without hesitation. Then, with equal immediacy, he added, "But I pray that my lord king would never do so, for though a truce exists, the Muslims only take advantage of that peace to use the caravans along the hajj routes to conceal their movements of troops between Egypt and Syria."

"Right now, Reynald, I am more concerned with the factions that have arisen within the kingdom. While there is a truce of peace with Salehdin, I must heal the divisions of the High Court before it erupts into a civil war. We averted war once with Raymond of Tripoli, but next time we may not be so fortunate."

The lord of Kerak snorted his disdain. "Raymond has ever been a fool and a coward in my mind. The lords of the kingdom may trust him, but not his abilities or his willingness to pursue war when necessary. He thinks there is always a chance for peace, even when the enemy holds a sword at his throat."

Baldwin glanced away, staring at the small islands of religious importance alight with torches to the East. He needed to proceed carefully with the man standing next to him. No matter which direction Reynald's sword swung, so too would the kingdom; and if he chose to side with malcontents and schemers, the kingdom would fall. Reynald was too important and too powerful. To that end, he had his own plan to keep Reynald loyal to the crown.

"When I am gone, whom will you stand behind, then?"

"I will stand with those who offer the best hope of preserving this kingdom against the Sarrazin dogs."

Baldwin chuckled softly. "And just who do you reckon they might be?"

"I will defend Sibylla's right to the throne," Reynald said, "and therefore, your mother and uncle, as well as the Lusignan's, and of course your mother's husband, the Lord of Sidon."

"I see," Baldwin said. "Not my other sister, Isabella?"

Reynald turned and leaned next to him. "Why all these questions, Baldwin?" It was not very often that he used the king's given name when addressing him. "Do you question my loyalty?

"No," Baldwin said and looked at Reynald. "I want to propose a marriage between your stepson, Humphrey, and my younger sister, Isabella."

Reynald's face lit with the sudden prospect of a royal alliance with the king's family. The implications were enormous for a man who was already one of the most powerful barons in the kingdom. He laughed aloud. "What you actually hope to propose is seeing Balian of Ibelin and myself huddled merrily around a cup of mulled wine, whispering about alliances and truces as our children exchange their marriage vows."

"Is it too bold a plan to think possible, my friend?"

"Christ on the Cross, no, Your Highness! It's brilliant, if it works as well as you imagine," Reynald said, laughing again. He clapped him on the back. "It's not so much Ibelin that gives me fits—it's Tripoli, and his blatant attempts to sit on the throne of Jherusalem. Balian's loyalty to his brother is all that keeps him in the faction of the native barons. Such a waste of a good lord and a valiant knight, too."

"That is why I want your children to wed. Balian's claim to power in his faction rests in his wife's daughter. You are my right hand, Reynald. Ibelin would be a fool not to betroth Isabella to Humphrey," Baldwin said. "Just make sure that Stephanie keeps her daughter-to-be tucked away from my stepmother at Kerak. I don't need Raymond or the Ibelins plotting to make a bid for control of the Court or the throne behind our backs."

"As you wish, Sire," Reynald said with a nod. "Is there anything else you require of me?"

"Tell my mother you found me and she need not worry," he said, feeling much better than he had when he first came up onto the roof of the Tower. "And Reynald, make sure you tell my mother to start planning for a feast. I want to make sure no one forgets this betrothal."

* * * * *

The autumn night breeze off the Mediterranean had a chill that cut through William's clerical robes and thick riding cloak with the ease of finely honed Damascus steel as he raced hustling and bustling from his See in Tyre to Jherusalem. Only a fortnight past Michaelmas and the weather had already begun to turn foul. It was not very encouraging for what the winter might hold, nor did it do anything to lighten his increasingly foul mood.

That mood had turned from bad to worse, much like the weather, with the saddening news that Aimery, the elderly Patriarch of Jherusalem, had passed on in his sleep to join the Lord and all his heavenly angels in Paradise. The news was sad, but not, unexpected. Aimery of Nesle had been Patriarch for over two decades. What was most disheartening—no; infuriating, unacceptable, and unbelievable— was that the canons of the Chapter of Jherusalem had nominated and chosen his rival, Heraclius, the Archbishop of Caesarea, as Aimery's successor. Even now, the king was considering their choice. Of all people—Heraclius! A pompous, arrogant, profligate specimen of a man. To choose him as Patriarch—what was the Church thinking!

Oh, their reasoning was easy enough to see. The canons— though not for any good reason that he good see—had long ago fallen under the spell of the Courtenays and their allies. Heraclius had charm and wit; he was handsome (or so all the women at Court constantly remarked) and intelligent, despite what rumors and lies others claimed of him. He was also ambitious. Everyone saw it and knew it, but those same witnesses also turned their blind eyes and called him humble.

Oh, yes, and as everyone else knew and conveniently forgot, Heraclius was Madame Agnes de Courtenay's former lover. The rewards for that much-desired distinction seemed to last long after she moved on to some other prey to bring to her much abused bed. Of course, Heraclius of Caesarea had moved on to another new lover as well: Pascua de Riveri. Perhaps that was the deficiency William lacked in his desire to ascend to the higher levels of ecclesiastical success. He had few sins he could exploit for his gain.

He certainly did not lack for foolishness. Particularly, when he realized an hour or so after he had departed from Tyre and the dark curtain of night had fallen so completely around him, that his anger had led him out into the wild alone, without escort to protect him from thieves or worse.

It really was not Heraclius, though, or his anger that had caused him to act so foolishly; at least not completely, although they certainly contributed to it. It was that Baldwin actually considered accepting the canons choice of Heraclius for Patriarch over him. Him—the Chancellor for the king since his coronation. Him—the delegate to the Lateran Council who the Pope himself had sent to the Byzantine Emperor to formalize negotiations for the reunification of the Church. Him—who shared the secret of Mary Magdalen. Him—the friend and tutor and confessor of the king who loved him like a son. Had he imagined that there was more between him and his young king than actually existed?

William had been much concerned since his return from Rome and Constantinople about his relationship with the king. Baldwin had scarcely called him for advice; he had found new advisors in his absence, namely, his mother and sister, as well as the new Constable, Amalric de Lusignan, who was now his brother-in-law. The boy he had left had become a man—a man with his own opinions and answers that no longer needed an aged tutor to mentor him. Baldwin had suffered loss, and known victory and defeat in battle. Men had died in great numbers on his account—by his wisdom and by his folly. His disease had changed him body and soul; the vicissitudes of life had bent his mind bent to other thoughts.

Somewhere in the midst of the last two years, a change had been wrought between them, a suspicion—a distrust—which gnawed at the core of the king's heart. No doubt, it was due in large part to Raymond of Tripoli's foolish attempt to take the throne by force and marry the Princess Sibylla to his leading supporter, the lord of Ramlah. Whom among the lords at Court did they account as one of Count

Raymond's closest friends? He knew the answer well enough: The conveniently absent Chancellor of Jherusalem who gained his position by the said Count of Tripoli.

William prayed God would give wings to his horse, and drove his heels into the animal's flanks, urging the panting beast into a gallop over the Judean hills, flying towards Jherusalem. He prayed he was not too late.

The vote, of course, was not nearly as close as the Chapter of canons tried to pretend. Heraclius sat opposite him in a high-backed chair in the midst of the High Court. Baldwin sat enthroned at one end of the hall, mute and silent behind his white veil and gold-crowned kaffiyeh; the canons of the Church of the Holy Sepulcher in their ceremonial robes, gathered at the other end. Heraclius eyed him as the prior read the decision, a pretentious smile tickling ever so gently at the corners of his mouth. Adding to the shameful scene of ecclesiastical hypocrisy, a shaft of sunlight happened to angle through an upper story window of the hall, falling with celestial glory round about Heraclius' humble self.

William was furious; first beyond words, then, as his anger and disbelief settled, he dove into a combative mood that only an argument would assuage. He stood up abruptly; the legs of the chair scraped loudly across the floor as it slid backwards. The hall fell silent. He glanced towards the king; Baldwin refused to meet his gaze. The king's new cabal of advisors had gathered collectively around him like a pack of wolves protecting their young pup from the threat of lurking danger.

William stood alone in his defense. It felt more as though he waited before a judge for a sentence against his crimes, rather than an ecclesiastical court considering him for the honor of advancement towards the throne of Peter. A sudden chill swept through the Court, subtle, stealing the heat of his anger and the words of his quarrel. He had felt such coldness before. It was the chill presence of evil. It could only mean that far more hinged upon this election than ego and selfish gain—more than the leadership of the Church in Jherusalem.

William walked purposefully to the center of the hall. All eyes turned to him; whispers abounded. Clearing his throat discreetly, he began to recite the history of the True Cross from its return to Jherusalem by the Emperor Heraclius to its rediscovery by the lords of the First War of the Cross. He related its connection to the Kingdom of Jherusalem and the miraculous events that accompanied its presence before the armies of Christendom. Lastly, he pointed a finger at the Patriarch-elect as he spoke to the king.

"Six years you have ruled this kingdom, King Baldwin, despite the increasing effects of a disease that most men would consider too debilitating to rule, and in that time you have successfully kept the Muslims at bay. But mark my words and my firmest warning, Your Highness, if you and the canons elect this man to the Patriarchate left vacant by our beloved father, Aimery of Nesle, your long-fought-for kingdom will fall to the enemy. I tell you that the Cross, recovered by a Heraclius, will be lost by a Heraclius, along with Jherusalem and the kingdom."

Snickers of laughter and an animated conversation burst out from various quarters around the hall in response to his warning. Heraclius smirked and shook his head.

He argued eloquently enough against Heraclius' election, but in vain: the canons made their decision before they had ever met in conclave with the king and the Court. It ended as quickly as it began; the vote counted, the decision read, and his words of warning unheeded. Heraclius would become Patriarch of Jherusalem, and he would return to Tyre, his hopes, his dreams of ever rising above the office of Archbishop ruined beyond repair, except by the miracle of his rival's death. He had reached the height of his career. Whatever chance he had of achieving more for himself, and for the kingdom, had died with Aimery. However, he felt a quiet embrace of peace that calmed him, and left him knowing God had ordained everything in spite of the dark spirit of enmity that pervaded the hall.

Chairs scraped the floor as the hall began to clear with the end of the session. Before William could address the king on his decision to support Heraclius' election, his pack of wolfish advisors herded him towards the rear entrance of the hall and down the stairs. His chin fell to his chest prayerfully. He made the sign of the cross on his body and turned to gather his cloak to leave. Heraclius was waiting. A malignant smile curled the lips of the new Patriarch.

"You should have known it would be pointless for you to come here, my old rival," said Heraclius. "The Church has no use for your old and antiquated ideas. You are a relic of the past, William. Go back to Tyre and finish writing your worthless *Historia* in peace. The king has no use for you any longer."

"It is a pity, Heraclius, the Church and the Court does not know you as I do."

"Perhaps, they know me better than you think, brother."

"The sin of concubinage is hardly becoming to one in your position, my lord Bishop—forgive me, Your Grace," William sneered. "By the way, how is Pascua? I expect she will be overjoyed to learn that your income will be increasing substantially now that you are Patriarch. You best make sure that Madame de Riveri—or should I call her, *Madame la Patriarchesse*—is never found with your child. You'd have a devil of a time trying to get her hands out of your coffers."

Heraclius' gaze narrowed briefly as his deep blue eyes brightened with amusement. "Careful, brother. Envy is a sin equal to concubinage and most unseemly to a man with such a righteous mien."

"Men like you are not deserving of the honor that has been given you. You are a disgrace to the cause of Christ and Holy Mother Church."

"And yet, I am the one who will wear the miter of Aimery. Perhaps, if you had paid more attention to the rights of Mother Rome, rather than your See in Tyre, or your master, the Count of Tripoli, you might have been elected to the throne of the Church of Jherusalem," said the pompous cleric in parting. "I bid you a good day."

William found himself alone in the sunlit hall of the Tower of David. He wandered back to his chair in the center of the great hall and sat down wearily. The day had certainly not gone as he had expected or hoped. His head fell into his hands with a heavy sigh. He laughed soberly and shook his head. Tomorrow would be the day God ordained it to be regardless of the outcome of this one.

Turning wistfully towards the king's throne, he discovered he was not alone after all. Baldwin stood beside a near pillar. He held a decanter of wine under his arm and two empty glasses in his hand. William stood respectfully.

"If it means anything, Your Grace, I'm not particularly fond of the man either."

"We live in troubled times, Sire. You did what you thought best. You need not explain your actions to me," William said, trying to be cordial, keeping his deep disappointment hidden beneath a weak smile.

"But I do, Father William. You must understand why I elected Heraclius."

"There is no need, Baldwin. I do understand."

Baldwin poured a glass of wine and handed it to him. "No, my lord Bishop, you do not," said the king, shaking his head. "I know how much you wanted to be Patriarch, but I couldn't risk losing you to the continual intrigues of the Court."

William could hear the frustration in the king's voice, the utter regret. "I still could have advised you from a throne of the Church; perhaps, with much more authority and power."

"Perhaps," Baldwin said. "But then, you wouldn't be at my side when I needed you more than the Church." He glanced uncertainly at William and paused, battling some inner daemon of his thoughts. William waited him out, determined to let the king explain himself. "For too long, Father William, I... I have made the terrible mistake of believing that only I could keep this kingdom together in the face of its enemies. In so doing, I trusted the advice of men who have done me far more harm than good in your absence."

"These advisors you speak of," William said, hesitating. "Your mother—"

Baldwin cut him off with a strangled, hissing sound in his throat. "No—say nothing of my mother or those of my family. I know what you think of her and my uncle, whether right or wrong, but it was none of their doing that I chose Heraclius to replace the Patriarch."

They walked the sword's edge now between reconciliation and further hostility. William offered a conciliatory nod to the king's rebuke, but he would not keep from setting blame where even the king could not deny the truth anymore than he could deny his own guilt. "Forgive me, Sire—but if not your mother or uncle, than those who seek to use them to gain your ear as well as your favor."

Baldwin at least could see the truth in his words. He nodded his head, if only reluctantly, and said: "That is why I need you back at Court, my old friend." He took a hand, touched it lightly to William's shoulder, and squeezed it roughly. "The Magdalen has finally made me see that pursuing peace is the only thing I can do to protect this kingdom, but there are forces within that are just as determined to break it and bring war down upon us before peace is ever given a chance to grow. I need you now more than I ever have before."

"For that I am most honored," William said. "You are, indeed, a good king, Your Highness, but you really are a terrible liar. Certainly, you do not think that I have become so old that I would believe your only reason for electing my rival, a man known for his profligate lifestyle, to the office of Patriarch of Jherusalem, was so that I could continue serving you as Chancellor. Please, Your Highness, I'm no fool."

"No, you are not," said Baldwin and fell strangely silent. Reaching for a column, he suddenly stumbled. His wineglass shattered on the stone floor. Only William's quick reaction prevented the king from falling himself. "Your Majesty, you're ill."

"No, my friend... only weary." Baldwin's voice, along with his body, was well past the point of exhaustion. He could hear it in his tone, in the very words he spoke. The desperation of his thoughts made him stronger than his body would allow.

William held the sick young man who had been like a son to him in his arms. Baldwin had wasted away to nothing more than flesh and bone now, although he still possessed a strong hand. His muscles had shrunk beneath his diseased flesh to sinewy whipcord. All the strength of will and mind that he possessed filled his eyes with a gleam that challenged the dark shadows of death that ever stalked him.

"These men, William—they have done everything in their power to persuade me to distrust you and break our friendship," Baldwin said. "Almost, I gave into their influence; but then, I thought that I could thwart them at their own game by making you Patriarch. I should have known better. Magdalen told me once not to elect you Patriarch should Aimery die during my reign. She warned me you would be humiliated and disgraced; worse, that you would most likely die as a result."

"I don't understand."

"The prophecy you spoke of concerning Heraclius and the loss of the True Cross. Whether you meant it or not, it will come true when I am gone."

William drained his cup and held it out to the king. Baldwin obliged him without question. "I see," he said. "And how much else has she told you about the future of this kingdom?"

Baldwin's eyes broke from their gaze and wandered about the hall. William had caught him in some secret and he had no way to escape. "More than any man should know—certainly more than any king should know of his own reign."

* * * * *

The newly elected Patriarch kissed the embroidered emblem of the Church and laid the white linen stole of his office in the vestment press to keep it from soiling. It was the night of the vigil of All Saint's: the All Hallows' Eve of the pagans. Heraclius had sung the prayers for Matins and joined them in the small, candlelit sacristy of the Church of the Resurrection. Amalric knelt at the *prie-dieu*, elbows resting on the cushion, his fingers steepled piously beneath his chin as he prayed. To whom, or what, he prayed as they waited on Heraclius' investiture ceremony as Patriarch, Agnes could not begin to imagine. Nor did she wish to. Amalric de Lusignan was a man with too many secrets.

Heraclius walked over to a side table and poured himself a glass of dark red wine. He raised his glass to his two guests. Agnes realized for the first time that both men in the room were her former lovers, and that both had risen to their present positions by her influence. The irony was not lost on her.

"Well, my friends, it seems that congratulations are in order," the Patriarch said. "We have accomplished what some thought might never happen. We are now but one or two generations from seeing the vision of Christian and Muslim lands united under one banner and one crown with both faiths under the See of Jherusalem instead of Rome."

Amalric rose from the *prie-dieu*, accepted the glass from the new Patriarch, and passed the other to Agnes. "Oh, yes, we have, indeed, won a great victory, my friends," he said, "but there is still some unfinished business we must attend to. This unsettled situation with Raymond of Tripoli and his faction cannot continue. His supporters must be silenced or removed once and for all. That includes our ever-constant friend, the Archbishop of Tyre. William has made himself enough of a nuisance this past year, here and in Rome."

"How do you propose we rid ourselves of these 'nuisances' without drawing too much attention?" Agnes asked, sipping her wine.

Heraclius answered her. "We need to find some evidence to bring against them."

"Trust me, my friends, we need not look too hard for evidence to lay against either of them," Amalric said. "If it proves otherwise, I'm sure it shouldn't be too hard to fabricate something damning against them, am I not right, Your Grace?"

"No, my lord, it should not," Heraclius said, nodding, and raised his glass the smallest fraction.

Agnes glanced at her fellow members of the Order of Sion. The unspoken words that passed between them gave her cause to wonder how much of this conversation was for her benefit. It was not unlike Amalric de Lusignan to share secrets with only certain individuals he found worthy. The more she demanded her former lover to confide in her, the more he seemed to ignore her request. Still, there were questions to which she wanted and needed answers, if she was to be of any help to her son. It was her sole reason for conspiring with Sion against the kingdom and the Church.

"What about the new Master of the Templars?" she asked. "Will he prove himself any more of a problem to us than Saint-Amant since he is the Pope's man? My son has every confidence that Messire de Torroge will work closely with him to keep the peace he has made with Salehdin."

The Master of Sion glanced at her and set his empty wineglass on top of the *prie-dieu*. He sat on the kneeling board. "The papacy may not be filled at present with a man of our choosing, but Alexander is a man easily influenced by thoughts of power and his own arrogance, not unlike most men that sit upon the throne of Peter. Negotiations are moving forward, however tenuous, for the reunification of the Church. He has taken steps to bring the Templars more directly under the control of the Pope as we have witnessed by choosing his own master for the Order. It is of little importance what he does, so long as he removes all suspicion from them about certain rumors making their way around the Lateran of late."

Amalric picked up the wine flask and judiciously filled his cup. "For now, I have named a man to Saint-Amant's position to act on our behalf until we can name a new master of our own. Messire de Glaise will report to us all that Arnaud de Torroge plans for the Templars. Have no fear, Madame; even without his knowledge, the Pope has only brought our plans that much closer to fruition." He let his dark gaze fall completely on the new Patriarch. "In the meantime, we must continue nurturing a relationship with the *sheikh al-Jebel* and his Assassins. Only the Shiites will ever accept a man of our making as their *Mahdi*. With any luck, the Jews will follow their example. If you must, Heraclius, send word to our contact in Cairo. He will know what can be done to open dialogue with his people."

A sudden knock at the door interrupted their deliberations. Agnes moved to the sacristy door and opened it a crack. The ancient, yet beatific smile of the Abbot Renaud of Mont Sion du Notre Dame greeted her.

"Good evening, my lady de Courtenay," he said, bowing his head. His voice was thin and reedy. "If I may, I need to speak with His Grace about a small ecclesiastical matter. He is, after all, the new Patriarch of Jherusalem. His needy flock of canons and bishops are unwilling to give His Reverence even the smallest fraction of time to settle in."

"Certainly, Father Abbot," she replied, taking his hand, and stood back from the door. "You need not apologize to me."

After a brief exchange of pleasantries and well wishes again on his election, Heraclius made his excuses, and was out the door with Abbot Renaud. Agnes and Amalric stood alone in the sacristy. Once, she had cherished and plotted such moments of intimacy with the handsome, dark knight from Poitou; now she only felt uncomfortable, used, particularly with the silence that he seemed all too delighted to let go on indefinitely. She cast it aside with a word.

"With Sion's plans coming together so quickly, what do we do now?"

Amalric sipped at his wine, his smile all but containing his smug, self-satisfaction. He glanced up at her. "We watch and we wait, my lady. We watch and we wait until we see the signs of the end and the coming of the One who will destroy the works of the Devil." He drained his cup with a gulp and a move to leave her as well. Her hand touched him as he passed. He stopped and looked down at her.

"And who, Messire, is this one for whom we wait?"

He removed her hand and gently kissed it. "I guess that depends on what you have learned and believe. If you insist on an answer, I tell you we wait not for one, but two men—two Messiahs—to lead us into the coming kingdom of God. A priest and a king of the holy blood," he said and left her alone in the sacristy.

It was important that they all not be seen leaving the room together, if at all.

Agnes swore under her breath. The vague answers her former lover gave had long since begun to annoy her. He refused to answer her for reasons of his own; or had he baited her to see what reactions she would give. Either reason she would not accept, even if she was helpless now to do anything about it. One way or another, she would discover Amalric de Lusignan's true plans for Jherusalem, and what place her son had in them, if any. She would wait for the answers to be revealed, but not too long.

KERAK
1183

† CHAPTER TWENTY

Fear ye not, and be not dismayed at this multitude: for the battle is not yours, but God's.
—*II Paralipomenon 20:15*

It was cold in the old scriptorium of the cathedral of Tyre. The chilling blast of a late spring wind blew in off the choppy, grey sea in a glistening mist that clung to the ancient stone of the house of God.

For William to work so late into the night was most unusual, particularly on the eve of so great and somber of an occasion as Easter. Holy Saturday had become one of his favorite days in the liturgical calendar. He had given the brothers a rare night off from work in the scriptorium so that they could attend the vigil in the chapel with prayers and contemplation of their own about the meaning of the Resurrection.

William sat on his customary stool at the tall wooden desk. Candlelight illuminated the sheets of the unfinished manuscript beneath his quill. After so many long hours of writing, indelible black ink stained his stubby fingers. The stains were something of a conversational piece on Sundays when he performed the mass in the finery and robes of his office; many of his students whispered rumors that the stains were scorch marks from wrestling with the Devil in his nightly battles for the souls of the kingdom. The origin of such cleverly invented and colorful stories were ever a source of wonder to him.

In the two and a half years since he had lost the leadership of the Church in Jherusalem to the pompous and iniquitous Heraclius, he had resigned himself to obscurity for the sake of the king. It gave him time to finish writing his *Historia regum*, even if that record brought him less joy than he had hoped.

He sifted through the loose sheaves of parchment and found the one he was looking for, a page half scribbled with his particularly cramped Latin script. It was a portion of his latest chapter dealing with events surrounding yet another feud between the Count of Tripoli and the king from the previous spring, a feud in which Raymond tried to enter the kingdom with the secret design of removing the king from the throne. Such was the lie the king's advisors maliciously insinuated to the king, hoping to use Baldwin's infirmity to their own advantage against the Count. The king unwittingly obliged their wicked schemes to create discord and unrest within the holy city. After Raymond's attempted coup two years before, Baldwin was ill inclined to trust any action on the part of the Count and refused him entry into the kingdom or his seigneury of Galilee.

Despite the humiliation of the illustrious count, those of wiser judgment and foresight managed to avert civil war, and William worked out an uneasy reconciliation between the king and the count. It was only the beginning, though, of troubles for the kingdom after more than two years of relative peace with the Muslims.

By midsummer, the situation forced Baldwin to assemble the army at Sephorie to prevent an invasion by Salehdin from the north. On the eighth anniversary of his coronation, Baldwin met the invasion force and won another miraculous battle at Le Forbelet in the tremendous summer heat. Although the king distinguished himself yet again as a brilliant commander of only twenty-two, the campaign soon wore down into a series of minor skirmishes as both sides tested the strength and resolve of the other. As a matter of convenience, Baldwin moved his Court to Nazareth and the army remained encamped at Sephorie under the command of Reynald de Châtillon. With neither side willing to capitulate nor withdrawal, the war ground to a halt. Salehdin found other interests to occupy his thoughts: Aleppo and Mosul, and the consolidation of his hold over the Muslim territories of Northern Syria.

The king, however, chose to remain in the field. There were other enemies afoot than just the Sarrazins. As long as he was not in Jherusalem, neither were those who might cause the most damage to the kingdom. Now, though, word had come that Baldwin had taken ill with a fever. William feared what new intrigues or trouble it would bring with Raymond of Tripoli if the *Haut Cour* named a new Regent. Whether the king saw it or not, there were too many troublemakers close to him: those that gathered around his throne were like moths to a flame.

William's eyes fell to the manuscript. He picked up the pen and, after thoughtful consideration of the record, changed the last line to reflect a truer picture of the situation at Court, and his personal opinion of the true conspirators: the king's mother, a grasping woman, utterly detestable to God, and her brother, the king's Seneschal. *Let the record show*, he thought, *that the situation with the Count was less the king's doing than it was of others.*

Despite the distraction of his writing, William's thoughts strayed; they came back to the king in a circuitous route that brought his emotions from anger to frustration to sorrow. He remembered the last time he had seen the king: the Feast of the Nativity in December, before the turning of the year four months before.

Even then, the man he found praying before the lighted altar in the cathedral of Tyre shocked him. Bent and hunched beneath the weight of riding armor and disease, Baldwin had grown taller, more kingly. He had that ability of his father and grandfather to command attention, whether in a large group or an audience of one. The more his leprosy took from him, the more his bearing bore out the king that lay beneath.

The scuff of his footstep on the stone floor and the sound of his voice in greeting had brought the king's head up. The eastern style of his robes and white silk kaffiyeh over his Frankish riding-armor seemed so alien in a house of worship to the Christian God. When Baldwin's eyes locked on his, the deep gaze of a vacant stare looked straight past William, seeing and not seeing at once. Although he hid it well enough behind the veil, his blindness had grown considerably worse. William saw it in the slight turn of his head as he listened for the slightest sound. When the younger man drew himself up to his full height, William grieved at the sight of the tall and handsome king he might have made had he not been plagued by a magic gone afoul from an enemy who thought him an acceptable sacrifice to their ambitions.

The thought squeezed his heart like a mailed fist. He remembered how Baldwin had been like other boys his age—fearless, brave, and prone to tests of courage among his friends. One particular day, as he was playing with some other boys of noble birth, they took to pinching each other with their nails to see which of them could withstand the most pain. Despite repeated trials of this sort, even to the point of drawing blood, Baldwin endured the hurt as though it was nothing to him as befitted a prince of the blood, or so his comrades believed. When word of this reached William, he became immediately suspicious, fearing what it might portend. He told the boy's father, the king; he consulted several doctors. When it became clear that Baldwin suffered from a form of leprosy, the doctors prescribed a regiment of treatment to cure the disease, if possible. Such hope proved vain.

He knew the day would come when that bright, young boy he had tutored as a child would eventually come to the end of his short life. He still had not prepared himself for that day. Not yet. He prayed that there was still time for hope, for healing, for an end to the long night of the king's suffering. As long as Baldwin still breathed, there were all of these.

He wished now that their visit had gone better on such a solemn occasion as Christmas—not that they had parted on angry terms, but they had argued. It was, after all, his responsibility to point out the foolishness of the king's actions, even when that advice was unasked for and contrary to the king's liking. Despite the continued tension between Baldwin and the Count of Tripoli, Reynald de Châtillon caused the greater source of contention.

In the week leading up to the Feast of the Nativity, word spread through the kingdom that the war-mongering lord of Kerak had built a fleet of ships, which he planned to launch on the Red Sea to harass the sea-caravans to the Muslim holy cities of Mecca and Medina. If possible, Reynald even planned to steal the body of the Prophet Muhammad from its tomb in Mecca. To William's great surprise, Baldwin supported the enterprise.

With a gleam in his red-rimmed eyes, the king had sipped a glass of wine and answered him. "Don't worry, Your Grace, its only five galleys and Reynald does so with my support, though I rather think he would probably have done so regardless. I assure you, it is a precautionary measure only should Salehdin decide to break the truce. I want him to think twice about which front he would rather fight against first—Damascus or Mecca."

It had proved a wise precaution in the end with the sultan's renewal of hostilities. William wondered if word of the venture had reached Salehdin and caused him to see the pointlessness of abiding by a new truce. Either way, Reynald had cast the die and it remained now, nearly a year later, to see what outcome this renewed war would bring. He knew he should have counseled Baldwin to greater caution, to greater patience with the Muslims. Perhaps he might have averted another war. With Salehdin busy in the north, harassing the ever-rebellious Syrians and Baldwin lying close to death in Nazareth, all they could do was wait.

* * * * *

Aleppo had fallen; Aleppo of the seven gates and bone-white walls, queen of the caravan routes and whore of the troublesome Zengid dynasty.

The grand army of Islam bowed their heads to the ground and, with one voice, gave praise to Allah for their victory. With the last of the northern strongholds removed, the lands from the Nile to the Tigris lay firmly under the yellow banner of the House of Ayyub.

For weeks, Yusuf had sent impatient dispatches to the court of Khalifa al-Nasir in Baghdad, pleading with the heir of the Prophet to support his actions, but with no reply. It mattered not to him whether the Khalifa backed him or not, he would act. If al-Qihara and Dimasq were the cornerstones of an empire, then Aleppo became the keystone of a fabulous dream: the union of all Islam. Through that mighty doorway, built upon blood and stone and years of ceaseless toil, the *jihad* would finally drive the infidels of Urshalim into the sea.

If for no other reason, he would seek a truce with Antioch to protect his newest possession. With the infidels of Urshalim, however, he had no interest in a continued peace that only delayed the inevitable. He had put off the *jihad* until he could unite the people of the crescent to one cause, and one cause only: to rid their land of the unbelievers. One thought had driven him these past few years, one thought that haunted his every waking moment and his dreams.

Urshalim will fall.

Five days before, Imam ad-Din, the governor of fallen Aleppo had surrendered and fled the city to the shouts and jeers of its people with his tail tucked neatly between his legs. As a condition of his capitulation, he gave Imam ad-Din his former possession of Sinjar far to the east of the Euphrates, away from the intrigues of Aleppo and Suriya. He had gained the position of lord of Aleppo only two years before in the midst of the turbulent chaos of Aleppan politics caused by his murder of Nur ad-Din's thirteen-year-old son and heir, as-Salih Ismail. He had sown the seeds of discord and strife, and reaped the violent whirlwind of an Ayyubid conquest.

The Commander of the Faithful knelt in prayer with his men before the gate of the mighty city, contemplating the success of his war against Suriya. It had proven a very long year, indeed. Mosul alone had defied him; but Sinjar and impregnable Amida, along with many of the lesser satellite villages throughout the Jazireh, had fallen—and now, lastly, Aleppo. Even the stunning naval attack in the Red Sea by the notorious Nasrani, Brins Arnat of al-Keraq and Shaubak could not keep him from the path ordained by Allah.

The year before his departure to Suriya, he had spent setting the affairs of Egypt in order under the governance of his brother Saif ad-Din al-Adil. He had told no one, but somehow, he had known that he would never return to the ancient red land of the Nile. Egypt had been a diversion, a necessity. His destiny lay in the indomitable land of Suriya. He would die in Suriya, but not before he had recovered Urshalim for the sake of Allah and removed the embarrassment of every Muslim across the breadth and width of *Dar al-Islam*. He needed only to hear that Al-Abras lay close to death to know that the greatest day of his life had dawned.

The success of his campaign had not come without sacrifices, however. He had lost a younger brother: Taj al-Maluk Buri died in the minor fighting before Aleppo. So fell another warrior who would enjoy the blessings of Paradise for his death in the cause of Allah. It was the second such loss in his family in a year. Beside his brother, his favorite nephew, Farrukh-Shah, had died suddenly in Dimasq nine months before. The shadows and the harem whispered of poison and Hashshashin, but it was only a test of Iblis, challenging his resolve to renew the *jihad* and see it through to its end.

The prayer ended. The army rose as one and marched forward like a lumbering behemoth; the same assorted lot that witnessed the final conquest of Suriya under the yellow banner of the Ayyubids and the crescent of a unified Islam: the armies of Egypt and Dimasq, the Jazireh, Sinjar, Amida, and the Turkoman clans.

Riding his favorite stallion, Yusuf entered the gate of Aleppo to the skirling pipes and the clashing of drums. The downcast people of the fallen city crowded the street, cheering expectedly and obediently, but obviously half-heartedly. He had publicly executed the officials who had counseled the previous governor to resist him as an example to those who might still harbor thoughts of defiance. There were no such incidents today as he rode through the city towards the Citadel, nor did he expect any.

The fortress of Aleppo in the heart of the Old City brooded upon a vast truncated mountain of rock and the accumulated debris that stretched back hundreds, if not thousands of years. The massive walls of white stone rose to a dizzying height; the stairs of a bridge spanned a deep moat, and was wide enough for only a few men to walk abreast at a time—a precaution against armed invasion. The stairs, pitted and worn with age, lent an impression of fragility to the tall, arched supports that seemed would crumble at the slightest noise. An earthquake a number of years before had damaged the steps as well as the Citadel and the city. More than two hundred thousand of Aleppo's people died in the disaster. The city, nonetheless, was still well fortified, the Citadel impregnable.

Dismounting at the large outer gatehouse, Yusuf walked through the arch and acended the crumbling stairs of the narrow bridge to the main gate of the palace. He had put aside his armor and donned his familiar robes of black touched with silver and gold. His second-in-command waited for him at the tall iron door of the gatehouse. The yellow banners of the Ayyubids flapped atop the wall in the breeze. It was a proud moment for him, even for a man with deep religious convictions and humble desires.

"Everything is in order, Excellency," said Isa al-Hakkari. "The *imam* waits for you within."

Yusuf followed his aging emir through the vaulted Gate of the Lion into the wondrous adorned throne room of the palace. Sunlight illumined the grated windows onto the floor. Four Mamluks kept a discreet, but vigilant, distance from their lord. The presence of a conquering army was anything but welcome in a city that had surrendered only at the connivance of their spineless prince.

The man who met him in the palace looked far older than the stones of Aleppo. Wrinkles creased his dark brown face and round, balding head. His toothy smile presaged a greeting in a reed-thin voice marred with an Aleppan accent.

"*As salaam u'alai kuum Al-Malik Salah ad-Din.*"

Yusuf bowed deeply. "*Wa'Alai kuum as-Salaam,*" he said. "*Alhamdulillah.* I most desire to pray with you in your mosque for the blessing of Allah's goodness on this city."

The imam closed his eyes and touched a hand to his head and heart with a bow. "*Allahu akhbar.*"

Making his obeisance to the aged spiritual leader, Yusuf and the *imam* proceeded in quiet conversation through the palace towards the small old mosque built in the courtyard to pray. He had done what the Ifranj had twice before tried to accomplish and failed.

He had much to pray for and give thanks to Allah. There was much, though, he needed still to do.

Urshalim will fall, Maryam had said. *Urshalim will fall.*

* * * * *

The king lay close to death. She had seen more signs of life in a fresh corpse than what she saw in her brother's frail and emaciated body. He had not spoken in more than a week. When he did, he spoke as though in the midst of some tortured dream.

His veil had slipped, exposing the edge of his disease ravaged jaw. She reached out impulsively to pull the cloth down to see his face. Her hand froze in mid-air; her fingers closed in a loose fist and fell, unable to unveil the hideousness it hid.

She remembered when they were children, before their father had become king, when he and their mother were no more than the Count and Countess of Japhe and Ascalone. Before Baldwin had become a leper and her life had changed. She remembered far more of their childhood than her brother. Their uncle should have reigned for many long years and begotten an heir. Baldwin should have become a mighty lord and knight of the realm, and she, the lady of some prince in Europe or a lord of Outremer. Things should have been different; but they were not.

However much she tried, Sibylla could not hold back her tears. She was never more thankful that her brother had grown blind from his illness. It made it easier to hide her sorrow. So she had thought.

—Don't weep for me, Sibylla. I no more fear the Angel of Death, than I do the just judgment of God.

Her hand recoiled from his arm. Half startled at his words, half in wonder that she heard him as clearly as the ringing of the cathedral bells. He plucked the thoughts from her mind. It was magic, his magic; the magic he had shown her once on the road to Ascalone. She still wore the gold ring as a reminder of her promise.

"You cannot die yet, Baldwin,' she said. "I'm not ready to rule the kingdom alone."

—You can, Sibylla, and you will. It is your duty. You must be strong. For yourself... and for your son.

Sibylla was frantic. She did not care how her brother could speak to her in her thoughts, only that he did. Ever since he had taken ill with the Court at Nazareth, she had known and she had feared that Baldwin would leave her alone with a war to be fought and won—or lost. The word of a spy had come, warning that Aleppo had fallen and Salehdin was massing his army at Damascus for an attack on the kingdom. It was only a matter of time before he acted and struck at Jherusalem. Baldwin's illness had rendered the royal army impotent. Without him, infighting and squabbling among the lords of the Court had turned every minor decision into a debate. Day by day, her brother drew closer to death and Jherusalem towards the final hour of her existence in Christian hands.

—Jherusalem will not fall while I still live.

"How can you know that—can you foretell the future now as well?" she said, trying not to lose her patience and failing hopelessly.

—Trust only that I know, sister. You must believe me.

Sibylla pulled her hands back and wrapped her arms across her chest. Her fingers clung to her upper arms like claws. Her thoughts betrayed her and scattered, leaving her mind bereft of sense or will. She feared she might suffer the same fate as her mother had at the hands of the Church and the Court when Amaury had become king—her marriage annulled, her children taken away, her reputation forever maligned. She wanted simply to be with Guion and her two small children, Baudinouet and her daughter Marie, who had been born eighteen months ago.

"I can't do this, Baldwin. I do not want to be queen. Father raised you to be king. I was trained to be a lord's lady and to breed his children."

Her head lifted, meeting the vacant, blind gaze of Baldwin's blue-grey eyes. He plucked the secret thoughts from her mind. *The life you chose to have with Guion is sealed. You cannot change it, sister. If Guion is to truly reign as king of Jherusalem one day, then he must prove himself capable and worthy of the crown. He deserves to be Regent and so he will be by my command.*

Sibylla sat in stunned silence at what her brother offered and promised. He was giving Guion the Regency and the crown for the taking. There was no question whether Guion had the support he needed—he needed only to prove himself to win the rest to his favor. Baldwin could have done so long before now. Why now? Why here on the verge of war?

—Because I must.

"Stop doing that and answer me aloud," she demanded.

He obeyed her, and more; he fell into a combative quiescence. Several moments passed as they both sat, refusing to acknowledge the other. His sudden sour mood gathered like a breaking storm, rumbling with fire and flashing lightning. She startled when he spoke, not with the volume with which he spoke, but at the softness of his words.

His voice sounded like the soft whisper of dried and rustling leaves. "Do you truly love him?"

"I do."

"Does he make you happy?"

"Very much so," she said, her eyes tearing.

"Then make sure he continues to do so."

"You still haven't answered me, brother," she said.

"Nor will I," he whispered. "My reasons are my own. Consider it a gift."

Sibylla sat back in the chair. "You don't trust Guion."

"I trust you, don't I, even if you are a spoiled and pampered princess." He always knew how to win through to her heart.

"That is because you love me."

—And you me. Even in her mind, his voice was no more than a strained whisper.

Sibylla touched his arm. The back of his bandaged hand caressed her cheek. She leaned into his touch and held his hand gently. "Why must you always be so stubborn?"

He shifted in his bed, trying to sit up in the nest of pillows around him. The effort took all his strength. "Because I must be king before all else."

"Even with me, Baldwin?"

His head turned as though his eyes sought to look at her. "Especially with you, Sibylla," he said. "One day, perhaps, you'll understand."

Sibylla held his hand tighter. Her brother knew her far better than she ever thought. She did not understand, but she was beginning to and it frightened her even more.

* * * * *

Dust hung in the air as the army marched along the old road from Sephorie and Nazareth, down into the Esdraelon Plain, which the ancient Israelites named the Valley of Jezreel. It was far worst for the fifteen hundred infantrymen that had to walk that long way through the choking dust, particularly those at the rear of the column. Such difficulties were always common when an army moved, especially in the midst of a drought. Ordinarily, the mounted knights usually fared better sitting atop their tall horses. This was no ordinary day, however. Sweat and dirt caked knights and soldiers alike before they even reached La Fève in the midst of the plain of Armageddon. Sixteen thousand men and animals were sorely in need of water and rest. Neither was forth coming. Had it been midsummer, all of them would have died.

Reynald rode at the head of the army alongside Guion, the new Regent of the crown. His eyes stared blankly ahead, fixed on the gleaming gold of the Life-Giving Cross. He dreamt of water and the clear, cool springs of Goliath and Tubania near Bethsan.

For the better part of the last few months, the army had remained encamped at Sephorie, waiting for the Muslims to make some move towards Jherusalem. Salehdin had made some minor forays in the past year, but the main invasion he kept in wait. The king unfortunately had fallen ill; the Court feared he lay close to death. Their fear crippled the army. With Baldwin sick, Reynald had assumed nominal command, but the Court remained divided over what course of action was best. It would remain so it seemed until the Muslims forced them into a decision none of them wanted.

Despite his friendship with Guion, it was uncomfortable without Baldwin at the head of the army, leading them into battle. It would be their first encounter with the Sarrazins without the king; it would be Guion's first campaign as Regent. Consequently, events forced Guion to rely on Reynald's experience to help him lead the army—a bit surprising given his brother's position as Constable.

The full flower of the Frankish nobility had answered the summons of Guion's muster to Sephorie. Even Raymond and Bohemond had responded to the summons despite Salehdin's four-year truce with the Prince of Antioch. In addition to the infantrymen and the thirteen hundred knights of the realm, the army's numbers were swollen by scores of Venetians, Pisans, and Genoese who had left their ships along with a good many pilgrims and hastened to join in the defense of the kingdom. At their head marched two brilliant warriors of the West: Godfrey III, the Duke of Brabant, and Ralph de Mauléon of Aquitaine. Their combined strength of arms represented the single greatest force ever assembled by the Christians to face the enemy since the First War of the Cross.

His wife's young son, Humphrey, fourth of the name and grandson of the late Constable, rode at Reynald's back with the remnant of the troops of Oultrejourdain. The day before, an advance party of Mamluks had ambushed Humphrey near the slopes of Mount Gilboa as his knights made their way up the Naples Road to rendezvous with the royal army. The knights were routed, a hundred men captured. The remainder, a mere twenty men, limped into Sephorie with word of Salehdin's movements about Tubania.

Contrary to consistent murmuring that his stepson was rather effeminate and less of a man than a knight of Outremer ought to be, he gave a good account of himself for a young man of eighteen under his first command.

"I'm sorry, my lord," his stepson had said, stammering as badly as the king. "I... I did my best, but the Muslims took us by surprise. They... they have split their army into three groups. They have attacked Forbelet, Bethsan, and even harassed the brothers of Saint-Elias on Mt. Tabor. I lost nearly all your troops, sir."

Uncharacteristically, Reynald had grabbed Humphrey by the shoulders and embraced him fiercely. "I don't care. As long as you weren't captured or killed."

It was his report on Michaelmas that had roused the army from their long encampment at Sephorie. Guion ordered their march the following morning to make a stand against the Sarrazin invasion before it could advance any further into Galilee and the kingdom.

By midday, reports of skirmishes began to run back through the long column: the advance guard under the lead of the Constable had come under heavy attack. Guion immediately ordered the Ibelin brothers and their troops to lend support to his brother, but only at Reynald's urging.

Mounted reinforcements rode forward from the center of the column. The advance guard fell back, even with help from the Ibelins. The Muslims followed them. A hail of arrows rained down into the center of the column. Only the tight discipline of the seasoned troops kept the army from falling into chaos.

Reynald took command and ordered the knights in the first few ranks to charge against the Sarrazins. At the last moment, the charge executed a difficult maneuver and split into two wings that swung wide and crashed into the left and right flanks of the enemy. Forcing the Mamluks into a narrower column, Reynald gave the signal for another charge using the core of the knights from Sidon, Caesarea, and the remainder of his own troops from Kerak. He held the Hospitallers in reserve should they be needed.

The attack was short-lived, more spectacle than substance. Ill prepared to face the full onslaught of a Frankish charge, the Sarrazins broke off their attack and scattered. These were not the seasoned troops of Salehdin's vast army, but only skirmishers sent to harass the enemy.

Guion quickly resumed command of the army from Reynald. Everyone noticed, however, how he had hesitated in the face of battle. Raymond of Tripoli rode up, agitated, but hiding it well enough. The Prince of Antioch, his omnipresent shadow, rode at his side.

"Well-handled, my lord of Japhe," said the Count. "That was rather too close for any of our comfort. Perhaps, it would be best if we camp for the night at one of the nearby pools and discuss some course of action before we move forward."

Having made his insult, Raymond rode off to rally his troops, leaving a visibly irritated Guion to confront his inner daemons. Guion angrily pulled his horse around and glared at Reynald. "Perhaps, Raymond is right. We should probably make camp and regroup. Salehdin has had time to prepare for us. He won't likely let us make plans to dislodge him from this valley."

Reynald sheathed his sword, making a deliberate show of his action. He raised the nose-guard of his helmet and looked at the younger man. "If you are to be king in Baldwin's stead one day, you best learn now to make these decisions for yourself. Do not let the Count of Tripoli command you. *You* are the Regent, my lord de Lusignan, not him. So long as you hold such office, your word is the word of the king."

Guion's hard face softened, listening to his rebuke with care, which was well and good since Reynald had far more to say. "I warn you, Your Grace, you best decide now how you will handle yonder Count. His will is to have the throne and the crown any way he can. Do not let the other lords see you give any quarter to that man. And for God's sake, don't let him cow you into any decision you have already chosen against." Reynald backed his horse away and turned the animal with a heel. "If I have your leave, my lord, I'll see about setting the order of the camp."

"Do as you will, my lord of Kerak," said the Regent. "But I'll expect you at my tent tonight to discuss our strategy."

Guion tried to keep his voice firm and commanding, confident, but Reynald was not convinced. Guion was still an untried, foppish youth from Poitou who aspired to a throne that should have been far beyond his reach. This was Outremer, however, and here the grandest dreams were as common as sand. Reynald made a salute to Guion and touched a heel to his horse, leaving the Regent to make what commands and decisions he could handle alone.

* * * * *

The Regent's crown weighed far more than Guion ever expected. Worse still, six days of infighting and squabbling amongst the lords of Jherusalem was beginning to take its toll on him and on the army. The men were as divisive as their lords. He wondered how his wife's brother managed to bear such a heavy burden with leprosy draining strength and life from his limbs.

He began to wonder about the position his own brother had worked so long to secure for him to hold… and whether or not it was worth the trouble.

Over the last few days, Salehdin had proven himself once more a cunning leader. No sooner had Guion called a halt to make camp, than the wily old fox abandoned the springs of Tubania and moved further downstream towards Bethsan and easy retreat across the Jordan. For the first few days of October, the Muslims scoured the countryside, harassing the local townspeople. After ravaging the peasantry, the sultan finally turned his attentions towards the true object of his enterprise, the

Frankish army and their defense of the Christian kingdom. The Muslims stole their supply of food, threatened their holy places, and encamped so close to the Franks that Salehdin's much larger army was able to extend its wings to nearly encompass them. It was only the miraculous discovery of fish in the Pools of Goliath that saved the army from starvation.

Guion glanced irritably at his quiescent brother. Amalric offered as little help as usual in these predicaments. The air had grown unbearably hot in his palatial camp tent by the Pools of Tubania. The wine and the flames of the copper braziers added only slightly more heat than the tempers of his quarreling lords. Most of the barons had already retired for the evening; only Guion and his brother remained behind to argue the difficulties they faced with Raymond of Tripoli.

"You're the Regent, my lord de Lusignan. Tell us what action we are to take," Raymond said softly in his anger. His quiet voice echoed like the loudest shout. He sat comfortably in a camp chair in the corner of the tent, the elected representative for those who agreed with his plan. "In case you haven't noticed, we are nearly surrounded by the enemy. Day by day, Salehdin attempts to lure us out by various stratagems."

"Exactly what action do you want me to take, my lord of Tripoli? Or do you hope I will attack and fail miserably, so you could blame me once more for another so-called error in judgment?" He glanced at his brother. "My lord of Kerak and the Hospitallers, along with the visiting lords from Europe all urge me to attack now, while we have the choice and the means to do so. On the other hand, you wish me not to attack at all. Listen to reason you say, and yet you offer no council as to how I am to accomplish such. You blame me for not protecting the holy shrines. You accuse me of not supplying our troops with much needed food. You claim I dally and hesitate, and call me indecisive. But where is the council you swore to give as a lord of the Court, my lord of Tripoli—or have you nothing but scorn and ridicule to offer us? If the king stood before you now, you would give him your advice without hesitation; instead, you withhold it and make demands of me without reason."

Guion laughed in a rather affecting manner, shaking his head. It was not often that he spoke so much or with so much anger. He held his hand up to forestall the Count's remark. "And yet, despite all this, I happen to agree with you. It is best we watch and wait to see what the enemy intends. And for that, you hate me all the more."

It was enough to make the intransigent man squirm uncomfortably. Raymond had remained unusually quiet through the course of Guion's tirade and he seemed equally determined to continue in his silence. It only made Guion all the more frustrated and angry. He was not sure if he should drink his wine or toss the remnants at the arrogant count.

"It seems that no matter what I do, you will find fault with me," he said. "I truly begin to think that you wish for me to fail because you hope to win back the Regency for yourself by making me seem unworthy of the trust given me by the king."

Raymond stood and shrugged his dark red cloak over his shoulders and mail. He was shorter than Guion was by a hand or two, but his physical presence made up for his middling height. Guion refused to give the slightest ground as the former Regent passed by him; his hand clenched nervously on the hilt of his sword.

"I need not do anything, Messire, to make you look inept and unsuited to the office of Regent," Raymond said. You have proven the fact simply by your inaction these past few days. I am sure the king has had word of the campaign thus far. Goodnight, my lords."

Amalric's arm shot out across his chest as Guion turned and lunged towards the empty doorway where the Count of Tripoli stood a moment ago. His anger gave thought to the malicious gossip he had heard over the past three years. His grip tightened on his sword. The gossip complained that he was untried and undeserving of so much favor from the king. That he had gained the hand of a princess, and the titles and land, and wealth of an important seigneury that went with it. That the king had granted him authority and power in Court, and now, the Regency of the crown and the command of an army he had no experience to lead.

He was the third son of the lord of Lusignan, a minor, petty noble of Poitou, with no greater claim on history than its participation in the holy wars, and their ignoble descent from the water-faerie Melusine. If he could not prove himself worthy of all the blessings of the crown, then his opponents would think themselves right and continually murmur against him.

"No, brother. Not here; not now," the Constable whispered in his ear. "His time will come I assure you."

"Not soon enough," Guion growled through clenched teeth. "Not soon enough."

* * * * *

Do not fear, brother, that the enemy surrounds us. Allies far greater and powerful than any seen by mortal man protects the army.

Such were the words that his stepson, Hugh, related to Raymond as he walked back to his tent after meeting with the Regent, Guion de Lusignan. Hugh had hung close to the tent after Raymond had made his exit—at Raymond's command, of course—hoping to gather whatever evidence he could overhear in the dark about the Regent and his brother, the Constable. He had expected to learn something of the Lusignan's plans for the kingdom, some word of treason or conspiracy against the king, but nothing so damning as their commerce with the black arts of the devil. For what else could the Constable mean by referring to allies *far greater and powerful than any seen by mortal man*?

Magic, he breathed. Somehow or another, it was being used to protect the kingdom. He wondered what else it might protect.

"Are you certain those were the Constable's exact words, Hugh?"

"Aye, my lord."

"Did you hear anything else, or what they might have meant by these allies?"

Hugh shook his head. "After that, the Constable bid his brother a good evening and left. I tried to follow him, but I was too late. He seemed to disappear into the darkness," he said, glancing around the camp. The incident had rattled his stepson's nerves. "I found you as soon as I could. Is there anything else you need of me tonight, my lord?"

Raymond clapped Hugh on the back and shoved him towards the tents of the knights of Galilee. "No, no. Go and get your rest, my boy. You've done enough for me for one night."

"What do you think the Constable meant?" Hugh asked as he turned to leave.

Raymond let the question hang in the air for several long moments as he sought for an answer. At this point, he needed to be careful about what he said, even to his stepsons. "I'm not sure—but I do intend to find out. Say nothing to anyone for now. I don't want to arouse any suspicion."

Hugh nodded his head and walked off into the night.

Raymond stood outside his tent for a time, contemplating the new wrinkle that presented itself in the ever-changing political landscape of the kingdom. It was not something one rushed to blurt out in a public accusation, but rather, a secret to mete out judicially in a way that was most advantageous to the discoverer of the said secret. After all, lives and reputations were at stake; the safety of the kingdom to consider in light of a Church Hell-bent on excommunicating anyone that consorted with the Devil. Hedge-magic and love charms, which were so common among the peasantry, could be overlooked; but the Holy Father in Rome would never abide outright alliances with daemons and dark magic. Raymond was no saint, but neither was he a monster that would see the kingdom suffer under an interdict that would leave the kingdom weak and vulnerable to an enemy bent on its destruction.

Of course, no one need know of such damning fraternization, only a small circle of intimates who shared his concerns for the well-being of the kingdom. The king, out of a certain necessity, he would have to tell, even if it was for no other reason than to cast suspicion on the Regent.

Raymond chuckled to himself and tucked the secret away in his mind for the time being. He had several guests waiting within his tent, eager to hear what excuses and recriminations the Regent had made for himself and his actions—or rather, his inactions. Bohemond and the Ibelin brothers would certainly be as indignant as he had been to know that King Baldwin had placed a man near the throne who was not the fool they had all claimed him to be. Oh, no. Guion de Lusignan was every bit the man his brother, the Constable, had made of him. Moreover, it meant he was a problem. If he could not persuade the king that Guion was inept and indecisive, then there was little chance of keeping the Poitevin upstart from taking the throne after Baldwin's death. Whether he liked it or not, they might have to lie in addition to refusing to cooperate with Guion to cast doubt on the Regent's actions. Of course, there was always the small matter of magic on the part of the Lusignans he could use to win this game of kings and thrones.

No matter what action it took, Guion must never take the throne of Jherusalem.

* * * * *

"It is said Al-Abras lies close to death in an-Nasirah, Your Excellency," said Isa al-Hakkari. The aged Egyptian commander waited for his response. When none was immediately forthcoming, he spoke further: "If we assemble the army now, we can crush the Ifranj once and for all."

Yusuf took no pleasure in hearing of the Ifranj king's losing battle with the *Malak al-Maut*, the Angel of Death. Ezra'il had struck down his young body with his terrible sword of death and disease; the blade sunk deep, cleaving flesh and bone and soul. Leprosy was a horrible way to die, seeing your limbs and body slowly eaten away by an unseen terror. It was a fitting death for the most vile of men; only the burning fires of *Jahannam* prepared for the unbelievers of Islam compared with the wasting disease with its devouring, yet never consuming flames. There was only one difference. Leprosy offered the promise of death; Hell promised everlasting torment. His was not a death meant for kings and valiant soldiers of war. Such was the depth of Allah's displeasure with Ifranj arrogance that he had stricken their king with such a terrible death.

Salah ad-Din Yususf turned to his commander and clasped him by the near shoulder. The westering sun struck the man's polished bronze armor and splintered into a thousand and one rays of dazzling light.

"No, my dear friend," he said. "The ordained moment Allah has meant for us has not yet come."

Isa al-Hakkari's wide mouth opened and closed voicelessly. His obsidian-black eyes narrowed as an argument struggled to battle its way from his mind to his tongue. "My lord Salah ad-Din, say it is not so. Surely, this is the day of our glorious victory over these uncircumcised swine. How can you calmly say it is not?"

Yusuf glanced around at the other commanders gathered around him on the hilltop. A breeze rose, stirring the saffron silk fabric of his palatial camp tent and the banners of his vast army. The long knife scar seaming his left cheek and down into his beard suddenly began to itch. He fingered it, stroking the puckered flesh and the long grey-black hair of his beard. He remembered the words of the *ifritah* as he had so many times before. *So long as the Leper King lives, Urshalim will not fall.* He dared not challenge that promise with unbelief.

"You are all of the same mind?" he asked. No one dared to defy him. Wisdom bound their tongues with silence. "I tell you now, one and all, as long as Al-Abras lives, we cannot meet the Ifranj in direct battle."

"This is madness and folly," the least wise of his emirs cried. He was a Damascene and proud of his heritage: a man whose family could trace back their lineage in the city to before the coming of the Prophet with the Word of Allah. "We have the infidels nearly surrounded with our camp and you council us to wait. From here, we can press onto Urshalim and capture the Holy City without resistance."

Yusuf walked forward without a word through the circle of his would-be advisors and stopped at the edge of the hill. The valley lay before him, crowded on the north and south by brownish-green mountains and cut by a small river fed by the springs around which his army and the Ifranj had encamped. He pulled his arms together behind his back and clasped his hands. The small spot between his shoulder blades began to itch, waiting for a knife to plunge into his flesh. Time and the silence stretched on indeterminably long and the itch soon faded from his notice.

"I had a dream last night," he said. It pained him with guilt to lie to his own men, but he must either lie or explain to them about the visits of an *ifritah* by night that disclosed to him the secrets of the future. Obedience and loyalty could only expect so much. It could not instill a belief in the miraculous.

"I dreamt of a great lion and a small frail lamb that devoured the lion when it was attacked." He paused, gauging the effect his lie had on his commanders. Their frustration and irritation with the Ifranj resolve to remain on the defensive and not fall prey to any attempt to lure them from their position only made them susceptible to the influences of his lie. He had never lied before about something of such importance, and yet his commanders believed him.

"I am the great lion; the small, frail lamb, the king of the Ifranj. If we attack now, war will devour us." He turned back to them, waiting on their response. He did not have to wait long.

"It is a sign from Allah," cried the youngest of the emirs and fell to his knees in prayer. The others followed the youngest's example of piety. It was, indeed, a sign that his men saw it as such, even if one or three still murmured about wasted opportunities.

Baha ad-Din Qaraqush, his chief commander of the horses, murmured the loudest. He, more than anyone else, had tried to pry the Ifranj from their position around the life-giving pools and bring them to battle. Even the imminent death of their well-beloved king was not enough to break their spirit or throw them into a state of confusion.

"What do you council, then, Your Excellency," Qaraqush asked. "Withdrawal to Dimasq?" For the Egyptian captain to take the lead as representative for the others given his own opinion on the matter was an indication of his deep loyalty.

"Only for a brief time, my old friend. Only a brief time," Salah ad-Din Yusuf said with a rare smile of satisfaction. Six days ago, they had captured nearly a hundred knights on the day after his crossing of the Jordan into the Ifranj kingdom. He knew all too well the banner of those prisoners. They belonged to the pig of al-Keraq, Brins Arnat. "I have another plan that will draw the Ifranj away from an-Nasirah."

† CHAPTER TWENTY-ONE

He will keep the feet of his saints, and the wicked shall be silent in darkness; because no man shall prevail by his own strength.
—I Kings 2:9

Dark silhouettes slipped through the rising mist. A giggle of laughter echoed among the trees, fading quickly into the silence of the ancient forest. It came unbidden and unwanted, the memory of another time, another place.

Gathering shadow and mist and the small, illuminated Psalter she prayed from, Mary fled upon the shadow-ways, the straight paths that deer and rabbits trod unseen. Her steps were silent upon the detritus of countless years, silent as the leaves that fell from the trees and floated down and down upon on the breeze. She turned, glancing over her shoulder. Other, more elusive shadows of the forest slipped through the grey light of dawn following at a distance.

She had not come this way for many a year; a way she dared not come for the certain sorrow lay at its end. Time made its slow way here as it did in the world of men. Its crawl was imperceptible, but it moved and had its subtle influence. This *otherland* was mortal enough, even if death had yet to claim a reward.

She stopped suddenly. The mists had grown thicker on the path that led near the edge of the worlds. Whispers rose, riding on the breeze. The voices of man drifted through the thin veil bordering the land of Faërie. Almost she could hear their murmuring words, echoing like prayers through the mists. Churches seemed to draw nearest to the bounds of her realm; they anchored it firmly, never letting it drift wholly away into dream and forgotten memories. Sometimes, when the worlds and men were at peace and she ventured close to the edge of the shadows, she could hear the church bells ring soft and clear. Dreams collided with reality in this borderland of whispers and shadow and the soft hazy light of a morning sun.

Few of her kind ventured along these pathways anymore. Eden reminded them too much of the truth they had long ago abandoned, and so they chose to stay away and forget the place that the children of Adam were once forbidden to enter. They remembered only in their dreams and trembled at the judgment awaiting them.

Her dreams, however, were not theirs, nor were they the distorted images that plagued mortal men as they slept at night. Hers were the memories of her shattered past, vivid and unforgiving; less often, though, they came as the unfolding of a future day—a *Seeing*, as the enemy of her kind, the Church, would accuse—shadows of things not yet seen.

An oak tree grew in this place of mist and dreams and shifting time. It was old, the tree, ancient; its massive limbs were thick with moss and overhanging vines. Its roots sank deep into the moist, primordial earth. A gleaming jewel on a silver chain hung from the lowest branches of the swaying giant. It called to her, willing her to take its glowing light in hand and speak with her treasured memories once more.

The stone was all she had left of her only daughter, a voice among the many that haunted her during the long and many dark years of her captivity to the enemy. Such was the irony of her fate. All she had left of her daughter was the memories the enemy had sealed inside the stone—the one thing for which the enemy had no need.

Its soft radiance warmed at her touch. Fear and anxiety mixed with regret and her gnawing guilt, threatening to chase her away. With all her heart, she wanted to feel the stone's warmth again, but it pained her, knowing the images she would see and remember once more.

Holding the prayer book close to her heart, she closed her eyes, and took the precious jewel in hand. It blazed to life at her touch, flooding her mind with memories she could never quite recall no matter how hard she tried to remember.

—**Salome**, *she breathed in a whisper and no more.*

Mary startled with a sudden break from the thoughts and memories of her daughter. A voice familiar, yet not, called to her. At first, she thought Salome had returned from that place she had long ago disappeared. It was not Salome; it was another who had learned to call her wherever she might linger. She remembered his name. *Baudinouet—Baldwin. The king of Jherusalem.*

—**Magdalen. Help me. I have lost my way into the mist.**

In that moment of her sudden remembrance, she turned towards his voice. He stood before her, healed and whole, his sickness gone. Forgetting the jewel she held in her hand, it fell, shattering on a stone half-protruding through the leaves and moss. It blazed into a thousand shards of light and memories lost forever.

* * * * *

A tear slid from Sibylla's eye; anger had all but burned the rest of them away. She could not believe what she was hearing. Frustration and dismay got the better of her, tempering that great anger into something far less threatening to her royal brother.

"And who told you this fantastic tale of witchery and the black arts—Raymond of Tripoli," Sibylla said. It was a rare day that she felt such anger and resentment towards her brother, but his accusations against her husband was intolerable. If magic and the trafficking of the black arts—particularly given the secrets she kept about Baldwin's own abilities—was the only argument he could bring against Guion and his inability to govern the kingdom, then she would certainly challenge him. "Thank God and the heavenly angels we have such an unbiased opinion as his to trust. We both know that Raymond has far more to gain than lose by making such accusations against Guion."

"Sweet Jhesú, I swear, Sibylla, there are days when I think I should take you and put you away again in a nunnery," Baldwin said and shook his head.

"You wouldn't."

"I would, Sibylla, if I had a need." He paused, calming himself to a more civil tone. "Perhaps Raymond does have more to gain than lose, but I also know that it is a little beyond him to just dream up so scandalous a charge as magic and sorcery to discredit Guion."

"Then where is the proof of my husband's guilt, brother? Or is there none—only lies and rumor?"

Baldwin sighed. "It doesn't matter whether it is true or not, Sibylla. It is bad enough that our much-beloved cousin in Antioch faced excommunication and interdict two years ago because he put away his Byzantine wife to take a witch to his bed. A witch mind you, that rumors say is in the employ of the Sarrazins," he said, his strained voice giving way to a harsh whisper and a fit of coughing. He struggled to begin again, stammering badly. "I... I... I will not risk the same chance of having the kingdom put under interdict by the new Pope because of a rumor floating around that the Lusignans are, in some way or another, trafficking in the black arts of the Devil."

Sibylla paced the confined grounds of the lower courtyard of the palace gardens. It was an unusually warm day for mid-November.

The birds were in song; the last flowers of the season lifted their weary heads and smiled at the shining sun.

"Sibylla, please. Sit down and quit pacing," Baldwin said.

She obeyed him, but not happily. She refused to meet his vacant stare, though she was on the verge of tears again. Instead, she glanced up, looking along the walls at the guards stationed on the heights. She wondered if any of them had overheard their conversation. Knowing the king talked with her, they would be fools to give her more attention than they ought.

In the month since her brother's fever had broken in Nazareth, the Court had returned to Jherusalem so that Baldwin could convalesce at home. He had cheated Death, yet again, but it would be months before he recovered enough to lead the army, if he ever did. Either way, his leprosy confined him to a litter. Seeing his failing health only made it more difficult to argue with him, even over a matter of such importance. Argue and defend her husband she must, if she wished to keep the life she had found with Guion. She could not—no, she would not—let fate force her to live in the shadow of her mother's shattered life. It did not mean her brother would not try.

"I beg you, Sibylla, let the Church annul your marriage for the sake of the kingdom," Baldwin said, more softly this time, more to the point. "We can say I forced you to marry Guion against your will while betrothed to another man. Trust me; no one will argue the point."

It came as no surprise, what he asked of her. Only that he had come to it so quickly. The shy, uncertain boy she knew as her brother had become a man and king without benefit of such youthful indirectness.

"How can you ask this of me, knowing how much I have sacrificed for you?"

"Because I must, sister," he said. The tone of his voice brought her eyes up to meet his. "I am removing Guion from the Regency." He held up a twisted and diseased hand to silence her outcry. Her eyes fastened on the ulcerated, snow-white patches of skin and missing fingers of his hand. She fought down the sudden revulsion and desire to vomit. It was enough to silence her, where his royal authority had failed. She used her anger as an excuse to take flight, but not before he gave her something more to consider. "I told you before, sister—Guion cannot expect to rule if he doesn't have the respect of the other lords at Court."

Her escape brought her running from the sunlit courtyard to the shadowed colonnade of the palace to hide her sudden flood of tears. Throwing herself against a column, her anguish and her anger welled up in great, heaving gasps that stole her breath and strength. She had nothing left within her. For all her years shut away in the convent of Saint-Lazare with her great aunt, she could not recall a single prayer or homily to give her comfort. All she could do was question her brother's actions. *How? How can you do this to me, Baldwin?*

In her sorrow, she lost all track of time. It was a miracle no one had crossed her path. Wiping tears and smeared black kohl from her eyes, she stiffened her back and her resolve not to let Baldwin destroy her life without at least a fight. Running through the twisted halls of the palace in a manner most undignified for a lady, she made her way to her former rooms in the women's tower. Her fierce determination and the prospect of yet another marriage for the good of the kingdom against her will, gave her clarity of thought and a peace about what she knew she must do to preserve the husband she loved.

Even while she packed the last of her belongings, she ignored the nagging voices in her mind that whispered to her that the actions she was about to set in motion bordered on the edge of treason and betrayal of the worse kind, the turning against one's own blood.

An hour later, Sibylla and twenty mounted knights in the silver and light blue of Japhe and Ascalone thundered from the western gate of the palace and rode for the sea. Her brother did nothing to stop her. It was her right to come and go as she pleased; she was a princess and a countess, a woman well able to guide her own actions.

By nightfall, they had ridden as far as Blanchegarde at the edge of the Judean hill country as it descended onto the plain of Ascalone. Rather than riding on through the dark of night, Sibylla pressed upon the lord of the castle for his hospitality. She had done so many times before. Walter Brisebarre III was a pleasant, elderly widower who was always overjoyed at her unexpected visits. Only this time, having dined and drank far more than was her usual wont, she spent the night in a restless slumber, half in tears, half in fear of the sudden turn her life had taken. Being the gentleman he was, Walter saw her safely escorted to her room by her own guard, overlooking the youthful indiscretions of a heartbroken princess.

They woke to a grey fog rising over the hills. The weather had changed overnight. A scent of rain hung in the air. Bidding farewell to the lord of the manor, the soldiers mounted their horses behind her and guided her away from Blanchegarde through the mist-enshrouded morning.

Guion was holding audience when she rode through the rain-soaked gates of Ascalone. After nearly a year in the field with the king, a backlog of grievances had accumulated in the office of the castellan. As soon as word reached him of his wife's unexpected arrival in the fortress, he called a recess and met her eagerly at the door of the palace. He was understandably concerned at the occasion of her overnight flight; her answer outraged and shook him. Everything hung in the balance: their lives, their marriage, their plans for the future. It all hinged on the words of a rumor.

In the midst of her tears, she found comfort in his embrace. He took her in his arms and carried her upstairs to their room; her mouth found his and he gave into her need. Later that evening, as they lay naked and entwined in the deepest luxury of their bedchamber, Sibylla betrayed her brother's most hidden secret. Why should he accuse Guion of dabbling in magic and daemons, and not feel the sting of his own *just* judgment?

Ten days later, Baldwin summoned them to Jherusalem to appear in an emergency session of the *Haut Cour*, along with the rest of the kingdom's lords.

* * * * *

Gerard de Ridefort knelt before the sacred altar for the evening vigil. He held a naked sword before him, his arms raised in prayer. Two golden braziers stood aflame on each side of him, diffusing the air of the Templar preceptory with the bittersweet scent of frankincense and myrrh, the symbols of holiness and sacrifice, of a life consecrated to God. The top of his head where the good brothers had shaved his tonsure in solemn song still tingled with the razor's keen edge.

Even stripped to his trews in the midst of November, the heat of the burning lampstands and the effort to hold the heavy sword warmed his body unbearably. A trickle of sweat beaded between his shoulders and ran the long, smooth length of his scarred back. He resisted the urge to shiver. He turned his attention to his task. With every drop of sweat that fell, he sought to rid his mind of the worldly pleasures that so easily encumbered it.

He had much to consider during his long vigil, much to confess and renounce. He had much, indeed, to renounce for a simple knight from Flanders. From a young, inexperienced knight of the Second War of the Cross, he had risen high in the service of the Count of Tripoli, and later, even higher as the Marshal to the king. In all that time, he had lacked only a wife and lands to call his own. Now, he loved a woman he would never have and he hatred the man who was the cause of that loss.

Their story was simple enough for the day. As a reward for his faithful service to the Count of Tripoli, Raymond had promised him Lucia de Botrun, a wealthy heiress, in marriage. After pledging his heart to Lucia, though, Raymond broke his promise to Gerard by exchanging his lover's weight in gold to a wealthy merchant from Pisa. Gerard was infuriated and distraught. He left Tripoli and came to Jherusalem, swearing he would have his revenge on the Count of Tripoli.

That revenge began now, as he knelt alone in the preceptory of the Templar hall, awaiting admittance into the Order by the word of the holy brothers. Amalric de Lusignan and the secretive Order of Sion promised to give him the opportunity to seek his revenge, if he would only serve them by becoming a Templar.

His love for Lucia he could renounce for the cross of the Templars, but the hatred he harbored for his former liege, he never would. Her memory he consigned to the fire along with the single token of her affection she had given him: a lone strand of her long, raven-black hair.

In the end, he remembered very little of the induction ceremony; but then, he cared little about it, only that he passed from postulant to brother knight. The Master of the order, Arnaud de Torroge questioned and lectured him. He waxed eloquently enough about his calling from God, likening his chosen pursuit strangely enough to a marriage, and finally came to the point. This, the final step in the process, had come only after moving from one tedious examination to another, until he stood before his new master. Gerard knelt before de Torroge as though in prayer, his hands raised, and pleaded his request for admittance.

"I have come before God, before you, and the good brothers of this Order, and I beg—nay, I require you in the name of God and of Our Lady—that you accord to me the benefits and company of this house, as one who will from this day hence always be its servant and its slave."

Having made his request, there remained now only the words of acceptance. It all rested in the word of the Master of the Order alone.

He closed his eyes and thought of Lucia his love, and of the sweetness of the revenge that one day would be his on Raymond of Tripoli. The Master made his final exhortation and Gerard replied, "I will accept all that you require and suffer all that is pleasing to God."

Arnaud stood and stretched out his sword above Gerard's head to pronounce his acceptance into the Templar Order of knighthood. "In the name of God, of Our Lady, and our father the Pope..."

It all seemed rather trivial to Gerard, given the assurances of the Amalric de Lusignan. In a few months' time, as they had planned, he would rise to the rank of Seneschal; and one day when the time was right, he would become Master in Arnaud's place. It was not God or the Templars who ordained his future. It was the will of the Order of Sion.

* * * * *

The battle had turned to near chaos when Baldwin finally signaled for a truce. Even that momentary peace, though, was fraught with difficulties: minor skirmishes and tactical maneuverings plunged the combatants into fresh outbreaks of renewed fighting.

In the center of the battle strode the Count of Tripoli. His fellow defenders of Jherusalem banded themselves together behind him, a united front against their common enemy. They struck hard, exposing the enemy's weaknesses with an accomplished ease of grace and pressed Raymond's own advantageous position. The battle was a rout.

Had it been an actual battle of clashing swords and battered shields against an enemy bent on victory, it would have been a terribly bloody affair. As it was merely a heated session of the High Court meant to decide the issue of a new regent, its outcome amounted to nothing worse than a few bruised egos and none more so than Agnes' son-in-law, Guion de Lusignan. His removal as Regent was a heavy blow to the carefully laid plans of the Order of Sion, but it was not a defeat. At least it would not be, so long as Baldwin did not pursue the annulment of his sister's marriage.

Agnes sat to the left of her son's throne with a clear view of the proceedings in the hall; Sibylla sat to the right with her young son standing beside her. Baldwin reclined quietly upon his throne, wrapped in the black shadow of his blindness and his thick woolen cloak. A soft haze of sunlight angled across the hall; incense and shadow filled the crowded wings of the Court. The only evidence that her son still breathed was the occasional flexing of his gnarled fingers upon the arm of the throne.

Outside, the weather had turned wet and cold. Grey winter clouds clung to the heights of the Judean hills; the dismal rains dampened the city and the mood of its people. A chill seeped through the grated windows into the hall where numerous burning braziers around the room stood guard against the cold.

Removed by the king as Regent of the crown, Guion dismissed himself from the heated proceedings and stormed from the hall alone. No one followed him in support, not even his brother the Constable. Too much needed to be decided for any one lord to absent himself from the Court should a vote be taken.

Raymond took advantage of the tense situation to tout his own qualifications as *bailli*. The fact that he had acted as Regent before weighed heavily in his favor; few could argue against his abilities as a war commander. Not surprisingly, the native barons supported him fully. They added their voices to his, trying to drown out his opponents arguments. With Raymond's chief detractors, Reynald de Châtillon and Joscelin de Courtenay, the Seneschal, away in Oultrejourdain to attend the wedding between Reynald's stepson, Humphrey de Toron and the Princess Isabella d'Anjou, there was little opposition to stand against the Count's claim. Only Amalric de Lusignan voiced his opinion about the former Regent. The council could not have taken place at a more opportune time for Raymond.

Watching Raymond, Agnes wondered why she had never tried to bed the troublesome northern count. He certainly was easy enough on the eyes with his swarthy Occitan features so common among the people of southern France and the Mediterranean. She prefered her lovers to be a bit younger. Of course, he had spent much of his better days in an Aleppan prison. Even after five generations in the East, his family still bred the familiar Languedoc arrogance.

From all she had learned of the history of Sion, the family of Saint-Gilles de Toulouse had been instrumental in the earlier years of its affairs and plans. It was a shame its youngest scion had never played an equally important part. An argument between Godfrei de Bouillon and the first Count of Tripoli had ended their association. It was too bad, for Raymond would have made a powerful ally for the cause of Sion.

The Constable's dark, calculating gaze found hers amidst the crowded hall. He signaled to her discreetly and glanced away. Baldwin held his silence. She stood abruptly. She wondered if her son took some perverse pleasure in watching the ever-demanding barons of his Court trying their best to destroy each other with words. "Enough of this bickering," she shouted.

The hall quieted, if only slowly, which in itself, was a small miracle of sorts, given the importance of the heated debate and the over-inflated ambitions of its combatants. She prayed her carefully orchestrated outburst in the midst of the argument was convincing. Amalric's plan depended on it.

Of a necessity, the plan had to come from someone who had nothing to gain from its implementation. That she was a woman and outside any chance of becoming Regent herself, only gave the plan greater credence. If Amalric de Lusignan knew her son, Baldwin would see the wisdom of the secret plan. In light of Guion's inevitable removal, Sion gambled they could salvage something of their long-held plans.

"I propose that my grandson, Baudinouet, be crowned and anointed king with power equal to my son's as his legal heir to the throne."

Pandemonium ensued with obvious rancor at her suggestion. She expected such would happen and planned for it accordingly.

The younger Baldwin was a frail and sickly child who would probably share his uncle's fate and die young. It was a tragic truth, but it would also make the boy's mother, the heir to the throne, should both die. Sibylla's husband would become king by right of marriage.

Her hand slid discreetly up to her son's arm and rested there. He responded with a slight turn of his head, his blind eyes searching her out. No one, but his family, knew that Baldwin planned to move his Court to Acre in the spring where the humid sea air was less troubling to his illness. Only Agnes knew that Baldwin planned to die in Acre. He needed a strong hand to occupy Jherusalem in his absence; he needed someone whose ambition did not necessitate taking the throne by force or subterfuge.

Raymond's outcry echoed loudest amid the chaos. "Is that really the wisest course of action you can propose?" he shouted, turning to address the Court. He spun back around to face the king's throne. His gaze fastened on Agnes. "You wish to replace one sick king with another, which no more than saddles us with a boy of five as king, and a very, very long Regency."

"My son is not dead yet, my lord of Tripoli—or is your lust for the throne so great that you would see him laid in the grave so soon?"

"I would see Baldwin healed and married, with an heir of his own without need for a Regent, but that, we all know, is most unlikely. However, putting a boy on the throne of Jherusalem will only invite disaster for the kingdom."

Agnes opened her hand to her grandson. She took a step towards Raymond. "This *boy* is the rightful heir to the throne and your future king, regardless of his age or ability."

The argument between Agnes and the Count of Tripoli proved far more than the other members of Court could endure in quiet. A murmur rose at the back of the room and spread, multiplying in a crescendo of competing voices that clamored for recognition. None of the voices, however, moved the Court towards any useful decision. Raymond took his seat amidst the chaos, smug and triumphant, and awaited the outcome. The lord of Ramlah leaned close to him, chattering quietly.

The Master of Sion had worked his long, slow way towards the dais. He whispered discreetly in Agnes' ear, warning her to be ready for the king's response. Amalric's subversive little plan to manipulate the High Court was about to bear new fruit.

It was a miracle that anyone in the hall could hear her son's whisper of a voice. The lifting of his jeweled and gloved hand held the power to quell the riot, the same hand with which he could no longer even sign his name. The room fell silent. Agnes began to wonder if the magic Sibylla claimed her brother possessed had the power to control the wills of men.

"My nephew will reign with me and Lord Raymond of Tripoli will assume the Regency for Baudinouet after my death until he reaches his majority."

Again, uproar came from both sides of the Court, threatening to disrupt the proceedings and the king's decision. Again, Baldwin raised a hand and the hall fell into silence, though with less willing compliance this time.

"What say you, cousin?" Baldwin whispered in his harshest voice.

The Count of Tripoli bowed his head. "I will do so, Your Highness, only if Lord Joscelin, as Seneschal and uncle of the boy, swears to act as the young king's personal guardian."

"Agreed," Agnes said and took her seat again beside the throne.

Raymond glared daggers at her. "You, a woman and another lord's wife, presume to answer for the lord Seneschal, *madame?*"

Agnes met the challenge of his gaze without hint of a smile. "I do, Messire. And my brother will abide by my answer, I assure you."

"So it will be written." Baldwin sighed. He motioned to his attendants to come forward and carry him away. He stopped them briefly. "Excuse me, my lords, but I need to rest now. I leave it to you to choose amongst yourselves how best to undertake this decision. But I advise you to do so soon, before you find you have acted too late."

* * * * *

"Sweet Jhesú," William murmured and swore. Just as quickly, he made the sign of the cross on his body and prayed for forgiveness. Seeing the size of the Templar record hall, he swore again.

Under the guise of writing his *Historia regum*, the Master of the Templars, Arnaud de Torroge, had given him permission to search through the Templar records to verify certain facts within the documents in their possession. He had not expected it would be so daunting a search. Obviously, the Templar record hall was not the size of the Lateran library, but it was surprisingly large.

For the sake of secrecy and privacy, the master bid him come during the hour of Vespers and the evening chores that followed. They both hoped it would give him enough time to find something of value for his work. William hated to lie to the kindly Arnaud, but it was necessary.

He had come in along the narrow eastern arcade since it lay in the deepest shadows just after sunset. Slipping through a side door, he made his way through the sacristy and smaller prayer cells used by the Templars for private prayers and meditation. William had never stood within the hallowed halls of the former palace and mosque. He had come to the Holy Land long after the palace had moved to the Tower of David and the empty hall given to the fledgling Order of the Temple for their headquarters.

With massive pillars and columns supporting spacious interior arches reaching to the heavens, the *Templum Salomis* rivaled any cathedral built in Europe for its grandeur and beauty. The halls echoed such that he could hear the brothers beginning to sing the evening prayers. He made the sign of the cross on his chest and prayed the Lord would forgive him for avoiding his own prayers in his search for the answers he sought.

Having recovered from his initial shock of the library's size, the opulence of the Master's private office adjoining the room struck his senses numb. Tapestries of various exotic scenes and expensive Persian carpets adorned the walls and floors along with other Eastern, and perhaps, Muslim extravagances. A large mahogany desk lay in the middle of the room. Treasures captured from the enemy over the many years he expected to find; but these other luxuries were, to be honest, rather surprising. It seemed that not all the Poor Knights of the Temple of Solomon lived in poverty.

William played the part of the cat and let his curiosity get the better of him. He prayed it did not end up killing him. Taking up a candlestick from the small table in the center of the room, he lit it using one of the burning braziers near the door and quickly launched into his search of the archive.

The volume of material the Templars had amassed in only sixty-five years of their existence amazed him. Not only the volume astounded him, but also the wide assortment of subjects the small library covered. There were full shelves of writings on the beliefs of Jews and Muslims, Christians, and even a smattering of lesser-known volumes of religious thought and philosophy. Three full shelves were devoted to History alone. His hand slid across a work by the Roman Emperor

Theodosius in the fourth century entitled, *The Holy Grail.* A rare find, indeed, even in his day.

The books smelled of old and dusty parchment. He would have loved to peruse the shelves of this exceptional library, and plumb the depths of its treasured lore, but his hunt for the archivist's records gave him little time for other quarry. Tearing himself away from the books, he made a quick search of the shelves for anything resembling... what? Scrolls? Missives? Charters? He was not quite sure what he expected to find.

In the corner, he found a cabinet filled with a nest of diagonal cubicles containing a horde of scrolls. At once, he started pulling out individual rolls of parchment and scanned through them.

A sound brought William to the door, listening. The brothers had finished singing the last of the Psalms that, ironically, emphasized Sion and Jherusalem as the holy sanctuary of God. He had little time to finish and he was no closer to finding anything of importance. After about fifteen or twenty scrolls—he lost count—he began to understand the archivist's system of filing. He had no system. The scrolls lay in pigeonholes at random. Most were grants or donations of land made to the Templars from all over the kingdom, some beyond the borders. One was a ledger of the annual tribute of gold the Assassins had paid to the Templars over the past several years.

In the midst of the varied documents, his hand pulled out a scroll he least expected to find. He read it twice just to be sure of its contents. He had found a proverbial needle in the haystack.

It was a charter of a land grant signed between a Prior Arnaldus of the Abbey of Mount Sion and Hughes de Payens, the first Master of the Temple, dated to *Anno Domini* 1125. It must have been a coincidence, the similarity in name between the Abbey of Sion and the Order of Sion. Only William did not believe in coincidences. By the time he had finished his search, he had found three similar documents linking the two groups.

He wondered if it was possible that the Templars and Sion were, or perhaps still were, the same. At the very least, they were in close league with one another in some fashion. Slim evidence he knew, but evidence all the same. It gave him a place to start looking.

* * * * *

Guion de Lusignan clenched his hands as the coronation for his stepson began to stretch on into an eternal torment of the soul. His fingers went white; they began to go numb with the loss of blood.

Voices rang out from the choir loft of Holy Sepulcher Church as the monks and priests sang a psalm. The sound echoed into the great sunlit dome of the Rotunda. Incense mingled with the hovering shadows of late afternoon. The Patriarch offered the blessing of prayer as he poured the holy oil upon the young king's head.

...*In nomine Patris, et Filii, et Spiritus Sancti. Amen.*

With Joscelin de Courtenay absent and away at Kerak in the older Baldwin's stead for the Princess Isabella's wedding to Humphrey de Toron, Guion's brother, the Constable, stood in for him as a witness to the solemn event. Amalric stood behind the younger Baldwin in his full armor, and the blue and gold of the royal house, a naked sword laid flat across his hands. Candlelight gleamed along the keen edge of the blade.

I should be kneeling before the altar, receiving the holy unction, Guion protested in his thoughts. Sion had crowned him as the sacred king. He stood so close to the throne, and yet, Raymond of Tripoli kept him so far from it.

Guion allowed himself the small luxury of a smile. He directed it towards his wife to hide his true feelings. He played the part of a proud stepfather well. Inside, his thoughts seethed. Oh, how easy it would be to seize the sword from his brother's open hands and kill the little brat where he knelt. Such actions would be far too obvious, too desperate; he needed to wait the game out. Sion cared little about such minor inconveniences as murder—they had killed kings and princes before. A child of five was no different.

Sibylla remained the key. Unfortunately, he needed her alive. Without her, he could not reign as king. Her blood legitimized his claim to the throne. At least she had proven herself good for something besides her beauty. She certainly was not much good in bed. Too many years shut away in a convent had spoiled her sense of wanton pleasure. Of course, he had known a nun or three in Poitou that never thought twice that their *marriage* to God was a hindrance to a good toss in the hay.

As the coronation wound down finally towards its tedious conclusion, the congregation lifted their voices with the priests and monks in singing a psalm. Guion lent his voice to theirs and smiled at his wife. If he had time, and could get away from Sibylla's smothering presence, he would find one of his favorite mistresses in the city and celebrate the day in another fashion.

* * * * *

Blindness gave Baldwin a certain kind of clarity of thought and inner Sight. He could sense her presence amidst a forest, smell the earthy loam beneath her feet, hear the whisper of a leaf as it fell gently to the ground. A breeze blew, sighing through the trees. She still closed her mind to him, but he could feel her distress. A great sorrow stalked her like a horrible, dark dream.

In light of recent discoveries made by Raymond and William about the Lusignans and the probable connection between the Order of Sion and the Abbey outside Jherusalem's walls, it was imperative that he find the Magdalen, even if it meant going to that place beyond the edge of the world. There was risk in that he knew. Mary had told him once that not even all her kind could find their way through the shadows, especially those so new to their power.

Try he must, or else lose the chance to unmask the conspirator who sought to destroy the kingdom by handing it over to the powers of darkness. It had seemed simple enough, stepping through space from one place to another when the Lady had taken him to negotiate a truce with Salehdin. What remained unseen was whether he could duplicate her actions. He tried not to think about how much the magic would exact from him.

Calling up the fire of his power, he let go of his thoughts, willing himself towards that place his senses took him... towards her.

He found himself lost in a thick grey mist that clung to everything around him. Immediately he feared he had erred terribly and gone astray into some unknown place beyond his ability to return. He forgot to breathe. He fought down the sudden instinct to scream. He called to her.

—*Magdalen.*

He took a step forward, unsure which direction he should go. The leafy ground beneath his feet was soft. A twig snapped. He stood in a forest; the mist made silhouettes of the trees. He realized only then, that he had gained the ability to use his feet to walk once more. The leprosy had disappeared.

His hands and his feet were whole in this enchanted land. He touched a hand to his face and found it remade; smooth, soft skin and a strong, firm nose met his fingers. His eyes could see clearly, until tears blurred the world into a watery kaleidoscope of color. They were tears of joy. They swiftly turned to anger for the life that Sion had taken from him. He flexed his right hand, his sword-arm, feeling the renewed strength in flesh and bone that had long ago become dead.

Suddenly, he felt dizzy from the use of his power. It could be a cruel master, the magic.

—Magdalen, he cried. **Help me. I have lost my way in the mist.**

He found her at the edge of the mist where the colors of the forest began to take on depth and vibrancy and the singing of birds in the trees sounded less distant, less enchanted. She turned as though waking from a dream. A shimmering globe of light fell from her hand and shattered into a thousand sparks of blue fire on the ground. She cried, crumbling into a heap at the foot of an aged tree and wept.

Unsure what he should do, Baldwin came and knelt beside her. He laid a hand upon hers as she tried to piece the broken glass together. Mary dropped the shards hopelessly onto the soft green moss and looked up at him. She smiled weakly at his feeble ministrations to comfort her.

"I never thought to ever see you whole again, King Baldwin," she said, taking his hand and turned it in hers, examining the non-existent wounds. "The darker side of magic is only illusion here." She pulled her hand away. "The leprosy will return when you come again to your own world."

He ignored her. The truth could be so very, very cruel. Instead, he reached for a shard of the broken jewel and held it up to Mary. She glanced away.

"What is this, my lady?"

"It is all I have left of my daughter."

"Your *daughter?*" he said. He had never thought of Mary as anything other than the Magdalen of the Evangels. That she might have once had a husband and children—that they might very well have died as well—unsettled him. The Order of Sion claimed she had married the Christ, and had a child by him, but that was a lie. Or was it?

Her laughter at his surprise and bewilderment, despite her obvious sorrow, was even more amazing. "Did you think my kind incapable of such things? Or did you think I sprang fully made from the mind of God, without mother or father as the ancients once believed of their pagan gods?"

"No," he stammered. "I just... I just never thought that you... not that I thought you couldn't... I just..."

She reached down, picking up a shard, and began placing the broken pieces in his hand. "Her name was Salome," she said. "And she meant more to me than my own life. Her father was a rebel named Judah who hated the Romans and the Herods only slightly less than I. He died a hero of our people, as did his sons for the cause of Jewish independence."

She paused. Her head dropped. "I used him, as I used his sons; and for my sins, I suffered the loss of them all, including my daughter."

Baldwin caught her hand in his. She fought his gaze. "Tell me what happened to Salome."

"She was taken from me, and from the world, by a man who claimed he loved her and then he used her for his own selfish desires. His name was Simon Magus, the same false magician that Peter and John condemned for trying to buy the power of the Holy Spirit. Once, he was a disciple of the Baptist, but when Herod Antipas killed John, he tried to claim his master's place, but for the wrong reasons. He corrupted the teachings of Jhesú, who he said had taken John's authority and power from him, and so he began to attract disciples of his own who claimed to follow the true teachings of the Messiah."

Mary's eyes welled up with tears. She wiped them away and continued. "Salome fell victim to Simon's charms and deceits and to his false assurances of his undying love. Knowing the truth of her being, they had a daughter together named Sarah, whom Simon plotted to sacrifice for the sake of his ambitions. When he learned that Sarah was mortal and without power or the abilities of our kind, he stole Salome's magic instead by bringing her to within a single breath of her death. To this day, she remains a prisoner of his hatred for Christianity. So long as he keeps her spirit imprisoned in her body, he has control over her power."

The tragic story of Magdalen's daughter intrigued him, but she only gave his curiosity more questions than she had answers. He could sense the pain Mary felt. Her mind was a blur of partial images and fragmented memories that each struggled to gain her attention, even as she tried to block them all from her thoughts.

He caught a glimpse of a face seemingly familiar, but not. It had far less beauty than her mother's, but a certain glimmer in the eye, a turn of the head, the arresting smile that was all of Mary's. He understood the importance of the jewel to a mother who had mourned the loss of a child for more than a thousand years. He hated to cause her any more hurt or sorrow.

"Magdalen, what happened to Sarah and Simon?"

"I took Sarah from Simon and hid her away in Gaul." She forced a smile and murmured a soft laugh. "No doubt, it was the source of the legend of my supposed sailing to France after the Crucifixion of Jhesú with the other Marys. Sarah married a Jewish exile sent to Southern Gaul by Titus after the destruction of Jherusalem. Her granddaughter eventually married into the family of James, the brother of

Jhesú, and founded a line of princes that governed our people in exile for many years."

"And what of Simon?"

The light of her eyes flared with an intense fire. He felt her power gather, blazing with the depth of her anger and hatred. It startled him, but he felt no fear—only pity for the traitor who was the focus of her millennia-worn wrath.

"Haven't you guessed, King Baldwin," she spat. "You know him, as do I—or rather, of him. He is the Master of the Order of Sion."

The truth was an astounding blow. His mind staggered. He closed his eyes, trying to draw upon his power to conjure up the enemy in Mary's mind. Simon glared at him, smiling wickedly, but it was not the face of the ancient magician. It was another face, one quite different and far more recent in his memory.

Amalric de Lusignan.

—Amalric de Lusignan, *she repeated, nearly shouting in his mind. He felt the subtle sensation he had learned to recognize whenever she searched his thoughts.* **How did you know?**

"It is why I came here to find you, my lady," Baldwin said. "Two months ago, Count Raymond discovered by accident that the Lusignans may be trafficking in magic in some way to protect the kingdom. Guion has only recently come to Outremer, but Amalric has been in Jherusalem far longer."

"As Constable, he made sure he is in the perfect position to know almost everything that happens in the kingdom."

Baldwin stood, still trying to understand everything Magdalen had told him so far. Asking her to explain anything else would only confuse him more and cause her greater grief. She needed to destroy the works of the enemy more than he needed to protect his kingdom from the threat of heresy. He clenched his hand around the shards of Salome's jewel. The shards bit into his skin like the fangs of a serpent. His head began to throb with the use of his power.

"There's more, my lady. William has found what he thinks is evidence of an association between the Abbey of Mount Sion and the Order of Sion—perhaps, even, the center of the Order's activities."

Mary hissed as she leapt to her feet. Cold blue fire flashed suddenly around her body in a glowing aura of power. "The Upper Room of the Last Supper," she breathed, looking off into the grey swirling mists suddenly rising around them as though drawing them back towards the world of the mortal sun. "How could I have been so blind? The hill upon which the abbey rests is the very place the first church was established, and then later, rebuilt after the fall of Jherusalem and the

Tribulation by Simeon, the cousin of Jhesú, who ruled the Church after James' death."

Mary turned slowly towards him and stood staring. "If these two Sions are the same, then I am all the more a fool for not having seen it before. The truth has been before me all this time, and I missed it. I see now the canons desire to rebuild the shrine of the Last Supper." Her face relaxed, her gaze growing far and distant. She murmured to herself. "How could I not see this before? I never thought that he would try to lay claim to the throne himself. This is bold even for him." Her eyes lifted slowly to his. "Baldwin, you must return to Jherusalem before it is too late."

Tears sprang to his eyes; he sunk to his knees on the soft green moss glistening with the mist and the rays of sunlight piercing through fluttering leaves above him. He breathed deep, taking in the freshness of the air and earth and the living world around him that seemed so unreal. It had been a long time since he had enjoyed the scent of something other than the fetid stench of decaying, corrupted flesh.

"How can you ask me to leave this place?" he said, holding up his hand and arm for her to examine. "Look at me. I have no illness, no blemish—I have nothing of the leprosy I have borne since I was a child. Please, Lady, do not make me return to that awful existence. Let me stay here for a while with you, and enjoy the life that was taken from me."

She came towards him and set a hand upon his head; she combed back his hair with her fingers. She smiled with great difficulty. "You can't, Baldwin. It is not what God has ordained for you."

"Now that we know who the Master of Sion probably is, I am not needed. You can confront him and finally see your enemy defeated."

"Yes," said Mary, "if that was the only reason for my long hunt for Simon. You know there is more to it than that, Baldwin. Even if my hand defeats Simon, it would change nothing. He is not alone in his heresy. Now more than ever before, Sion must not be allowed to gain control of the throne."

He looked up at her. "We may have more to worry about than just Sion right now. Salah ad-Din has laid siege to Reynald de Châtillon's castle."

Mary staggered and fell against him. He took hold of her hands, searching her thoughts. Chaos swirled; and in its midst, a blood-red turmoil that was war and slaughter. "You must go and relieve the siege, Baldwin. If not, and Kerak falls, Sion will accomplish all it has ever planned to achieve."

—I cannot go. Please do not make me return.

—You must.

Baldwin clasped her hand, squeezing it with all his strength as the world began to fade into grey and misty shadow. *I am afraid to die.*

—*I know,* she said, pulling him close and holding him tightly. *But you must not be. I will go with you. I promise I will stay close to you, even to the end.*

† CHAPTER TWENTY-TWO

A conspiracy is found among the men of Juda, and among the inhabitants of Jerusalem.
—*Jeremias 11:9*

The stones of the Muslim mangonels pounded the walls of Kerak with thunderous ferocity. For weeks, the bombardment continued; day and night Salehdin reminded the people of the besieged castle and the surrounding town of his presence and their fate. Night was the worst. Darkness and fear stalked the inhabitants of the desert fortress. Wind and the howling of jackals echoed from the east and the rocky hills that rose into the wilderness. Had it not been for the wedding between Reynald's stepson, Humphrey, and the Princess Isabella, the multitude of guests might have despaired. He assured them that there was still time for hope and for rescue. The signal fire in Jherusalem burned; the king was on the march to relieve the siege, even if he was three weeks late.

The courtyard lay filled with townspeople and the Syrian Christian farmers and shepherds of the countryside who crowded around their small campfires. Reynald had tried to hold off the Muslims from taking the lower town, but they breached the walls and overwhelmed the faubourg. The fighting was brief, but fierce. Everything of value they left behind for the enemy to seize. Reynald and his soldiers owed their lives to a single knight who valiantly held the narrow bridge over the fosse to the castle against the Sarrazins while they made their escape.

Stephanie did her best to make sure she saw the displaced peasants fed and made as comfortable as possible given the circumstances. The fortress had enough food in reserve even without the added stores for the wedding banquet. More than a few times, Reynald told himself that it was better this way, than trying to defend the castle and the town together. He had no real concern for the town.

He stood at the narrow window of his tower keep, just out of range of Salehdin's siege engines. Another stone crashed into a lower wall; the castle shuddered with the thundering impact. The Muslims had caused a considerable amount of damage to the exterior curtain walls of the fortress, but nothing lasting. The Christians built Kerak to withstand a prolonged siege. Still, something troubled Reynald. Salehdin seemed content to wait and simply hurl stones day after day at the fortress without care. He began to wonder if the man had some other purpose in mind.

Even after the faubourg fell and the sultan brought six of his eight mangonels within the lower town, he casually took his time. That by itself was certainly peculiar given Salehdin's avowed hatred of the lord of Kerak, particularly after Reynald's brazen naval attack in the Red Sea a year ago. He had failed in men's opinions, and terribly so; but it had given the Muslims something to think about, a reason to believe that the success of their *jihad* was not God-ordained.

He had come close to doing the unthinkable and it scared the sultan. The son of the devil learned that there was more to Frankish warfare than simply armor and horses and a bloodthirsty urge to kill. They possessed a cunning will to live, as well.

He had thought that with the army of Egypt held in reserve after arriving the week before, Salehdin might finally intensify the attack. He did not; nor was hesitancy the only strange behavior he saw. On the night of the wedding banquet, his wife sent down dishes of food prepared specifically for a Muslim's taste and bid him enjoy the blessing of her son's wedding. In reply, Salehdin ordered the siege engines moved away from the couple's tower so that they might enjoy at least one night of marital bliss.

There was more to the sultan's act than plain and simple chivalry: Isabella and Humphrey would command a pretty ransom if he captured them. Dead royals fetched nothing in ransom if a misaimed missile killed them by accident. Salehdin, however, was not the only one that would benefit from keeping them alive and well, safe behind his stout walls and strong towers.

With his stepson having married a princess, it gave Reynald a greater voice at Court, especially in regards to what was best for the kingdom, even if that advice prompted war. Humphrey might well be king one day should some evil befall Sibylla or her son, and Isabella rise to the throne. That would give Reynald even greater influence and power, indeed, in the affairs of Outremer. Humphrey was young and impressionable; he looked up to him as a father and as a great lord of the realm.

Of course, there was also the issue of Raymond of Tripoli. Stephanie still blamed Raymond of murdering her previous husband, Milon de Plancy, the former Regent of the king. Nor could he forget that Isabella was the daughter of the former Queen, Maria Comnena, the current wife of Balian of Ibelin, Raymond's staunchest ally.

Oh, there were certainly wheels turning within wheels in the king's own masterful maneuvering of the pieces upon the chessboard. No one could call Baldwin a fool when it came to the ordering of his kingdom, no matter how ill he had become. Reynald was only thankful that the king had recognized and rewarded his many years of faithful service.

Stephanie came up next to him and slipped her long arms around his naked waist. She smelled of fragrant rose water and the subtle, musky scent of their lovemaking. She set her chin upon his shoulder. They were nearly of the same height, he and his wife; he needed never to look down at her. They peered out the narrow window slit onto the night-dark plain of Moab and the light of the setting moon playing among the shallow wavelets of the Dead Sea. Their mutual silence drew them closer. A cool, faint draft found its way through the slot of the window; the castle breathed as a living thing. Another stone whistled through the air and pounded against the lower curtain wall. The tower shuddered with the impact. Stephanie buried her face in his shoulder.

"How long will it be before the king sends us relief?" she asked.

"It takes time to gather the army and march from Jherusalem to Kerak, my love," he replied, caressing her hand. "Don't worry. Payens and your father built this castle to last a siege of several months. As long as Salehdin is content to just throw stones at us, we have nothing to fear."

"But this fortress wasn't built to house the entire population of the castle and the town, as well as the guests of a large state wedding."

A loud explosion, followed closely by a second louder and closer blast, shook the keep to its foundation. The force threw Stephanie against Reynald's back. He caught her before she fell to the floor.

Outside in the courtyard, the frightened townspeople began to scream for their lives.

* * * * *

For a friendship once shared between children.
The note had come with the plates of food and the small gift of a silver bell molded in the shape of an acorn. The simple message

331

evoked a host of memories that broke in upon Yusuf's solitude like an army of charging horses.

Not that he had forgotten; he had just chosen to push those troubled times into oblivion for the sake of expedience, and perhaps, for his pride. The thought of the grand sultan of Egypt and Suriya having once been held prisoner behind the walls of al-Keraq was not the image his people, and for that matter, he, could abide—even if it had been for only a few weeks. That was before he had become Salah ad-Din, when he was just Yusuf ibn-Ayyub.

He remembered clearly the day he met the Sitt al-Keraq, Saifineh al-Mileh, now that the girl he once knew reminded him of it. He was thirteen; she was eight. His father ruled as governor of Ba'albek; hers, a great lord of the Ifranj. They met in the aftermath of battle when their fathers clashed at a tiny village outside Dimasq. He had disobeyed his father and ridden out with his older brother to see a battle. What he saw was a pointless skirmish fought to a draw, but not before the Nasrani had captured and taken him to al-Keraq as a servant for a little girl he never expected to like. But he did.

She treated him as though he was some eastern prince who had traveled a long away for the sole purpose of entertaining her. Despite their differences in age and gender and religion, he enjoyed every moment of their brief time together. He became the famed King Shahrar, and she, Sharazad, the ill-fated storyteller of a thousand and one mythical tales of adventure. Only in this case, Yusuf told the wonderful stories of Arabia to Saifinah.

Their joy lasted only a short while. Upon learning that he was the son of a great Muslim lord, Saifinah's father sent him home quietly for a small, yet modest ransom as befitted his position—and to teach the boy the importance of obedience and sacrifice. He learned the lesson well; his father beat him sorely and sent him off to his uncle, Shirkuh, the following year to learn the arts of war.

He repaid that debt of gratitude to his old childhood friend by moving his mangonels away from the tower of the young couple celebrating their nuptials.

Yusuf picked up the small silver bell and smiled; he shook it gently. It tinkled softly with music. He fastened the bell on the halter of his white stallion and fondly rubbed the animal's head between its twitching ears. It was warm inside his palatial tent; the fire in the large copper brazier blazed, heating the air on such a cold winter's night. He always stabled his horse in his tent like the tribesmen of his ancestors, no matter the season. The fire sputtered and popped. The horse snorted from the smoke and tossed its head with a whinny.

"Easy, my beauty. It's only the fire," Yusuf laughed, slipping the feisty stallion a cube of sugar. He picked up a brush and began grooming the horse's long, white mane. Tomorrow, the army was marching for Dimasq.

The gaze of the stallion's black eyes rolled towards the door of the tent. Yusuf turned. His brother, Saif ad-Din Al-Adil, stood scowling darkly in the doorway. Two armed Mamluks guarded him. A foul mood had followed him when he had arrived two weeks before from al-Qihara with the army of Egypt to supplement his older brother's siege. Yusuf's command to break the siege only worsened Al-Adil's temper. He waved the Mamluks away.

"How long, brother, will you shamefully run from these impure infidel dogs?"

Yusuf turned back to grooming his horse's mane. His brother could be emotional and irrational. He needed to remain calm and detached from his own emotions when dealing with Al-Adil.

"Until I wear the Leper King into the ground with fatigue," he said. "Al-Abras is close to death. I plan to nudge him ever closer by leading him around by his sense of duty to his people until he collapses."

Al-Adil grunted. "You have the vilest lord of the Ifranj holed up in his castle like a jackal. He is useless to them now. If the Leper is so close to death, then why not crush him now and end this game here in the desert?"

"Because, while he lives," Yusuf said, "the Ifranj remain united behind him, despite the petty differences between them. Once he is dead, that unity will disintegrate and make them vulnerable."

"You have brought the entire Egyptian army here, only to have us run at the first sight of the worthless Ifranj. You risk too much, brother. And for what—a greater advantage of attack? Why do you insist on hesitating?"

"Don't worry, *brother*. I will compensate you quite well for your humiliation, I assure you. I need someone I can trust to govern Aleppo in my son's stead."

Al-Adil glared at him from across the tent, his arms crossed. His black brows knit into a dark and ominous line of storm clouds. Yusuf trusted his brother more than most, but they still often saw things quite differently. Saif ad-Din had more of their uncle, Shirkuh, in him than their father. His brother laughed, which was most unusual. "So, is that your answer?" he said. "Mollify me with gifts to keep me quiet and loyal, all the while, the infidels slip through our fingers again. I wonder, brother, if you have truly given yourself to your vow of *jihad* this past year; or is this siege only another in a campaign of spurious offenses

333

meant to strengthen your image in the eyes of our Muslim brethren and the Khalifa of Baghdad."

His brother's words stung, even if they were not true. His brush strokes became firmer, more rigid. Faster. Until he could no longer hold back his anger. His horse shied, tossing his head. When he finally turned to comment on his brother's accusation, Al-Adil had gone.

* * * * *

The beacon fire on the Tower of David burned brightly; the flames of other watchtowers blazed brightly from Jherusalem to Kerak, offering the hope of salvation.

With the Patriarch Heraclius marching before them with the reliquary of the Life-Giving Cross, the army set out from Jherusalem, taking the shorter route east and west to Kerak. Against the advice of his councilors, Baldwin insisted on being present with the army. His presence impeded their progress. There would be no race to relieve the siege. The fate of Kerak was in God's hands.

Baldwin rode in the vanguard of the march, his litter placed in sight of the True Cross just behind the Patriarch and his fellow unarmed clerics. The two white Arabian stallions he once rode into battle now carried his litter of purple silk. Despite his frail condition, he had his horses caparisoned for war, with long mantles of white and gleaming *chamfrons*, plaited headpieces with a long spike in the center of the brow; it gave them the semblance of unicorns with golden horns.

Crossing the Jordan opposite Jericho, they passed over by Mount Nebo and took the olden road aptly called, the King's Highway, which ran eastwards of the Asphalt Sea through the barren landscape of Oultrejourdain. Even in ancient times, the highway was a well-traveled avenue of kings and conquest. In the days of Abraham, the Kings of the East had marched down the same olden way to make war against the Cities of the Plain. Those cities, of which Sodom and Gomorrah were part, now lay beneath the black, mineral-crusted waters of the Sea of Salt.

By the time they reached the road beside Mount Nebo where Moses once looked down upon the Promised Land, he was too weak to continue, so he laid down his authority and put it into the hand of Count Raymond of Tripoli, the newly elected Regent.

Baldwin slept most often thereafter. True to her promise, Mary rode with him in the litter, invisible, unseen, unheard; usually her hand rested on his for comfort and company as he lay beneath a heavy woolen blanket. She spoke mostly in his thoughts. After his experience on the borders of Faërie, his magic had all but devoured the last of his strength and health. Only her presence kept him from death. Even in his sleep, he felt her nearness.

She told him stories to wile away the hours of the long march... but nothing of war or bloodshed. Instead, she told him of the Christ and the early days of the Church. It was not what he expected, nor did the stories she related resemble anything of the Church he knew. He found an image of the Christ that the world had lost long ago: a God of love and a man of passion.

Although sight and his sense of touch were taken from him, Baldwin could still *See* the land they traveled, even without Mary's description. What his eyes and hands had lost to disease and magic, his ears and tongue and nose more than compensated. Sounds and scents gave him a truer sense of the land that most would never know or notice. The wind whispered through canyons cut deep and narrow by the elements; water, that rarest of commodities in the desert, ran just below the dry and thirsty ground. A herd of gazelles on the hills fled at their approach. The air, itself, tasted of sun and salt. They passed a stand of acacia trees earlier that morning.

His thoughts and senses learned to perceive more than just the land with his growing Sight. A hint of fear, most palpable amongst the knights and soldiers, lay hidden just beneath the more common scents of war: horseflesh and sweat, oiled leather and the acrid tang of whetted steel.

Near the ruins of Machaerus, the ancient fortress of the Herodian and Hasmonean kings where Herod Antipas beheaded the Baptist because he feared the prophet's power and charisma, Raymond called a halt to the march at the end of the second day. Baldwin was thankful for the rest, but he would never have told anyone beside Mary. He would not willingly have the army slow its advance because of his insistence on being present.

The fortress lay well fortified on its flat mountaintop. The wind whistled through its scattered ruins, giving it shape in his mind. Herod had built well on the foundations of the earlier Hasmonean stronghold. Baldwin could see the strength the fortress once had in his mind; its three large corner towers, extensive ramparts, and thick walls; the magnificent palace itself was a strategic wonder.

However, so complete was the destruction at the hands of the Romans years later that no one had occupied the site for over a thousand years. Strangely, though, almost as soon as they had made camp, he recognized a powerful presence among the jumbled stone: a brooding, solitary essence of thought. It seemed somehow familiar to him, like seeing a shadow passing through a morning mist. Magdalen noticed it too. Together they tried to put a name to it, but could not. It was too elusive; too insubstantial.

For days now, since their return from that other place, they had kept a close eye on Amalric de Lusignan and his brother, the former Regent. In that space between the worlds, where even those with the smallest spark of power glowed with a faint aura of bluish light, he was invisible. It was little wonder that Mary had been unable to identify the Master of Sion. That is, of course, if they had come to the right conclusion about him.

The day proved far too long for Baldwin. Simply reclining in a litter began to exhaust him. His strength was fading. He felt the Shadow of Death lingering near, waiting patiently. He tried to ignore its whispering beckon. Mary ordered him to rest and sleep, while she went hunting. His mind and body were far too tired to care what she meant.

Baldwin woke abruptly and immediately sought out Mary with his thoughts. It had become an instinct with his blindness and her ever-constant companionship. He reached into that grey void where they often met to talk. It was a place of magic he had learned of late, not a place in each other's mind or heart, but a greyness between the worlds.

He found her easily enough; she was not alone. Mary had found the quarry of her hunt. She argued with him, her great enemy Simon who had become Amalric de Lusignan. It was a carefully waged battle of words and wills they fought—a contest of magic too deep for him to comprehend.

She stood opposite him. Between them, a shrouded figure lay on a raised platform cut from the living stone of the earth. At first Baldwin's senses recognized only the smell and echoing sound of ancient masonry; the taste of its dust hung in the air. He knew this place, seemingly out of time. They were inside Machaerus—but in no place the annals of history knew.

—Does it comfort you, Mariamne, *said the sorcerer, holding out a hand to her,* **to know you have found her after all these years, and yet you can do nothing to bring her back?**

Mary fought the desire to look down at the face before her. Baldwin could feel her pain, the ache of a sorrow greater than he could ever bear. **You will pay for this treachery, Simon. I promise you.**

—Vengeance is God's, is it not, Mariamne? *Simon sneered.* **Or are the words of your prophet, your precious Jhesú, meant only for the weak and ignorant, the unenlightened of your faith?**

Mary ignored his blasphemy. Her hands balled into fists at her sides.

Baldwin could see through her teary eyes as though they were his own. Simon smiled cruelly with a mouth he knew too well as the Constable's. He shuddered. Mary felt his sudden presence and cautioned him to silence.

—*You should not be here, Your Highness. It is too dangerous, she whispered, even in his thoughts. I cannot protect the both of us.*

—*What is this place?*

—*A dungeon, she said. The cell where the Baptist died.*

—*The king knows who you are now, Simon, she said. Or should I call you Amalric de Lusignan? Your plotting, your scheming—all of it is exposed. It is only a matter of time before I find what I need to rob you finally of your power and end the conspiracy of Sion. How long do you think it will be before Baldwin removes you from your position and that of your fellow conspirators?*

Simon laughed at her, moving slowly around the raised platform towards her. Mary retreated from him. Baldwin felt her sudden fear. Simon lowered his head, gazing at her from beneath hooded black brows.

—*How foolish do you think I am? Raymond of Tripoli was easy enough to lead astray. He learned nothing about me that night at Tubania that I did not intend for him to know. You proved just as easy to lead here. I needed only to make my presence known, and you came looking for me. He laid a hand on the shrouded body on the platform. Think about your lovely daughter. I am giving you a gift, Mariamne. Swear to me that you will not pursue me any longer and I will not hide Salome from you ever again.*

—*Don't listen to him, lady, Baldwin cried out. It is a trap.*

Suddenly, a flash of light appeared in Mary's hand. She held a silver athame above Salome's heart. And what if I take her life first?

Simon laughed. He leaned over the body of the near dead woman, looking towards Mary's face. Baldwin could see the cold hatred in his eyes. Do so, my lady. Kill your only daughter. I will not stop you. I doubt even you could slay your own child—or have you become so cold-hearted over the centuries?

—*Do what he says, Mary, Baldwin shouted in her thoughts. She gave no thought to the command he gave her. You have to do this. Do it now, before it is too late.*

For a moment, he felt the struggle of her mind and body as she considered the consequences of her actions. He tried to lend her what little strength his mind and body had left, but she resisted him, pushing him away towards the edge of the grey void between the worlds.

She growled suddenly with a feral, unnatural sound. The dagger went clattering across the ancient broken floor. He called to her; but her thoughts went red with overwhelming anger. He could no longer sense anything that happened in the cell.

—*Leave me*, *she commanded and forced him from the void, back into his cold and lonely bed.*

Quietness filled the tent. He was not alone. As his overwhelmed senses began to calm, and his weakened power reached out around him, he found her at his side in bodily form. She touched his hand. The throbbing in his head subsided.

"You have need of sleep, Your Highness. Rest now."

His mind felt the sudden weight of slumber bear him down into sleep.

—*Why*, *he asked.* *Why?*

"Do not venture into that place again without me. It is no longer safe. The enemy is watching," Mary said. "Promise me, Baldwin."

"I promise," he replied. "But you haven't answered me."

Again, she forced to him to sleep. He had no strength to fight her.

"There is a time for everything, King Baldwin. This was not the time for Simon's end. You must trust me. His time will come soon enough."

He tried to question her further, but his thoughts began to wander; his head grew heavy. He dreamed, then: first of ancient walls of stone enclosing him, sealing his broken body within a dark tomb; and then, of mist and trees, of bright green sunlight and the fragrant scents of dawn.

Two weeks later, with the army of Jherusalem at his back, Baldwin relieved the siege of Kerak, much to the everlasting praise and adoration of its people and its lord, Reynald de Châtillon.

* * * * *

With the siege of Kerak relieved, Salehdin packed his army off to Damascus. Once more, Baldwin had proven himself the savior of his people. However, barely a sennight past Twelfth Night and the end of the Christmas season, and fresh trouble between Guion and the king erupted anew. Civil war threatened.

Guion had ridden directly for Ascalone with his troops. The insult of his removal from the Regency still stung. He had brooded over it during the long march towards Kerak and back until a desperate plan of rebellion had formed in his mind.

Returning to Ascalone had proven wise, for the king immediately summoned him and Sibylla to Jherusalem to stand before the Court. Fortunately, Sibylla had warned him of Baldwin's intent to annul their marriage. With both of them out of reach in Ascalone, they forced the king to come to him.

Now the king and the entire army of Jherusalem, the heroes of Kerak, waited at the gate of his city. Twice the king had come forward in his litter and knocked upon the wooded gate with his own hand, demanding admittance with the Court in attendance as prescribed by law. Guion stood upon the ramparts, silent and rebellious, in his full battle-armor, daring to refuse a king an order. Such was the legacy of his family.

The blue and silver banner of the House of Lusignan snapped in the stiff breeze above his head. Having thrown off his allegiance to the Crown, the banner of the kingdom no longer flew over the city. Sibylla stood with him, determined to defend her husband even before her brother the king. Guion's second-in-command, the Seneschal of Japhe and Ascalone, the post his brother once held under Agnes de Courtenay, looked up at him from the gatehouse, pleading for some answer to their dilemma. He held his hands in the air as if to say, *Should I open the gate?*

Guion slowly shook his head. *Let the king see what it means to wait.*

He was not the first vassal of the Crown to rebel against his sworn liege; Hugh II Le Puiset had helped spark a civil war on behalf of Queen Melisende in her bitter feud with Fulk, her husband and king-consort, the current king's grandparents. Ironically, Hugh himself had likewise been the Count of Japhe in his day.

Baldwin patiently waited for his surrender, but the gates remained closed and barred. The gates would remain closed until the king rescinded his request for the annulment—that, or Hell froze over with snow and ice.

His brother had advised him to do so four days ago.

Amalric had appeared to him out of the shadows of the tilting-yard that day. He had mistaken him for an intruder of the keep and crossed swords with him. His brother's skill had improved during his time in the East; it was like sparing with a complete stranger. Until Amalric knocked him off balance and threw him to the ground on his back.

"Your swordsmanship is sloppy and slow," his brother said, shaking his head. "If I had been even the least skilled soldier in

Salehdin's army, you would be dead. You've grown lazy, brother, playing the part of a Christian lord in Outremer."

"Swordplay in the practice-yard is not the same as actual battle," he complained, scrambling to his feet. He turned away from Amalric and returned the practice sword to the barrel.

The flat of a sword struck his back, sending Guion sprawling to the ground again. He grabbed a handful of straw and threw it at his brother. Amalric batted the straw into chaff and dust. Guion struggled backwards on all fours; his head bumped against the wall. He had no weapon to defend himself. Fear paralyzed his thoughts and limbs. His brother struck at him.

"What was that for?" he cried, glancing sidelong at the quivering sword blade sticking out of the wall beside his head.

"Never turn your back on anyone—especially those you trust."

Blood dripped from Guion's nose. He wiped at it with the back of his hand. Anger replaced the tight knot of fear in his stomach. "Christ on the Cross, Amalric! Look at what you did—I'm bleeding."

"Better that, than a knife in your back when you least expect it. You have enemies, Guion—not the least of which, the king and the Count of Tripoli. Now that Baldwin knows how close Sion stands to the throne, he will stop at nothing to keep you from the crown."

"I have friends—allies," Guion snapped and scrambled to his feet.

"Trust me, brother, you don't, except those who are loyal to Sion," Amalric said. He twisted his sword loose from the wall and pointed it casually towards Guion. "The king is coming here with the High Court to demand your submission; but we could have a bigger problem to deal with when it comes to Sibylla. Are we completely certain where her loyalties lie?"

Guion laughed. "She is an empty-headed young girl who still fancies herself in love. Trust me, her loyalty is all mine."

"You best be right, brother. So long as you keep your wife in line, Baldwin can accomplish nothing. Remember your oath to the Order of Sion, and I will take care of the king. And for all that's holy, Guion, under no circumstance open the gates of Ascalone to the king."

His brother had instructed him to play a dangerous game with the king. His enemies would not hesitate to call it treason. If he wished to be king in more than ceremony alone, however, he could not let Baldwin annul his marriage to Sibylla.

For the third time, Baldwin came forward in his litter and knocked upon the gate, demanding that Guion appear before him to answer and give an account of himself.

Guion refused.

* * * * *

Patiently, Baldwin had adhered to the letter of the law. Guion was insubordinate; Baldwin had acted in accordance with the *Assise sur la ligèce* laid down by his father and the High Court. He was free, therefore, to act according to his own demands of justice. Guion de Lusignan would learn now the depths of that kingly authority.

Baldwin just never reckoned that the lords of his own Court would plead leniency for a rebel whose actions were paramount to civil war.

Having failed to draw de Lusignan from Ascalone, Baldwin rode for Japhe and seized the city under the authority of the Crown. The confused citizens wisely opened the gates for him and received him with all due respect. In place of their rebellious count, he appointed a royal governor over them. Having deprived Guion of half his income, Baldwin headed immediately up the coast to Acre and called for a *curia generalis* to discuss a call to the Pope for a new holy war in the wake of Salehdin's renewed hostilities—and to begin proceedings to divest Guion of his fief.

At this point, his lords thought themselves wiser, or perhaps, they feared his wisdom, and balked at the prospect of divesting a fellow lord of his tithe, his lands, and most of all, his income. It cut too close to the question of loyalty for many of them. He read it in their thoughts. He heard it in their voices. *Whom else might the king choose to dispossess if they disagreed with him?* A blind man may not see, but it did not render him sightless.

Cunningly enough, three of the very lords that had stood with him before the gates of Ascalone—the Patriarch and the Masters of the Temple and Hospital; all three of which had no titles or land or income he could confiscate—now knelt before him. Heraclius foremost among them, begged him to see reason and not give Guion any more reason to start a civil war. It appeared that Guion had more powerful allies than he first suspected. His grasp of authority in the kingdom was beginning to slip from his decaying hands. Perhaps, but he was determined not to lose face over such a clear act of defiance.

He sat on his throne in the enormous arched hall of the palace of Acre. Sunlight filled the windows; it angled down, warming his sick body on a morning chilled with more than just the cold of a late winter's day. With more sunlight shining down into the hall than in Jherusalem, the spirits of darkness could hide in far fewer shadows.

William had come from Tyre to offer him his council, but he needed none in regards to his vassal's defiance. He elected to sit alone on the throne, wrapped in his cloak and veil. It was easier to think without anyone else's thoughts crowding too close.

—*Does that include mine, Your Highness?* *Mary said, a hint of humor in her voice*

—*Never, my lady*, *he said, casting about for her with his senses.* *Your council is far wiser than those within this hall.*

He reached into the shadowy void only far enough to find the bright glow of the Magdalen's presence. She stood among the ladies of Court. No one seemed to pay her any attention.

—*Let us hope that your praise does not prove itself empty.*

—*Yours is all I can trust.*

"Your Majesty, King Baldwin," Heraclius began, bending his knee before him. "We come before you to ask that you please reconsider your request in regards to his Lordship Count Guion de Lusignan. Although he has openly defied you and made a mockery of your royal authority and person, please, find it in your heart to show mercy and clemency. Do not repay spite with spite. Think of your royal sister and her son. Do not deprive them of your favor. Deal with the Lord of Ascalone as your sworn vassal, not as an enemy of the Crown."

It angered Baldwin foremost, that of all people, Heraclius dismissed his proposal for a new holy war to defend an inexcusable act of rebellion.

A very, very long silence followed the Patriarch's impassioned plea. Baldwin took his time to consider a reply; he needed time to control his wrath. Heraclius was, after all, an anointed servant of God, however profligate.

Baldwin wanted nothing more than to accuse both Lusignan brothers of witchery and heresy before the Court and the Patriarch, but he realized now that any one or more of those assembled in the hall could also be in league with Sion. No doubt, Guion was nothing more than a pawn in a much larger game of conspiracy. He needed more proof of the Lusignans' guilt than just whispers overheard outside a tent at night by their sharpest critic and adversary. He needed solid, incontrovertible proof. For now, though, all he had was a headstrong, intransigent brother-in-law bent on defying his commands at every turn.

Baldwin shook his head. He gave the only answer he could to the Patriarch. Heraclius pressed the issue. "For the good of the kingdom God has given you, Your Highness, you must. I implore you; see the consequences of not restoring the Count of Ascalone to your favor. We cannot risk the chance of open civil war."

"Tell that to *Messire* de Lusignan," Baldwin said in a voice that he kept purposely soft. He raised a heavily bandaged hand and pointed at the Patriarch. "Christ did not show mercy on the one who betrayed him; rather, he condemned him to his own place. I will do no less for Guion. My forgiveness comes only at the price of his humbleness before me."

It was only a matter of time before someone in the Court waded into the fray. William filled that expectation. "If I remember aright, my lords, this Court acted as one in removing Messire de Lusignan from the Regency," he said, making his way into the center of the sunlit hall. All eyes turned towards him. "Ascalone has defied this Court, as much as he has defied the king. Is this how you deal with oath breakers and unruly men—by overlooking their trespasses?"

"Your Highness, please, I pray you will reconsider your judgment," argued Arnaud de Torroge, the Master of the Templars. "This kingdom can ill afford to defend the rights of two kings at war with each other."

Baldwin grew agitated at the petty bickering over his decision. His agitation put him into a fit of coughing. "This kingdom can ill afford such a war only if men who are like-minded as Guion rally to his banner. I pray that those in attendance here will remember the oath of fealty they swore before me, and before God."

Resplendent in his elegant robes of office, Heraclius slowly rose from his knee. Baldwin watched the entire pageantry of the Patriarch's action in his mind. He was certain that the image his senses lent him were not the same as those the Court witnessed.

"I pray you have considered the seeds of discord you are sowing here today, Your Majesty, just as I hope you remember the precedent you have set in regards to those who defy the will of their lord."

Baldwin sunk down into his throne, brooding in the dark depths of his voluminous cloak and veil. "I can see now, my lord Bishop of Jherusalem, where your true loyalties lie. I pray you show Guion de Lusignan the same loyalty you have shown me should he manage to become king someday when I am dead."

Baldwin's words were finally enough to render the Patriarch speechless. A commotion broke out through the hall. He heard the sound of retreating footsteps. Heraclius fled the palace, he later learned, with the masters of the two military orders. It troubled him. The proposal to send a new delegation to the West had gone undiscussed. Guion's actions had caused more than just a simple argument between the Crown and one of its vassals; it had put the kingdom in jeopardy of not receiving new recruits to help in the defense of the Muslim *jihad.*

—You did what was necessary, Baldwin, Mary said, hovering just behind his ivory throne. **We have to see now what becomes of it.**

—And what if it fails to make Sion act in desperation?

* * * * *

The Archbishop of Tyre bore the brunt of Sion's frustrations with the king. In reality, the Order meant to demonstrate to the king the scope of its power. On Maundy Thursday, the celebration of the Last Supper three days before Easter, William suffered the humiliation of excommunication by the very man the Church had chosen over him as Patriarch.

William was understandably distraught. He was also furious. That it was a political move on the part of the Patriarch was undeniable. That Sion had made a move to separate the king's allies from him came as no surprise, and all of it based on fabricated lies and misrepresentations of the facts. At the heart of the matter, lay the accusation that William had defied his ecclesiastical lord, the Patriarch of Jherusalem. The shadow of Guion's rebellion stretched farther than even the Magdalen had imagined.

Considering the tension between William and the Patriarch during the last few months, it was only a matter of time before Heraclius resorted to such underhanded tactics to prove his authority over William. It began with the renewed discussions between Baldwin and Heraclius about sending delegates to Europe to rally support for a new war. The king and the patriarch had come to terms; Guion de Lusignan brooded still in Ascalone, unrepentant and undisciplined. In the end, they decided that the same three men that had pleaded the cause of Guion, would be the delegates sent to the West.

Of course, it put the Patriarch in a difficult situation—one that necessitated keeping William from acting as his vicar in Heraclius' absence. Since being elected to the patriarchate, Heraclius had demanded that the Archbishop of Tyre yield to his authority, an untenable situation that caused the suffrigan Sees under William's jurisdiction to be cut off from the patronage of the Archbishop of Antioch. At best, it presented a very confusing predicament, one over which William became quite defensive. It bordered heavily on the question of rights and privilege within the Church.

Heraclius saw fit to remind the king of the warning he gave him at the proceedings following Guion's rebellion. *Remember the precedent you have set in regards to those who defy the will of their lord.* That precedent resulted in the king's pursuit of divesting Guion of Japhe and Ascalone.

William paced the floor of his office in Tyre, wringing his hands and venting his outrage. His secretary glanced at him when he swore not a few too many times. Brother Giles quickly finished packing the little belongings William chose to take with him and fled the office with a brief, parting embrace for his mentor.

With the shadow of excommunication hanging over him, William forbade the priests and brothers under his authority to speak with him lest they fall under the same judgment at the hand of the Patriarch.

If he was to have any hope of reaching Rome with the spring sailing, he needed to leave immediately. Several merchant ships from the Italies lay in the harbor at Acre, waiting to return to Brindesi after disgorging their load of pilgrims and refitting for the voyage home. By some small miracle, he might return to Jherusalem by year's end. It was something towards which he could direct his prayers, that, and the Holy Father's clemency and restoration.

Another brother, hooded against the chill of night, stood in the doorway following Brother Giles' exit. He waited, standing silently, for William to address him. *Ignorant fool.* "I told you before, brother, you shouldn't be here," he said, throwing the remark over his shoulder. He folded a stack of freshly scraped parchment sheets and stuffed them into his already overfilled satchel next to his manuscript. "Or do you truly wish the Patriarch to excommunicate you as well?"

"I should like to see him try," the dark-eyed brother laughed as he removed his hood and made his way into the smallish room. "How *does* one go about excommunicating a dead person, let alone a saint?"

William spun around to face his unexpected guest. He—or rather, she—crossed her arms and stared intently. She shook out her mane of wine-dark hair. Her eyes shone like emerald jewels mirroring everything upon which she gazed.

"Magdalen," he said, breathing her name with great relief. "You don't know what a relief it is to see you."

"I can well imagine, my dear William," she said, touching his hand. "You do know that none of this is a result of anything you've done? It is an attempt to separate you from the king's council."

He glanced up at her. She smiled. "I know it, my lady. But it changes nothing. I still must leave the kingdom, or risk drawing the king under the same judgment of excommunication."

Mary moved around the desk, keeping a hand on his. Her touch was gentle, reassuring. Events were tilting swiftly now towards their conclusion—or oblivion. He felt little fear looking into her bright, immortal eyes. She seemed to read his thoughts. "Baldwin's illness is getting worse and you can't let him die unshriven."

"I am a priest, a servant of God," he said. "It is my duty to care about such things. He doesn't deserve to die this way—not after all he has been made to endure."

Mary pulled back her hand and stood up. He had forgotten how tall she stood compared to most women. "Those are things— rites—made by the traditions of man. They have no truth to them, however much faith you place in them. What resides in the heart determines the final reward of a soul. Baldwin believes that Christ is the Son of God, that he alone is the Savior of man. You taught him that, William—not the age-worn traditions of a Church that have clouded the simple gospel of Jhesú. Baldwin's eternity is secure with God because of his faith, not because of words mumbled over him at the last moment of his life."

William sighed and laughed softly for a moment, relieving the tension and emotion that had bottled itself up inside of him. He smiled. "Be careful of the words you speak, my lady. They are like a fire that could reform all that the Church holds clear."

"Truth has that reaction, my friend."

A sudden melancholy came over him at the thought of his leaving the kingdom for Rome. There were some fears he refused to name, others, which he knew he had no choice, but to confront. One such fear was that he would not see Baldwin again in this life. He knew the king would likely not live much longer, but William held out some small measure of hope that Mary could heal him if only he could abide just a little longer with the suffering of his body. Mary dashed his hopes before he could even voice them.

"He will be dead by this time next year."

"Promise me you'll keep him from acting rashly in my defense," he said, trying not to think on her words. "Sion has effectively cut him off now from those who can offer him the best advice—or at least they've tried to. They'll come after you last of all, my lady."

Mary laughed coldly. "Let them try. I think the Master of Sion underestimates the king's ability to defend himself. They believe him to be weak and enfeebled by his leprosy. You need not fear for your young king, William. He has strengths of mind and body that he has not yet begun to test—strengths that they take for weakness. In the end, it will be their undoing. Go, and make whatever farewell you need with Baldwin."

She came to him around the desk and embraced him fiercely. She had never done so before. He still thought that she was the most beautiful woman he had ever seen. Only she had ever made him regret the calling that brought him into the service of the Church.

She lingered; he felt her hesitate before breaking their long embrace. He knew, then, the reason. He would not likely see her again either.

* * * * *

Baldwin set a tall cushioned chair in the midst of the hall in the palace of Acre. He thought it important for Heraclius, His Grace, the Patriarch of Jherusalem, to sit comfortably. A man of such importance was certainly used to the luxury of a soft cushion to uphold his saintly backside.

Having set his stage, he bid Heraclius to come and give an account of his actions against the Archbishop of Tyre; miracle of miracles, Heraclius came, not that he needed to. The matter belonged to the Church, but Baldwin was a king in need of his excommunicated Chancellor.

The Patriarch was punctual if nothing else. At the stroke of Nones, he presented himself at the door of the throne room. Two armed guards escorted him in. Baldwin listened, hearing the whispering swish of silken robes. Heraclius strode arrogantly towards the chair; Baldwin could hear it in the casual, yet confident gait of the profligate prelate.

Heraclius had many sins for which he needed forgiveness. Baldwin doubted he would ever seek absolution for any of them. If anything, the man seemed unashamed of his sins or of the fruit of those sins, and none more so, than his year old daughter by Pascua de Riveri. The girl could often times be found toddling about the Patriarch's residence at the Holy Sepulcher. Heraclius made no effort whatsoever to conceal his paternity, and none so much as when he allowed a servant to burst in on the Court to announce Pascua had delivered the child.

Concubinage was not a sin in the eyes of Mother Church, but neither was it encouraged. Everyone knew about the secret. The Church had a way of turning a blind eye to those who struggled with certain appetites of the flesh. Heraclius' sin was in keeping a wealthy widow as a mistress and never once repenting of it.

He sat at Baldwin's silent invitation—a mere wave of the hand; the soldiers closed the door and barred it behind him. They were alone, king and cleric in a hall abounding with shadow and sunlight, the echoing sound of their voices. Well, almost alone. The Magdalen stood huddled in a dark and voluminous robe at the back of the hall, guarding the door. In the grey space only she and he could enter, the glow of magic rimed the door. It crackled with cold blue fire. Mary warded them safely within the hall. They would not be disturbed. No one or no thing could pass beyond that ward that they did not allow.

"Do you fear me, Your Eminence?" Baldwin asked abruptly. He reached up and slowly pulled off his crown and the kaffiyeh that veiled his face. He felt the revulsion register in the Patriarch's mind. It seemed to confirm some secret thought the cleric held about him as a leper and his suitability to sit upon the throne of Jherusalem.

Heraclius replied cautiously in a snuffling tone. "Why should I fear you, Your Highness?"

"You shouldn't," he said. "And yet, you haven't stopped fingering your talisman since you sat down." His Sight showed him that Heraclius' hand switched to another artifact on a chain around his neck. "And no, I don't mean your silver crucifix."

Heraclius' hand fell into his lap. Baldwin felt and heard the minute gesture. "The Church condemns all forms of magic, Sire. You'd best be careful of whose presence you use it in."

—It is not me he fears, my lady; it is you. I can smell it. He reeks of fear.

"Do you think it magic for a blind man to hear the rustling of fabric or the whisper of a dry hand upon rough-hewn wood? I am blind, my lord Patriarch, not deaf. Even so, forgive me if I gave you cause for fear. I thank you, as well, for the warning against magic and all forms of deviltry. It is comforting to know that the Church still stands for something—even if it excommunicates innocent men based on false charges."

Heraclius laughed softly. "Ah, so we come to the crux of the matter so quickly. You question my integrity."

"I question your motives," Baldwin countered. "What manner of threat could the Archbishop of Tyre possibly be to you that you found it necessary to excommunicate my Chancellor?"

"His influence over you." The arrogant cleric let the words linger a moment on the air. He obviously took pleasure in the cat and mouse of their conversation. "You are sending me to preach a new war in the West. William would have become vicar in my place, as is the right of the See of Tyre. That, I could not allow."

Just by the tone of his voice, he could tell that Heraclius was smiling. He wanted to strike the smug grin from his pretty face.

—Careful, Baldwin, Mary warned him. Do not let your anger cloud your thoughts.

—Yes, my lady, he replied tersely.

"Your arrogance is astounding," Baldwin said, "but you forget, Your Grace: I put you into the position of Patriarch. I can remove you just as easily."

"You could try—but you would fail, miserably so, I assure you, Majesty. Interfering with Church affairs is a chancy venture at best. I warn you: do not underestimate my influence within the Church. To break faith with me, is to break faith with the Church and the Holy Father in Rome. Consider how your people would feel to find their king excommunicated and the kingdom under interdict."

"You dare threaten me, Your Grace?"

"I give you warning, King Baldwin. I will not give you such council again. You continue to reign only by the will of Sion."

"*Sion*, my lord Heraclius?"

—Why would Sion reveal itself so openly now, after so many years of secrecy?

There was a disturbance in the grey void between the worlds. Darkness gathered there. Baldwin sensed the Magdalen's irritation, her utter contempt for her age-old enemy.

—They grow bolder with each victory they think they win.

—And every victory brings the kingdom that much closer to its destruction.

—But not at the hand of Sion, Mary said, again reminding him of what he already knew. You cannot change that outcome, Baldwin. You can only prevent a greater calamity.

"I'm sure you know the name, King Baldwin," Heraclius said, his smile smug and defiant. "It controls your Court, just as it controls the Church. The House of Anjou has betrayed the sacred trust through which the throne of Jherusalem came to them. You reign only because my master wills it."

"*That* is a lie, *Your Grace*," Mary said, stepping out of the air at Baldwin's side. Her voice echoed through the air at her sudden appearance.

Heraclius gasped and leapt from his seat. His surprise, however, did not live long enough to still his tongue or dull its sharpness. "Do not speak to me, witch." He fumbled with the silver crucifix and held it up, stepping towards them—towards her. Heraclius' body burned suddenly with lust at seeing Mary's exquisite beauty. He yearned to give into it and let it have its way. Images flashed in his mind; images of what her body

349

was like beneath the folds of her garments. He brandished the crucifix like a sword. "I command you in the name of Christ to be silent."

Mary shrieked like a caged animal and disappeared.

He felt her presence. She hovered close still. **Why did you do that, my lady? He has no power over you.**

—Let him think that he does, *Mary said laughing.* **I tire of this man's endless ramblings.**

Heraclius retreated to behind his chair and stood behind it as though it had become a shield. "Your Majesty imperils his immortal soul by consorting with daemons and spirits of the air."

—Fool. He denounces all those whom God created a little higher than man as children of the Devil.

Baldwin shifted in his seat. He, too, had grown weary of Heraclius' ranting. "According to His Holiness, Pope Alexander, I am condemned already by the just judgment of God," he said, reclining back into his throne. "If I were you, my lord Bishop, I would fear she who God has set as the protector of His Holy City. The Order of Sion will never have the throne or the kingdom so long as she stands against you."

"You and your pet witch are no threat to us, King Baldwin," Heraclius sneered.

"We are done here, Your Grace," Baldwin said, dismissing the arrogant prelate. "But this is far from over."

"Oh, I rather expect it's not, Your Highness," Heraclius chuckled softly and strode from the hall. At the double-door, he turned back. The wards fell at Mary's command. "I fear for you, Majesty. You forget that daemons have the power to appear as angels of light; even one who calls herself by the name of Magdalen and confesses the name of Christ."

The door closed. The sound echoed through the hall with a disturbing effect. Baldwin brooded in his blind darkness upon the throne. Mary appeared at his side, her hand resting lightly upon his arm.

—Is it true, lady, what Heraclius says of you? Are you a daemon that has led me astray into darkness?

"What does your heart tell you?"

"It tells me that you are Mary Magdalen, the beloved disciple of Jhesú."

She touched his face with her fingers and turned his head towards hers. "Then believe your heart, Baldwin, rather than your mind which can easily be led astray."

The Church had its reasons to fear and hate the elvenkind, reasons far beyond simple ignorance and blind jealousy of their beauty and immortality, their grace, their power, and their strength. To some, they possessed too many of the divine attributes of the Christ to be children of God's handiwork; they were spirits born of the fires of Hell and of their father, the Devil. He wondered how much the early Church fathers knew about the Magdalen that some went to such lengths to malign her. Still, he had his own questions.

"What are you, my lady? Who *are* your people?"

"Creatures created in the image of God," she said, "without the innocence of man. We are servants of the Most High on earth; a people gifted with power and glory much like the angels. God meant us to be a living testimony of His grace—of what might had been had Adam and Eve partaken of the tree of life in their sin. And so shall we remain until the Judgment or until God no longer has any use for us as He has ordained."

He took her hand and squeezed it gently. It was a joy not to have her pull her hand away. "Can you—I mean, your people—die?"

"Oh, yes," she said soberly, "but not easily. And for that reason, King Baldwin, we must not take the power of Sion or its master too lightly."

† CHAPTER TWENTY-THREE

For the fear which I feared, hath come upon me: and that which I was afraid of, hath befallen me.
—Job 3:25

The bells of the basilica of Saint-John Lateran tolled across the Seven Hills of Rome. Rain and the dismal, lowering grey clouds deadened the sound into something more like a funeral dirge than a call to prayer.

The people of the ancient papal city huddled at their windows, peering out on another Michaelmas celebration ruined by a late September storm. William leaned against his own window frame in the small room he had rented in sight of the Lateran Palace. The king had given enough gold in coin to stay in Rome as long as he needed to gain the Pope's pardon.

The cobbled streets were narrow in this older section of the city, and ran with rivulets of water along the gutters. A horse and wagon trundled up the gently sloping hill towards the Lateran; the sound of hoofs and wooden cartwheels echoed off the walls of the densely packed stone houses.

It was more than five months since his arrival and he still awaited an audience with His Holiness, Pope Lucius III. With Lucius in the north at Verona under self-exile due to his on-going feud with Emperor Frederick, it would likely be many more months before he could meet with the Papal Father, if ever.

Meanwhile, William spent his days wandering about the city and the countryside. With the blessed Alexander asleep in his grave, he had no chance of obtaining permission to visit the Lateran library. It was heartbreaking for a historian of William's reputation. Rome, though, had more to offer than old scrolls and dusty books.

There were a good many sites and wonders to see, shrines and churches at which he could pray. And pray, he did; often. The Church may have cut him off from her sacraments and her privileges, but she could not keep him from exercising his faith through pilgrimage or the observance of the holy days. Rome was a city of wonder; a city of deep faith built upon the ruins of a long-dead pagan religion; a city where one could lose themselves in the sanctity of so many saints whispering for adoration, even by an excommunicated archbishop from Outremer.

A knock came at the door. William startled; he knew no one in Rome, only a few cardinals at the Lateran palace. A flash of lightning sheeted the heavens. Thunder rumbled softly in the distance over the seven hills. It was certainly no day for anyone to be about his or her business.

Opening the door, he found a white-robed Cistercian brother standing in the rain. He remembered that Pope Lucius had risen through the ranks of the Cistercian Order. He prayed the Holy Father had sent the good brother with word of an audience.

"Can I help you, brother?"

"It's raining hard, my friend," the stranger said. "Please, if I may come in, I promise I will explain everything."

William stepped back, confused. "Forgive my manners, brother. Come in; come in. You'll catch your death in this rain and cold."

The man drew back his white hood and tried to shake out what little rain he could from his thick robe by the small fireplace before introducing himself. He wiped a hand across his tonsured head and chuckled at his obvious bedraggled appearance. "Despite what you may see before you, I am Cardinal Giovanni di Pietri, a secretary in His Holiness' service."

William offered his grey-haired guest a chair at the table. He had just set out a board of bread, fruit, and cheese for an early meal before the rain had drawn him away to the window. He invited the cardinal to dine with him. Giovanni di Pietri nodded and produced a flagon of wine from a heavy satchel he carried with him.

"This seems rather appropriate, then. It is Falerian. The best the Italies have to offer," he said, handing the flagon to Wiliam. "The wine of Caesar and the emperors of Rome. A gift from His Holiness for causing you to wait so long for an audience. He regrets that he cannot meet with you in person, but this affair with the Emperor has him rather entangled at present. He prays, Bishop William, you will forgive him and enjoy the wine with his blessing."

William nodded appreciably, nearly struck dumb with such a magnanimous gift from the absent Pope. "His Holiness is, indeed, a generous man. Shall we drink to his good health?"

Di Pietri brought his hands together at his chest in an attitude of prayer and bowed towards William with a smile. William poured wine into two earthenware beakers and handed one to the cardinal. They raised their cups to Lucius and drank deeply. "Please forgive me, but these rather crude cups are all I have."

"You need not apologize for your poverty, brother. We are all poor in the sight of God."

William nodded silently and sipped his wine again, watching his guest do the same. He was about to ask after the matter of the Pope and the Emperor, when the wine suddenly turned bitter in his stomach and on his tongue. A tingle of fear twisted into a knot of pain in his abdomen. He felt dizzy. He set his cup down heavily, sloshing the wine. Giovanni di Pietri did the same, but slowly and deliberately.

"What... what have you done?"

"What do you mean, brother?" the cardinal asked. "You don't look so well. Perhaps, it was something you drank. You should probably lie down."

William's stomach clenched and fell to the floor in pain. Fire seared through his limbs and head. The poison spread quickly; faster than any poison he knew. His assassin watched him with amused indifference.

"Who are you?" William groaned. "Who sent you?"

"Does it truly matter, now, my lord Bishop?" said the white-robed cardinal stoppering the wine flagon and slipping it into his satchel along with the two cups. "You'll be dead in a few moments."

With his last few breaths, William's only thought was for Baldwin and his safety. Darkness fell over his eyes as Giovanni di Pietri opened the door. "By the way," the Cistercian said, "His Grace, the Patriarch of Jherusalem is passing through Rome at the moment with the Masters of the Temple and the Hospital to meet with the Holy Father at Verona. Lord Heraclius sends you his greetings."

William heard nothing more. Nor did he care. He had already passed from the darkness of the world into the glorious light of God and the heavens.

* * * * *

Salah ad-Din Yusuf knelt before the *mirhab* in the wall of his small, private prayer chamber in Dimasq. He held a Qur'an in his hands with a string of *dhikr* beads wrapped around his fingers. He had prayed *alhamdulillah* so many times that his thoughts were lost in the rhythm of the words. Nothing else entered his mind but the cadence of the prayer. Only the beads and his fingers kept count of the repetition of his words. Ninety-nine beads for the ninety-nine names of Allah.

Alhamdulillah... Praise to God... Alhamdulillah... Praise to God...

His prayers gave him a sense of oneness with Allah; they centered his every thought on the majesty of the unknown. It blotted out the bloodshed and the war, the death, the utter hatred that made enemies of men who believed differently than their neighbors. It helped him forget who he had become.

The silence that came at the end of his prayers fell suddenly and completely; it blossomed, swelling into a peace that comforted his soul. Only his sigh of contentment broke the quiescence. It called to the night and the dark shadows that inhabited the world. Familiar troubles began to disturb his thoughts once more. His fingers began to rub the *dhikr* beads.

"God guides to His Light whom He will," a familiar voice said; a woman's voice and one as familiar as the troubles that tormented him. She stepped from the air all in white and gold and the beauty of the *jinn*.

"Your knowledge of Holy Qur'an is surpassed only by your beauty, my lady Maryam."

The *ifritah* nodded and bowed her head at his praise. Her eyes glowed as her gaze fell upon him. True to her infidel self, she refused to wear the veil of a proper Muslim woman in his presence.

"Nor will I, my lord Salah ad-Din,' she said. "I am a Christian and a Jew, not a proper Muslim woman."

He laughed, but nervously. "So, it is true that the *jinn* have the ability to read the hearts of men."

"Just as I can see the good that is in men's souls. Men like you, my lord." Maryam opened her hands to him. "King Baldwin's death is near now. He will not last the season. I have come to give you warning, friend Yusuf, that with his passing, the *Qiyama* may soon be proclaimed."

"The Day of Resurrection." Yusuf lowered the Qur'an into his lap. "By whom? The *Qiyama* can only come once the *Mahdi* and Isa al-Masih—your Jhesú—defeats the Evil One."

Her hands went to her mouth, fingertips pressed to her lips. He could see this was hard for her. "There is a group of Nasrani and Jewish heretics that call themselves the Order of Sion, men who are in league with the Old Man of the Mountain to hasten the appearance of the *Mahdi*. The *sheikh al-Jebel* believes your holy war will bring only greater war and unrest across the lands of Islam."

"Surely, this is some trick of the *jinn*; some mischief of your kind, my lady."

She arched an eyebrow. "Do not Shi'a clerics teach that the last battle will begin with war in the lands around Jherusalem?"

"There are some who believe such," he said, rubbing a wooden bead with his thumb. "But still, only the *Imam Mahdi* can proclaim the *Qiyama*."

"I think this Order of Sion has convinced Sinan that *he* is the Lost Imam and that *you* are *ad-Dajjal*, the Deceiver."

He snorted. "The only deceiver is the Old Man of the Mountain and his Hashshashin," Yusuf said, twisting his prayer beads tighter around his clenched fingers.

"That is why you must take Jherusalem from the Franks only after the Leper King is dead," she said. She knelt down in front of him. "Otherwise, everything we both hold dear will fall into darkness and deception."

Yusuf laughed uncertainly. "Why do you insist on continually telling me what I already know to be true?"

"To assure you that what you do from here on is just and right, and that it is ordained by God."

"God guides to His Light whom He will," he said with a smirk. He pulled on the point of his beard. "I will not fail, my lady Maryam."

"Of that, I have no doubt," she said. "Only do not act in haste, or you will play into the hand of the enemy and all their lies. Do not become the very thing the enemy claims you are. I will come to you when the moment comes for your great victory."

"You told me I had to wait only for the death of the Leper to have Urshalim."

She set a long, thin finger to his lips. Her touch felt soft and gentle; her scent was rapturous. "Trust me, my lord. Look to the north and Mosul before you strike. The day of Jherusalem's fall swiftly approaches."

Maryam stood abruptly and stepped back from him towards the wall, wrapping her cloak around her thin shoulders. He set aside the Qur'an. He called to her before she could fade. "What does an *ifritah* care about the affairs of men or of Urshalim?"

She did not fade, but stepped back towards him. "In my anger and my grief, I helped let loose a terrible evil into the world that has conspired since before the birth of Christianity or Islam to corrupt all I hold dear. As long as that evil continues to exist, I will do all I can to destroy it."

"And Urshalim?"

"Jherusalem is what it is. Holy. Beloved. The City of God," she said, closing her eyes. "It is a nest of vipers; a prize for the strongest and the most ambitious. Christians and Jews long ago gave up the right to it. Perhaps under Islam, it will finally have the peace it deserves and wants."

* * * * *

Gerard de Ridefort spat on the shining gold cross of Christ. It was blasphemy certainly; a renunciation of everything his vows as a knight and monk held most dear. His blasphemy would make him Master of the Poor Knights of the Temple of Solomon.

He owed his rapid rise through the ranks of the Templars to the promise of Sion and the sudden, untimely death of Arnaud de Torroge that autumn in Verona while visiting the Pope with Patriarch Heraclius. Unfortunately, his death had come close on the heels of the former Chancellor's. Too close. It aroused too many questions. Whispers of poison abounded; none of them proven.

Gerard wore the armor and tabard of his Order. He knelt, not in the grand hall of the *Templum Salomonis*, but in the small chapel of Sion deep beneath the ancient Church of the Apostles.

Robed and cowled in black, Amalric de Lusignan gestured stiffly towards the spittle-covered cross, pointing. Despite the silver mask that hid his face, Gerard knew that powerful voice. "Put no faith in this—it is only illusion, a lie. It is a deception for those who are weak and ignorant of any truth or enlightenment. *This* has no power to save you from sin or from the darkness of the world."

Candlelight cast shadows across the floor. The shadows wove together in a swirl of black robes and silver masks, each one indistinguishable from the next. He had long heard that Amalric de Lusignan was a master in the art of magic; he believed it now. The air of the chapel crackled with arcane power. This was no simple ceremony; it was an initiation into the sacred rites of a magic that traced its secrets to Alexandria and the East.

He replied with the words that the master had instructed him to ask. "What must I do? What must I believe?" he said.

Another voice spoke behind him: "Believe only in the Highest God, the Lord of Light and in the perfect knowledge of his Holy Name. Trust not in the words of the Church that calls itself the way of truth."

Again, the shadows shifted about the room as the cloaked figures wandered about him in a circle. His head swam with the pungency of burnt incense. The candle flames guttered and settled.

Amidst the swirling robes and gleaming masks, the crucifix disappeared. When Gerard looked again, a skull and a chalice had replaced the cross on the altar. He knew their importance, their history. He had learned enough of the secret behind them in recent weeks as he had the steps of the ceremony and their connection to the true traditions of Christianity that the Church hid from the world.

He bowed before the reliquary of the *caput mortuum*, the dead head: the Baphomet, or *abufihamet*, the head of wisdom as the Arabs called it in their tongue. The chalice was the equal of the skull and its opposite: life and death, light and darkness, female and male, repentance and sin. The cup held a mystery, the *arcana arcanum*, the secret of secrets.

A masked figure moved towards the candlelit altar and picked up the gold and red agate cup, raising it above his head. A woman spoke. Her voice sounded cold and hollow behind the silver mask. "Know you the meaning of the sacred chalice?"

Gerard raised his bowed head and answered. "It is the Holy Grail, the cup of the divine, which the Magdalen hid away until the time that its true nature should be revealed."

The cup lowered. A voice commanded him to drink. The bitterness of the wine burned his throat; it tasted of blood and ash. He choked.

Warmth filled his stomach, turning to fire, making him dizzy and nauseous.

The room spun. The black robed figures blurred in a watery confusion of darkness and light.

Then, suddenly, it passed.

Only a slight buzzing of voices remained, whispering in his ear. Confusion struck him with fear.

A new figure in black, much taller than the woman, took up the skull from the altar and held it out with both hands. His voice was deep and booming like the rumble of thunder on the hills. Dark, penetrating eyes pierced him through with their gaze from behind the mask. He felt cold and hot at once; sweat beaded on his brow.

"Know you the meaning of the severed head?"

Gerard cleared his burning throat and spoke. "It is the head of the true Christ, who is called John and Baptist; the head that speaks and utters forth truth and prophecy."

Instantly, two men grabbed him roughly from behind, extended his right arm and hand outwards. He resisted the urge to fight back. His captors produced a small silver athame and slit his hand. Blood welled brightly in a thin crimson line. After a moment, it filled his palm in a pool. The skull lowered before his face.

Hollow, vacant sockets gazed at him darkly. The toothy jaw grinned with a malevolent, ill-humored smile. The black robed figures released him and stepped back. He knew what he had to do. Even having rehearsing it beforehand, something inside him gave Gerard reason to pause. Slowly he set his bloodied hand atop the skull and closed his eyes.

"Do you renounce all allegiances to the Papal Father and the Church of Rome?"

"I renounce all allegiance."

"Do you swear to keep secret upon the pain of death all that you have heard and seen?"

"I swear it."

The questioning continued, making the round of the circle hemming him in about the altar and the skull, now smeared with his own blood. His head hurt with so many questions. The fire in his abdomen had diffused, radiating to the ends of his limbs. The dizziness had passed, but his thoughts swam, becoming more incoherent and confused. Then, it stopped, just as it had before.

He knew how the ceremony would end. He would swear his allegiance and fall unconscious into the arms of his new and secret brethren among the Order of Sion, only to wake on the morrow in his own place, in his own bed.

"To whom do you swear your allegiance and your oath of service?"

Gerard raised his voice for all to hear in the small underground chapel. "To the Church of John and the Order of Sion. This I do by committing my sword, my life, my faith, and all that is commanded of me."

* * * * *

A light dusting of snow lay upon the brown and withered garden; it swirled in the wind, piling into small drifts in the winter-shadowed corners of the castle walls. Moonlight spilled over the garden, riming the snow with a silver-white glow. It was a cold night in Ascalone, even for the eve of the Savior's Nativity.

Sibylla sat in the solar with a thick blanket wrapped around her son's legs and body. Baudinouet had taken ill again. His fevered body kept them warm beneath the blanket. He had been sick only two weeks before. Earlier, she had let him test his skills with the new sword his great uncle Joscelin had commissioned for him as a Christmas present. Jherusalem was a warrior state. Its king, no matter his size or his age, should have a sword to wear and to wield with pride.

Despite Baudinouet's excitement over his gift, he quickly wore out with exhaustion and his sickness. Now he lay in her lap while she sang lullabies to him. Usually, he was quick to complain and remind her of his age—he was seven, after all—but tonight, he seemed not to care about such things as motherly concerns and displays of affections.

He curled next to her, letting the moonlight fall upon him. Two years had seen him grow into a gangling youth; all knees and elbows with large hands and feet, but still, he had a subtle grace about him. She saw it when he moved or held a sword. He reminded her of the king, her brother, before he was stricken with leprosy.

He adored the king and worshipped him as a hero out of the ancient myths and legends of Greece or Rome. Baldwin was most often the subject of all his conversations, and he usually begged her to tell him stories of his exploits, particularly of the Battle of Montgisart.

Of course, his worship became a source of great annoyance to her husband, his stepfather. They were too much alike, her son and brother. How much so, she was only now beginning to learn. What she was about to discover, however, would haunt her the rest of her days.

They had fallen into silence, Sibylla and her son. She rested her head atop his head, watching his hands idly play with the moonlight slanting across her shoulder from the window. Closing her eyes, she listened to the sounds of merriment and revelry going on down into the lower hall. Baudinouet squirmed, snuggling closer to her. Guion had wished her to stay and join in the feast and the dancing, but she had no desire for such fun tonight.

Her days in the convent as Saint-Lazare were never so loud or filled with such clamor, but they were joyous. Their vow of poverty had prohibited the receiving of gifts of material worth. It did not stop the sisters, though, from giving gifts of another kind.

On the eve of every Feast of the Nativity, they gathered around the altar in the chapel and, after giving thanks for the birth of the Blessed Jhesú, they would tell each other the one thing they would give if anything in the world were in their power to give. The most precious gift she ever received was a crown of stars that shone with the fires of Heaven. That was the Christmas before her father died.

Baudinouet squirmed again in her lap. Sibylla opened her eyes to find him gazing up at her with wide blue-grey eyes. He took her hand, pressed something cold and round into it; when she looked, she found a bright silver coin. When she tried to touch it, the coin slowly faded back into moonlight.

It amazed her, and then, it horrified her.

She knew instantly what he had done, and how, as surely as the small gold ring on her finger that Baldwin had once given as a gift the first time she had married. It frightened her beyond words. If her son could work even the slightest enchantment, then she had betrayed more than just her brother to Guion and his faction. Secrets were power to those who chose to use them to their own ends. If the wrong people discovered her son's abilities, it would put him in grave danger.

"How…" she said, barely able to speak. It took all her strength of will not to scream her fear.

Baudinouet sat up, turning to look at her. "It is *magic*, mama," he said, whispering the forbidden word with a care that belied his age. "But I'm still not very good at it."

"I know what it is, young man! I want to know how you learned to use it."

"Uncle told me."

"The king?"

Baudinouet giggled. "Of course, mother. But Uncle says I'm not to ever do it when people can see. He said that kings need to keep things secret sometimes."

Sibylla lifted a hand to her son's brow, and combed back a stray lock of golden hair. "Your uncle is a wise man, Baudinouet. You would do well to listen to him." She pulled him close and hugged him fiercely. "Promise me, Baudinouet, that you'll never use your magic again."

"Why?"

"Because your uncle is right. If the wrong people learn of your magic, you could be in danger. Some people are afraid of your kind of power," she said.

"But it's only magic."

"Promise me, Baldwin."

Baudinouet pouted, but he obeyed. "I promise, mother."

* * * * *

Guion's knuckles turned white on the hilt of his sword. He gripped it in ever-constant readiness against the shadow that stalked him: as if a sword would have any power against a spirit of the air. He could almost feel the daemon's presence at his back, smell the sulfurous stench of its breath.

This is supposed to protect me from her, he thought, referring to the spirit his brother had summoned from the depths of Hell. He dared not speak *her* name for fear that she would come at his bidding. Better the daemon, than her. He wished now that his brother rode with him on the raid against the Bedouin of Daron.

The nomads lived on the edge of the Sinai under the protection of the crown. Most of the nomads were Christian Arabs; the rest embraced Islam. Daron was a royal fief south of Gaza important to the southern defenses of the kingdom. In exchange for protection as they pastured their flocks in and about the fief, the Bedouin paid a small tribute to the king and supplied valuable information on Egyptian troop movements.

More than once, Guion had voiced his opinion about the unfairness of the tribute going to the king, rather than the County of Japhe and Ascalone. The king had always ignored his complaints.

What Guion contemplated now was paramount to further treason and war. A year ago, he had done much the same when the king had sought to deprive him of half his fief and his income. In his anger, he had acted rashly; he ordered the Bedouin massacred and their flocks confiscated. He would not make that mistake again. Raiding Daron could never make up for his loss of Japhe, but it certainly made him feel better, especially since his actions amounted to thumbing his nose at the king and his authority.

The thought had crossed his mind more than once over the last year that, if he chose, he could easily take the southern half of the kingdom from Baldwin's hand. Hebron, Blanchgarde, Bethgibelin, Montgisart, Ramlah, Lydda, Ibelin—all of them could easily fall to him before the king could even act. Hebron was the fly in the ointment along with its notorious lord, his friend Reynald de Châtillon. He could not simply take the fief from him, and yet he needed the strategic position to safeguard the south. Without Reynald, a civil war would prove fruitless. Therefore, he had to content himself only with inciting the king's ire.

Even still, his brother tried to keep his hand from the temptation of war. He suspected that that was the true reason his brother had called up a spirit of Hell to protect him, just as he summoned a devil to hound the king's every waking moment. More likely, the daemon protected the interests of Sion should he prove too indiscriminate in his actions.

The knights of Ascalone rode past Gaza and its small contingent of Templars unharrassed and into Daron like a sudden storm in the desert. Many of the Christians among the Bedouin were beginning to gather at the small castle on the edge of the Sinai to celebrate the Purification of the Virgin on Candlemas a week hence.

For the first time, Guion felt the oppressive presence of his infernal companion. Even the cold of a grey, late January morning did not chill him to the bone as much as the whispering voice of his fiendish companion.

"Give me thy leave to hunt."

"Go," Guion said, just to have the daemon away from him.

He gave the signal to his marshal to sound the attack. The horn blew.

Twenty knights and one unseen daemon overwhelmed the unsuspecting tribesmen, scattering them to the four winds. Wearing only light armor on swifter, more gracile mounts, the men of Ascalone used dulled swords and blunted spears to stir up chaos in the nomad encampments outside the walls of Daron. The daemon caused havoc in its own particular fashion by spreading fear and panic among the fleeing Arabs.

Guion made sure this time that there was plenty of the Arab Christian mongrels alive to fill the king's ears to overflowing with complaints about his raiding. He would he continue to do so until the king gave Japhe back into his possession and he gave up his intentions of annulling his marriage to Sibylla.

* * * * *

The dove's coo broke the solemn silence of the king's bedroom. Her son lay close to death on his richly ornamented bed with its golden posts and silken draperies. Fluid rattled in his lungs. His doctor, Dawud, gave him a week to live, perhaps two, if God and the Goddess were merciful. But no more.

Now, at the end of his life, a fever was about to overtake him rather than leprosy. He had taken ill again with the same malarial fever that had so often times taken him unawares. The last bout had struck him down at Sephorie a year and a half ago.

The Order of Sion had failed her. They had failed her son. For all its talk of ancient crowns and sacred blood, it had turned all its attention to Guion and Sibylla. Their failure found her now following the ramblings of a local hedge-witch to heal her son, rather than the incantations of some revered, half-forgotten sage of ancient Egypte.

Agnes cast such angry thoughts from her mind; they were no help to her son or to the task at hand, not that she could look upon her own child and not have her emotions distract her.

She had stripped Baldwin naked and laid him out on a sheet of white muslin. The illness made him too weak to care much what she did to him; only that his mother was trying to do what she could to comfort him. He remained quiet, silently enduring pain and the grief of his mother.

She could barely stand to see his frail, skeletal body so eaten away by disease. Fingers and toes had rotted away, his nose was gone, and his lips shrank back in a snarl that exposed yellow teeth and bleeding gums. She had placed candles at his head and feet. In their dim light, his sunken blind eyes stared vacantly at the ceiling. Raw, putrid sores erupted like bright red anemones along his protruding ribs and skin blotched white as the new fallen snow that lay upon Jherusalem in a thick blanket. The leprosy ravaged even his genitals. Tears sprang to her eyes, knowing that her beautiful boy would not see his twenty-fourth year.

The ritual was simple enough; it required more faith than action. Darkness attended her; the grey and purple shadows stood as a witness to her efforts. *"Terribilis est inquit locus iste! Non est hic aliud nisi domus Dei et porta caeli,"* Agnes intoned, recognizing the precarious position her son lay in between life and death. *Terrible is this place! This is no other but the house of God, and the gate of Heaven.* They were ancient words from the Scriptures in Latin—certainly an odd inclusion in the mummeries of a local Arab witch; but then, Jherusalem was a Christian kingdom afloat in a sea of other faiths and beliefs. If any magic existed in the words she spoke or the things she did, she ignored them and carried out the ritual as the witch had described it to her.

The dove thrashed its wings against the bars of the cage as Agnes began the rite. First came an anointing just as pagan as it was Christian: the candle and a burning of a strand of Baldwin's hair lay somewhere between the two. Taking holy oil, she touched it to his head, his navel, and the heels of his feet, making the sign of the *tau*, a symbol far older in ritual and tradition than the Christian use of it for the cross. To the ancients, it represented life and resurrection, not death, as the Church of Rome was wont to believe all too eagerly.

The anointing, however, was only the beginning. There was blood, afterwards, and water from the Jordan; blood from the dove, which she dispersed with a sprig of hyssop and an invocation to the archangels that guarded the four quarters of the earth; and water, which she poured gently over her son's all too numerous sores. *"Vade et lavare septies in Jordane et recipiet sanitatem caro tua atque mundaberis,"* she said. *Go, and wash seven times in the Jordan, and thy flesh shall recover health, and thou shalt be clean.* Such was the command the prophet Elisha gave to Naaman the leper in the Book of Kings.

Each time the water lathed over Baldwin's open sores, his body stiffened and he moaned in his fevered sleep. For the ritual to succeed, though, she had to ignore her son's pain as well as her own fears and proceed. Neither one proved easier than the other.

Seven times, she repeated the rite proscribed by Scripture and by witchery. Seven times, she felt the same unseen presence lurking in the shadows, watchful and protective. She had felt such things before.

The shadows were always harboring the agents of the enemy. She feared it might be the Angel of Death, waiting and watching, abiding his time as her son drew closer to his final rest.

The candle flames guttered in a sudden gust of an invisible draft, threatening to wink out. Agnes spun around to confront the lurking shadows. A figure cloaked in black and shadow separated itself from the darkness that lay in the deepest corners of the room and strode purposely towards her.

"Why not simply ask for your son to cry out, *O God, my God, look upon me: why hast thou forsaken me?*" a strange voice said. "It would have about the same result as your worthless ritual of blasphemy and witchery." A hand pulled back the hood from the hidden face, revealing a woman of startling beauty. "Magic of this kind cannot be easily undone by the simple magics of a village hedge-witch, my lady de Courtenay."

Agnes stepped back, setting a protective hand on her son's arm, but only briefly as the question of magic won out over her fears of the dark-robed intruder in her mind. "Or by the power of a mighty spirit of the air," she accused. In a flash of sudden understanding, it all made sense. She could not begin to understand what it meant, but it rang strangely true, even in the mouth of a woman of the immortal kind. "Who are you and what do you know about my son's illness?"

"I am one who knows that your son lies close to death's door because certain men found him expendable in their pursuit of power and the throne of Jherusalem," said the stranger. "Men who have set their own popes on the Chair of Peter and secretly plotted two holy wars to wrest control of Jherusalem from the Muslims. Men who call themselves the Order of Sion."

The accusations against such men stunned Agnes, not for what they claimed, but that they spoke the truth. Men that a stranger now claimed were responsible for her son's leprosy.

If she had cause to fear the woman before her, she knew she would be powerless to defend herself against one of the ancient Watchers of Hebrew legend. Still, she stood between her son and the mysterious woman who confronted her. "How do you know such things?"

The woman circled the large, drapery-hung bed towards the far side, her gaze never falling from Agnes' eyes. Agnes stood rooted to the stone floor. She watched as the beautiful woman bent down to Baldwin and whispered in his ear.

"I have long stood guard over your son, trying to protect him from those who would betray the crown. Men with whom you have had a long and secret association it seems."

"You couldn't *possibly* know that," Agnes said.

"And yet, I do know it, my lady?"

Daemon, she thought, tensing. *Seed of Satan*—

The strange woman caught Agnes off her guard by replying to her unfinished thought. "A Watcher, yes; an *ifritah*, an elven-maid, a faerie. But I am no daemon, my lady. Or would you have me touch holy relics to see if I fly off shrieking into the night." She reached for a nearby blanket and spread it out over Baldwin's naked body. She set a hand on his fevered head and sat down beside him. He groaned in his sleep; she calmed him with a word and a gentle stroke on his shoulder. "You wish to blame someone for what has happened to your son, my lady. This, I understand, for I, too, have sought revenge in my time, but I assure you, the fault for this tragedy belongs to Sion and its master alone. Baldwin's leprosy is not the unfortunate happenstance of nature. It is a spell of magic meant to destroy the power born of his father's noble house. The blood of Anjou and the Merovingians."

"They would not do so without my knowledge," Agnes said. "I was promised that he and his rights as king would be guarded."

"Sion cursed your son with leprosy long before that promise was made to you. Protecting him after the fact is a small price to pay for them to have your trust and help in dealing with both your children." The woman turned her head to Baldwin; she touched the edge of his brow, stroking back the golden blonde hair with long thin fingers. "Amalric de Lusignan is not the man he claims to be. But by now, I think you know that, or at least you have suspected as much."

She could not deny it. She had known it from the day he had told her about the Order of Sion when he first came to Court after Baldwin's coronation. Agnes sunk to the edge of the bed and sat, staring off into the dark shadows of the room. The weight of knowing was almost too great to bear. Yet, she needed to know more about the man that had betrayed her and her dying son.

"He once said that he has worn the faces of many men, but I did not understand him. I did not *want* to understand."

"I doubt very much that your fellow conspirators are any more knowledgeable of his true name and motives than you," said the woman. Her eyes flashed green with some inner fire of emotion. She proved herself a woman of little patience. "Who else, my lady de Courtenay, has *Messire* de Lusignan ensnared in his web of lies and deceit?"

Agnes barked a short, uncomfortable laugh. She rose from the bed and began to pace the floor. She glanced at her visitor and stopped. "Tell me first who you are, and then I will answer whatever you wish to know."

"If I tell you, you will do more than believe, Countess. You will curse yourself for having believed the many lies that you have come to learn at the hand of Sion."

"Tell me anyway," Agnes demanded. "I must know."

"I am Mary, whom men call the Magdalen," she said and stood to face her. "The same which the Order of Sion falsely worships as the Goddess and wife of Jhesú the Christ."

Mary, whom men call the Magdalen.

It was an obvious lie. She could not possibly be the same woman mentioned in Scripture as a disciple of Christ. The Magdalen died in the Languedoc over a thousand years ago. Tradition said she lay buried in Marseilles or Vezelay.

"Traditions are exactly that, Agnes; stories meant to explain what men don't understand—or truths they wish to keep hidden. If you doubt me, then ask the master of your Order. He knows the truth; he will not deny it. Would I lie, and then admit that I, too, unwittingly had a hand in your son's sickness?"

"You?" Agnes accused. "What did you do to him?"

"I tried to protect him with my power and his, but Sion turned the spell against him so that it would devour his magic even as it destroyed his body—the same Sion that had your marriage to Amaury annulled and then had him slain when he turned against them. Did you think the marriage of a king of Jherusalem to a Byzantine princess came about by mere chance?"

That cut her sharply, but it was truth. Agnes' thoughts were beyond words now. Her mind reeled with what even *she* knew she could not deny. She answered without considering the depth of the Magdalen's reply. If she did not, she might never have the courage to do so again.

"I hold the title of *Apostola Apostolorum* as the only woman of the Order, but there are eight others as well. Those whom you would know by name, are Amalric de Lusignan..." she said, hesitating before each name, as though it pained her to speak them aloud. With each name, she betrayed the betrayers... "Patriarch Heraclius... the new master of the Temple, Gerard de Ridefort... Renaud, the Abbott of Mt. Sion Abbey; Raymond Embriaco, the lord of Gibelet and Constable of Tripoli; and several others who you may not know. Alexius Angelus, a cousin and envoy of the Byzantine Emperor to Jherusalem; Bartholomew Domenico de Acre, a merchant of Genoa; and Count Rodrigo Alvarez of Sarria in Leon and Master of the new Order of Montjoie. There are others, of course, who live outside the kingdom— Jews and Muslims, as well as Christians—and all of them bound by their oath to Sion and its desire to destroy the Church of Rome."

Her admission was a cathartic release of her long-held guilt. She had closed her eyes as she named the last of the traitors against the king, and against Christ. In the blindness of her revenge against the Church, she had succumbed to heresy and the betrayal of her people just to spite those few small men who had given in to their jealousies against the heirs of Courtenay. And for what? After so many promises, so many assurances, her son lay closer now to death than he ever had before.

"I can end this, my lady, if you'll only trust me."

Agnes was on the verge of tears. She reached for Mary's hand and clenched it tightly. "This is my fault. I was such a fool, and I knew it."

"You tried to protect your son in a world dominated by weak, grasping men."

Now the tears sprang to her eyes and she laughed softly. "No, my lady Magdalen, if you truly are the blessed saint—it hardly seems to matter now. I believed a lie all too cleverly wrought of flattery and deceit to use me against my son for the sake of Sion."

Between the sobs of despair and hope, a spasm of uncontrollable couching wracked Baldwin's body. Blood spattered the sheet and blanket as he rolled to his side, curling into a ball. For a moment, Agnes feared that her healing ritual had only made his condition worse. She panicked; and froze in horror of her son's gasping for air in between the coughs.

Magdalen knelt on the bed, cradling him in her arms for comfort. She prayed over him, murmuring words into his ear. They were strange words she heard, familiar, yet not. They might have been Hebrew; perhaps the language of the faeries for all she knew. Either way, she felt their power. It came from the faintest light in the room, and gathered about her in a softly glowing aura like golden halo of an illuminated saint in a Greek icon.

Suddenly, he cried aloud in a hideous, strangled groan, and went slack. Agnes wailed, crumbling to her knees in grief as she cried out to the God she had tried to abandon for mercy on her son. Miracle of miracles, God answered her. Baldwin still lived, but he clung to life by the thinnest of threads.

The Magdalen sat back and took a deep breath. She looked visibly more tired, almost fragile. Her face had aged in the space of a few moments; grey streaked her long wine-dark hair. She was still beautiful beyond human compare, only now she bore the heavy burden of her long years of concern upon her.

"I've done what I can for him for the time being," said Mary, wiping a hand across her brow. She sighed. "Even with my power, I cannot heal him completely. The fever should pass in a day or so. I dare not tax his strength too much." Her eyes turned towards Agnes. "This is only a very temporary measure, my lady. This must end… now. For your son and for the kingdom."

"What must I do?"

"Amalric de Lusignan has in his possession a certain ancient treasure of my people called the Seal of Solomon. I need to know where he has hidden it if I am to have any chance of defeating him and destroying the power of Sion."

Mary's answer startled her. She expected something a little more than just a simple question as a penance for her many sins. It also gave her a choice: she could betray the man she once had called lover, or she could give into the hand of that same man, a woman who was certainly his enemy. Either way, she needed only to give the Magdalen an answer to her plea.

"I know where it is."

† CHAPTER TWENTY-FOUR

Weeping, she hath wept in the night, and her tears are on her cheeks: There is none to comfort her among all them that were dear to her: All her friends hath despised her, and are become her enemies.
—Lamentations 1:2

The king, through his uncle the Seneschal, called for the reading of his will on the twelfth of March, the feast day of St. Gregory the Great. Being high in the councils of the king, Reynald de Châtillon already knew what the will contained, the provisions made for the succession of Baldwin's nephew to the throne. Many of the barons would be severely annoyed or outraged by its wording and the unstated mistrust Baldwin obviously had for his High Court. A much smaller few would be pleased. The will, however, for all he knew in advance, put Reynald in a difficult situation.

In effect, Raymond of Tripoli retained the Regency with the Seneschal acting as guardian for the younger Baldwin. Although it put the government in the hands of the Count until the child king reached his majority at fifteen, it stripped him of all temptation to the crown and kingship by setting all the royal castles under the control of the military orders. The sticking point to the whole mess came with the provision that came into play should the new king die prematurely. Here was the condition that made no one happy, except the dying king.

Blind, cripple, and too weak to even hold himself upright, Baldwin valiantly slumped on his throne, propped up with pillows to keep him from falling over. His family surrounded him on the dais: his mother, his uncle, his nephew, the heir apparent, even his sister and brother-in-law. Guion and Sibylla had come from Ascalone under a flag of truce. With the Patriarch traipsing through Europe, drumming up support for a new holy war, Heraclius' vicar in Jherusalem, Bishop Bernard of Lydda, had sworn he would make no moves for annulments or excommunications in his master's absence. Sion had rendered Baldwin powerless to do anything against the traitors.

Reynald's gaze settled on the crowd of assembled lords and ladies of Court; his wandering eye fell upon his wife. She stood near one of the columns rising towards the vaulted ribbed ceiling. She was deep in conversation with the comely daughter of one of the minor lords of the kingdom. The men—great lords that they were—rarely mingled with the women in Court.

An overblown courtier drifted between them. A redolence of heavy perfume hung in the air, mixing with the ever-present haze of incense. Reynald raised himself upon his toes, trying to peer over the many heads that separated him from Stephanie. The young maiden remained, having moved on to another lady and another conversation. Stephanie had disappeared. Reynald glanced around, ignoring the Seneschal as he read the will. He already knew its contents. A murmur of protest rumbled through the hall at the reading of one of the stickier points.

A hand touched him lightly at the elbow; an arm slipped under his and around his waist. "This is proving to be quite the drama. A spectacle worthy of any Greek poet," Stephanie whispered. "The king has a particular knack for annoying his lords, and yet, keeping them loyal. I, for one, will miss him when he's gone."

"Baldwin knows not to let any one person or faction think their position is more secure than the welfare of the kingdom."

Stephanie pulled a face; her dark, Occitan eyes glittered with wicked amusement. "With Guion in some measure of disgrace, Baldwin might have made you Regent for our young king-to-be, if you would have pushed the issue."

"He needs—" Reynald began, and caught the tone of his voice. "He needs the sword of a strong southern lord to support the claimant to the throne."

His wife jabbed him in the ribs. "Which my son would be quite capable to provide if you controlled the crown. Humphrey would be far more loyal to you than you have been to Baldwin," she said in a soft purr. "Sibylla and her sickly son are not the only royal heirs worthy of the throne."

"I promised Baldwin I would defend the kingdom," he said. "I can only do that by siding with the strongest faction—not by pursuing the Regency or the crown."

"What's happened to you, my darling? When you were Constance's plaything, you had ambition to spare as Prince of Antioch."

"Revenge and years of anger have a way of tempering a man's ambition. The day may well come when our ambitions will secure the throne to protect it, but for now, I will do what I can to prevent any division. Civil war will certainly come if the kingdom is divided."

His wife embraced him and whispered in his ear. Her soft breath distracted him; it was warm and arousing. "Power does not only rest in the man beneath the crown, my lord—sometimes, it is the man behind the crown who yields the greater power for good or evil. Isabella has a claim just as good as, if not better than, Baldwin or Sibylla; and her claim certainly has none of the... shall we say... entanglements of her brother's or sister's position. Isabella and Humphrey would provide stability to the throne—and they both could bring with them the support of lords no less than Reynald de Châtillon and Balian d'Ibelin, not to mention his wife, Maria Comnena."

Reynald chuckled morosely. "I thought you despised our former queen."

"I still do, my love," Stephanie said. She glanced up at him demurely. "But I love my son more. For the sake of Humphrey and his beautiful princess-bride, I can put aside my differences with Maria for a time, if necessary."

His wife's bluntness took Reynald back apace. He had never looked upon her as a particularly ambitious woman. Of course, he had only to look at the identities of her father and three former husbands to see that she would not have married such men if she were not. Stephanie was not some innocent heiress held up as prize to whatever lord could win her hand. As a great lady of the realm, she might not have ambition for herself, but for her children, she had an infinite supply. That mild-mannered, stately ambition had seen her eldest daughter packed off to Rupen III of Cilicia, and now, her son poised to reach for the throne of holy Jherusalem, if only he dared to reach for it.

"I hadn't realized my wife was so politically adept. Your father taught his daughters well in place of sons. I'll have to keep a closer eye on you, Stephanie de Milly."

"Trust me, my lord," she said, squeezing his thigh, "there are a great many things you have yet to learn about me."

* * * * *

Mary stepped from darkness into darkness in the Abbey of Mt. Sion. Powerful wards protected the door and the window. A silhouetted lampstand rose out of the floor beside her; moonlight spilled through the window in a white square on a richly patterned carpet. Her senses detected no trace of the man Baldwin had lured away by the reading of his will. She knew exactly where to look to find the object of her hunt.

Holding up her hand, she called forth fire. A faint glow of bluish-white light filled her palm. She discovered that the small study held far more than just the Seal of Solomon.

There were books and scrolls—a great many of them copies of texts she knew were a thousand years old—none of which surprised her a great deal given Amalric de Lusignan's secret identity. Among the texts, she found several leather-bound tractates and codices reputedly written by the Apostles and others among the first and second century Church—nothing that she had not come across before in her many long years of watchfulness.

Agnes' directions lead her to a small chest of ornately carved wood concealed behind a secret panel in the bookcase. Simon had hid it well. Pushing in a volume of St. Augustine's *De Civitae Dei*, The City of God—what else would Simon choose—she heard a faint *click* behind the shelving. A panel sprang loose. The handfire exposed a wooden chest in the dark recess. Mary stood there; numb and uncertain, wary of any trap the Master of Sion may have left as a defense against theft. She detected nothing in the hidden space, not even the seal.

Once she opened it, she found the box thickly lined with lead. She smiled. Simon had taken no chances. The lead shielded her senses. The seal lay in its midst, its bronze face and etchings of Hebrew script glinting in the bluish-white light of her handfire. At a thought, she felt its sudden presence wake. Released from the captivity of its lead prison, she could feel its ancient magic; its power grew when she took it into her hand. Her hand clenched around it. She could end it here, all the long years of grief and anger she had known in pursuit of Simon's demise. She had only to use the seal and see it done. However, she wanted the chance to see her enemy face to face, to see his face when she stripped him of his magic.

"Why not do so now, then, my lady Magdalen. I am here."

Mary turned to Amalric de Lusignan, throwing up a shield of magic in defense. She cursed Agnes de Courtenay for her treachery; the fire in her hand flared to a reddish-orange with her anger.

"I should have known she would betray me."

"Who betrayed you, Mary?" The candles on the stand suddenly lit with flames, casting shadows across the room. "Ah," he said and smiled. "The king's mother. It's not like you to make such a mistake, let alone two."

Her own thoughts had betrayed her just as they had betrayed Agnes. She took her time in answering, afraid to give too much away by her thoughts. "Two mistakes, Simon?"

He stepped towards her out of the shadows. "Did you think I wouldn't notice the seal's presence when you opened the chest?" he said. "Now, hand the seal over to me."

Mary had no choice but to flee. Gathering the darkness about her, she fled into the night. She felt Simon's malevolent presence pursuing her even in the grey space between the worlds. He chased her, though he could never quite catch her. She fought the temptation to use the Seal of Solomon against him.

Mary nearly stumbled into the altar in the chapel of Calvaire in Holy Sepulcher Church. She startled a pair of Benedictine brothers; Simon arrived a moment later, nearly catching her unawares. She fled again, stepping into the air between Jherusalem and Damascus, daring him to follow her into the lair of the lion. The murmur of the black-robed brothers of St. Benedictine mumbling prayers of angels and daemons followed them into the void.

The chase continued from church to mosque, from mountaintop to coast, from city to city throughout Outremer; Simon proved relentless in his pursuit. To him it was a game. She heard his laughter pursuing her through every dark corner she fled towards through the long night.

He had her briefly in the garden of the Lord's Passion.

Dawn brought the early morning crowds of pilgrims to the roads out of Jherusalem and the opportunity to end the chase. The untimely interference of a crowd of predawn pilgrims, however, bearing their candles along in procession towards the Cave of Gethsemane, allowed him to grab her arm.

She struggled as he drew her back into the grey shadows of the space between the worlds. She could hear the pilgrim chants rising from the ancient shrine that bound the worlds together.

"I grow tired of this game, Mary. Give me the seal," he demanded. His hot breath on her neck made her tremble. "Give it to me, or I'll simply kill you and take it from you."

As the pilgrims passed them by, she wrenched free of his grip and stomped his foot with her heel. She fled before he could grab her. He would follow in a moment. She needed a plan—a distraction. She knew exactly where to go—the one place where more daemons congregated than at any other place in the world. Rome.

Stepping down into the woven shadows of the Lateran Palace, Mary cast her thoughts ahead towards the brilliant sunlit gardens of her own place in elusive Eden. A moment later, Simon appeared and pursued her towards the East, unaware of her deception.

THE LEPER KING

Quickly, Mary held up the seal and summoned a minor devil to her command. For her plan to succeed, she needed to hurry. "In the strength of the Name, I command thee, Ornias, to come, for I hath need of thee."

With a shrieking whine of protest, the daemon flew to her—he had not too far to come—groveling and hissing at her feet with all manners of curses and blasphemies towards God for allowing her to have power over him.

"Silence," she commanded, and it fell as one dead at her feet. "Keep your tongue, or I will send you back to the pit of Hell where you belong. If you would be free from the seal's bondage, you need only give me your service in exchange. Are we agreed?"

"What doth thou biddest me to do?" whimpered the daemon Ornias.

"To lead the man who follows me here astray."

The daemon purred, hissing venomously. "For *this* you offer me freedom after two thousand years?"

"You were the first that Solomon bound to the seal," Mary said, holding the seal before the daemon's face. "Even Solomon in his wisdom would agree you have earned your freedom from it."

"Give me thy word you'll not cheat me," Ornias whined.

"It will be as I have promised," Mary said to the fallen creature's great pleasure.

She did not have long to wait for Simon's return. His anger made him blind with rage. Her heart beat rapidly, pounding in the echoing cavity of her breast. She could hear nothing else. She had rarely ever felt such panic or fear.

At once, the daemon attacked him, wrestling him back against a statue of a saint. The air around the daemon shimmered with light as Ornias blurred between fiend and lion as he pounced upon Simon. His leonine roar echoed through the church. Mary did not waste the tiniest moment by lingering to watch the battle. Drawing her power about her like a cloak, she stepped into the shadows of *between* and disappeared from Rome. By the time Simon freed himself of the daemon, she would be waiting for him at Machaerus.

* * * * *

The Count of Tripoli knelt at the foot Calvaire, praying for wisdom and for the soul of the dying king. The Prince of Antioch knelt at his side. Bohemond had little regard for religious matters, but he copied his cousin's pious example for the sake of the king. Behind them, filling out the hallowed chapel of the Lord's Passion, other knights knelt in a silent vigil for the king. A priest of the church led them in prayer; two white-robed boys stood by his side, censing the room with incense.

Even as he prayed, Raymond cursed the Court—no, his cousin, the king—for what they had done to restrict his power as Regent.

The midmorning vigil in the Church of the Holy Sepulcher was only a ruse to cover his greater plan already at work; he sent messengers the night before through a prearranged contact with an envoy from Damascus. The fact that he needed to send word at all was damning proof that the Court had had their way through the king and the wording of his will.

By right of birth and the king's decree, he would be Regent for the younger Baldwin—that much was assured; his power and his income, though, would be little more than what he already held as Count of Tripoli. Any hope of peace lay in his hands. With the likes of Reynald de Châtillon and Amalric de Lusignan at Court, war was a likely and inevitable probability. What he did, he did for the kingdom, not for himself. If he could insure peace for the space of a few years, he would do so, no matter the cost to his reputation.

His was a chosen duty to defend the Church against the enemies of Christ. Generation after generation of his family had seen too many pretenders make false claims of royal descent, albeit quietly in the innermost circles of influence for reasons of political exploitation. None more so than in the wake of the First War of the Cross, when the first Count of Tripoli, Raimon de Saint-Gilles, his great-great grandfather, had refused the crown as the first king of Jherusalem, while others eagerly sought it. Instead, Raimon sought only to serve, not to rule after the example of the Lord and his brothers.

Raymond rubbed his thumb over the enameled surface of his father's signet ring. It bore the *Chi-Rho* in scarlet and white, the initials of Christ. It was an heirloom of his family's ancient house from the days of Charlemagne. It reminded him of his current situation. Vicious rumors already flew about the city that he plotted to make himself king, hence the Court's desire to restrict his power. The sources of such gossip were ignorant fools; then again, they might very well be the weapons of his enemies. Too often the servants of the Cross had become the object of ridicule and scorn—even ones whose duties were sworn to secrecy. Few were the secrets the servants of Hell could not learn.

He had failed his cousin, the king, in keeping the forces of the pretenders at bay. They gathered about the dying king like vultures. Raymond knew the families that were part of the great messianic conspiracy—they were aged, revered names that had risen to prominence through the secret claims they made to restore an ancient house to its rightful inheritance. Wealthy, influential families that always seemed to hover like a shadow court around the crowned heads of Europe—names of families that even now threatened the security of Jherusalem's throne: names like Monthléry, Anjou, Payen, Blanchfort, Bouillon— and Lusignan.

Raymond *had* tried to serve the king—by force sometimes, if necessary—but still he had failed to keep the conspirators from getting close to the crown. The damage was done. He would not fail again, if he could help it.

Raymond turned his face upwards to the mosaic of the Savior glowing softly in the flickering, wan light of the prayer candles, pleading for an answer to his prayers. The large, round iconic eyes of the image seemed to hold some sadness as he gazed down on him. They were eyes that seemed to say, *'Blessed are the peacemakers, for they will be called the children of God'*. An answer of sorts— but not one would endear him to the enemies of the cross or the crown.

* * * * *

Agnes was frantic with worry and fear. She worried for her ailing son; she feared for her own life. Less than a day had passed since she had betrayed Amalric de Lusignan and the Order of Sion to the Magdalen, and she still waited for the swift sword of his wrath to fall against her.

Her husband, Renaud, the Lord of Sidon, had returned to Court with the other lords of the realm, to discuss Baldwin's will and to hold vigil for her son who lay dying in his bed. While Renaud remained away at Court, so too, would the traitor.

Agnes paced the carpeted floor of her private room in the Queen's Tower at the palace. Bells rang outside the window from the numerous churches about the city. They signaled the midmorning hour.

She swore under her breath; her words would have made even a knight blush. Where had her fool of a servant disappeared to now?

Her hands trembled; she rubbed them on the smooth fabric across her abdomen. A knock came at the door, one soft and hesitant. She startled; her gaze darted towards the sound. Her breath caught in her throat. "Come in."

Dura made her late entrance and bowed before Agnes. Agnes breathed a sigh of relief and lifted her Christian-Arab servant hastily by the hand. There was no time to scold the simple girl for her usual dawdling.

"Dura, my dear," Agnes said, giving the henna-dyed girl her sweetest smile. She handed her a small sealed envelope. "I need you to take this letter and find my daughter. This is urgent. You must find her at once. Do not let anyone distract you from your task. Do you understand?"

"*Oui, ma dame*," she replied and hurried away, remembering only at the door to curtsy. Agnes shooed her out the door and closed it behind her. She leaned against the dark paneled wood and sighed with deep relief. As much as she feared for her son, she feared more for Sibylla. Baldwin lay on his deathbed and had obviously known of his Constable's treachery for some time from the Magdalen; but Sibylla was married to Guion. Her fate remained inescapable; particularly with a Church and a wicked Patriarch who would make sure she remained so.

Agnes startled at the sudden knock at the door. Her heart leapt into her throat. She cursed Dura for her incompetence. "You stupid girl," she yelled through the door. "Simply find my daughter." Her hand clawed at the door handle and flung it open.

Amalric de Lusignan stood before her.

Her blood froze. His icy stare made her back away; he followed her through the door and closed it behind him. She had no escape. He had trapped her in her own room.

"My lord Amalric," she stammered, calling him by his given, Christian name. She made a slight nervous laugh. "You gave me a fright. I thought you were my cow of a servant. She's as forgetful as a stone."

Her former lover stepped closer and lifted a hand to her cheek. He fondled an earlobe. "My dear, dear Agnes, did you truly think I wouldn't learn what you've done?"

"What do you mean? What have I done, now? I assure you, my son's will is entirely his own doing. I couldn't persuade him from his choice."

"There is little use in hiding your actions from me. I've been at this game for a very, very long time," he said, shaking his head. "You reek of treachery."

She backed away from his hand and into the tall post of the bed. Her hands found their way around it and held the post firmly. "Treachery, Messire?" His accusation turned her fear into anger. "You dare to accuse *me* of treachery. You used me to work against my son. You promised me you would protect him and his rights as king. You never told me, though, that *you* are responsible for his leprosy. Your treachery was at work long before I ever heard of the Order of Sion. How dare you accuse me," she said and spit on him. "I trusted you and yet you lied to me about everything. I hope you rot in Hell."

Amalric's dark gaze fell upon her in a very disconcerting way. He stroked his beard. "You disappoint me, my lady," he said. "I offered you a chance at immortality—a chance to stay beautiful forever. Now, you risk it all for a child you cared little about until he inherited a throne."

"I would rather die, than sacrifice my son for your *gifts*."

"And die you shall, I assure you, my lady de Courtenay. Perhaps, sooner than you expect."

"At least I'll die in the knowledge that you will, too, soon enough. Your precious little seal is in her hands now. By the time you find her, it will be too late."

"Too late? I think not," he said, smiling wickedly. "If I didn't want the Magdalen to find the seal, do you really think I would have told you where it is hidden? I had hoped you would prove worthy of the secrets you have been given. Instead, you proved yourself weak and too attached to the things of the flesh. No matter. Your betrayal only made it easier to lure the Magdalen into my hand. Besides, I know her better than she thinks. If she truly had the power and strength of will to stop me, she would have done so by now. Thanks to you, I know *exactly* where to find her. Before I confront her, though, I have a few loose ends to attend to first."

Agnes had often thought that the sparkling depths of Amalric's dark eyes were his most handsome features—his eyes were what had first attracted her to him. Now, they held only terror. She turned away, her chin resting against her shoulder. His gloved hand lifted, grasping at the air. His fingers stiffened and curled, squeezing the breath from her throat like a gnarled claw. She gasped for air.

"No matter what other lies you believe me to have told, believe me when I tell you, my lady, I will enjoy nothing more than watching you slowly die."

Agnes tried to scream, but nothing came out—only the strangled sound of her own dying breath. Slowly she fell to the floor beside her bed, her fingers raking desperately at her throat for breath. She thought of her children; how she had brought them to ruin. It was her final thought before she slipped beneath the surface of consciousness into darkness and oblivion.

† CHAPTER TWENTY-FIVE

And I will destroy thy graven things, and thy statues, out of the midst of thee: and thou shalt no more adore the works of thy hands.
—Micheas 5:12

The stones of the crypt far beneath the ruins of Machaerus glowed orange-red in the flickering torchlight. By Mary's reckoning, morning had passed into afternoon, but the light in the ancient subterranean hall remained unchanged. All magic had fled this place. Only the power of the seal and slumbering bond that kept her daughter on the sword's edge between life and death, lingered in the air. Lesser magics hovered in the shadows of this long-forsaken place where the Baptist had died, but they were dormant or disinterested in the troubles of the present.

Simon knew she would be here, waiting. Yet even that could not bring her to fear. She had waited too long for this time—his time—to come.

Mary held Salome's lifeless hand. It felt cold. It had not always been so. She remembered that much from the past, like other, simple things. A laugh; a touch; a smile brighter than the sun at dawn. It was all she had left now of her daughter with the loss of the stone of memories. Salome was beautiful still, even in suspended death, just as she had been as a child. Mary's clearest memory was of her as a little girl with a crown of white and yellow flowers woven through the dark curls of her hair.

Although her daughter had all but died long ago, now Mary would suffer that loss again. This time, it would be her own doing. Tears blurred her eyes.

After more than a thousand years, the battle would end here, not with a sword, but with a single spoken word—a name. *Salome*. The ritual was complete, the command given. Her daughter's spoken name would release the magic of the seal, and the spell would break. First, though, she had to contend with the enemy.

Once, Simon used to taunt her with seeing Salome's enchanted body whenever she wanted, daring her to slay what was already slain. Hiding her away, however, proved an even greater wound to her grieving heart. Destroying Simon's power would not bring Salome back to life; it would not even destroy the Order of Sion, just as the fall of Jherusalem would not.

—Then what do we gain, my lady? Baldwin's voice echoed across the grey void between the worlds. His body lay alone in his great bed in the Tower of David in Jherusalem. It belonged to death now; his time was near.

Mary felt his presence. He waited in the grey shadow-realm where his power was greatest, and his body was almost whole. Here, he stood as tall as the warrior he should have been had not the machinations of Sion struck him down in his youth. Even in his weakness, the flame of his magic shone like a raging fire. It consumed his spirit as the spell that consumed his body. This last working of his magic would kill him, but he insisted on being with her even to the end.

Mary could hear the terrible weakness in his mortal voice. She blotted it from her thoughts. She looked down at her daughter's face. *We gain time, and the upper hand, my lord king, which we will need if the power of Sion is ever to be broken and destroyed.*

She did not want to think about how that would happen. She had enough to deal with at present. Even if she prevailed today against Simon, he might remain alive far longer than the allotted span of a mortal's life. Even a lion without claws could be dangerous—and deadly.

Therefore, Mary waited, knowing that he would come when he thought it most convenient and advantageous for him. It made the waiting all the more dangerous. He would not come lightly, knowing she had the seal and had not yet chosen to use it.

* * * * *

Tears stung Sibylla's eyes. She hid behind a column, waiting for Guion to return from Court. Anger burned through her blurring tears, concentrating on the door. She clutched the small dagger at her chest so tightly in her hand that her white-knuckled fingers began to go numb. She shook the tingling pain from her nervous hand and wiped a sleeve across her eyes. Her other hand held the crumpled letter her mother had sent to her earlier in the day. Sibylla feared that if she let it go, she would lose the nerve to carry through her plan.

A myriad of candles glowed about the room, lending their soft, flickering auras of amber light to the false mood she had created to lure

Guion into their bed; the sheets were strewn with blood-red rose petals. Sibylla prayed Guion would come to her without question.

It was not often that her husband came to her anymore without some word of enticement. She had long ago learned, as most women of high rank, that her husband took other women to his bed, and often. She could never fulfill his insatiable lust. As long as his heart belonged unwaveringly to her, she could overlook his many indiscretions. Her mother's letter, however, had changed everything...

Guion is not what he pretends to be. He does not love you. He uses you only to gain the throne in his own name... The Lusignan brothers and this Order of Sion of which I write have played us falsely... Your brother's death lies on their heads... Magic—not leprosy—devours him...

The words came back to her in brief snatches of memory that held no real meaning or understanding for her—except one: Guion and his brother, Amalric, must pay for their actions. It was a promise. She would begin with Guion for his betrayal. She owed that much to her dying brother.

Not long after midday—she remembered because she had just put her two daughters, Alix and Marie, down for a nap—her mother's servant girl, Dura, found her at the door of the women's solar. She had hoped to enjoy an hour or two of rest and sewing. She felt a sense of foreboding at hearing the urgency in Dura's voice.

Breaking the seal, she sunk down onto a bench as she slowly read the enclosed letter. Dura disappeared in the midst of her reading. The second reading brought a scream of anguish to her throat that she stifled only by bringing a fist to her mouth.

She knew what she must do. It filled the emptiness she felt. Only now, when anger gave way to a broken heart, would tears come to her eyes. The tears only angered her more.

Her daughters were still asleep in the nursery. It was long past their time to wake up. With the passing of the hour, the silence of the room, rather than leeching away at the iron-willed core of her emotions, stiffened her fierce determination to kill her husband as he had helped kill her brother. Later, she would consider the consequences of her actions.

A noise echoed outside the door— Guion's voice. Her body shuddered and tensed with sudden fear and anxiety.

Her hand closed tighter around the hilt of the dagger. It rose slowly to her chin. Sweat beaded across her brow and shoulders, trickling down her spine. The heat of the flickering candles grew hotter.

Guion whispered her name lustfully. Fabric rustled as he removed his outer tunic and flung it aside. His shadow crept past her hiding place behind the column. She closed her eyes, drawing herself further back into the shadows.

She lunged.

Guion turned at the last moment with the trained instinct of a knight and soldier. The blade bit into his left shoulder and held fast as she fell past him. He cried in pain and blind rage. The dagger clattered across the floor. She had failed.

He grabbed her by the hair as they both spun with the force of the blow and threw her down on the flower-strewn sheets. She scrambled back, kicking, and crying; he grabbed her legs and dragged her towards him, straddling her body on the bed. Thrashing wildly, she slapped him hard.

"You stinking whore," he sneered and backhanded her across the cheek. Pain exploded in her head. He grabbed the throat of her gown and tore the bodice open, baring her naked body beneath him. "You want to play games with me—I'll give you a game you'll not soon forget."

"Get off me, you bastard," she cried, pulling a corner of the sheets across her exposed chest.

"Better a bastard, than a whore's get."

"I hate you," she screamed, her anger all but spent. "How could you do this to me?"

"It's simple enough, Sibylla. I don't love you," said Guion, bending down to kiss her shoulder. "I never loved you."

His words pierced her heart like the cold blade of a sword. "You used me as well as my brother to gain the throne. How long did you and Amalric think you could go without someone finding out? Why did you have to kill my brother?"

"You have a vivid imagination, my dear."

She shoved the letter from her mother in his face. "This says differently, *messire.*"

"What is this?"

"A letter from my mother explaining everything about you, your brother, and your Order of Sion. Do you still think I'm imagining all this?"

Guion sat back on his heels, staring at the letter. He sighed and smiled. He flung the letter aside. Several candles fell off their stand and went out. "That was a mistake on her part. The kind that can end in a person's death."

Sibylla felt the subtle, threatening tone in his voice. The sheet in her hand twisted into a knot. "You wouldn't dare! If I die, you'll never have the throne."

"I'm sorry, Sibylla, I didn't mean you," he said. "Haven't you heard? Dura found your mother dead in her room a short while ago. She seems to have died in her sleep. That's why my brother sent me to find you."

Fresh hot tears sprang to her eyes. Sibylla tried to slap him again, and again. He laughed at her. His hand lunged at her throat and pinned her to the bed, squeezing, as he pulled the sheet from her hand. Touching a hand to his wounded shoulder, he smeared the blood on her face and breast, and kissed her roughly. She spat on his face. He slapped her again and laughed.

"If you so much as whisper a word of your mother's accusations or try to betray me, I will mingle the blood of your daughters with your own," he said, kissing the smooth curve of her neck just beneath her earlobe. His breath felt hot on her skin. His own cruelty aroused him.

"Please, Guion," she cried, cringing beneath his body. "I'll do whatever you tell me. Just don't hurt Alix and Marie."

"Swear to it," he breathed into her ear and slapped her hard.

Tears sprang to her eyes. "I swear it."

* * * * *

Baldwin had only to reach out into the grey between the worlds and he could touch the ancient magic in the stones of Machaerus, just as he could feel Mary's presence beside her daughter. He felt the heaviness of her heart, the sorrow that threatened to draw her away from the world of men forever. All he could do was offer his thoughts as company. It was enough that he cared and would soon release her from her long torment.

All morning and throughout the afternoon, a steady stream of visitors made their way to his bedside to pay their last respects. Even his quiet cousin, Bohemond, came from distant Antioch with Raymond of Tripoli to offer his prayers. It was a magnanimous gesture given Bohemond's well-known disdain for religion and the Church in general.

No one troubled him with news of his mother's death. He just knew. He sensed her sudden fear of not knowing her fate—whether it would be Heaven or Hell. He had long known the Church's teaching concerning Purgatory and the expiation of a person's sins, but he also knew from Mary that such beliefs were nonsense.

Christ had promised the thief beside him on the cross that he would be with Him in Paradise that day because of his faith. Mary had heard the Savior's words herself from the foot of the cross. There would be no release from Hell for his mother on account of her good works; she had refused the Christ as the Savior of man. She would be condemned forever, separated from God, and tormented by the eternal fires of Hell.

Both he and Mary grieved for each other. He had lost his mother; she would soon lose her daughter again. Each had lost a loved one to the man who claimed to be Amalric de Lusignan.

By late afternoon, the line of visitors through his room had dwindled to nothing. For that, he was grateful. He ordered the doors closed and guarded. He rested and tried to eat the simple porridge Cook had brought in for him. His stomach refused it. After choking up the food and blood, his doctor gave him a physic to help him sleep. What sleep he got was fitful and restless.

He startled awake to find a familiar, yet unwanted, guest in his darkened quarters. Guion had a taper and was making the round about the room, lighting the candles for the evening. Blind as was, he knew Guion by the whisper of his footsteps, by the odor of his sweat, and the small, imperceptible habits that others might easily miss. The scent of blood filled the room; the blood was his, which he certainly found strange, if not disturbing for what it might portend.

Baldwin lay propped on a nest of pillows to ease his breathing. Only a thin sheet covered the skeletal, disease-riddled remains of his once strong body. He wore no veil to hide his face. He no longer cared what men thought of him. They knew little of his suffering, only that he was a leper. He let them see what he had mercifully hidden from them the last eleven years while he wore the crown. The scented candles served to mask the stench of his rotting flesh, not to provide light.

His halting, whisper of a voice caught Guion off his guard. "Have you come, my lord of Ascalone, to gloat over your brother's triumph in my death?"

"I thought to see for myself the truth of it," he said, and added, "Your Majesty."

Baldwin coughed with mild amusement. Black blood smeared the cloth. "Are you pleased, then, by the hideousness and ruin of what you see before you?"

"You still live. It would suit me better if that were not so."

"I'm sorry I disappoint you, Messire," Baldwin said. "Take heart, my death won't be long in coming I'm told. Even then, you still will have not won my throne. I've made sure of it."

Guion circled the bed lighting the candles; he bent close, whispering in Baldwin's ear. "I assume you refer to your pathetic attempt at a will. A clever bit of maneuvering, I must say, Your Majesty. It matters only as long as my stepson lives to inherit the throne. Once Sibylla is crowned queen, the kingdom will be mine."

Mary listened to their conversation with intent and concern. She urged him to caution with the arrogant Lusignan upstart. *Be careful how you answer, Baldwin. He is baiting you. Do not provoke him.*

—Guion is not the one we have to fear, my lady. He has no stomach for regicide. He is only a puppet of his brother.

Baldwin turned his hollowed eyes towards Guion. "Your brother uses you as a pawn, my lord, and you don't even know it. Everything you think you know… is a lie. My death will not further your ambitions, Guion… it will only hasten your demise," he said in his halting, whispering mockery of a voice. He felt the disgust and contempt his brother-in-law had towards him and his leprosy. "You and your brother have under… underestimated me and the protection of this kingdom."

"If you refer to your precious Magdalen, she is no match for Amalric, as she is about to discover. Both of you will die this day at the hand of Sion, just as your mother has," said Guion. Baldwin's gnarled and fingerless hands twisted the sheets into fisted balls. Guion noticed. "I am sorry, Your Highness, has no one told you of your mother's unexpected demise? I heard she died a violent death. One your sister can certainly expect if she tries to stand between the throne and me. It is mine by a right of blood stretching back much further than even your own."

Baldwin was thankful that his eyes were beyond the ability to see. He had had enough of Guion de Lusignan and his aspirations for the crown. He would rather slay the Poitevin where he stood with the same magic that had killed his mother. "Get out, my lord of Ascalone, before I order you thrown in prison for the rest of your miserable life."

Guion left willing enough. He had done what he had wanted to do in coming: torment him with the knowledge that he would sit upon his thrown. Baldwin, though, had knowledge of things that Guion would not believe. "Enjoy your reign, *King of Jherusalem*," he whispered to the empty room, "for it will last less than a year."

* * * * *

Mary felt Baldwin weakening with each passing hour of her strange vigil at her daughter's side. She felt his weakness, just as she felt his fear at Guion's threats against Sibylla and his grief over the unexpected loss of his mother in sacrificing her life to lure Simon into the trap laid for him.

There was at least one consolation for Baldwin: he would witness the downfall of Simon's power through her.

—He is here, she called to the dying king. She felt his grief again over the death of his mother. She hated to disturb him. His blind eyes gazed at her in that place, acknowledging her warning.

—I am ready.

"How long to you plan on waiting in the shadows, *Messire* de Lusignan?" she asked, taking hold of her daughter's hand one last time.

Simon moved far more quickly than any mortal could. He stood opposite her across the stone-cut bier in the space between one breath and another. Her hand tightened on the hilt of the silver sword she held at her side.

"I thought I would give you a few moments with your daughter," the Constable of Jherusalem replied. "I hadn't realized you were in such a hurry to die, my dear Mariamne."

She glanced up at him. "You dare threaten me, knowing I possess the Seal of Solomon? You are bold, indeed, Simon Magus, if not foolish. The spell is cast, the command given. I need only to speak my daughter's name, and your spell will break. The Seal will release her from your bondage. Your power is all but broken, Simon."

The man behind the living mask of Aimery de Lusignan's face laughed at her. "If that were so, your hatred for me would have ended this already. I doubt you have the strength of will to carry out this charade."

Mary turned away, her gaze falling to the closed eyes of Salome. She looked so peaceful, so at rest, ready to awake at any moment. One word, one spoken name, separated Mary from a millennium-long search for vengeance against her most hated enemy.

Salome, she thought. *Forgive me.* "You are here by your own power only because I wished to confront you one last time."

"I'm sorry, my lady," he said, his voice thick with condescension, "are you under the belief I am here because you think you somehow lured me here? Do you honestly think I would let you find the seal so easily? —Or let you escape?" He shook his head as he walked around the bier towards Salome's feet. Mary moved in response, stopping above her daughter's head. She stroked Salome's long dark hair. "That was a clever trick, though, sending a daemon to waylay my pursuit. What did you offer him—his freedom? It almost worked. You should have sent a daemon with more power, though, if you wanted to stop me. I suspect he's tormenting some poor, pathetic monk in England with dreams of beautiful, young river nymphs." He smiled annoyingly. "You doubt me?"

"It matters little to me how you came to be here, Simon—only that you came, as I needed," she replied, letting the faintest hint of a smile play at the corners of her mouth.

Simon laughed, thoroughly amused, but she felt a sudden fear rise in his thoughts. "Clever, my lady. It seems I underestimated your skill of deception, even after all these years. Is that some spiritual gift of your faith—the ability to lie and deceive? Certainly, it is not a quality all Christians share; except of course, for those in Rome."

"What I know of deception, dearest Simon, is what I have observed in you," Mary said. Her hand slid from her daughter's head to her shoulder. She glanced up into Simon's dark eyes. "And this is the cruelest work of your deception."

"Then you have learned well, indeed, my lady Magdalen," he said, laying a hand lightly upon Salome's feet. "Have you told your pet king that you are the last heir of your ancient house—that you have a better claim to his throne than he? Or have you left that out?"

Mary struggled to control her anger against his twisted accusations. Her heart raced, pounding in her ears. "Baldwin is the rightful king of Jherusalem. The heirs of the Hasmonean crown lost that right when we betrayed our people to our enemies," she said, keeping her voice calm. "Only those of the House of David have the right of the throne. Ours was a priestly line never meant to reign as kings, no matter how well it did so."

"What a noble sentiment. It's a shame your father's house didn't share your opinion."

"What I've done, I did to protect Baldwin from those who would use him for their own means, just as you have used your fellow members in the Order of Sion and their long-held ambitions to your own ends."

Simon glared at her. He sighed with annoyance. "It is enough for now that we share similar goals in regards to your false Messiah's claims."

With each word they spoke, Simon took a small step around the bier, trying to get closer. Mary watched him warily, waiting for him in case he tried to grab her. He paused each time she glanced up at him. Her hand tightened on the sword in her hand. She was afraid.

"Where is the Cup of Christ?"

"In a safe place. One you'll never find," he said with a smile and struck at her with the subtle agility of a deadly serpent. Even with her vigilance, he took her by surprise. His hand closed around her throat. Her sword fell useless against his iron grip to the ground. She could not speak or breathe. He would strangle her if she even tried.

"Your obsession for vengeance has become your own downfall, my dear Mariamne. If only you would bow to me and serve me, I might choose to restore your king's worthless life."

—*Serve you?* *She laughed sarcastically in his thoughts.* **To what purpose? So you can slay me, as you have done to others of my kind. I would rather die first.**

"Kill you? —Hardly, my dear. Give me the seal or you will serve me as your daughter has these past thousand years."

Mary laughed at his blind arrogance. **Simon, Simon, did you truly think me foolish enough to trust my own heart to do this? Kill me now if you wish. Either way, you will see how your own deception and treachery has caused your downfall.**

Drawing her power inwards, she called out through the grey space to her dying friend, the true King of Jherusalem.

* * * * *

—**Salome,** *Baldwin shouted with all this strength into the grey shadows bordering the world where he stood whole and healed, his body having cast off its semblance of leprosy and death. The Seal of Solomon blazed with a blinding light as he spoke the dead woman's name.*

A rush of wind and noise rose through the crypt at the sound of Salome's name. Light gathered from every corner of the crypt, swirling in a raging tempest around the bier; her body burst into sudden flames as the spell broke with a roar.

Simon Magus threw Mary aside to protect himself from his unexpected assailant. He laughed at them and drew his sword. **Enjoy your victory, my dear Mariamne Alexandra, for it will be short-lived.**

Mary's arm shot out, throwing Simon backwards into the air against the wall, and he disappeared. Mary collapsed beside the charred remains of her daughter's clothing and wept.

In breaking the spell, however, it had unleashed a daemon to destroy the bearer of the seal.

Simon Magus had planned well for any threat against his life.

With a hideous, fiendish shriek, a shadow unfolded before him into the wings and face of a daemon. Baldwin raised his sword in both hands, poised to defend himself against the spirit of Hell.

Eyes like burning embers flared with the daemon's laughter. Its taloned hand drew a sword of orange-red flame out of the air; smoke and fire and choking, sulfurous fumes enveloped them in the darkened prison-crypt of Machaerus.

—We meet again, King of Jherusalem. This time thou wilt suffer death, as thou should have on the field at Montgisart.

Baldwin slowly raised his sword, pointing it at his infernal adversary. I **command you in the name Jhesú Christ to leave this unholy place.**

—You, nor the Son of God, have any power to command me, *the fiend of Hell laughed with a hideous, shrieking whine.*

The daemon's flaming sword swung at Baldwin's head, missing only by a hair's breadth. His arm shuddered with the blow as it fell upon his sword. Sparks and lightning lit up the prison cell. It illuminated Mary's tear-streaked face as she huddled on the dusty floor. Baldwin struck back, a glancing blow that caught the daemon across its shoulder. The daemon shrieked and howled in anger and pain.

Baldwin summoned all the power his magic held and attacked the shadow creature with a fury. He pushed his attacker back against a column cracked and faded with age. Only for a moment, though, as the creature lunged back at him, driving him towards the bier where Salome had once lay.

As the daemon battled his body, fear and doubt besieged his mind. His thoughts sunk into a mire of dark images that threatened to drive him mad. The dead faces of those he loved most; his kingdom in ruins, Jherusalem in flames. Baldwin fought back, raging against the red-eyed angel of Hell.

The more he struggled, though, against the daemon, the stronger the fiend seemed to become. Time after time, he struck with his sword, but he received just as many blows in return.

They were evenly matched, he and the dark spawn of Satan; it was odd that it should be so, for the daemon loomed over him, cloaked in smoke and the black shadows of the nether world. Stroke matched stroke; blow fell upon blow. Neither gave or gained ground to the other. Even in the grey space where his magic made him whole, he knew he would eventually weaken and the daemon would not.

Mary tried repeatedly to call to him, but the clamor of battle drowned out her voice. At the last, in a moment of brief and sudden silence amid the clash of arms, he caught a single word of her thoughts and acted without hesitation.

—Flee.

Gathering his thoughts of Jherusalem and the Church of the Holy Sepulcher, Baldwin fled, trying to gain the advantage of sacred ground. The enemy boldly followed.

In the church, the priests were about their nightly duties, singing the offices of prayer. Candles illuminated the nave and the Rotunda. The priests were oblivious to their clash of swords as they battled towards the entrance and the steps into the Chapel of Calvaire. The canons and monks of the church saw and heard only shadows and whispers of noise that they attributed to the angelic hosts of Heaven defending the holy shrines of the Savior's Passion. Piously making the sign of the cross upon their heads and breasts, the reverend clergymen returned to their prayers, but not without keeping an eye or ear to their surroundings, hoping to catch a glimpse of the divine combatants.

Slipping on the polished marble floor, Baldwin fell back against the Stone of Unction where tradition claimed Christ's body had been prepared for burial. The fiery sword of the daemon struck the stone casing beside his head, casting off a shower of sparks into the air heavy with incense. Rolling backwards over his head, Baldwin brought his sword up to defend himself; the daemon leapt atop the Anointing Stone brandishing his fiery sword.

—Do you truly believe this place holds any power over me? It is but stone and mortar and the wishful imagination of man's foolish thought, *whined the daemon, and hurled itself at him.*

Weaving together candlelight, shadow, and incense with his magic, Baldwin threw up a glimmering wall between him and his attacker. The fiend shrieked as it flew against the ward and fell. Its howl of rage terrorized the chanting priests. Using the few moments he had gained to think, Baldwin turned and ran for the steps of Calvaire.

In the shadowy grey borderland between the worlds of men and magic, the church looked far more different. Stones and walls, long ago removed, stood as faint silhouettes demarcating the lines of an ancient power. The white columns of a shaded portico surrounded a courtyard filled with the hazy warm light of the sun. From the great double-doors at the eastern entrance to the floating dome of the Rotunda, the focus of the earlier church looked to the empty tomb of Christ, not the cross.

The rebuilt church had weakened the sacred power of the older, larger Byzantine basilica. Decades of natural magic left long untended had formed stagnant pools that fouled the air of the holy site. Miracles had ceased in the church shortly after the arrival of the first Warriors of the Cross and the first renovations on the church they began.

The Holy Sepulcher of Emperor Constantine's grand basilica glowed in the grey void with a soft amber radiance that reflected the glory of Paradise. Once, a gateway had opened at the tomb between Heaven and Hell with the shedding of sacred blood—divine blood. Even after a thousand years and more, the stones of the church still held the gateway open.

In the world of shadow, however, Calvaire had become one of those stagnant pools of sickly green light. He felt it immediately as he stumbled in the shrine with the daemon in close pursuit. The greenish light made him feel weak and sick, confused.

He turned at the top of the narrow stairway alongside the large rock of the crucifixion to face the servant of Hell. A blow sent him sprawling atop the shrine of Calvaire. Rolling slowly onto his back in pain, his eyes glanced heavenward and to the mosaic of Christ for help. Blood trickled from his split lip.

Baldwin cast aside his sword. He refused to fight any further. The fiend's eyes glared bright red; it stretched out its huge, black leathery wings and beat the air menacingly. It thrust out its hand, grabbed Baldwin by the throat, and lifted him in the air; Baldwin fought back. The daemon raised a sword to Baldwin's breast. They struggled over it, each trying to gain the advantage and run the other through with the blade. Baldwin choked on the daemon's foul and noxious breath; it reeked of death and sulfurous fumes. His strength began to fail against his overpowering enemy. Its taloned hands grasped Baldwin's sword-arm and wrenched him to the ground.

—Do battle with me, little king, or die.

Baldwin shook his head and knelt on the floor. The air about him changed as he tried to use his remaining magic to bring him to a place of safety, but fear and doubt brought him only to failure. The daemon howled its victory. Weak and weary with battle, Baldwin finally began to understand the source of the daemon's strength. It was the same as that at Montgisart. Fear.

His sudden doubt broke the power of his magic. It shattered like a pane of stained glass; it collapsed in upon itself, shrinking to the tiniest ember of fire. He began to feel the weakness of his spell-riddled body. Fresh wounds appeared among the innumerable sores of the leprosy; his hands and feet bled from where the sword pierced them after the fashion of the Savior's. Blood welled from his side.

—Begone, fiend of Hell, *Baldwin cried.* **I have no fear of you. You can do nothing to me, except what I allow through my own fears.** *He held up the glowing Seal of Solomon and intoned a command the daemon could not refuse.* **In the name of Christ and the power of the Seal whose power you know, I command you to return to the pit of Hell.**

Darkness descended suddenly with his words in the chapel of the cross. A rumble echoed from the deep bowels of the earth. It shook the church to its very foundations; the floor cracked with a terrifying noise. The air itself seemed to split asunder. Baldwin scrambled away from the narrow chasm that opened between them. He pressed his back against the Rock of Calvaire, praying for help of any kind.

The dark spirit, knowing its time had come, raised his fiery sword to strike Baldwin down. A hand's width from his face, a flash of magical light from Mary's thin sword blocked the blow as she stepped suddenly from the air. She cast the fiend back and shouted a command: **Begone, Asbiyel. Go back to thy master whence you came.**

With a piercing, desperate wail, an unseen force tore the daemon from the shadowy spirit realm and dragged it down through the crack in the floor to the pit of Hell and the everlasting fire below. The crack slammed shut, leaving the church as it was before, but the daemon's hideous shriek echoed through the nave, even after it had disappeared, sending the faithful priests scurrying for safety from the visitations of the hellish fiends of the night.

With the daemon defeated, the last remaining strength of Baldwin's magic failed him. The ineffable name of God glared brilliantly on the seal with a reddish light; the light streamed through his fingers, even after he covered it with his hand. Everything went black around him.

A hand lifted his head and cradled him. He was beyond understanding what had befallen him. He drifted in a dream. Battle raged all about him. His men were dying, but the Sarrazins had lost far more to his charge. Darkness and rain covered the land in a grey shadow.

The battle had an ordered chaos to it; war had that quality. He limped through the heart of the battlefield, unnoticed. Dead men, and those far closer to death than life, littered the ground. Most were Muslims. Although they were the enemy, he felt for them. They were men, the same as he, defending what they loved. Blood soaked the ground; Muslim and Christian blood. Baldwin was drenched with it. He had lost his sword at some point along with his helmet and shield. The Muslims were in flight. Weak from combat and the loss of blood, he collapsed in the midst of the field.

A sudden chill swept over the field of his victory—a darkness that blinded them born of fear and doubt and the stark terror of their dreams. Lightning flashed across the heavens; thunder rumbled through the earth. Only Baldwin could see the source of the darkness. It centered on a daemon locked in battle with an angel armored in silver, wielding a sword of purest light. A cross overspread the skies above their heads. Suddenly, the daemon fell beneath the angel's sword. Light split the heavens at its fall and the malevolent darkness scattered. The shadows fled. Rain still fell upon the battlefield, but it brought with it a cleansing that washed the world of the stench of blood. The angel called to him with the voice of the Magdalen.

—Baldwin, she called to him. **Baldwin. Arise; shine, for thy victory has come.**

He awoke abruptly. Candlelight shone brightly about him—he could smell the hot beeswax. Voices echoed nearby; the chanting of brothers singing the offices of prayer. His senses reeled, causing him terrible confusion. Had he died?

In his mortal blindness, he felt a sudden fear; he struggled to move, to escape. His mind and his body were too weak to command. A woman's hand held him.

"Baldwin," Mary whispered. "You are not dead. You still live."

Baldwin grabbed her hand, felt the warmth of solid flesh and blood. "Did... did we win? Were we victorious at Montgisart?"

"Montgisart was eight years ago, Baldwin. Do you remember nothing of this night?"

A flicker of memory returned. The daemon. The seal. The dim memory of it swelled in his thoughts and blossomed into a profusion of connected events that had filled the evening.

—Salome, he shouted into the familiar grey space of the worlds.

"Did... did she... did he...?"

"You defeated him, Baldwin," Mary said. Her arm wrapped tighter around him. "Simon's power is broken. He is Amalric de Lusignan now. And so shall he remain until death claims him."

The memory of his ordeal returned, and with it, the hurt and pain he had endured. *His mother's death; Guion's threats against Sibylla and his nephew, the anointed heir of Jherusalem.* He had not failed, but he had not won, either. Sion would accomplish its goals for a season, but Salehdin would also accomplish his. He could do no more, except to await his death. At least Mary would be with him.

—You have done so much more than save Jherusalem, Your Majesty. Nothing you have done with your life has ever been in vain.

He understood her meaning as well as her tears that came in abundance.

—Take me home, my lady*, he whispered.*

Mary gathered him in her arms and cast her thoughts towards the Tower of David. The priests sang the office of Compline, ushering in the Great Silence of the night.

In te, Domine, speravi;
non confundar in aeternum:
in justitia tua libera me...

In thee, O Lord, have I hoped,
Let me never be confounded: deliver me in thy justice.
Bow down thy ear to me: make haste to deliver me.
Be thou unto me a God,
A protector and a house of refuge, to save me.
For thou art my strength and my refuge;
And for thy name's sake thou wilt lead me, and nourish me.
Thou wilt bring me out of this snare,
Which they have hidden for me: for thou art my protector.
Into thy hands, I commend my spirit:
Thou hast redeemed me, O Lord, the God of truth...

† EPILOGUE

Call for the mourning women, and let them come:
and send to them that are wise women, and let them make haste.
Let them hasten and take up a lamentation for us:
let our eyes shed tears, and our eyelids run down with waters.
—Jeremias 9:17-18

M ary speaks…

      Baldwin is dead. Sibylla buried him at the foot of Calvaire beside his father and the other kings of Jherusalem. At last, he is at peace in the presence of our Lord in Heaven. This I know, for I held his weak and trembling hand in those final moments with Sibylla as Michael the Archangel himself, and an army of shining angels led him away into Paradise. So passes the saddest chapter in the short history of these Christian kings who came so boldly out of the darkest West to wrestle the holy city of Jherusalem from the fist of the Muslims.

      Of those whom I have called to help defend the Light, I will mourn him as I have mourned few others. He truly was the bravest, the most noble of the knights of Christ. His people loved him dearly; the Muslims honored him as a king who knew how to make his authority respected. He was, indeed, a rare light in this age of darkness, where unbelievers hold to a greater truth of love, while Christians spread only bloodshed and war. Despite his best effort to pursue peace, though, Jherusalem will fall to the army of Islam as ordained by God. Until then, I must watch over Sibylla and her children.

      Summer is upon us in all its infernal misery. It is the feast day of my sainthood. If only the Church truly knew me, they might think differently. Everything is circling quickly now towards its consummation. The younger Baldwin reigns as king after his uncle—another sick king to stand between Sion and its prize. Mosul and northern Syria presently occupy Salehdin's attention, but he will return once he hears of Baldwin's death.

I fear most for the young king's life. Simon will surely exact a terrible vengeance on those under my care for his loss. It is not enough that I lost my daughter forever. The Order of Sion will not run to ground for very long; the conspirators are far too close to their seeming success to allow Raymond of Tripoli to gain too tight a grip on the crown. Through it all, either Sion will triumph or it will destroy itself. Baldwin's sacrifice has crippled its power, but it continues in its plans to set a creature of its own making upon the throne of Jherusalem. That miserable creature can only be Guion de Lusignan. He is as crafty as he appears inept; a man without a shred of love within him that is not devoted to himself. He is not a man who should be king, and yet, I have no doubt he will. How could I have been so blind not to see how far the ambitions of the conspiracy had already reached?

Even as I speak, the warning of my dearly departed friend, William, has come true: a rebellion certainly encouraged by the Order of Sion, has overthrown the House of Comnenus in Constantinople and replaced it with another, the Angeloi, the family of one of the Order's members.

Perhaps in my zeal for Sion to expose themselves by their carelessness, I refused to see the full measure of their conspiracy. Still, I regret that I could not tell Baldwin everything. He, of all people, deserved to know the whole about Sion, and my part in it. But even to him, dear friend that he was, I could not trust revealing the hidden most secret of my past, or how I used him to lure Simon out of the shadows by not healing his leprosy when I had the chance. Secrets are the greatest power and I could not let Simon learn mine from Baldwin's thoughts in a chance, unguarded moment. His death, and his terrible suffering, however, is on my head. May God judge me if I sinned.

Regardless of my guilt or innocence, I cannot let Baldwin's death be in vain. He lived long enough and ruled wise enough, to frustrate Sion's plans; he broke Simon's power when I could not. Whether or not Simon is truly bereft of all his power, I do not know. I wonder even now, what truly happened in the crypt beneath Machaerus. In order to keep Simon from ever using the Seal of Solomon again, I set it inside the same lead box in which I found it and hid it with Baldwin in his tomb. To that end, it falls to me now to prevent Sion from gaining any more influence or power.

While the forces of providence circle and collide about Jherusalem, I keep watch with the sisters of Saint-Anne's convent near the Gates of Jehoshophat, knowing the end is coming soon. I am weary from grief and the use of magic. Even now, the mist and grey shadows of Faërie surround me, drawing me from my prayers in the chapel. I dare not rest, though, for there have been too many casualties in this long war, but I must. There is still too much I have yet to do.

I will wait out this new season of uncertainty by ministering to the women among the pilgrims visiting the holy city. Many are sick and elderly. They have come to die in the place their Savior died. On the faces of so many of them, I see their beloved Mary, Deo Mater, the Mother of God, who has become the object of so much devotion in these past many years—another sign of the influence of the enemy.

I know not why God has called me to defend His Church against heresy. I have proven myself a poor defender of the faith. My blood alone makes me the least likely vessel of His most holy will. I pray, even now, before the symbol of His grace and mercy, that He will send another to stand with me in the hour of my need, to help defend and protect the Church in this uncertain time.

I am alone now, even among the aged sisters who are but children to me; but I will abide here in the city, dividing my time between prayer at Saint-Anne's and ministering to the poor in the Hospital for Women, waiting upon the answer of God to my prayers. Perhaps, He has already and I am too fearful to recognize it. Only yesterday, as I bandaged the raw and tortured soles of the women's feet—the Abbess tells me I have some skill in healing—a vision came to me. I Saw a very young man on a horse, wearing the colors of Ibelin, a stranger with a Christian face and Muslim eyes. He looked up at me and smiled, as if he knew me. I watched him: his face and the gleaming brightness of his mixed-colored eyes have haunted me since.

I will not quickly forget his face. I will remember him when I see him again this unnamed child of my dreams with the magic of faeries in his blood. In this land of such ancient histories and so much mixed blood between Europe and the East, there seems always to be some unnoticed heir to the magic that once filled the earth with such abundance. I see him, a child as bright as the morning sun in its rising. He will prove a powerful friend in the never-ending war with the powers of darkness. His name remains hidden from me for now, but I will know him when the time comes for his revealing.

I, who am Mary Magdalen, tell you these things; Mariamne, called apostle and saint, priestess, prostitute, princess, and daughter of Satan, promise I will not desert these hapless Christians of Jherusalem, even in the day their kingdom falls.

AUTHOR'S NOTE

BALDWIN IV was indeed an historical king of Crusader Jerusalem—and he was a leper. He was born in 1161 and ruled between 1174 and 1185. He died at the age of twenty-three. Until recently, historians have long looked upon Baldwin's reign as a period of decline that culminated in the disastrous loss of the kingdom to Saladin at the Battle of Hattin. As the king succumbed to his disease, so too did the kingdom. Historians thought the young king a weak and ineffectual ruler who, because of his disabling infirmity, could not keep his conniving lords at bay. Even William of Tyre, Baldwin's tutor and Chancellor, wrote that those closest to him easily manipulated the king. Certainly, this is an odd observance given the opinion of a personage no less than Imad ad-Din Isfahani, a Muslim chronicler of the time, who expressed the view that Baldwin was a king who "knew how to make his authority respected"—among his own people and among his enemies.

Fortunately, modern scholarship has begun to see Baldwin's reign as a brief period of stability and growing prosperity in the face of war—a view that certainly throws into sharper contrast the unexpected and devastating loss of Jerusalem by Guy de Lusignan only two years later. As for his illness, it must have come as a complete shock to the kingdom. Leprosy is a disease that slowly comes upon a person from long exposure—hardly a condition one would expect from a prince born of royal blood. It is certain that the Crusaders held a far more tolerant opinion of the disease than did the Muslims or the rest of Western Christendom. In a bull issued by Pope Alexander III in 1181 calling for new crusade to the Holy Land, he expressed his solemn opinion that the king was "severely afflicted by the just judgment of God."

As for Baldwin's own people, they saw their young ruler as a hero and a savior. They loved him and mourned his death greatly no matter whether he was a leper or not. In a time of war, the barons of the Christian kingdom unanimously stood by Baldwin's claim to the crown by electing him king. Quite easily, he could have refused the throne or laid aside the crown as he so often desired in later years and no one would have thought any ill will towards him. Repeatedly, despite his leprosy and continual bouts of malarial fever, he proved the worth of his election to the throne and managed to help keep Saladin from his treasured prize of Jerusalem for more than a decade. As to how or why he contracted leprosy at such a young age is a mystery, especially since he spent most of his youth under the personal tutelage of Archbishop William in Tyre. Perhaps, a nurse or close childhood friend infected him—or perhaps, it *was* an affliction of God sent to chastise the war-mongering Crusader kingdom. We will never know.

Turning to **MARY MAGDALEN**, she has always occupied a peculiar place in Scripture and other mundane writings. She seems to appear and disappear almost at will. Aside from a few meager though very important scenes in the Gospels (which only seem to conflate the problem of her identity), she remains a mystery to even the most learned scholars. But just who was this woman about who so much is written and believed? The Gospels give just enough information to make some speculate wildly beyond the bounds of common reason. What we do know is that: 1) she had seven demons cast out of her; 2) she was a woman of some means (in other words, she had money) who followed Jesus and his disciples with several other women and supported him; 3) she was present at the crucifixion; and 4) she was the first to see the risen Lord.

Beyond these scant, tantalizing facts, we know absolutely nothing more of her. These few tidbits, however, in the way they are presented, are enough to give the overwhelming impression that the Magdalen was sufficiently well known and important that it was not necessary to explain her presence in the Gospels. The early Christians knew her well, even if she disappeared completely from the historical record after the Resurrection. We are left then with traditions that claim she traveled westwards into France and the cultural backwater of Europe that evolved into the late Roman and Medieval periods of history.

By the 11th and 12th centuries, legends about the Magdalen had blossomed in the south of Europe, particularly in the Languedoc whence many of the first Crusaders originated. By then, however, the Church and various heretical groups had done much to malign Mary's growing reputation. The Church made her out as a harlot and sinner; the heretics claimed she was the wife of Christ, or worse. The

Magdalen of the Gospels disappeared into a cycle of legends and cultural stories that bore little resemblance to her true historical character. In fact, in the millennium between Christ and the Crusades, Mary Magdalen, because of her attachment to the Christian story, became a figure of myth herself.

When it comes to the **ORDER OF SION,** we are on far less certain ground. Despite claims to the contrary by modern historians, it is obvious that it existed. In 1099, after Jerusalem fell to the Crusader armies, Godfrei de Bouillon founded an abbey on the ruins of a Byzantine structure located on a hill south of the city called the Abbey of Notre Dame du Mont de Sion, just as he instituted another order of knights and monks in the Church of the Holy Sepulcher. There is evidence, albeit thin, in the form of charters, that there was some connection between the Abbey of Sion and the newly formed Order of Templar Knights. But were the Order of Sion and the Abbey one and the same? Beyond these few simple facts, we can only speculate. A strong case can be made, as some notable conspiracy theorists claim, that the Templars actually began to function several years before their official founding in 1118. But does this necessarily mean that the continued bad press the Templars have attracted of late is true or that some secret history exists?

Given their known thirst for knowledge of the religious and the arcane, it should come as no surprise that some Templars would be guilty of such. Perhaps, some members of the Order could have formed some sort of esoteric society, but the overwhelming majority of the knights believed that they served God and his Church in defense of the Holy Land. Some have argued that Sion's influence extended even to the throne of Peter, particularly during the long and dark years of the 11th and 12th centuries. This was the Middle Ages after all, and many strange and unorthodox ideas were beginning to ferment under the oppressive system of feudal Europe. That a group of powerful and influential nobles might think to try and control the Church is not outside the realm of possibility. The Holy Roman Emperor Frederick Barbarossa certainly tried for many years to put his own popes in the Lateran Palace.

The sudden and dramatic demise of the Templars at the hands of the Pope and King Philip IV of France has forever fostered all sorts of rumors as to the cause of their downfall. Were the famous warrior-monks devil-worshippers or heretics? Were they too powerful and rich for the Church to allow them to exist? Did they protect a sacred bloodline descended from Jesus and the Magdalen? Were the Templars the military arm of the Order of Sion? The answer to all these questions is an emphatic *no*, despite the supposed *evidence* of the conspiracy theorists. The Templars were certainly not saints—but neither were they heretics.

Why write a story about the Leper King with the Magdalen and a heretical conspiracy? My answer is simple: Why not? In the past thirty-some odd years or so the world has become fixated by conspiracy theories bent on uncovering some elusive mystery lying at the heart of Christianity. Namely, that the Church has long suppressed a hidden secret about Jesus and Mary Magdalen and that various groups have guarded this faith-shattering secret until the present day. In writing *The Leper King*, I set the story in the timeframe in which the origins of many of these supposed theories are said to have been given birth. By bringing Mary forward in time it gives her the opportunity to answer for herself the charges laid against her by the heretics and a chance to defend her faith against the enemies of the Church. And if such diabolical power and elemental magic was called into play during the turbulent times of the Crusades, could not a curse disguised as a disease devour the life of a young king sworn to defend the holiest place on earth? If the purveyors of wildly heretical nonsense can make such fantastic claims on history, why can't an historical novel demand any less from the realm of fantasy? Is there really any difference between the two? After all, is it is only a book.

As an additional note, an astute reader may perhaps have noticed that I used the name *Urshalim* as the Arabic form for Jerusalem. The actual name is *al-Quds*. I chose the slightly more Jewish-sounding name instead of the Arabic simply to aid the reader in remembering it amongst all the odd-looking spellings of names, places, and things. I hope I may be forgiven this slight derivation. SRR

Recommended Further Reading:

While the below list is by no means an exhaustive list, these books constitute my primary sources of history and heresy in creating this novel. There are simply too many books, articles, and websites to make a detailed list.

Baigent, Michael, Richard Leigh, and Henry Lincoln. *Holy Blood, Holy Grail* (New York, 1983).

Benvenisti, Meron. *The Crusaders in the Holy Land* (Jerusalem, 1972).

Hamilton, Bernard. *The Leper King and His Heirs: Baldwin IV and the*

Crusader Kingdom of Jerusalem (Cambridge, 2000).

Lyons, M. C., and D.E.P. Jackson. *Saladin: The Politics of the Holy War* (Cambridge, 1982).

Maalouf, Amin. *The Crusades Through Arab Eyes* (New York, 1984).

Payne, Robert. *The Dream and the Tomb: A History of the Crusades* (New York, 2000).

Runciman, Steven. *A History of the Crusades,* 3 vols. (Cambridge, 1951-55).

ABOUT THE AUTHOR

Scott R. Rezer was born in Doylestown, Pennsylvania in 1963. He met his wife while serving in the United States Air Force. They have two grown children and live in the Southwest. A writer since his youth, his grandmother, a respected town historian, taught him a deep appreciation for history and religion. It is no surprise, then, that he turned to those two great passions in writing this imaginative tale of medieval fantasy.

He is also the author of two other books—*Shadow of the Mountain: A Novel of the Flood* and *Love Abideth Still: A Novel of the Civil War.*

Made in United States
Orlando, FL
20 November 2022

24800065R00248